Vets in Love

Cathy Woodman was a small-animal vet before turning to writing fiction. She won the Harry Bowling First Novel Award in 2002 and is a member of the Romantic Novelists' Association. She is also a lecturer in Animal Management at a local college. *Vets in Love* is the sixth book set in the fictional market town of Talyton St George in East Devon, where Cathy lived as a child. Cathy now lives with her two children, two ponies, three exuberant Border Terriers and two cats in a village near Winchester, Hampshire.

Other books by Cathy Woodman

Trust Me, I'm a Vet
Must Be Love
The Sweetest Thing
It's a Vet's Life
The Village Vet

Cathy Woodman

Vets in Love

arrow books

Published by Arrow Books 2012

2 4 6 8 10 9 7 5 3

First published in Great Britain in 2012 by
Arrow Books
Random House, 20 Vauxhall Bridge Road,
London SW1V 2SA

www.randomhouse.co.uk

Addresses for companies within The Random House Group Limited can be
found at: www.randomhouse.co.uk/offices.htm

The Random House Group Limited Reg. No. 954009

A CIP catalogue record for this book
is available from the British Library

ISBN 978-0-099-57094-3

The Random House Group Limited supports The Forest Stewardship Council
(FSC®), the leading international forest certification organisation. Our books
carrying the FSC label are printed on FSC® certified paper. FSC is the only
forest certification scheme endorsed by the leading environmental
organisations, including Greenpeace. Our paper procurement
policy can be found at www.randomhouse.co.uk/environment

Typeset by SX Composing DTP, Rayleigh, Essex, SS6 7XF
Printed and bound by CPI Group (UK) Ltd, Croydon, CR0 4YY

Acknowledgments

I should like to thank Laura Longrigg at MBA Literary Agents, Gillian Holmes and the rest of the wonderful team at Arrow Books for their enthusiasm and support.

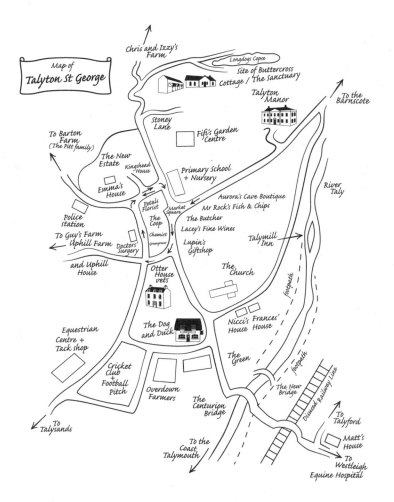

Map of
Talyton St George

To Chris and Izzy's Farm

Longdogs Copse

Site of Buttercross
Cottage / The Sanctuary

Talyton Manor

To the Barnscote

Stoney Lane

Fifi's Garden Centre

To Barton Farm
(The Pitt family)

The New Estate

Kingshead House

Primary School + Nursery

River Taly

Emma's House

Petals Florist

Market Square

Aurora's Cave Boutique

Mr Rock's Fish & Chips

Police station

The Coop

The Butcher

Lacey's Fine Wines

To Guy's Farm Uphill Farm

Chemist

Greengrocer

Talymill Inn

Doctors' Surgery

Lupin's Giftshop

and Uphill House

Otter House vets

The Church

footpath

Equestrian Centre + Tack shop

The Dog and Duck

Nicci's House

Frances' House

Cricket Club + Football Pitch

Overdown Farmers

The Green

footpath

Disused Railway Line

The New Bridge

To Talysands

The Centurion Bridge

To Talyford

To the Coast Talymouth

Matt's House

To Westleigh Equine Hospital

Chapter One

A horse is worth more than riches – Spanish proverb

It's just before nine on Monday morning and the rush has already begun. There's no time for appreciating the bright June sunshine that slants in through the blinds across the window, catching the red, white and blue profusion of geraniums and lobelias in the hanging basket outside the practice.

Having picked a stray strand of hay from my skirt, I sit at my desk, take down the sign that reads 'I am at the Stables', and press the button on the computer. While the system loads, I check I have everything to hand – stethoscope and formulary – but I'm still looking for a pen when the door flies open and Claire, the practice nurse, appears, her face almost the same shade of cerise as her uniform.

'Nicci, it's going to be one of those days.' She runs one hand frantically over her fringe, disturbing the red stripe running through her sleek brown hair. 'Would you be able to see Mrs Green? She's turned up without an appointment, even though she knows perfectly well that she shouldn't.'

'Is it urgent?' I ask, detecting a hint of desperation in Claire's voice. I've been working here for eighteen months, having returned to the area after completing my training, whereas she's been employed by the practice in Talyton St George for several years. She's in her early thirties, like me, and in spite of her experience, she doesn't deal with confrontation well and Mrs Green, or Fifi, as she is better known, gives the impression of being someone who isn't used to being denied.

'Apparently it's a matter of life and death, but—'

'Anything for peace and quiet,' I finish for her. 'I'll see her.'

'Thank you.' Claire smiles with relief. 'You've saved my life.'

'You'd better send her in before I change my mind.'

For a woman in her sixties, Fifi's heels are high and her nails are long, and it looks as if there's nothing wrong with her, yet she's suffering from every condition to be found in the medical textbooks lined up on the shelves behind me, according to a quick glance at her notes. She stands in the doorway, dressed and made up as if she's on her way to a garden party, with a red fascinator in her copper and blonde curls and a bag decorated with a strawberry motif on her arm.

'Good morning, Mrs Green.'

'I really wanted to see Dr Mackie.' She looks me up and down with a critical eye. 'He's done wonders for my bunions, you know.' Fifi is referring to Ben, my colleague who, having been established as the family GP here in Talyton St George far longer than I have, has earned his place as the oracle when it comes to medical matters.

'Dr Mackie isn't here until later. I'm sure Claire's told you he's making house calls.'

'Oh dear. You'll have to do, Dr Chieveley,' Fifi goes on as I offer her a seat.

'You must call me Nicci.' Very few patients call me doctor, even though I have a framed certificate behind the desk at reception that confirms Dr Nicola Jane Chieveley is a Member of the Royal College of General Practitioners.

'I couldn't do that, not in the surgery. It doesn't feel right.' She flashes me a smile, sits down and turns her attention to the gallery of photos I have on the wall. There's one of me, a blonde, blue-eyed woman in jeans and a T-shirt, with a young girl at my side and a baby in my arms. 'What lovely children.'

'They're my sister's,' I say quickly, not wishing to let Fifi create any misunderstandings about my personal life. She's a terrible gossip.

'Haven't you got a picture of your young man?' she continues.

'You must know something I don't,' I say lightly.

'I just assumed that at your age you'd be settled.'

'I'm thirty-one. I'm in no hurry.'

Fifi leans forward, apparently warming to her theme. 'You'd make a great catch for someone. I wonder . . .' She taps her lip with her finger as if she's creating a

3

mental list of eligible bachelors for me, while I divert her back to the topic in hand, her health, thinking that it's no good because unless one of them is Daniel Craig or Orlando Bloom, I really won't be interested.

'That's enough about me,' I say, making a brief comparison between Fifi's beautifully manicured nails and the state of mine. 'What about you?' I thought I was supposed to be the one asking the questions here, but for all my training in the art of doctor-patient communication, I can't stop her. Like the river Taly in flood, Fifi Green is in full flow.

'The Women's Institute has an evening of music and poetry tomorrow night. You will come along and join us.'

'It's a lovely idea, but I'm afraid I'm rather busy.' My eyes drift towards another of the photos, that of a dapple grey mare, the most beautiful and talented horse in the world (okay, so I'm biased) flying over a rustic spread on a cross-country course with her ears pricked and her flaxen tail streaming out behind her.

'I assume it's you riding that horse, Doctor? Do you compete?'

I nod. I'm definitely a competitive person, but I'm finding it hard to compete with Fifi in conversation.

'Willow's an eventer. I'm aiming to qualify with her for Badminton within the next couple of years.'

'How marvellous,' Fifi gushes. 'Of course, I couldn't possibly ride a horse with all my problems. I'm in chronic pain the whole time. My wrist is sore, my hips are aching and my back is playing up again.'

'Let's take things one at a time,' I say firmly.

'I don't think Dr Mackie would approve. He has a holistic approach to medicine, treating the patient as a whole person, not separate body parts.'

I give Fifi one of my 'looks', something I have practised in front of the mirror over and over again, and she backs down.

'I'm sorry, I shouldn't be telling you your job.' Her eyes flash with good humour. 'Dr Mackie has a lovely bedside manner, doesn't he?'

'I couldn't possibly comment,' I say, flashing a quick smile back. 'He's a happily married man.'

'More's the pity.' Fifi sighs.

She's married, so I can only assume she isn't serious. As for me, I have no regrets that Ben has a wife and family. I have my career and an all-consuming hobby. Having a man in my life is an optional extra, not a necessity, whereas keeping a horse is an entirely different matter.

I examine Fifi's wrist and discuss her back pain at some length, and as I'm winding up the consultation, thinking that she'll probably be back to see Ben at the first opportunity, there's a sharp rap on the door and Claire is back.

'Nicci, I need a word.'

'Will you excuse me?' I say to Fifi, detecting from Claire's expression that this is urgent.

'Of course.' Fifi stands up, looking from me to Claire and back, gleaning clues. 'I do hope nothing's amiss.'

I join Fifi and usher her out, pressing a prescription for pain-relieving gel into her hand.

'Let Dr Mackie know how you get on. Give him a call or make an appointment for two weeks' time.'

'Thank you, Dr Chieveley.' She hurries out to reception, but fortunately Claire had the foresight to show our next patient into the nurses' room, so Fifi is left with the impossible task of extracting the gossip she wants from Janet, the receptionist, while Claire and I enter the nurses' room where a man in his fifties is sitting slumped on the edge of the examination couch. He's pasty and overweight with a flabby paunch, as if the only exercise he takes is lifting a pint or two in the pub.

'You needn't have jumped me up the queue.' He wipes sweat from his brow. 'I can wait, you know. I have all day.'

'This is Steve Wilde. He's complaining of chest pains,' Claire says quietly.

'How are you doing, Steve?' I move across the room and take his pulse, which flutters like a dying butterfly – too fast and missing beats – under my fingertips.

'You can hold my hand for as long as you like, Doc,' he says weakly.

'Take no notice, Nicci,' Claire says. 'He's always the joker.'

'Has he had any aspirin?' I ask her.

'I'll get some.' Claire wheels across the trolley with the ECG and crash kit. 'Steve's in charge of our local Am Dram group and famed for his roles as a panto dame.'

'Have you had chest pains before?' I notice how he's

shaved the stubble from one side of his face and not the other.

'I thought it was indigestion.'

'When did they start?' I say, checking his blood pressure, which is sky-high.

'A couple of days ago.' He touches his chest and forces a smile. 'Not this bad though. I put it down to acid.'

'Claire, can you call an ambulance?' I say, wondering why he didn't think to call one himself from home. Steve's in denial. This has nothing to do with acid. He is one very sick man.

'It's done,' Claire says, handing him some aspirin and a glass of water.

'There's no need for an ambulance,' Steve says. 'I'll feel like a fraud.'

'It's just a precaution.'

'I don't like to be a bother.'

'Better safe than sorry,' I tell him, waiting for him to swallow the tablets. 'I'm going to check your heart.' I get him to lie propped up on the couch, help him remove his shirt, which he appears to have put on over his pyjamas, and set up the ECG, but my fingers are all thumbs as I stick the electrodes to his chest.

'I feel like I'm an extra on *Casualty* and you're about to start spouting medical terms at me.' He can hardly force a smile any more. 'It's all mumble jumble to me.'

'Don't you mean mumbo-jumbo, Steve?' Claire says, giving me a look of concern. 'I'm going to get Janet at reception to call your wife,' she goes on. 'I think you should have someone with you.' Without waiting for his response she goes outside.

At the same time, Steve gasps and clutches his throat, his lips turning blue. I glance at the trace of the electrical activity of his heart – it's all over the place.

'On a scale of one to ten, where is the pain now?' I ask calmly, although my heartbeat is all over the place too. This isn't looking good.

'Oh, about a five, no, make that a . . .' He can't speak, let alone decide on a number, confirming my suspicions from the evidence so far that he's in the grip of a major heart attack. He's trying to be brave, but I can sense his growing panic, and panicking will only make his condition worse.

Although I'm afraid that he's about to go into cardiac arrest, I concentrate on keeping him as calm as possible, distracting him while we wait for his family and the ambulance, which is probably trying to make its way through the holiday traffic that jams the lanes into Talyton St George on hot summer days like today.

'I don't think I've met a panto dame before,' I say, keeping my hand on his, partly to reassure myself that he does indeed still have a pulse, and partly to reassure him. He's breathing more steadily now and his colour is returning.

'I love it,' he says. 'I don't act professionally any more, but I still tread the boards for the Am Dram group's annual Christmas show. My wife is used to me borrowing her lippy and blusher, but my daughter hasn't always appreciated me dressing up in women's clothing.' His grin quickly turns into a grimace of pain. His breathing quickens again and to my relief I hear the sound of a siren.

'The ambulance is here, Steve. I'm going to call ahead to let the right people know you're on your way.' He doesn't argue with me – he's exhausted and in too much pain. Within a short time, he's on the way to hospital with his wife, and all I can do now is hand over to the consultant in A&E and hope that he makes it.

The next few patients sympathise when I explain that I'm running late because of an emergency, and two of them can tell me exactly what it was because they've already heard about Steve's condition on the grapevine, but my last patient of the morning is not so forgiving.

'Mr Warren,' I say, calling him through from the waiting room where he's sitting beside a striking young woman in her mid-twenties, with long, dark, glossy hair, full lips, brown eyes and lashings of mascara. I recognise her as one of my patients, a vet who came to see me with a horse-inflicted injury not very long ago, a needle-stick wound that became infected and required a course of antibiotics. She's wearing a crisp white blouse and jeans that emphasise her curvaceous figure, the kind that makes other women jealous.

'Do you want me to come in with you?' she says, touching the man's arm as he stands up.

'No, Mel. I appreciate you giving me a lift, but I can walk and talk for myself, thank you very much.' He pauses before going on more gently, 'Why don't you book that appointment?'

'I haven't got my diary with me,' she says. 'Go on, Matt. Now you're the one keeping everyone waiting.'

I watch my patient walk along the corridor towards me. He's a man of about my age and of average height dressed in soft moleskin trousers, a check shirt and light sweater. He has one hand clenched around a set of keys and the other around his mobile, and he moves with a slight stoop, his right shoulder dropped and carried forward of the left – okay, I'm a doctor, I notice these things.

'What time do you call this?' he says curtly as I step back to let him pass. 'My appointment was over an hour ago. I'm a busy man.'

'I'm sorry for the delay, Mr Warren. You could have rearranged, instead of waiting,' I say, finding it hard to apologise to someone who appears to lack both patience and common sense, and perhaps compassion too, or any powers of observation. Didn't he notice the ambulance? I suppress a sigh of annoyance at his attitude, especially when he appears quite healthy. This is one of the occasions when I'd very definitely prefer to be up at the stables, kicking about in my jodhs and polo shirt. I glance down at my work attire – an embroidered white vest with a lacy cotton cardigan over the top, a straight skirt and turquoise heels – I like to think I'm quite a glamorous lady doctor, and tall at almost five foot eight.

'How can I rebook when I don't have a spare

moment?' he goes on. 'Unless you'd consider opening up the surgery late one evening, say ten-thirty?'

I assume he's being flippant.

'Take a seat,' I say, returning to mine and checking the notes on the monitor.

Matt Warren, thirty-two years old – that's one great advantage of being a GP, having all the basics on record – blood type O, height 177cm which is – I make a quick calculation – five foot ten inches, and weight eleven stone six. As for the rest, he's rather . . . well . . . I appraise his figure and his face in an enquiring medical way, assessing him for signs of health, and I would have to declare, if pressed, that he is extremely fit, in more ways than one, being ruggedly handsome and lightly tanned, with short brown hair, hazel eyes and a determinedly square jawline.

It's a pity he's so prickly and off with me. I don't take it personally though.

As he catches me staring at him and I catch him staring at me, his irritation seems to disappear. His mouth curves into a smile and dimples form in his cheeks, at which I'm completely disarmed and almost forget he's one of my patients.

'It's a long time since I was sick,' he says ruefully, something I can understand – I never have time to be ill. 'I guess these things happen though. I'm a vet and I should know. I was operating on a horse until three this morning.' He yawns as if to emphasise the point before looking up at the photos on the wall. 'Is that you on the horse?'

'It is. I do a bit of eventing.'

11

'Professionally?'

'I'm a keen amateur.'

'Oh, I have lots of clients like you,' he says somewhat dismissively. 'Where do you keep the beast?'

'I keep Willow—' I resent him describing my baby as a beast '—at Delphi Letherington's yard.'

'I know it. My partner attends the equestrian centre. I spend most of my time at the hospital, Westleigh Equine. I'm more into sports medicine and surgery than the routine GP kind of stuff.'

I'm a little offended, but he doesn't seem to realise it.

'So what's the problem, Mr Warren?' I say rather sharply.

'Ah, I'm sorry. I didn't mean to—'

'It's all right. Let's get on. You obviously have far more important places to be.'

'It's my shoulder,' he says, tapping his right elbow.

'Can you be more precise?' I ask, wondering about his knowledge of human anatomy.

'Of course I can.' He gazes at me and starts giving me his opinion of what's wrong. 'I injured my shoulder in my early twenties, playing rugby, and since then it plays me up now and again.'

'Is it very painful?'

'It's agony, particularly when I'm doing dentals,' he says, flinching at the mere thought. Wuss, I think as he continues, 'At the moment, I can hardly lift my arm, which is bloody inconvenient. That's why Mel, our houseman, offered me a lift.'

'Are you right- or left-handed?'

'Right,' he says regretfully. 'Anyway, I'd like you to

confirm that it's a rotator cuff impingement and refer me to a decent orthopaedic surgeon asap.'

'It seems you don't need me. Have you got private medical insurance?'

'I haven't. There was an oversight.' He pauses and I find myself waiting to see who he's going to blame for it, but he goes on, 'To be honest, I was so busy I forgot to put the forms in.'

I'm relieved to hear that he isn't so perfect after all.

'Let me examine you and then we'll decide what to do.'

'Do you want me here or on the couch?'

'On the couch.' I smile to myself. I'm going to enjoy causing him some pain. I wash my hands and dry them on a paper towel while he settles on the couch. 'You'll have to take your shirt off.' My mouth runs dry and the words seem to stick on my tongue and my teeth. I sense that he's testing me.

I keep my eyes averted as he removes his shirt and hangs it over the trolley beside the couch.

'I'm ready now, Doctor,' he says, his voice bubbling with humour.

'I'd prefer it if you called me Nicci.' I move towards him, forcing myself to look at his torso, at the tan lines on his neck and upper arms, at the slab-like muscles of his pectorals, and the smattering of dark curly hairs across his chest that spill down towards his navel, which indents an admirably flat belly. I realise that although I see many bodies, embarrassing and otherwise, both male and female, it's been a very long time since I saw the body of a fit man.

13

'And you must call me Matt. None of this "Mr Warren" nonsense. I hope you haven't got cold hands,' he says as I reach out to touch him.

'You're lucky it's a warm day.' I palpate his shoulders and the surrounding areas, applying light and deep pressure, checking for symmetry in the swell and dips of the musculature. He has just the right amount of muscle, not so much that you would think he spent all his time working out, but more than enough to be manly. I check the shoulder joints, feeling for warmth and tenderness, but he's guarded and tense.

'Hey, you can relax,' I say gently, trying to put him at ease.

'I can't. I'm not used to being the patient.'

'I expect your patients are more co-operative than you are,' I say with irony.

'More?' I notice how his brow furrows briefly before he breaks into a heart-stopping slow smile. If I were attached to the ECG right now, it would have gone haywire, which is ridiculous because I never allow myself to respond to my patients, but then Matt isn't any old patient. He's utterly gorgeous. 'Okay, that was a joke, right. I hope you make a better doctor than a comedian.'

'What made you go into horses?' I ask him, changing the subject.

'I thought about going into small animals, but I don't like hamsters – or hamsters don't like me, I'm not sure which way round it is. No, I find horses a challenge. They can be such delicate creatures. It's very satisfying when you get one coming round after injury, or after colic surgery. That's my specialist subject – tummy ache in the horse. I'm running a series of evidence-based studies at the moment.'

'I see.' I don't know what I was expecting – for him to say he loved horses, like I do? It's clear he sees them as patients to bring back to health and as subjects to research.

Observing the pattern of moles on his skin, I ask him to place the palms of his hands at the base of his neck with his elbows pointing out to each side. I notice how he's biting his lip as I inspect his upper body for muscle wasting or swelling, anything that will confirm his diagnosis or suggest an alternative.

'I'm going to do a couple of tests to assess the state of your rotator cuff,' I say. 'The cuff is formed from four muscles—'

'I know what it is,' he cuts in. 'You don't have to explain.'

I decide that I don't need to explain the tests either, both of which are positive, judging by his reactions.

'Ouch!' He winces each time. 'Are you some kind of sadist?'

I ignore that comment.

'Much as it pains me to admit it,' I begin, 'I can confirm your diagnosis.'

'So you'll refer me.'

'My approach is to prescribe complete rest in a sling for a few days, followed by some physio. If that doesn't work, we can try a shot of steroid.'

'What if you're missing something?' he asks. 'Not that I'm suggesting you don't know what you're talking about.'

'I should hope not,' I say, standing tall and straight. 'If necessary, I'll refer you for a scan or X-rays.'

'What if I disagree?'

Undeterred, I flash him the flirtiest of smiles.

'I'm sure you'll let me twist your arm.'

'No no—' he holds his hands up, wincing again '— not that.' He chuckles. 'Anything but that, Nicci – what kind of doctor are you?'

'Take some time off to rest that shoulder.'

'That's impossible. We're always working at full stretch and this is the worst possible time for me to take time off. There's only me and Mel to cover the hospital and all the visits. My partner is on leave.'

I don't ask what kind of partner he's referring to, although I admit I'm a little curious.

'Can't you arrange cover for a few days?'

'You know how it is. Clients like to see the same vet each time, they like continuity.' He tilts his head to one side. 'And of course, when it comes to equine surgery, no one does it better than me.' Having lured me into believing he's arrogant and his ego is bloated with self-importance, like some of the consultants I met during my medical training, he breaks into another smile. 'Not really. I just don't like the idea of having to sit around doing nothing all day.' He drums his fingers on the edge of the couch.

'It's up to you, but I'd strongly advise you to—'

'Are you always this bossy?'

I ignore that remark. 'I would at least avoid rasping teeth for the foreseeable future.'

'Are you sure you won't just refer me straight away?'

'Quite sure. I don't suppose you can help being a surgeon,' I say. 'They always think the only way to solve a problem is with a scalpel.'

'You don't like surgeons then? In general, I mean, not specifically,' he says.

'What kind of question is that?' I ask, turning away from his intense stare. Is he trying to chat me up in a funny sort of way?

'Are you finished with me?' he asks.

'Um, yes,' I say, a warm flush creeping up my neck. 'I'll get dressed then.'

'Please do,' I say, before wishing I hadn't said it with such emphasis. I shouldn't care if he's sitting there with his shirt off. I've seen it all before.

I start to type some notes as he pulls on his shirt, fastens the buttons and rolls up his sleeves.

'Thanks for that,' he says, moving towards the door, where he hesitates. 'I'll make another appointment for next week.'

And I think, I didn't ask you to, but I don't attempt to dissuade him. I'd like to see him again, purely in a professional capacity, of course. Suddenly, I have a particular interest in shoulders.

'I'll see you soon,' I say.

'It's good to meet Talyton's new doctor at last.'

'I've been working here for eighteen months,' I say.

'You're new to me,' he says decisively. 'Goodbye, Nicci.'

'Goodbye.' I sink back into my chair when the door closes behind him. I believe this is an occasion when an old-fashioned country doctor might dig out a bottle of whisky from their drawer and turn to drink. I doubt very much that Matt will do as I suggested. I pick up the phone to call the hospital to see if I can find out what's happening with Steve.

Chapter Two

Horse Sense

With surgery over for the day, I ring the hospital. Steve is in theatre undergoing a procedure on his coronary arteries in the hope of preventing another heart attack. Confident that although still in a critical condition, he's in the best hands, I set out for the yard for my daily fix of horse, driving south along the road towards Talysands. I begin to relax at the top of the hill, where I catch the first glimpse of the sea glittering in the early evening sunshine. I take a deep breath and exhale slowly, letting go of my work worries. I'm glad I chose to come home and settle here in Devon. I think it's the most beautiful place in the world.

I turn off the main road into a driveway, passing a sign reading 'Letherington Equestrian Centre' and a small warehouse-style building that houses the shop Tack n Hack on one side, and on the other a field divided into sections by wooden posts and green electric tape where several horses are grazing, some of them looking like warriors, covered from nose to tail and ears to hooves in fly sheets and masks.

I continue past a modern barn half filled with the new season's hay and into the car park that faces onto the first yard of breeze block and tile stables reserved for the liveries. Beyond is a second yard of older, higgledy-piggledy part-brick and part-cob buildings where Delphi keeps the riding school ponies, and behind that are the indoor school, outdoor school, horse walker and two foaling boxes. There's also a wash-down area with a solarium – for the horses, not the humans.

Having parked, I grab Willow's head-collar from the hook outside her stable to fetch her from the paddock, walking between the fence and the hedge entwined with cow parsley, brambles and dog roses. Willow reminds me of a rocking horse with her grey dapples and flaxen mane and tail. I call her name and she raises her head from where she's been grazing with her muzzle buried in the lush grass. She flicks a fly from one ear and decides I'm not worth bothering about.

'Do you mean I have to walk all the way over there to catch you?' I say with a mock sigh as she returns to her favourite occupation – eating like a horse, so to speak. 'I spend all this money and time on you, so I think the least you could do is pretend you're pleased to see me.'

She turns her rump to me and swishes her tail as if to say, 'But I'm enjoying this far too much.'

Willow can detect the sound of a sweet wrapper

from miles away, so when I fish around in my pocket for a mint she makes her way over, pausing only to grab one last mouthful of grass. She stops and sniffs at my hand, then waits for me to uncurl my fingers and reveal the mint on my palm before taking it gently between her lips and crunching it with her teeth. I slip the head-collar on and lead her down to the yard.

There is a long-limbed brown gelding in the paddock next to Willow's. Dark Star is Willow's neighbour in the stable block and he's quite attached to her, so when I lead her away he starts trotting up and down whinnying for her. She doesn't feel the same way about him, a horse of half her age and experience. She doesn't look back.

When I tie her to the ring outside the stable, Dark Star continues his pacing up and down the fence until I take pity on him and fetch him in too, letting him into his stable. I remove his head-collar, stroking the white star in the centre of his forehead, and let myself out, keeping a close eye on him, remembering the adage 'The front end bites, the back end kicks' – and true to form, Dark Star tosses his head with his ears pinned back.

'Don't you even think about it,' I growl at him, and he backs down as if nothing has happened. 'You might have the rest of the yard under your thumb – or should that be your hoof – but you don't scare me,' I tell him. I watch him for a moment as he settles to chew on some hay. He's very well bred with a minor fault of a Roman nose, which I think gives him an air of gravitas, but he's a strange horse temperament-wise, whereas Willow is a darling, beautiful and kind. I return to her, running my hand down her neck and smiling to myself. There are times when I wish my patients were horses, and wonder why I didn't train to be a vet.

At the sound of another vehicle arriving in the yard, I turn to see a silver pickup spattered with rust-coloured mud pulling up between my car and a stack of big-bale haylage wrapped in pale green plastic.

It's Shane, my trainer, and I'm not ready.

I grab a body brush from the grooming kit outside the stable and give Willow a quick brush, concentrating on the areas where the bridle and saddle rest, checking where the girth fits to make sure there's no dirt that could chafe. The last thing we need is a girth gall that would put her out of action for the rest of the season.

I jog across to the tack room and slip into my long leather boots, zipping them up the back so they fit close to my calves, and tie back my hair before putting on my hat, grabbing a stick, and Willow's tack, and walking back across the yard with her bridle slung over my shoulder and her jumping saddle in my arms. She has three saddles, one for dressage, one for jumping and a general purpose one for hacking, which sounds like a terrible extravagance, but we have to have the right gear to compete.

I put the saddle on her and fasten the girth straps before slipping the reins over her head, something to hang onto her by if she should decide to wander off when I remove the head-collar and replace it with the bridle. Willow doesn't move though.

'Good girl,' I tell her. I talk to her like a friend. I've had her for six years now and I chose well. It's a pity I'm not so lucky at picking a good man, someone as loyal and courageous as my horse, someone who respects me as I respect them, and who can stay the distance.

My last boyfriend couldn't, and I don't know why he should enter my mind right now, when I promised myself I'd never waste another moment on him.

'You aren't keeping me waiting again, VB?' Shane says cheerfully, using his nickname for me as he comes up alongside. He's about my height, brown-haired, blue-eyed and skinny, his muscles well defined. 'How are things?'

'Good, thanks. How about you?' I lead Willow to the middle of the yard and Shane follows, striding along in a tatty olive green polo shirt, brown breeches and long boots. He's been my trainer since I brought Willow to Delphi's yard when I returned to the area to work as a GP. I've known him for years though. We used to be members of the Talyton branch of the Pony Club, but he was a couple of years older than me and utterly fixated on showjumping. He never had a girlfriend and people used to think he was gay, but he's married now to the greengrocer's daughter, and everyone jokes that he did it to make sure of an endless supply of carrots.

'Not bad,' he says. 'Ready for a leg-up?'

I bring Willow to a halt, gather up the reins in my left

hand as I'm facing the saddle and bend my left leg. Shane grabs me around the shin, and counts, 'One, two, three,' before propelling me into the saddle. He casts an eye over the position of my leg as I slip my foot into the stirrup.

'I really think you should put those up one,' he says and I adjust the leathers as we head through the next yard to the outdoor school. I warm up, taking Willow through walk, trot and canter on both reins with light touches of my legs against her sides, while Shane sets up three jumps across the middle.

'Okay, VB. Bring her down the centre line,' Shane calls as he slots a cup onto the wing of the last jump at the end of a blue and white striped pole, making a straightforward upright fence with a cross-pole underneath.

Coming around the corner at the end of the school, I ask Willow for a rhythmic canter and aim for the centre of the jump. She flies it.

'Good,' says Shane, 'keep the rhythm and come down on the left rein.'

By the end of the training session, Willow has jumped all three fences raised to one metre twenty. I pat her neck and it's dark with sweat. I'm sweating too, my face burning from exertion, even though the air is cooler now as the sun begins to go down and the shadows of the fences lengthen across the school.

'That's enough,' Shane decides. 'Let's end on a good note. Walk her around and we'll talk.'

'You'll talk, you mean,' I say brightly. I reach down and loosen the girth and let Willow walk on a long rein so she can snort and stretch and cool down. 'What do you think?'

'I think Willow's looking great, but you, VB, need to get yourself down to the gym. Your horse is fitter than you are, and that isn't good enough.' Shane doesn't pull any punches, which is why he's such a great trainer. He tells it how it is. 'When did you last have a proper workout?'

'I feel as if I've just had one,' I exclaim in mock protest.

'Make sure you get a couple of sessions in before the next event,' Shane says. He's strict. That's what I pay him for. 'The horse is ready, but I'm not sure about the rider.'

I pay him to make me feel guilty too. I need to sharpen up my act if Willow and I are going to break through to the next level. She's twelve now and if she doesn't make it in the next two years, I think that will be the end of it and we will go no further. There will be no trip to Badminton for us.

'Hey, stay positive,' Shane warns as if he's reading my mind. 'I can't stop, I'm afraid. I've got to get home – Michaela's parents are coming over for dinner.' He grins. 'She'll kill me if I'm not there this time.'

I want to tell him how lucky he is to have someone waiting at home for him, but that would make me sound a bit sad, so I don't. Instead, I ride around to the yard, say goodbye to him and jump down outside the stable where a tall, blonde woman with greasy hair, much of which has escaped her pony - tail, is waiting.

'Hi, Delphi,' I say as she grabs the end of a hose and turns on the tap.

Slightly unkempt, with dirty nails and weathered skin, she's in her mid-forties and fabulously fit. Her short-sleeved lemon-coloured showing blouse exposes her muscular upper arms, and her cream jodhpurs show off her shapely legs, wide hips and large bottom. She exudes, as always, an air of horse, Chanel and superiority. Some people find her difficult, some annoying, but I like her. I respect her for the way she cares for my horse – all the equines in her charge come first, before anything else in her life.

She had the wash-down area and solarium built recently, but on hot days like today, she prefers the old-fashioned way, washing the horses down with the hose. Willow takes exception though. As I take off the saddle and rest it on top of the stable door, Delphi flicks the end of the hose at Willow's neck. Willow snorts and fidgets, her skin twitching as she tries to escape the jet of cold water.

'Willow, stop that,' I say sharply and she settles down, allowing the water to run down her legs and under her belly. 'I think she likes it really.' I stroke her muzzle. 'Drama queen!'

'Was that a successful session?' Delphi asks. She's very well-spoken, like royalty.

'Not bad, except Shane's told me to get down to the gym. I'm not sure when I'll find the time.'

'Thanks for bringing Dark Star in for me. No one else will. I don't know why he's the way he is. I've brought him up from a foal, so he should know how to behave.'

Delphi takes the hose away and switches off the tap, while I grab a sweat-scraper to remove the excess water from Willow's coat before throwing on her cooler. 'I've got one of the vets from Westleigh coming up at the end of this week,' she goes on. 'Did you want me to book Willow in for her vaccinations then, or do you want to leave it until after the next event at East Hill? There's plenty of time.'

'Which vet?' I say out of curiosity.

'Matt Warren – I prefer his partner, Jimmy, but he isn't available.'

'What's wrong with Matt?'

'There's nothing wrong with him – Jimmy's more familiar with the horses, that's all. His wife's just given birth to their first child.' She smiles. 'It's lucky Matt isn't breeding yet because they wouldn't be able to cope.'

I smile at the way she talks about him as if he's some stallion.

'Is he married?' I ask, trying to maintain an air of casual interest.

'No.' Delphi opens the stable door for me. 'I think he has a girlfriend though, the other vet at the hospital.'

'Mel, the houseman?'

'Yes, that's right.'

'Come on, Willow.' I lead her inside and take off her head-collar before leaving her to have a roll on her bed of shavings. Matt is attached, so there's no surprise there then, except I *am* a little surprised because he was definitely flirting with me this morning and described the woman in the waiting room as their houseman rather than his girlfriend. It doesn't show much respect for her, and although I don't like to tar all men with the same brush, it reminds me of my ex and his lack of respect for women in general. Good men do exist. Shane is one of them, but I have no idea where the rest of them are.

'So what do you think?' Delphi says.

'About Matt?'

'Do you want him?'

'Want him?'

'Yes, to see Willow?'

I realise that I'm definitely on the wrong wavelength here. Blushing, I respond that I do.

After checking that Willow has cooled down and eaten her tea of competition mix, chaff and an apple, I go home, driving around Talyton's one-way system to get back to the house I'm renting until I find a place to buy. I park the car, a white Audi – not a good colour for a horsey person like myself because it's always dirty – behind a delivery van that belongs to my neighbour's man-friend. I can't bring myself to call him a boyfriend when they're both in their sixties. I live in a substantial terrace between Frances, the aforesaid neighbour who is the receptionist for Otter House vets and a longstanding member of the WI, and a family consisting of a woman I call Eternally Frazzled Mum and two or three noisy boys.

The house is perfect for now, but not entirely to my taste. It has three bedrooms, two bathrooms, a living room, dining room and kitchen spread over three floors. Although it's painted throughout in light creams and white woodwork, it feels dark. Perhaps my feelings about the interior are influenced by the view from the front of the imposing church and graveyard across the road. The church is more like a cathedral, tall and daunting and built from grey stone and adorned with gargoyles that dribble and spit water when it rains. The graveyard surrounding it is bordered with an iron railing and deep green yew trees beneath which nothing grows, and is filled with headstones etched with the history of Talyton St George.

There are always people coming and going, attending services and placing flowers on the graves. A handful of dog walkers take their pets for a wander around the churchyard – I often see Bridget, the florist and one of my patients, walking her bulldog and Labradoodle in the mornings. When the organist, Nobby Warwick, isn't playing, the bell-ringers are practising. This evening, the bells are ringing peals from the tower.

I jump out of the car and step across the pavement to the front door, which not only leans to one side but is so narrow that any furniture has to be taken apart and reassembled inside, or passed through the window. There's a jam jar on the step, labelled and decorated with an elasticated floral cap, along with a note from my neighbour, reading, 'Dear Nicci, thank you for watering the plants. Frances. PS I would have popped this inside for you, but you've left your door locked.'

I can picture her writing it, peering through her flamboyant specs, her lips pursed with frustration that in spite of her assurances that this is a low-crime neighbourhood and I don't need to bother about securing my home when I go out, I still can't break the habit of a lifetime and give her the chance to have a quiet nose around.

I pick up the jar and check the label: Home-made Prize-winning Green Tomato Chutney. I take my post indoors too, file it in my 'to deal with' pile on the breakfast bar and tuck the chutney away in the cupboard. I cook up some fresh pasta and a creamy sauce, throw on some pepper and Parmesan and sit down to eat at the garden table before calling my sister. Lately, I've tried at least once or twice a week to get in touch with her, but the last time we spoke was over two months ago.

I eat as dusk falls and the bats start swooping around the garden, then I phone my mum.

I never call my father. He calls me two or three times a year. My parents divorced when I was thirteen and my sister nine. It's strange because they used to argue all the time and really weren't suited but, even now, my mum doesn't seem able to move on. She's been out with other men, but each one has turned out to be 'just a friend'. I don't think she will ever truly accept that her husband walked out on her. He said he wanted his freedom – to travel the world with his new girlfriend, who was much younger than him – but now the girlfriend is his wife and they have teenage children – half-siblings I've never met. My father abandoned us to create a new family and, although I can deal with that, I don't think I'll ever completely forgive him.

'Hi, Mum,' I say when she answers the phone. 'I'm

just checking that you're still up for being groom for the one-day event. It's a week on Saturday.'

'Of course I am. You know I wouldn't miss it for the world.'

I'm very grateful to her because without my mum I wouldn't have made it this far as an event rider. She's been at my side for years, since I was a Pony Clubber riding borrowed ponies. We make a great team.

'I have news,' she says, once we've finalised arrangements. 'Someone has asked me out.'

'A man?' I say, failing to disguise the surprise in my voice.

'Of course, and before you say anything,' she says quickly, 'it isn't serious. He's just a friend.'

'Where did you meet him?' I ask, pleased for her and expecting her to say they met through Art Club or mutual acquaintances.

'I've joined an online dating agency. Nicci, you should try it – it's so easy.'

'Too easy,' I say. 'Mum, are you sure he's genuine?'

'We've been chatting for a while. In fact, I feel as if I've known him for years. His name is Robert.'

'But . . .' I'm not being a spoilsport, I'm worried for her, '. . . You hear all kinds of stories. I think it's a really bad way to meet someone. He could be a cheat, a fraudster, a thief, a con man . . . I could go on.'

'I did meet someone who turned out to be very short and orange, like an Oompa-Loompa,' she says drily, 'but I've asked Robert to confirm his height and that he doesn't use fake tan.' She chuckles. 'You really should have more faith in me.'

'You must give me all the details. Where are you meeting him?'

'Don't you worry, darling. We're having a drink at the Talymill Inn and then I shall go straight home.'

'You will text me to let me know you're all right?'

'I'll let you know when I get home,' Mum says, her tone wistful.

'I want you to text me every hour, otherwise I'll be worried sick.'

'Nicci, you'll be going on about safe sex next. I know what I'm doing. I'm older than I like to think.' She chuckles. 'I guess the tables have been turned. Now you know what it feels like.'

'What do you mean?'

'When you were seventeen and going out, and I didn't have a clue who you were with—'

'You did,' I cut in. 'I was with my friends.'

'So you said.'

'All right, but it was a long time ago. Things are different now. We knew the local boys. You're talking about a complete stranger you've met on the internet.'

'Not a complete stranger. He's a farmer, his wife passed away three years ago and he isn't in a position to meet women because he's always busy on the farm.'

'And you believe him?'

'One thing I've learned over the years is that not every man is like your father,' Mum says abruptly. 'Listen, I promise to text you every hour if it makes you happy.'

We hang up and I gaze around the garden at the tall

privet hedges that offer privacy from the plots on either side, at the laburnum which bloomed bright yellow in the spring, and the lilacs that are in flower now, mauve and white varieties with a beautiful scent. When I say the garden is private, it isn't entirely. The boys next door have a trampoline, and every so often I'm aware out of the corner of my eye of a child bouncing above the level of the hedges between us.

I smile to myself. I can't believe I'm worrying about my fifty-six-year-old mother, or that she has more romance in her life than I do – but internet dating? It isn't for me, although I wouldn't mind a companion. A dog would be great, but it wouldn't be fair to leave it alone all day. Or something low maintenance, like a goldfish or a hamster, neither of which have a reputation for being great conversationalists.

There's a shout from the other side of the hedge and something whistles past my ear, landing with a thud on the patio behind me.

'You kicked it over the other side, you idiot!'

I turn to find a battered football on the ground. As I pick it up a child starts crying and the voice of Eternally Frazzled Mum berates one of her sons.

'It's all right,' I say, trying to see through the hedge. 'No harm done. I'll throw it back over.'

'Thank you, Doctor,' says the voice of Eternally Frazzled Mum.

'It's Nicci,' I say. 'I'm off duty now.'

'I'm sorry if we're disturbing you. I was trying to let

33

the boys run around a bit to wear them out before bedtime. Goodnight.'

'Goodnight,' I call back, and I don't feel so alone after all.

Chapter Three

Doctor's Orders

On Friday a few days later I receive the good news I've been waiting for. Steve Wilde is out of intensive care and expected to leave the hospital in a few days. We – that's me, Claire and Janet – celebrate with chocolate brownies and custard tarts from the baker's shop.

After a quick break, I call in my next patient. I like to fetch them from the waiting room personally, rather than make them jump at the anonymous sound of a buzzer – and after two custard tarts, it's good for me. I smile to myself at our deception. When we're promoting good health, we really should be seen to practise what we preach.

When I step out to reception, I find Ed Pike, the local gamekeeper, struggling with a baby and a dog. I've met Ed and the baby before, but not the dog. Janet is clearly struggling with the dog as well, but in a rather different way.

'I'm very sorry, you can't bring that in here,' she says. 'It's against the rules.'

I love Janet. She isn't your typical receptionist; she just isn't fierce enough. She isn't the best advert for the practice either because she always looks under the weather – thin and pale, with lank, shoulder-length mousy hair – but she's the kind of person who will do anything for anyone, and within moments she's agreeing to keep the liver and white springer spaniel behind her desk.

'Please don't bring Jack again, Ed,' she says.

'He won't do any harm.'

'I know that, but this is a doctor's surgery, not the vet's. It isn't hygienic to have dogs in here.'

'Please, Janet. If I don't get the baby seen to the wife will kill me.'

That doesn't convince me – Ed's a broad-shouldered, outdoorsy kind of man. I can't imagine him feeling threatened by anyone, least of all his mild-mannered wife, Ellen, who works full-time in the local dairy, making specialist cheeses, while Ed looks after the children and does part-time gamekeeping and general maintenance in return for a tied cottage on a country estate just outside Talymouth, the coastal resort where I was born.

'Please,' Ed repeats.

'You'll get me into trouble.' Janet is wavering. 'I'm not a dog-sitter.'

'I forgot I had him with me,' Ed says. 'I can't leave him in the Land Rover in case the sun comes out.'

'I don't think that's likely to happen. The rain's set in

36

for the day.' Janet leans across the desk to take the dog's lead. 'Give him here. I'll keep him quiet, then no one—' she glances at me with a little smile on her face '—will know any different.'

'Thanks, my lover,' Ed says, using the peculiarly Devonian term of endearment. 'You've saved my life.' He moves the baby onto his hip and turns to me. 'Hello, Nicci. I've brought Milo back again.' He wipes his forehead with the back of his hand. I don't know about Milo, but Ed doesn't look so great. He stands round-shouldered, weary and overdressed for a summer's day, like an Arctic explorer who's lost his way. He's sporting an odd combination of green wellington boots, khaki shorts and layered tops under a shooting vest fastened very tight across his chest. In fact, the vest could be part of him – I've never seen Ed without it.

I'm tempted to feel sorry for him because he left it a bit late to have children, ending up with three under fives – Ivy, Peaches and baby Milo – in his fiftieth year, but I get the impression he wouldn't have it any other way.

I hold the consulting room door open for him, and as he passes I catch the scent of warm milk and baby sick on his clothes.

'How are you?' I ask when he's sitting down with the baby on his lap.

'I'm shattered. We all are. Milo won't sleep – he's got a terrible cough again. He sounds like he's barking.'

'Let's have a look at him.'

'Have you got kids?' Ed takes a non-spill cup out of

one of the many pockets in his vest and gives it to Milo, who grabs it with his chubby hands and sucks noisily on the spout. He's about fifteen months old, a funny-looking baby with a big round face, large blue eyes and blond hair crackling with static and standing straight up like a golden halo. His cheeks are chapped and he's wearing a vest, pink shorts (hand-me-downs from his sisters) and a nappy.

I shake my head.

'It's bloody hard work. We didn't think having a third one would make all that much difference. Not that it's put Ellen off having any more.' He smiles ruefully. 'She wants another boy to even up the numbers. I've told her one more and that's it for me. If she wants a fifth, she'll have to find herself a new husband.'

I find it strange that some people are intent on having as many children as they can, while others are keen to avoid having any at all.

I concentrate on Milo, who stares at me when I approach him with the stethoscope, warming the bell in my hand before I slide it under his vest. At first, he looks as if he's about to burst into tears, but when I tell him how clever he is, he offers up a placatory smile, revealing his gleaming white teeth.

He has a chest infection, the second in as many months. 'I'm going to prescribe him more antibiotics. Does he go to nursery or the toddler group?'

Ed nods. 'He has a better social life than I do.'

'It's pretty common for babies to catch coughs and colds that turn into chest infections. He's meeting all kinds of bugs that his immune system hasn't come across before and it takes a while to build up resistance against them.' I gaze at Ed, hoping he's reassured by my explanation, but he falls quiet. I don't know what it is but there's something different about him since I last saw him with Milo, and I can't put my finger on it. I'm not psychic, but I can sense from my experience as a doctor when there's something wrong. 'You're all right, are you, Ed?' I ask again.

'There's nothing wrong with me,' he says quickly – maybe too quickly. 'As I said, it's lack of sleep, that's all.'

'Hopefully Milo will sleep better once he's had a couple of days on antibiotics – this one's banana-flavoured, so he should like it.'

'But it doesn't taste of bananas, does it? And it isn't the colour of bananas. In fact, I don't suppose it's ever been near a banana.'

'Probably not,' I say, smiling at his analysis.

I pause while the prescription emerges from the printer on the desk. I hand it over to Ed. 'You can take this straight to Bev, the pharmacist up the road. I'd like to see Milo again at the end of the course, or before if you're at all concerned about his progress.' Not only will I have another listen to Milo's chest, I'll be able to check up on Ed too.

When we return to reception, Jack the dog is sitting on one of the waiting room chairs sharing a packet of ginger biscuits with Nobby Warwick, elderly church organist and heavy drinker, while Janet looks on.

Ed whistles between his teeth and the spaniel pricks

his ears but remains seated, apparently torn between following his owner's command and drooling over one last ginger biscuit which Nobby holds within snapping distance of his nose. Jack sits patiently until Ed says, 'All right. You may have it,' then he takes it very gently from between Nobby's trembling fingers.

'Would someone like to tell me what's going on here?' Claire comes waltzing in from the nurses' room where she sees her appointments. 'What on earth is that doing in here?' She turns to me at the same time. 'I thought you of all people would know better than to let that mangy mutt in here. All those germs . . .'

'He doesn't have germs,' Ed says in Jack's defence as the dog joins him, standing at his feet and looking adoringly up at his master.

'And he doesn't look mangy to me,' I join in. In fact, from the expression of pure joy on Nobby's face, I reckon it's a shame I can't prescribe a dog for every patient.

'You're not a vet, Nicci,' Claire says.

'No,' and I don't know why but an image of Matt Warren enters my mind, which turns out to be a bit of a coincidence.

Later, when I change into my jodhpurs and go up to the yard to spend my free afternoon with Willow, Matt is there in the stable next to Willow's with Delphi and Dark Star.

Delphi is hanging onto Dark Star's head, keeping him reversed into the corner of the box. Matt, unaware of my presence, is wearing a headlamp and looks more like a miner than a vet as he peers into the depths of the horse's mouth held open by a metal gag. 'We've had a bit of trouble with Dark Star,' Delphi says. 'Matt had to sedate him to do his teeth. You had to give him a double dose, didn't you?'

'You wouldn't think so,' he mutters as the horse leans back into the wall and throws his head right up. 'Mind yourself, Delphi.'

'Behave!' Delphi tugs at the end of the lead-rope attached to Dark Star's head-collar. 'Sometimes I hate this horse. I'm always having to tell him off.'

'I don't know why you've kept him so long,' Matt grumbles.

'Because no one else will have him.' Delphi rubs the horse's shoulder.

'He isn't all bad,' I say.

'Why don't you ride him then?' Delphi says abruptly.

'Because Willow's my priority.'

'And you're scared of this brute. Everyone is, except me.' I don't argue with her because if I'm honest, I've seen how Dark Star can behave in the school and I do want to stay in one piece for the rest of the season. 'He's six now, and if he doesn't come right by the end of the summer, I'm going to sell him on. He'll do a half-decent dressage test on a good day. He'll make a nice horse for someone, just not for me, which is very disappointing when we bred him ourselves.' Delphi is referring to herself and her sister – they own a couple of broodmares between them. Her sister and brother-in-law are working overseas, so Delphi is looking after the horses.

I don't think Matt is listening to us. All his attention and effort is centred on rasping the horse's teeth with a long metal implement that looks like something out of a torture chamber. The muscles on his upper arm bulge and swell in rhythm with the strokes of the rasp, but when it catches on the overgrown hooks on the horse's back teeth, I notice how he winces and bites his lip, taking a breath before starting again.

Gradually, the sound of metal against tooth becomes less grating as the enamel hooks grow smooth and Dark Star quietens down. Matt drops the rasp in the horse's water bucket and checks his handiwork.

'That's all good,' he pronounces. He loosens the gag and slips the headpiece over the horse's ears, removing it completely. 'He's going to go to sleep now,' he goes on, rubbing the horse's face.

Matt turns towards the stable door.

'Oh, hi,' he says, noticing me for the first time.

'Hi,' I say. 'Where's the sling?'

'I must have put it down somewhere,' he says lightly, 'or used it for polishing my boots. Anyway, I don't think I could put a sling on without assistance.'

'You could have asked someone to help.'

'Like you, you mean?' he says quickly. 'What, and let you stick pins in me?'

'I have steady hands,' I confirm. 'I could have been a surgeon, if I'd wanted to.'

'Well, I can't turn up to a yard in a sling.' He grins and my heart lurches. 'Besides, it isn't a good look.'

'You make a terrible patient,' I joke, then wish I hadn't said it in front of Delphi because she picks up on it instantly.

'Do you know each other then?'

'I'm Nicci's patient,' he says, as if he's the only one. 'She's caught me out. I'm supposed to be taking time off to rest my shoulder.'

'Oh dear,' says Delphi. 'Have you tried some of that nutritional supplement you suggested for the old pony? I swear by it. It's done wonders for my knee.'

'So, if we trotted you up now, Delphi, you'd be one hundred per cent sound,' Matt says with a twinkle in his eye. 'You're not supposed to take it yourself. It's designed specifically for equines.'

She snorts with amusement. 'I've been around them for so awfully long, I feel I can count myself as a horse. If that doesn't work, there's always the liniment.'

'The dreaded liniment?' Matt says. 'I thought I'd managed to convince everyone around here to leave that well alone.'

'It works though,' Delphi insists.

'It scalds the skin. I've treated more horses for the side effects of liniment than I care to count. Please, tell me you've destroyed all your old stock and you aren't selling it under the counter in the shop any more. The world has moved on.'

'Sometimes the old stuff is the best—'

'No, Delphi. Throw it away,' Matt cuts in. He looks at me, his eyes flashing with amusement. 'Why don't people listen?'

'That's funny, I have the same problem,' I point out with a chuckle.

'Well, I have a good excuse for disobeying doctor's orders. I can't find anyone else to step in for me. I'm indispensible.'

'I hope you remember that when you can't work because you have chronic arthritis.'

'That's a very harsh prognosis. I have no choice – my partner is on paternity leave for a couple more weeks, so I'll have to wait. It doesn't help that our houseman—'

'Mel?' says Delphi.

'Yes, Mel,' he says with a sigh of resignation. 'I don't know how she managed it, but she broke the electric dental burr so we're having to do everything manually.'

'I expect you can afford a new one,' Delphi says.

'A new burr or a new houseman?' Matt says brightly.

'Will she be moving on soon?'

'In about four months, when her contract runs out. We'll miss her.'

I notice that he doesn't specify that he in particular will miss her. He doesn't talk about her as if he's her boyfriend.

'It's a shame,' Delphi says. 'When Honey, the little Shetland pony, was in for her MRI scan, Mel was a great support. I spoke to her twice, three times a day. She was utterly marvellous.'

Matt changes the subject. 'Now, what else do you have for me today?'

'Willow's due her vaccinations,' Delphi says.

'Nicci's horse?' Matt says, looking me up and down, his eyes lingering briefly on my legs, making me glad that I chose my clingiest pair of jodhs.

'Is she due?' I frown. Sometimes I worry that I've let

Delphi take over my horse. I should know whether or not her vaccinations are due.

'I told you on Monday that I was booking a visit from the vet.' Delphi emerges from the stable and picks up a green booklet from the ledge alongside the door. She hands it over to Matt when he's finished washing his hands under the outside tap.

'Is she well?' Matt peruses the pages of the passport containing Willow's ID and record of her annual flu and tetanus jabs.

'Yes, awfully,' Delphi says. 'She looks amazing at the moment.'

'You'd better introduce me,' Matt says.

She steps forward with a head-collar, but I take it from her.

'It's all right. I'll do it. I'm sure you have plenty of other things to do.' I catch Willow and hold her close to the doorway, but Delphi's still hovering outside.

'Delphi, I can manage,' I say sternly, and she reluctantly disappears across the yard to the feed room to start mixing the evening feeds.

'Why aren't you at work?' Matt asks.

'I finish early on Fridays. I have a surgery every other Saturday and two late evenings a week,' I say, wondering why I feel I have to justify my time off to him.

'It's no wonder I pay so much tax – so that GPs can swan about on Friday afternoons.' I think he's joking. 'I bet you don't even have to do nights.'

'The surgery has an out of hours service.'

'I should have been a doctor – I was up all night with a colic. The horse is in recovery, but I doubt it's going to make it.' He glances at his watch. 'I've got the client lined up to come in after work to say their goodbyes.'

'That's so sad.'

'You win some and lose some,' he says philosophically. 'It's pretty gutting for me and the team when we've agonised about putting the horse through major surgery, opted to go for it and then it gives up.'

I watch how he approaches Willow, how she sniffs at his outstretched hand, her nostrils flaring as she decides that she and Matt can be friends. I smile to myself. I trust Willow's judgement. If she likes him, he must be all right.

Matt heads off to his four-by-four and returns with the combined vaccine, needle and syringe. Delphi comes back from the feed room, apparently afraid to miss out on any horsey gossip.

'Where are you going next, Matt?' she asks.

'To check on a horse with a nasty gash on its leg from some barbed wire. I don't know why the stuff hasn't been banned. It's everywhere, but it keeps me in work,' he goes on, smiling wryly. 'Nicci, how's the poor guy who was having a heart attack, the one who was taken off in the ambulance the other day?'

'He's doing okay,' I say, wary about how much I should reveal, but pleased that Matt is concerned. It makes up for his attitude when he first marched into my consulting room, complaining about my running late. It makes him seem more human.

Matt draws up the vaccine and injects it into Willow's neck. She doesn't flinch.

'You're a brave horse.' Stroking her, he turns to me. 'Are you riding at East Hill?'

'Yes, I can't wait.' My chest tightens with anticipation tinged with a touch of fear at the thought of galloping Willow around the cross-country course on Saturday. 'East Hill is my favourite course ever,' I go on.

'You're mad.' Matt's eyes fix on mine.

'I love it,' I say lightly.

Matt's expression is sober, his tone critical. 'I will never understand why people risk their lives like that in the name of sport.'

'You'd be out of a job if everyone thought like that,' I observe.

'That's true.' He changes the subject. 'I'm done here now, so you can go for your ride.'

'Oh no, I won't take her out tonight. I always give her a couple of days off after she's had her jab.'

'There's no need.' He smiles when I shake my head. 'But why take any notice of me when I'm just a vet and you're paying me for my opinion? There doesn't seem any point in paying for advice you're planning to ignore, although a lot of people do,' he goes on with a grin.

'It doesn't feel right,' I say adamantly.

'I don't think you should rely on feelings. I like your horse, by the way.'

'She's a good sort, isn't she?' Delphi cuts in.

'Yep,' Matt agrees, his eyes on my face and then my legs again. 'She has great presence and perfect con-formation.' He signs Willow's passport and hands it over. 'I'll see you next weekend.'

'Oh?' I say, confused.

'At East Hill – I'm the duty vet. Goodbye, Nicci. Delphi, I'll see you on Monday to check on the pony.' He glances back as he walks off across the yard to the car park, a grin on his face when he calls out, 'I'll make sure I bring my sling with me, Doctor.'

'Matt doesn't normally pass comment on a horse,' Delphi says later when we're drinking cans of diet Coke from the fridge in the tack room.

'I think he was talking about me,' I say, blushing. 'He's a bit of a flirt, isn't he?'

'If he was a horse, I'd describe him as a nice sort, hard to find. He's lovely, but he's very young. I couldn't believe he was old enough to be a vet when I first met him.'

'He's about the same age as me.'

'You seem too young to be a doctor.' Delphi pauses. 'Matt's a great vet. We used to have Alex Fox-Gifford and his father from the mixed practice in Talyton, but we had a falling-out and went to Westleigh instead. They aren't cheap, but you get what you pay for.'

'I don't mind how much it costs,' I say. 'I want the best for Willow.'

I want the best for my mum too, and I spend the rest of the evening, having showered and eaten, half reading a book and half waiting for her texts. I'm like a mother fretting about her teenage daughter, which is ironic, considering that's how she used to be with me, except that fourteen or fifteen years ago I didn't have a mobile phone. I can now understand how anxious she must have felt, and I can also see that she must have been worried sick over my sister when she disappeared at sixteen, running away with a man twice her age.

She texts me three times in total, the final one at midnight, saying 'Home safely, lol Mumx Ring me if you are awake.'

I smile to myself. She wants to tell me all about it, so it was either a complete disaster or a raving success. I call her.

'Did you get my texts?' she says.

'Of course I did, thank you.'

'It would have been quicker to phone you each time – I'm all fingers and thumbs when I'm texting – but I thought that would be just too embarrassing.'

'It would help if you used proper text-speak, not your archaic version. How many times have I told you "lol" means "laugh out loud", not "lots of love"? Oh, never mind. How was the date?'

'He's lovely,' she says with a giggle. 'He has a tan – a natural one – and he looks more like Roger Moore as 007 than an Oompa-Loompa.'

'That's a relief,' I say lightly. 'Does he drive an Aston Martin?'

'Um, no . . .'

'Are you going to enlighten me?' I say, sensing that she's holding something back. 'Let me guess, he's a farmer so he turned up at the pub in his tractor or his combine harvester?'

'It's better than that, darling. He arrived with a pony and trap – he's broken the pony to drive quite recently and added lights and reflectors to the harness and cart. It's wonderful.'

'What did he do with the pony?'

'He unhitched her from the trap and tethered her on the verge outside the pub. She's a chunky little black cob called Beauty with the longest mane and thickest tail you've ever seen, the polar opposite of Willow. Everyone loves her.'

'I suppose it's one way to cut back on the cost of petrol. Did he pay for the drinks?' I continue, wanting to know if he's tight-fisted and only after my mum for her money.

'He paid for everything,' Mum says sharply, and I apologise for having a suspicious mind. 'I know he sounds too good to be true, but I think he's completely genuine, a real country gentleman.'

'Do you have much in common? I mean, did the conversation flow?'

'Nicci, I wish you'd get a life,' Mum teases, 'then you wouldn't have all this time to worry about mine. Now, before you ask, I'm seeing him again.'

'You will text me? Same rules apply.'

'Goodnight, Nicci.'

'Goodnight, Mum.'

Chapter Four

Horsepower

'Are you sure you've got everything?' Mum asks as we set out in the lorry early on a Saturday morning in the middle of June.

'Isn't it your job to check, as unpaid groom?' I say cheekily.

I love driving the lorry. I have a great view of the countryside, looking over the hedgerows filled with flowers to the panoramic Devon hills bathed in pale sunlight. We pass a herd of black and white cows grazing in a field. Some are chewing the cud as if pondering the meaning of life.

'I wonder what those cows are thinking about,' I say. 'I mean, what do they do all day?'

'Nicci, what an odd thing to say.'

'Well, it is a bit of a mystery, isn't it?' I look briefly at my mother's face. Her eyes are downcast, her lips compressed into a thin straight line, and I know what – or who – she's thinking about. My mother, Kathryn, is resilient and usually quietly content with life. She used to event herself until she got married and had a family. She makes an excellent groom, and is also one of those annoying people who manage to stay clean and tidy when they're working around horses. She's been plaiting Willow's mane and loading the lorry, yet she looks immaculate in an ice-blue top, navy waistcoat and cream casual trousers.

'Everything's a bit of a mystery to me at the moment,' she goes on. 'Have you managed to get in contact with your sister recently?' I notice how she refuses to refer to Cheska as her daughter. When I don't respond, she continues, 'I understand you don't want to tell me, but I need to know that my grandchildren are safe, even if . . .' her voice fades then returns, '. . . I can't see them.'

'I spoke to her on the phone a while ago – I did tell you.'

'Have you given her money again?'

'It's a loan – she's going to pay me back.'

'You'll be telling me that pigs can fly next,' Mum says scathingly. 'Oh, slow down, darling,' she ex-claims, grabbing the edge of her seat as the lorry swings into a zigzag bend.

'I *am* going slowly.' I drive as if I have a dozen eggs loose on a tray in the back of the lorry with Willow. I did that for real once and I didn't crack a single egg, but Mum's comment and the thought of the competition ahead unnerves me. I have butterflies doing the salsa in my stomach.

'How is the lonely farmer?' I ask. 'What's he like? You haven't really gone into detail.'

'He's what *you'd* describe as an old man.' She laughs. 'I'm sure you don't want to know every wrinkle.'

'How old?'

'A few years older than me . . .'

'How much older?'

'Fourteen years.'

'Fourteen?' I say, appalled.

'Really, Nicci, fourteen years might seem like a huge gap to you, but to me it's nothing. Age is just a number.'

'But that makes him seventy.'

'He's very fit,' Mum says, her voice bubbling with happiness and humour. 'He has his own teeth and his own hair, and to be honest, I'd almost got to the point where all I was asking for was a man with a pulse. He's lovely and I hope one day I'll introduce him to you.' Mum changes the subject. 'Would you like me to run through the test with you?'

She's referring to the dressage test, but it's already etched in my mind. I glance at the side-view mirror, catching sight of a line of traffic, at least six cars, a caravan and behind that – I can see it as we start to climb the long Devon hill – a big red tractor. I put my foot down to the floor, but the lorry maintains its slow crawl. I can't believe I'm actually holding up an agricultural vehicle.

We arrive eventually and park in the field allocated as the lorry park at the end of the second row of horseboxes and trailers. I switch off the engine and take a few slow breaths before getting out and joining my mother, who already has the ramp down at the back and is leading Willow out on her head-collar. She ties her to the baling twine attached to the metal ring at the side of the lorry, tying her short so she can't snatch at the grass under her feet.

'You sort yourself out while I see to Willow.' Mum checks her watch. 'You have about an hour before your test.'

I start to walk towards the ramp to take a short cut into the living quarters that lie between the stall and the cab when a voice catches my attention.

'Hello, Nicci.'

'Henry?' I turn to find myself face to face with a black horse's gleaming shoulder. I look up, shading my eyes. It's my most recent ex-boyfriend, mounted on his horse, his fingers playing on the reins, his legs long against the horse's sides. He's looking incredibly cool in his hat, black dressage coat, white breeches and leather boots, while the horse is sweating already, its veins standing proud of its skin.

'How are you?' Henry leans down and runs his fingers under the girth to check it's secure.

'I'm well, thank you.' I was warm, but my blood runs a little cold at the sight of him. 'And you?'

'Oh, I'm on top form.' He grins. 'As always.'

Arrogant . . . I refrain from swearing, even under my breath. He just isn't worth it. No more tears. No more pain. It's over.

When I returned to Talyton St George to work at the surgery after my GP training, I went out with Henry. Like Shane, he used to be a member of the Talyton branch of the Pony Club. He was a couple of years older than me and was in all the Pony Club teams: eventing, showjumping and tetrathlon. He was ambitious even then and had his heart set on becoming an international eventer, which he's achieved, riding for the British team at the European Eventing Championships on one of his more experienced horses.

Tall, gangly, blond and blue-eyed, he always had the girls flocking around him. At Pony Club camp, he never mucked out or cleaned his tack or his boots. There was always some willing volunteer to do it for him. But I wasn't one of them, something he pointed out to me when we met again eighteen months ago, and maybe it was something I should have heeded when he was pursuing me like a huntsman after a fox.

I went out with him for several wonderful months. We had so much in common with the horses. It was perfect, too good to be true. But soon Henry was off in pursuit of his next prey, his new groom, although I didn't find out about it until I turned up at his flat one evening to find his new lover spanking him with a horsewhip.

I wanted to do more than spank him. I was furious, embarrassed and devastated, and in spite of his attempts to dismiss it as an isolated incident, a moment of weakness, I drove away, blocked his number on my mobile and refused to see him again.

I can hear the ripping sound of Velcro being pulled apart as Mum removes Willow's travel boots.

'How about catching up sometime, Nicci?' Henry says. 'For old times' sake?'

55

'In your dreams, Henry,' I say sharply.

'You could make my dreams a reality,' he wheedles. 'Come on. You're so bloody serious. What's wrong with having a bit of fun?'

Because it wasn't a bit of fun for me, I want to say, but I know it isn't worth it. Henry will never understand.

'Are you attached, or something?' he says, his expression still hopeful.

'Well, yes, I am actually,' I say quickly, grabbing the opportunity to put him off.

'Anyone I know?'

'I'm not saying because it's none of your business, but I do have a boyfriend. I have done for a while,' I elaborate. 'Did you really think I'd sit around moping over you for the rest of my life?'

'Go on. Who is it?' Henry persists. 'You know I won't believe you if you don't tell me. Is it one of your doctor friends?'

'If you must know,' I say stiffly, 'it's Matt Warren.' I'm not sure what's come over me. I wouldn't normally dream of making something like that up, but then Matt has hinted that he likes me.

'Matt, the vet?'

'Satisfied?'

'Surprised.' He smiles ruefully. 'He's kept that one quiet.'

I keep my mouth firmly shut as Henry continues, 'I'd better get on and warm up. This is one of my novices. What do you think?'

'He's a good-looking sort.'

'I see you're still flogging a dead horse.' Henry looks

towards Willow. 'You really need something bigger and with more scope.'

'She does a good test.'

'But she's inconsistent jumping. You can't make a horse more careful.'

'I'm not going to give up on her.'

'You should have a couple of youngsters coming along behind.'

'If wishes were horses . . .'

'Good luck.' Henry turns his horse on a sixpence. 'You're going to need it,' he adds over his shoulder as they walk away.

'I never did like that boy,' Mum says when I start stripping off my sweatshirt and waterproof trousers to reveal my shirt and jodhs.

'He's hardly a boy any more.' I grin at her. 'You thought he was amazing when we were going out together.'

'Did I? I don't remember,' she says, but I'm sure she does. 'Hurry up, Nicci. Just make sure you beat him today. It would give me great pleasure.'

Although I'm happy to go along with dissing Henry for his behaviour, I'm not stupid. I did play a part in the demise of our relationship. When I look back, it was all a bit too convenient, everything falling into place when I started working in Talyton. I was single. Henry was available. It seemed as if it was meant to be, and although I was heartbroken for a while after his betrayal, I sensed that I was never as committed as I could have been. I thought I loved him, but on reflection, I didn't love him enough.

Dismissing thoughts of Henry, I fasten my stock around my neck, keeping it in place with my lucky pin, and pull on my jacket. I tie my hair back and tuck it inside a hairnet before putting my hat on and slipping into my leather boots. I fasten my gloves at the wrists, pick up my long dressage whip, adjust Willow's bridle after Mum's tacked her up, and we're ready to go.

I lead Willow up alongside the ramp so I can jump on and walk her down to the warm-up area.

'I'll catch up with you in a minute,' Mum calls after me, and I wave back as I ride to the top of the hill.

Although it's a warm day there's a breeze at the top of the escarpment where the ground falls steeply down to the valley covered in scrub and gorse. There are a few stands of tough firs and a tumbledown stone building, marking the highest point where the locals used to light beacons. The views stretch to the sea in the far south, and to rolling green hills to the north.

I give myself a mental nudge to concentrate on Willow rather than my surroundings, but it doesn't have any effect at first. I'm aware of other riders cantering past me and the crackle of loudspeaker announcements attenu - ated by the wind. There's a tack stall, a stand advertising Devon dairy ice cream and a hotdog and burger van emitting the scent of fried onions, which contributes to the nausea I'm feeling at the thought of entering the main dressage arena with its sand and rubber surface, the gleaming white marker boards around the perimeter and the judges' box at the end.

As I gradually ease Willow into trot and then canter on both reins, I forget about everything. It's just me and the horse, working in harmony. The nerves disappear and the test crystallises in my head, and when the steward calls me over to the arena, I'm ready.

I enter at a trot, straight up the centre line. The test flows, each movement leading into the next, and at the end, when I salute the judge, my throat tight with love and pride for my horse. I know we couldn't have done any better.

Mum is in the warm-up area, waiting with Willow's cooler, which she throws up over her back.

'That was fantastic,' she says, giving Willow a mint.

'She was brilliant, wasn't she?' I couldn't be more pleased.

As I take Willow back to the lorry for a break until the showjumping phase, I keep an eye out for Matt. I don't like to admit it but I'm slightly disappointed when I don't see him.

With a change of jacket, hat and tack, I'm ready for the jumping phase. Mum swaps our dressage saddle for the jumping one, and leads Willow around for me while I walk the course with my fellow competitors. Henry is there, but I keep my distance, concentrating on the route I'm planning to take and how to make the most of the corners to ensure Willow stays at a balanced and controlled canter while not lingering anywhere because the time allowed is tight. Shane and I walked the cross-country course yesterday, but the jumps in the arena weren't set up. It's a fair course, except for the treble, a row of three fences, related by one and two strides between them, and I wish I had him walking with me again, not so much for advice as for moral support.

I rejoin Mum and she gives me a leg-up. I adjust my stirrups and Willow and I are off again, warming up in the collecting ring over an upright fence and a small spread. I don't jump too big before my round because, as Henry kindly observed, Willow isn't the most reliable showjumper. If I push her now, she'll decide she's done enough and will put less effort into her jumping when we're in the ring. I could wear spurs like Henry and let her know who's boss, except that for Willow the saying 'You can tell a gelding, but you have to ask a mare' holds true.

I have a view of the main jumping arena, where Henry is first to go with his black horse, Karizma. Willow and I walk around, keeping half an eye on how he approaches each jump. It's useful watching another competitor – you can get a sense of where the problems are on the course – and Henry jumps it perfectly and within the time. He makes it look easy.

I stroke Willow's neck and give her a pep talk as Mum comes walking over to give me the news that I'm in the lead after the dressage and Henry is second.

'No pressure then,' I say with a nervous smile.

Within twenty minutes, we're in the arena, cantering down to the first fence, a plain rustic upright that Willow clears with ease. I keep the canter steady, although she's fighting for her head, wanting to go faster and fly them like a steeplechaser, which is not good because she'll flatten out and take the poles with her.

'Steady,' I murmur. 'Steady.'

We jump the next four with a good rhythm, then

turn away from the entrance to the collecting ring to face a double spread of blue and white poles gleaming in the sunshine. Willow's ears flick back and she slows the pace, knowing very well she's close to the exit, but I'm ready for her, giving her a good nudge with my heels to send her forwards to the next fence, another spread with a spooky filler painted with tiger's eyes. Willow doesn't hesitate, flying that one and extending nicely for the water jump. And now it's the penultimate obstacle, the tricky treble. I'd like to take a pull to steady her up, but I'm aware that time is ticking away and every tenth of a second counts.

Willow flies the first element, takes one stride, flies the next and takes two short strides to the third. I hear the rap of her hooves against the back pole when we're suspended in the air, and I'm listening for the sound of the pole hitting the ground as we canter away, knowing that our chance of a placing let alone a win could be over.

But it doesn't fall and I can focus on the last obstacle, another spread. I feel Willow lifting herself into the air, tucking her forelegs under her chest and arching her back to make the height before she stretches across the parallel bars and lands well beyond as I push her on through the finish.

Clear! We're clear! I lean forwards, patting Willow's neck as she steadies her pace. I can't believe it. We've been close before, but not so close that I can almost smell victory.

'And that's a clear round within the time allowed, so no penalties to add to the dressage score for Nicci

Chieveley and Willow, keeping them in the lead just ahead of Henry Belton-Smith and Karizma,' the commentator says over the loudspeakers.

I let Willow canter a half circle before bringing her back to a trot.

'That was fabulous,' Mum says, meeting us in the collecting ring. 'Whatever she's on, I'm having some of it.'

'There's no magic ingredient,' I say, smiling as I catch my breath and thanking Shane inwardly for making me go to the gym for a couple of sessions on the cross-trainer.

Willow doesn't care. All she's interested in is nudging Mum's pockets for another mint.

'Hi, Nicci. I caught the end of your round,' Matt says, strolling up to join us. 'I'm impressed.' He's dressed in a short-sleeved check shirt and chinos, and there's no sign of a sling.

'Thank you,' I say a little awkwardly.

'I haven't had too much to do as yet. I've sent two horses home, one with a nosebleed and one that came off the box lame.' He smiles broadly.

The heat from the sun burns into my back and my hair is damp and sticky under my hat.

'Aren't you going to introduce me?' Mum says, hovering. I can see her eyeing him up, and I think please, please, please, don't say anything embarrassing.

'This is Matt, the vet. Matt, this is Kathryn, my mother.'

'And groom,' Mum adds.

'That as well,' I say cheerfully. 'I couldn't do it without her.'

'We'd better be moving on,' she says. 'Willow needs to cool down before the cross-country.'

'Ah, I won't be watching that.' Matt looks at me through narrowed eyes, his mood more serious now. 'As I said before, I don't understand you horse people. You'll break your neck one of these days.'

'Don't be so dramatic, I've been on horses since I was three.'

'Doesn't it ever worry you?'

'It doesn't.' At least it didn't, until he mentioned it. 'If I thought I was going to fall off every time, I wouldn't entertain it.' I imagine Shane speaking to me, 'Stay positive, VB', and it helps.

'Good luck,' Matt says. 'I'll catch up with you later.'

'What did he mean by that?' Mum asks, watching him walk away towards the marquee, where the organisers are calling for the last of the jump judges to make their way to their positions on the cross-country course.

'I don't know.' I shrug. 'He's a patient – and my vet.' Having seen him working at Delphi's yard, I realise I don't want anyone else looking after Willow from now on.

'You kept that one quiet.'

'Any interest I have in him is purely professional.' I look down and fiddle with the buckle on the reins.

'I don't think he sees it that way. Come on, Nicci. I'm not blind. He came across especially to talk to you. He couldn't take his eyes off you.'

'Delphi says he has a girlfriend.' I'm flattered by the attention, but nothing can come of it if he's attached. 'Mum, please don't distract me. I've got to get Willow's bandages on and get changed.' I dismount and take the reins over Willow's head to lead her back to the lorry. Henry is already in his red and black cross-country colours. He frowns and jams his skullcap on his head when he sees me, then bends down and picks up his crop, slapping it against his boot.

'You reckon that old nag's going to get round the course clear today?'

'It's her favourite phase,' I say. 'She'll fly it.'

'We'll see.' Henry whistles between his teeth and a girl of about eighteen emerges from the side door of his lorry with a can of cola in one hand and an apple in the other. She sticks the apple between her teeth and hangs onto Henry's horse while he vaults into the saddle.

'All the best,' I say generously, in spite of his criticism of Willow.

Henry gives his mount an unnecessary slap on the flank and the horse breaks into canter with a buck that almost unseats him.

'Serves you right,' the girl mutters, before turning away and disappearing into the lorry.

It isn't long before I'm back in the saddle, wearing my pale blue and purple silk over my skullcap, and an air vest for protection. Willow knows what's coming next and she's on her toes, shying at everything on the way to the warm-up area at the start of the course.

We pop over the log a couple of times between the red and white flags, listening to my competitors' progress via the loudspeaker announcements. Henry has gone clear within the time, so I know we have no room for error as I run through the course in my head, visualising the approach to every obstacle, as planned with Shane when we walked the course.

The starter calls me into the box. Willow prances about on the spot, jerking her head forwards in a vain attempt to snatch the reins from my hands, but I know her too well.

'No way,' I tell her, chuckling in spite of my nerves at the thought of jumping a course that's at the top end of Willow's limits and mine. 'That little trick doesn't work any more. Remember?'

The starter calls the countdown. 'Three, two, one.'

And we're off, straight into a fast canter down the gentle slope to a rustic fence filled in with straw bales which Willow jumps fluidly before we gallop across the grass for the next, an enormous log followed by a skinny fence, which catches some horses out. Not Willow though. She has no intention of doing anything but jumping them. It takes all my strength to pull her back under control when we jump off the bank, heading down to the tiger trap and beyond to the water, which is a straightforward trot in and jump out, followed by a pair of gates. It's fast, fun and exhilarat - ing, and I'm not worried about the time because Willow is going for it, her long strides eating up the ground.

The next is a ditch with a steep drop on the other side. I give Willow a kick and a 'Click, click' as she takes an extra stride into it.

'Trust me,' I tell her and she responds, throwing herself over the top. I sit back, letting the reins slip through my fingers and we land safely on the other side. The rest is a formality, a long steady gallop over the remaining fences to the finish. I let Willow slow to a canter then a trot, and finally we walk to the cheers of the crowd waiting at the end of the course.

Mum can't speak and nor can I. She grabs Willow's reins while I dismount and through a blur of tears relieve my wonderful horse of the weight of the saddle. I can feel Mum's arms around me and hear her barely audible whisper of congratulation as she gives me a warm hug. I can't believe it. It's going to take a while to sink in. With this win, my dream of competing at Badminton among the elite has moved that much closer. I watch Willow stand as Mum throws her cooler over her back. She's blowing, her nostrils flared and red inside, and her chest is heaving. She's put her heart and soul into this, and even though I'm breathless and too hot to think straight, my chest tightens – I'm so proud of her. I step close and hug her neck, inhaling the scent of steaming horse and sweaty leather. Noticing one of her plaits has come undone, I remove the plaiting band caught in the tiny curls of her mane and run my fingers through to straighten them out.

Back at the lorry, Mum washes Willow down with cool water and a sponge while I scrape the excess moisture from her coat with a sweat scraper, and throw on a clean rug before I walk her around to let her dry off. When she's stopped sweating, I let her pick at some grass while I brush her and tack her up for the presentation.

She swishes her tail when I put the saddle back on and gives me a look as if to say, 'Not again'.

'Humour me,' I tell her. 'You can have a day off tomorrow.'

'Your jacket,' Mum says, handing it over. 'You can't go in for the presentation looking as if you've been through a hedge backwards.' She brushes me down as if I'm about five and going to school in uniform for the first time. 'I'm going to find myself a good place to watch.'

Henry moves up beside me and we ride down to the main arena, almost knee to knee, our stirrups clashing. The arena has been cleared, the jumps stacked neatly onto a tractor and trailer, and the other prize-winners are waiting for us to take the lead and enter first. Willow is excited, jogging along to the presentation area in front of the small grandstand, but she seems a touch sore and I wonder if she's bruised her foot.

We stand at the head of the line with Henry beside us, his horse champing at the bit and flicking foam from his mouth.

'Congrats,' Henry says, his grim expression relaxing into a smile. 'Well ridden, Nicci.'

'Thank you,' I say, realising what an effort that must have taken him. 'I like your horse. He looks like he's got a great future.'

'Even though I can't believe he was beaten by a donkey.' Henry's eyes crease into a grin. We've come to a truce, I think, although I'll never forgive him for cheating on me. 'I had a chat with Matt about you and him.'

'Oh?' I say as nonchalantly as I can as a tsunami of blood rushes to the roots of my hair and the tips of my ears.

'It's all right. I can keep my trap shut.'

I cringe. What must Matt think? How will I ever face him again? I glance at the crowd of spectators gathered to watch the presentation, and there he is. I look away quickly, but it's too late, I've caught his eye. He smiles and waves. I nod back. Perhaps it isn't so bad. I can only hope that Matt assumes Henry has got the wrong end of the stick.

When I said Matt was my boyfriend I didn't think about the consequences. I should have guessed that Matt was Henry's vet – I knew Henry was one of Westleigh Equine's clients. I should also have had more than an inkling that Henry would pursue my statement because he likes to gossip. He'd relish being the first to spread the news among the horsey set.

I'm presented with a red rosette the colour of my face, a silver plate and a small cash prize, but these are mere tokens compared to how I feel. Winning is reward enough and I'm euphoric as I canter my beautiful horse around the arena for the lap of honour.

'The winner, Nicci Chieveley and Willow . . . Second . . .'

The sound of hooves and the wind in my ears blots out all other noise and it's just me and the horse and the scarlet ribbons on the rosette flying back behind her ear. I stand in the stirrups and let Willow slow to a trot as we leave the arena, looking for my mother to share what is turning out to be one of the best days of my life.

A pulse beats in the back of my throat and the butterflies are back when I notice Matt walking purposefully towards me. He raises his hand.

'Hi, girlfriend,' he says with a wicked twinkle in his eye. 'Henry thinks we're an item. How about that?'

'How about that?' I echo. I'm mortified. How could I have been so stupid? Matt must think I'm deranged, and although there's no particular reason why his opinion should matter, I realise how much I wanted him to think well of me.

'I wonder who on earth could have given him that impression?'

'I wonder,' I say inanely. Matt is teasing me, calling my bluff.

He moves up close and pats Willow's neck. 'What are you up to now?'

'I'm heading back to the lorry, then the yard.'

'I'll come with you as far as the lorry.' As we cross the grass, I'm aware of Henry watching us and Matt walking alongside me, one hand still on Willow's neck in a gesture of possession.

'How's the shoulder?' I ask quietly.

'You can take a look, if you like.'

'I'm being serious,' I say, challenging his cheeky attitude.

'I know. I'm sorry.'

'I wonder if you could have a quick look at Willow if you're not in a terrible hurry to get away somewhere to meet someone, or something.' I rush on making a real mess of what should be a simple request. 'She's pulled up a touch unlevel, and I thought if I trotted her up you could check I'm not imagining it. It's probably nothing, but I'd rather be safe than sorry.' I dismount and remove the saddle, resting it on the ramp of the lorry.

I'm tempted to take my hat off, but I would rather faint with heatstroke than reveal my hat-hair in front of Matt. I know it will be flat and damp and that the hairnet will have left a furrow across my forehead.

'Walk her up and back.' Matt points towards the aisle between the rows of horseboxes. I walk Willow away from him, turn her and walk her back. 'Now trot her up.'

I try to keep up with her as I let her have her head.

'It isn't the horse. It's you. You're one of those neurotic horsey owners.' Matt moves to join me when I bring Willow to a halt. 'She looks perfectly sound to me.'

'She might be sound, but she still looks like a bloody donkey.' Henry's voice interrupts us.

'I think she runs up pretty well,' Matt says, turning to Henry. 'She's supple and moves with a good rhythm.'

'Are you talking about the horse, or the girlfriend?' Henry says, his hands on his hips and his feet apart.

'My girlfriend, of course,' Matt responds, and I almost leap out of my skin when he pinches my bottom. I'm shocked and pleased, though I shouldn't be, but I'm particularly delighted at the expression of what could be a touch of envy and regret on Henry's face. 'We should be getting on,' Matt continues. 'I'm taking Nicci out for a drink tonight.'

This is news to me but I play along, until Henry disappears into his lorry to harangue his stroppy groom for leaving the water tap on and draining the tank.

'I know Henry – he's a bit of a prat.' Matt is grinning. 'It's all right. He's well aware of what I think of him.'

'I'm really sorry.'

'Oh, don't worry about it.'

'You know, you didn't have to go that far.'

'As far as what? You mean, pinching your bottom? Well, I couldn't resist.' His chuckle turns to an exclamation of regret. 'Nicci, I haven't offended you, have I?'

'No, no.' I can hardly accuse him of overstepping the mark when it was me who started the boyfriend/girlfriend thing.

'I don't know why you said it, but I'm more than happy you've decided to be my girlfriend, because it saves me having that awkward conversation where I ask you out.'

I stare at him, confused. His gaze is steady and his pupils are dilated, set in irises stacked with shades of brown, hazelnut and gold. His cheekbones are high and his complexion infused with warmth. His hair, although cropped short, is tousled in all directions.

'You are joking?' I say.

'Not really.'

'Oh?'

'Don't panic – you look like the proverbial hare

caught in the headlamps. I'm more than happy to play along, especially when you're trying to make your ex-boyfriend jealous. Henry told me. He said you were a bit of a spoilsport.'

'He would say that, wouldn't he?'

'It's all right. I know there are always two sides to every story.'

'I can't apologise enough for saying what I did,' I repeat, but Matt cuts me off.

'You aren't dumping me already? We haven't been on a date yet.'

'We can't date,' I point out quickly, and I'm about to give him a very good reason.

'You're right. We've moved way beyond the casual dating stuff. Should I ask you to marry me?'

'Oh, Matt!' I start to giggle at the ridiculousness of the situation. 'Stop it.'

'You have a lovely smile,' he says. 'I didn't see much evidence of it when you were being Nicci the doctor. I thought you were a bit . . . well, scary at first.'

'Thanks.'

'There's no reason to thank me. Let's go out for a drink tonight and we can discuss our living arrange - ments. Are you a live-out or live-in girlfriend?'

'I need to get Willow home,' I say, turning away and leading her back to the lorry where I tie her up and put on her boots and tail guard for the journey. Matt leans against the side of the ramp, watching.

'I'll pick you up at eight.' He pauses. 'I'm being serious now. I'd like to take you out to celebrate your win.'

'This isn't a date?' I blurt out.

'It can be whatever you want it to be.'

'What about Mel?' Matt frowns as I go on. 'What will she think about it?'

'It's none of her business.' His expression relaxes. 'I'm not involved with Mel, not now. I'll explain later.'

'Okay.' His reply seems genuine enough. I make my mind up. 'I'd like to meet up.'

'Where do you live?'

Mindful of what I've been preaching to my mum, I suggest we meet at the Talymill Inn.

'That's a great idea. We can sit outside.' He smiles that slow, heart-lurching smile of his and adds, 'See you later, girlfriend,' before walking away without giving me time to argue over the status of our relationship. I suspect he's never going to let me live this down.

Chapter Five

A Horse of a Different Colour

When I'm debating whether to walk or drive to the pub, my mother texts me to say she's going out. I'd forgotten in the excitement of the day. 'Keep in txt,' I text back. I don't mention that I'm going out too, because I don't want to spoil her date.

I eat eggs on toast, then shower, throw on cropped denims and a top, and keep everything simple with mascara and lip gloss. I check my look in the mirror – not bad for someone who was up at five. I grab my bag and drive to the Talymill Inn.

It's already eight-thirty, and I can see it's busy because it's a Saturday night and peak summer holiday season when everyone flocks to sunny Devon for the beaches and moors, the cream teas and cider. By now, every static caravan at Talysands and every pitch in the surrounding campsites will be taken. As I turn into the car park, there are several children and their parents on the verge outside, feeding a small fat pony with feathery feet, and I think OMG, I know who that pony belongs to, which can only mean my mother is here on her second date with her latest 'just a friend', the Roger Moore lookalike.

I suppose I should have known better because there can't be many pubs where you can park your pony and trap outside while you pop in for a drink.

I park the car alongside Matt's four-by-four and head inside the pub, an old mill that has been restored to its former glory by the previous owners, a couple from London, who sold it on to Tony and Max, a couple of young entrepreneurs who made their money buying and selling hotels along the south coast.

Matt is waiting for me, watching the door from the bar.

'Nicci,' he calls.

'Nicci!' My mum doesn't so much call my name as yelp it, such is her surprise. She touches her throat. 'What are you doing here?'

Acknowledging Matt, I walk towards the bar via the table where Mum's sitting with the man I assume is Robert. She's glammed up in a sundress and pale yellow shrug, and sitting beside – well, I say beside, but she's practically on his lap – an old man who was probably quite handsome in his youth. His hair is thick and salt and pepper grey, and he has magnificent bushy sideburns, lively blue eyes and a ruddy, outdoor complexion. He wears an old denim shirt, black trousers and shiny shoes.

'I'm meeting Matt,' I say sheepishly.

'Why didn't you think to mention it to me?'

'He isn't a stranger. Everyone knows Matt.'

'Harold Shipman was a doctor, and he turned out to be a serial killer.'

'Mum, you're overreacting.'

'Which is what you did when I said I was meeting Robert.'

'Okay, I'm sorry. I should have mentioned it, but Mum, it isn't a date. We're two acquaintances having a drink.' I lean closer and add in a hoarse whisper. 'So please don't go buying your hat just yet.'

'I believe you. Thousands wouldn't,' she says glibly. 'Why don't I treat us all to the next round? You and Matt must come and sit with us. There's plenty of room around the table.'

'I'll get them,' says Robert.

'No, it's fine,' I say. 'Thank you, but Matt's at the bar. We're going outside. It's a lovely evening.' To be honest, it's chilly and overcast, but there's no way I'm going to be seen 'double-dating' with my mother.

'Let me introduce you to Robert before you disappear,' Mum says. 'Nicci, this is Robert. Robert, this is my daughter, Nicci.'

The lonely farmer nods at me and smiles. 'I've heard all about you.'

I can feel myself blushing. How could this have happened?

'We're having a drink to celebrate Willow's win, that's all. I'll see you later.' I touch Mum's shoulder. 'Have fun.'

'Oh, we will, won't we, Robert?' she says, with far

too much certainty for my liking. 'Do you want me to text you?'

'No,' I decide. I warm to Robert immediately. Anyone less like a serial killer, I can't imagine.

When I finally join Matt at the bar, he looks straight into my eyes and gives me the biggest smile, making my heart skip a beat.

'Hi there, girlfriend.'

'Can we go back a step, please?' I say, smiling in return. 'I'd like to go back to friends.'

'Oh no, I don't want to give up on our relationship so soon. I mean, we've only been going out together for a few hours.' He chuckles. 'Tell me what I've done and how I can make it up to you? Why don't we talk about it over a drink? What would you like? I'm buying.'

'A lime soda, please.'

'I can stretch to a glass of wine, or a bottle of champagne to celebrate your win.'

'I don't drink. I'm teetotal.'

Matt whistles between his teeth. 'Are you sure?'

'Of course I am.'

'You're a rare creature around here,' Matt observes, 'quite an exotic species of animal. I thought everyone in the medical profession resorted to drink at some time or another. You know, you're full of surprises. I like that.' His voice is soft and gently caressing. I am mesmerised.

I take a step back to put some space between us as he hands me a glass of lime soda rattling with ice.

'Shall we go outside?' he says, and we walk

through the back of the pub into the beer garden where we find a bench by the river and sit down with the sun sinking behind the trees and a duck squawking somewhere in the shadow of the reeds at the bottom of the far bank.

'So let's hear your version of the story. Why did you tell Henry that you were my girlfriend?' Matt leans towards me. 'I'm curious.'

'We have history,' I say eventually. 'I went out with him for a while, but it turned out he was cheating on me with one of the many grooms and working pupils who pass through his yard. I should never have agreed to go out with him in the first place, because it was never going to work.'

'Never mind. It's his loss.' Then he asks, 'Have you ever thought of competing professionally, like Henry?'

'It was a dream of mine when I started riding, but I needed a proper job. I wasn't sure I was talented or tough enough to make it.'

'You seem pretty talented to me,' he says, pushing his glass towards me, chinking it against mine. 'Congratulations on your win.'

'Thanks. It's one of those days that makes all the training and preparation seem worth it.' I pause, sipping my drink. 'That's enough about me. What about you? Would your real girlfriend be happy about me having a drink with you? I mean, I can't officially be your girlfriend if you're already taken.'

'You are the one. There is no other. I was rather pleased that you offered to take up the vacancy. Do you have many patients who have a crush on their doctor?' he goes on, holding my gaze. 'You know what I'm talking about. One look at you and I was smitten. I am smitten, Dr Chieveley.'

'You can't be,' I say lightly. 'You don't know anything about me.'

I'm beginning to think that being friends with Matt is going to be tiring. He has a seemingly inexhaustible supply of good humour and I'm not sure how I'm going to know when he's serious and when he's joking.

'Well, this is a fact-finding mission,' he responds. 'You go next. Ask me a question.'

I go for the obvious one first. 'If you haven't got a girlfriend, are you married?'

He shakes his head. 'No.'

'Engaged?'

'I've never been engaged.'

'So you're afraid of commitment?'

'That's rather a harsh judgement. Maybe I haven't met the right person yet.' He breathes a sigh of regret. 'I was close to getting engaged once.'

'What happened?'

'She turned me down.'

'She must have been mad,' I say lightly.

'That's what I told her. It was a long time ago – when I was a vet student. She was right anyway. I was far too young and immature.'

'What was she like?'

'What is this, Twenty Questions? It's like you're at work, investigating a difficult case.'

'Are you a difficult case?'

'Come out with me again and you'll have the opportunity to find out. I'm not answering that now – I want to keep you in suspense.'

'You're pretty cocky, aren't you, if you think it matters all that much to me,' I say archly. Recalling something he said earlier, I return to my interrogation. 'You said you were involved with Mel, your houseman?'

'I was,' he admits. 'I committed the unforgivable sin of dating a member of staff. It didn't last long and I finished it about three months ago, because it just wasn't working. Mel didn't take it too well. It's been rather awkward since.'

'I'm sorry.' Matt seems genuinely upset.

'Nicci, I'm not proud of what happened. I made a terrible mistake and I'll never do it again.' He pauses for a while before regaining his good humour.

'Come on . . .' He smiles that heart-stopping smile. 'Ask me some more questions.' He flips a beer mat into the air. 'Fire away.'

'Can you play darts?'

'Can I what?'

'Play darts.' I can't help giggling at his expression of amazement. 'I like a game of darts occasionally. I'm checking that we're well-matched.'

'I'm a bit rusty, but I'm sure I can pick it up again quite quickly. I'll have to play left-handed because of my poorly shoulder,' he says. 'Go on.'

'Hobbies?' I start to get into the swing of what is turning out to be rather like speed dating, even though it isn't supposed to be a date. 'What do you do in your spare time?'

'I like running and sailing, and I keep bees.'

'That's unusual. What kind of attention does a beehive need?'

'It's all aimed at collecting the honey. One day, you can have honey for breakfast at mine.'

'You reckon?'

'I'm quietly confident.'

Matt is charming and the thought is tempting, but I'm not going to let myself be seduced by his offer.

'I thought it would be something I could do when I retire.'

I laugh. 'That's long-term planning!'

'You should always be prepared.' He glances towards his shoulder. 'Who knows how long I'll be able to work for. I've spoken to my doctor, but she hasn't a clue.'

I give him a dig in the ribs.

'Ouch.' He winces. 'You're supposed to relieve suffering, not cause it. What about your hobbies? I expect you spend most of your spare time up at the yard.'

We go on to talk about where we live and about the pair of farm-worker's cottages he's been trying to renovate for the past four years. The conversation plays out as if we're already best mates. I like the humour and the banter and I like him very much, but there are many reasons why it can't go further. He's my patient, I'm too busy for dating, and I'm not prepared to risk another man being reckless with my heart like Henry was.

'Hello there.' It's my mother calling across to me,

walking arm in arm with Robert, who looks the picture of health to me and hopefully many years from expiring, so I can forget any worries on that score.

'Do you always bring your mother along as a chaperone?' Matt says.

'She thinks I'm keeping an eye on her.'

'Is that your father?'

'My dad? Oh no.'

'I'm sorry I've put my foot in it.'

'It's all right. My parents are divorced. That's Robert, my mother's internet date.' My heart sinks as I watch her sit down at a rustic table, look into her beau's eyes and lock lips with him.

'Did I mention to you that I was adopted?' I say to Matt.

'Were you?' Matt frowns. 'But you and your mother look so alike . . .' His voice trails off. 'You're joking.'

'Yeah, but there are times when I think I must have been. What about your family?'

'My parents live in Sussex – they run a vineyard that makes English sparkling wine.'

'I'm not ideal girlfriend material then, am I, being teetotal?'

'My mother doesn't drink wine either,' Matt says, 'only gin. I have two brothers, the eldest returned home to take over the reins of the winemaking business, and the youngest is sailing charter boats in the Caribbean. I'm the one in the middle.'

'I have a sister. She has a couple of kids and lives in London.'

'Is she a doctor like you?'

'No, she left school at sixteen.' I don't elaborate – Matt's family sounds far more interesting than mine. He edges closer until his thigh is touching mine. I lean against his shoulder, his good one. It feels perfectly normal and natural, sitting close to him, breathing the scent of aftershave, beer and the river while listening to the sound of his voice and in the distance the laughter of the children clambering about on the climbing frame in the play area, and the occasional splash of a bird or fish in the water.

I relax, closing my eyes for a moment, when I hear the dreaded words.

'Dr Chieveley, how fortuitous!'

I sit up abruptly to find Fifi Green, resplendent in a sunhat, mauve dress and matching shawl, standing over me.

'I'm here to arrange a quiz night to raise funds for Talyton Animal Rescue,' she goes on, as if to make it clear that she isn't the kind of person who is normally found frequenting such an establishment. 'Matt, could I borrow your companion for just a moment?' Without waiting for a response, she rushes on, 'Dr Chieveley, it's about my wrist. I couldn't fasten my necklace by myself and I do so hate being dependent on anyone. I'm in agony.'

I resist the temptation to point out that if she was in that much pain, she wouldn't be here, dressed up to the nines. She'd be at home on painkillers, alternating with ice packs and heat, or in contact with the emergency doctors.

I recall Ben mentioning with a rueful smile that Fifi was a pain, always grabbing him for a consultation about her bunions whenever he ran into her socially. He gave me the impression he was fed up with humouring her and it made me wonder if he treats Fifi like the boy who cried wolf. If Ben isn't taking her seriously any more, perhaps I should at least listen to check that there really isn't anything wrong with her.

'If you're doing consultations in the pub, I wouldn't mind you having another look at my shoulder,' Matt says once Fifi has gone, pacified by my suggestion that she books an appointment with Claire for some blood tests.

'Not here, not now,' I say, blushing at the memory of his naked torso.

'Later then, after closing time.'

'Matt!' I exclaim as his fingers brush lightly against mine.

'I'm sorry. I've offended you.'

'It's fine.'

'I've gone too far.'

'Matt, I forgive you. I'm not used to being chatted up like this.'

'I can't believe that you don't have men chatting you up all the time,' he says.

'Well, I think you're more than making up for it.'

'I would like to see you again, on any basis of your choosing. How about dinner sometime? I'd prefer you to be my girlfriend, but if you want to keep up the "just friends" charade for a little longer, I'll survive.'

'I'd like that.' Despite my misgivings I really do want to see him again. 'Maybe we could have lunch tomorrow?'

'Unfortunately I'm working tomorrow,' he says with a sigh. 'Actually, I don't mind working on a Sunday. It can get busy, but I usually find some time to catch up with paperwork and the general repairs that need doing at the hospital.'

'Don't you have a handyman for that?'

'We employ a gardener to mow the lawns and keep the paddocks tidy, and we have contracts on the anaesthetic, X-ray and ultrasound machines, but Jimmy and I try to do as much as we can ourselves to keep the costs down.' He pauses. 'How about Monday for a meal out?'

'I have dressage training with Delphi on Monday after work, and late-night surgeries on Tuesday and Thursday.'

'Can you do Wednesday? No, that's no good.' He changes his mind. 'I'm on call. I know – give me your mobile number and I'll text you mine. I'll see if I can do a swap on the rota. Here.' He holds out his hand, palm down.

I take a pen from my bag and write my number in shaky figures on his skin.

Later, my phone rings, but it isn't Matt. It's Mum calling me to check that I'm home.

'What did you think of Robert?' she goes on to ask, and I can tell from the tone of her voice that it doesn't really matter what I think because she's made her mind up.

'He seems . . .' What can I say? I've never been interested in older men and May to December relation -

ships, so I can't say 'Yum, he's rather gorgeous,' as she does about my boyfriends, because it would make me want to throw up. 'Lovely' is too non-committal to count as an opinion, so I settle for, 'He seems very jolly.'

'Is that the best you can come up with, Nicci?' Mum sighs. 'I think he's wonderful – intelligent, attractive and civilised – for a man.'

'It's rather too soon to be saying that, isn't it?'

'What are you like? I know Henry let you down, but you mustn't let that influence you in the future.' She pauses. 'I like Matt. If I were you, I wouldn't hesitate to snap him up.'

'You have a spring in your step this morning, Dr Chieveley,' Claire says on the following Wednesday morning. I'm bringing the treats for today – cherry and almond slices and meringues filled with cream and sprinkled with hundreds and thousands. We'll have a cholesterol-free day tomorrow. 'I hear you had a good weekend.'

'I did. How about you? How was your long weekend off?' I ask her as I head into the staffroom with my armful of goodies. Claire follows me as I make my way to the consulting room to prepare for the day.

'Oh, I did the garden and went to the beach, nothing special. I believe you have a lot to tell me.'

'Willow won the one-day event over at East Hill.' I sit down, pull my mobile out of my bag and switch it to silent before putting it away in the drawer of my desk.

'That's amazing. You must be over the moon.'

'I am. Willow's such a great horse. I gave her the day off on Sunday, turning her out in the paddock to graze and relax. I hacked her out on Monday and started back on the training schedule yesterday in earnest.'

'I'm more interested in the fact you were spotted out with Matt Warren,' Claire grins. 'It's no good denying it – I've had it confirmed by more than one source. And if you'd wanted to keep it quiet, you shouldn't have gone to the Talymill Inn. The gossip's all over town.'

'Oh great,' I sigh, recalling that I spoke with Fifi Green. 'It felt like I was on a double-date with my mother.'

'So it was a date,' Claire flashes back.

'My mum was on a date. I wasn't. I'm glad she's found someone, for now at least. It takes her mind off my errant sister.'

'So?'

'So what?'

'You and Matt?'

'He's my vet.'

'In what way?' Claire teases.

'It's purely platonic.' I giggle, before growing serious. 'Claire, there's nothing going on. Matt's a patient and I'm well aware of the rules about doctor-patient relationships. I'm not stupid.'

'But you do fancy him?'

'Well—' I can't deny it '—he's pretty fit, but—'

'So you must do something about it.' Claire is excited. 'Don't let him get away.'

I smile to myself. There is something irresistible about Matt Warren, and he's asked me out for a second time. I'd love to date him, but there's no changing the fact that he's my patient, and nothing can happen between us, even if I wanted it to. And I'm too shy to raise the subject of him changing doctors – it would make me look desperate and cheap. And I'm not sure I'm ready for a relationship. What if I went through all that and found out he wasn't for me after all? No, it's best to let it lie, at least for now. Take it slowly, I tell myself. The problem is that Matt gives the impression of being an impatient kind of man.

'I won't be seeing him for a while now. We tried to arrange to meet for a meal this week, but we're both too busy. He was supposed to get in touch, but he hasn't.'

'You're in for a nice surprise then,' Claire says. 'He phoned for an appointment this morning.'

'Today?'

'You had a cancellation.'

'What time?' I scroll down through the patient list for the day. Ten o'clock. *Matt Warren. Shoulder still playing up something chronic.* It's Janet's explanation. The receptionist likes to put her own spin on things. Sometimes it's helpful and other times it isn't. I notice that Ed Pike is on the list too, without Milo this time. *Personal problems. Will only speak to Nicci.* There's also another of Janet's observations. *Nobby Warwick. Can't sit down.*

'That's quite a list,' Claire says, looking over my shoulder.

'It certainly is. There are times when I long for the cut and thrust and adrenaline rush of emergency medicine, and today might very well turn out to be one of them.' I glance at her. 'By the way, Fifi's coming in for blood tests. I thought I'd better warn you, so you can prime Janet to interrupt if she chatters on for too long.'

'Thanks for that, Nicci.'

'It's a pleasure. I'm going to look forward to the cakes at coffee time, I can tell you.'

I see Ed Pike first. For once, he's alone with neither a dog nor a baby, and he's nervous, clearing his throat without saying anything at all. He's sweating too in his skeet vest and long brown hunting boots.

'How can I help?' I say, offering him a seat. I wait for him to speak.

'I don't know why I'm here really,' he says eventually. 'I doubt there's anything you can do. And it's a cosmetic thing. I'm not ill.'

'But it was important enough to bring you here,' I point out.

'Actually, I'm fine, A-one.' He makes to stand up. 'I'm sorry, Nicci. I'm wasting your time.'

'Ed, sit.' I find myself talking to him the way he does to his dog. 'You aren't wasting my time.'

'I'll – um – make another appointment sometime.'

'And then you'll forget or not get around to it,' I say sternly. I notice the flush on his cheeks, like the baby teething, and the fine tremor in his hands as he rubs them along his thighs.

'I really should let you get on.'

'I promise you I've seen and heard it all, and whatever you say, remember it's in complete confidence.' I know Ed. He wouldn't have booked an appointment if it was nothing. Finding it hard to admit weakness isn't an exclusively male trait. 'If there's something bothering you, it's better to get it off your chest.'

Ed stares at me. 'That's just it, Nicci. It's so obvious, isn't it?'

I frown. I'm not sure what he's getting at.

'I feel like a freak,' he goes on, staring down at the front of his vest.

'Ed, you're going to have to be more explicit,' I say gently. 'What exactly is the problem?'

'I'm growing breasts, man-boobs, moobs, or whatever you like to call them.' He looks as if he might burst into tears. 'One of the guys at work on the estate asked me if I was having a sex-change the other day, and the guv'nor's wife calls me Edwina. She's a right stuck-up bitch too, but I have to kowtow to her to keep my job and the roof over our heads. I get a small wage and the gamekeeper's cottage rent-free, but I'm not sure I can stand the humiliation for much longer.'

'What about your family?'

Ed relaxes a little. 'I'd like to say they're supportive, but my brothers take the mickey out of me too, cracking jokes about which bra I should go for and how I should model for Victoria's Secrets.'

'And your wife?'

'She says she loves me the way I am, but it isn't helping our sex life.' He smiles ruefully. 'I don't feel, well, like a man any more – and I like to stay covered up.' He tries to make light of it, adding, 'At least we're both keen to undress in the dark now . . . And I'd hate to make her feel inadequate in the breast department.'

I let Ed unburden himself now he's found his voice.

'I get pretty depressed sometimes, because they seem to be getting larger. I've tried working out a bit to see if I can turn them to muscle, but that only seems to make them look like eggs on toast.'

'What about your health in general?' I ask. 'How are your hands?' Immediately, he rests them back on his thighs to control the tremor.

'They've been a little shaky recently,' he admits. 'But it's no problem. It doesn't stop me handling a gun.'

I realise there is more to this than meets the eye. Ed relies on his gun licence to work as a gamekeeper. He can't afford to lose it.

I ask him the usual questions about drinking and diet, before returning to any other symptoms.

'Do you feel unwell at all?'

'I've been feeling a bit panicky, but I put that down to my state of mind,' he says. 'I'm under a lot of stress with three small kids.'

I smile at the thought. I can't imagine living with one small kid, let alone three.

'One consolation is that with the situation I'm in, I'm not likely to have any more in a hurry.'

'I'd like to examine you now. I need you to undress.' I pull the curtain across in front of the examination couch for privacy, and wait for him to undress, running through the possible diagnoses for gynae-comastia, the technical term for moobs.

'I'm done,' he says, and I go to examine him. He's very self-conscious. He can't look me in the eye. 'Look, I'm almost a double D. It's like I've fallen asleep and woken up with bloody implants.'

'When did you first notice a change?'

'About a year ago. Yes, I should have come along sooner, but you know what it's like.'

'Have you lost weight recently?' I ask. He's carrying very little spare flesh, and obesity clearly isn't the cause of Ed's problem.

'I've been putting that down to stress as well.'

'I don't think this is stress-related at all. I'm going to ask Claire to take a blood sample and refer you to an endocrinologist – someone who specialises in hormonal disorders – for some investigations.'

'So it's possible to get rid of them?'

'We have to identify the underlying cause so we can address it, but yes, there are ways to resolve the problem.' I worry a little that the underlying cause might turn out to be more difficult to manage than the moobs, but for now, it's enough for Ed to know that something is being done.

I send him out to Claire for the blood tests, make a note to sort out the referral and check the waiting list. Matt is next. I can't help it – I run a brush through my hair before calling him in.

'Hello, girlfriend,' he says, entering the consulting room.

'Sh,' I say. 'I'm not your girlfriend.'

'I wish you wouldn't say that with quite so much conviction.' He smiles and looks me up and down. 'Are you all right, Dr Chieveley, only you look a little flushed, as if you have a fever.'

'Hang on. Who's running the consultation here?'

'How's the horse?' he goes on.

'She's fine now, back in work ready for the next event.' I sit behind the desk, keeping the barrier between him and me. 'What can I do for you?'

'What are you willing to do for me?' he says immediately.

'That would be telling,' I say, unable to resist.

'Tell . . .'

'Oh, stop flirting with me. You're wasting NHS time.'

'Do you have any compassion at all for your patients?' Matt teases. 'I've come back because I'm in pain.'

'Your shoulder.'

He lowers his voice and leans across the desk. 'Would you believe me if I said I've been aching to see you, Nicci.'

'You've come here to tell me that?'

'Well, yes. You haven't been returning my calls.'

'That's because you haven't called me.'

'I have – I've left messages on your voicemail . . .' he hesitates, '. . . on what I thought was your voice - mail. I wonder who's been receiving my messages? It must be your fault – no one can read a doctor's handwriting.'

'It was perfectly clear,' I say. 'You probably washed

93

some of the numbers off when you scrubbed up for some operation or other.'

'I transferred them straight to the mobile when I got home. Anyway, why don't I give you my phone now and you can type your number into my list of contacts? That way there'll be no more confusion.' He hands me his mobile from his pocket. 'I thought I'd better make an appointment to see you instead.' He gazes at me as a million thoughts race around my brain. Is he serious?

'I'm pulling your leg,' he says, grinning. 'Well, not entirely. I wanted to see you again and my shoulder still hurts. And before you tell me off for not wearing that sling, I have been resting it to a certain extent.'

'You know what I'm going to say, then. Go home and rest it. Properly.' I pause. 'Unless I refer you now, and hand you on to someone else to deal with. You might listen to them.'

'Are you trying to get rid of me?' Matt says with mock petulance.

'Of course not.'

'So you'll come out for dinner with me on Saturday? I'll pick you up at seven.' He gets up and heads for the door.

'Hey, you don't know where I live.'

'I'll call you, now that I have the right number,' he says. 'I'll see you on Saturday. Don't forget.'

As if, I think when he's gone and I'm making a note to organise his referral. I'm looking forward to it, but I'm wondering how we're going to remain friends through the rising mist of attraction that envelops me whenever I think of him. I bite my lip. I should have turned him down. That would have been the right thing to do.

Nobby Warwick takes my mind off Matt temporarily. He has a boil on his bottom, and the less said about that the better. Suffice to say, he won't be sitting down to play the organ for a while.

Chapter Six

Happy Hackers

On Saturday afternoon I have a jumping lesson with Shane before Willow and I go for a long hack. We take a circular route, the one we call the chicken run because it passes some tumbledown sheds that were once used for keeping poultry. Willow is fresh, snorting at all kinds of imaginary monsters in the hedge along the soft and peaty bridleway. I pop her over the log onto the open common where the grass has been mown short by deer and rabbits. I let her canter along the ridge between the clumps of gorse and bracken and the stunted trees, taking in the view of sea and the houses and hotels of Talymouth, my childhood home and where my mum still lives. Once Willow has stretched her legs, I bring her back to a walk and let her stretch her neck on a long rein while my mind wanders to thoughts of Matt.

I'm going to have to tell him what the problem is, why we can't be more than friends, unless . . .

Suddenly I find myself halfway up Willow's neck, the reins flapping and one foot out of the stirrup as she stops and shies.

'Hey!' I say sharply, sliding back and taking up the leather between my fingers. 'What do you think you're doing?' I look towards the ground and catch sight of a plastic bag.

'Honestly, Willow. When has a piece of plastic ever done a horse any harm?' I grumble lightly at her, relieved not to have fallen off.

She walks on unconcerned as if nothing has happened and I can imagine Delphi's voice in my ear telling me off for blaming the horse. 'It's your fault, Nicci. You had your mind on other things – Matt and your love life, for example. A good horsewoman NEVER blames her horse.'

When we return to the yard, I untack Willow, throw on a light stable rug and put her away. I lean over the stable door to watch her settle as she munches on the hay in her net. Dark Star whickers at me and I give him a mint so he doesn't feel left out.

'I'll see you tomorrow,' I tell the horses. I would normally add 'bright and early', but I doubt it somehow. 'I'm going out with your vet.' Willow doesn't show any interest in this news, but I can hardly wait.

It seems like a long time, but eventually seven o'clock arrives, and as soon as the long hand hits the twelve on the clock on the church tower opposite the house, Matt appears on the doorstep, which is flattering. It suggests that he couldn't wait to see me either.

I open the door before he has the chance to ring the bell.

'You found it then. My house,' I go on. I'm nervous – that's why I'm wittering, but Matt doesn't appear to mind. He's standing on the step, eyeing the wonky door with curiosity.

'I'll have to duck when you ask me in later,' he says, tipping his head to one side.

'*If* I ask you in.'

He looks me up and down. 'You look amazing, as always.'

'Thank you.' My pulse trips into a faster rhythm and a hot flush creeps up my chest and neck. The combination of a low-cut tunic top, leggings and silver heels is the fourth ensemble I've tried on this evening.

He's looking good too, dressed in a grey sweater with a white T-shirt underneath and blue jeans – designer, not the workmen's jeans they wear at Overdown Farmers, the local agricultural merchants. He smells good too, of shower gel and mint, overlaid with a hint of antibiotic. He's had his hair cut and his complexion has a healthy glow.

'Have you been hitting the bottle?' I say, still failing to engage my mouth and brain at the same time. 'The tan,' I add quickly when I realise he hasn't a clue what I'm talking about. 'I didn't mean the other kind.'

'I believe there are many varieties of bottle,' he says, grinning. 'I've been in the garden all day.'

'Catching some rays?'

'Mowing the lawn and trimming the hedges.' He

hesitates. 'I feel as if I should have been doing something far more exciting to impress you.'

'I'm quite impressed that you've been gardening. I didn't realise you were so domesticated.' I duck back indoors. 'Let me get my bag.'

When I return, I close the door behind me.

'Don't you lock up around here?' Matt asks.

'Um, I do usually, although my neighbour says I don't need to, but right at this moment, I can't find my keys.' I check in my bag. 'And I can't remember where I've left them.'

'You don't want me to come in and help you look for them. I'd hate you to get burgled while we're out.'

'It'll be fine,' I say, wishing I didn't look so dippy in front of Matt. 'Let's go.' I pause. 'Where are we going?'

'I thought about Mr Rock's to pick up fish and chips,' he smiles, 'but because I can remember what the food was like the last time I tried it and because I'd prefer it if you actually wanted to see me again after tonight, I'm going to whisk you away to a little place I know in the big city.'

'In Exeter?'

'All right, it isn't that big when it comes to cities, but I know this restaurant on the quay where we can eat pizza and listen to some jazz, if you like that sort of thing,' he adds anxiously.

'It sounds great,' I say.

Half an hour later we're sitting outdoors near the quay with the water lapping gently against the side of the canal. Behind us, dug into the sandstone rock face, are the warehouses where the ships coming up from the coast used to unload or collect their wares of wool, tobacco and wine.

We eat pizza and drink cola and listen to a jazz quartet while talking about where we've come from and where we think we're going.

'What do you think of the music?' Matt asks eventually, when the quartet have finished their first set.

'It's different, but it isn't really my thing,' I say tactfully. 'I prefer pop and rock.' I smile at his crestfallen expression. 'Matt, I'm glad you brought me here.'

'It's a great place for a first date, isn't it?' he says, his eyes flashing with amusement because he knows exactly what I'm going to say about that. We both start laughing.

As the music plays on, I catch the sound of the Scissor Sisters' track 'Only the Horses' coming from my bag.

'That's my mobile,' I say, rummaging for my phone. 'I'm sorry, Matt. No one ever calls me.' I cringe when I realise what I've said. I sound like Billy No-Mates, though I do have many friends all over the place but we tend to communicate via Facebook, unless we're planning to meet up. 'I won't answer it.' I glance at the screen, which tells me it's my sister calling and I change my mind. 'I need to get this.'

However, when I accept the call the line is dead.

'Is there a problem?' asks Matt.

'Do you mind if I . . .' My finger hovers over the CALL icon on the screen.

'You go ahead.' He stands up. 'I'll go and see if I can find the menu for dessert.'

I haven't heard from her for ages, and of all the times to choose to call me my sister has chosen now. I listen for her to pick up, but there's no reply and the familiar voicemail cuts in.

'This is Cheska here. Please leave a message and I'll get back to you asap.'

My heart sinks because I appear to have missed an opportunity to catch up with her to check she and the children are safe and well and happy.

'What's up?' Matt passes me a menu when he returns from inside the restaurant and sits back down beside me.

'My little sister. She's . . . Oh, it's a long story. I won't go into it now.' I look at the menu. 'What are you having? I'm not sure I can eat dessert as well.'

'We could share,' he suggests, moving so close I can feel his breath against my cheek.

'Do we have similar tastes?'

'What's your favourite?'

'Something chocolatey. How about the profiteroles?'

Matt calls the waiter over and orders two profiteroles.

'I thought we were sharing.'

'We are. I'll eat mine and share yours.' He raises one eyebrow. 'I have a good appetite.'

'Hey, I hope you're not—'

'Here we go again – "This isn't a date." Nicci, what's the problem? I feel like I'm getting mixed signals, as though you're attracted to me and you'd like to be more than friends, but something's holding you back.' He hesitates. 'Don't you . . . well, you know . . .'

'Fancy you,' I say for him. 'Yes, I do,' I add, but I don't think he hears me.

'If you don't want me to pursue you, I can stop. I don't want to, but—'

'I don't want you to stop,' I say quietly as the waiter arrives with two bowls of profiteroles and hot chocolate sauce. Suddenly, I'm really not hungry. 'Matt, I'm a doctor. I can't date one of my patients.'

'It doesn't worry me.'

'The principle is there to protect patients and doctors, not that I'm saying you need protecting from me, or vice versa, but I do believe in it. It prevents vulnerable patients being exploited.'

'I'm hardly vulnerable, and I like the idea of you exploiting me.'

'Matt, please, I'm being serious here. It protects doctors too, from accusations of taking advantage of their patients.'

'It's an anachronism. This is the twenty-first century.' He pauses to wipe chocolate sauce from the corner of his mouth. 'Anyway, who is going to bother about us? Neither of us is married.'

'I don't like the idea. I don't mean the idea of going out with you.' I lower my voice. 'I like that very much, but I work in the community. If someone catches on that we're an item, it'll be all over town.'

'I've seen stories in the papers of doctors being struck off for having relationships with their patients, but it seems highly unlikely that anyone would chase it up to the extent that it would jeopardise your career.'

'The risk is there and I've worked so hard to achieve my registration, I don't want to lose it.'

'You're right,' he sighs. 'Eat up,' he adds, changing the subject.

Later, we walk back along the waterfront in the dark, the reflections of the streetlights dancing on the water. On the way to Matt's car we pass the massive black iron rings where the ships used to be moored and the historic Customs House.

He reaches out. I step away but he catches my hand and interlinks his fingers through mine, squeezing them tight. He stops walking and turns so he's facing me. 'Nicci,' he breathes, his eyes shining in the shadows, and I'm almost lost when he presses his lips to mine, an exclamation of desire catching in his throat. My heart is saying yes and my head is saying no.

'You do want this? If it wasn't for the doctor-patient thing?' he adds huskily. 'Can I register with another doctor?'

'Yes, but it's a bit awkward, isn't it?'

'Well, I'm not going to give a reason, am I?' He smiles. 'Leave it with me. I suppose another kiss is out of the question?'

'I think you'd better take me home,' I say, afraid that one more kiss will lead to another and sweep away any resistance I have left.

'Okay,' he says.

He drops me outside my house. He leaves the engine running, and if I'd thought of throwing caution to the wind I would have been disappointed because he says,

'Before you invite me in for coffee, I have to decline, I'm afraid.'

'Oh?'

'There's no need to sound so—' he inclines his head towards me '—disappointed. It isn't you. As you've said, it's probably better that I'm not seen emerging from your house late at night, but I've also got to get home to let the dog out.'

'I didn't know you had a dog.'

'I'm just getting used to the idea myself.'

At first I think he's making excuses, but Matt is a vet so it's understandable that he would have a pet, I think, as his hand sidles towards mine, his fingertips touching my skin. My pulse quickens and my lips tingle with anticipation, but there is no kiss.

'When can I see you again?' he says gently.

'I'm not sure.' I reach out for the door handle, reminding myself that I have a choice. 'I think it's best to leave things as they are for a while. I don't believe I can do the "just friends" bit with you.'

'Same here,' he whispers, running his fingers down the inside of my wrist. It's an erotic gesture, highly charged and I have to summon all my resolve.

'Thanks for a lovely evening,' I say, opening the door. 'Goodnight, Matt.'

'I'll be in touch,' he insists. 'I'll get something sorted soon, I promise.'

I let myself into the house, turn and wave before he drives away, waving back. I go to bed, but I can't sleep. I used to wonder why on earth doctors left themselves open to accusations and threats to their livelihoods by entering relationships with their patients, but now I understand. I toss and turn and watch the moon and stars over the church roof opposite my bedroom through a gap in the curtains. Why did I have to go and fall for a patient?

A few days later I walk straight into Ben when I arrive at work.

'Hi,' I say. 'How are the girls?' and that's as far as our conversations normally go. Ben is quite reserved, aloof even, and doesn't like to partake in gossip like me, Claire and Janet. The price of fish and chips at Mr Rock's, Steve's daughter's recent engagement to the local animal welfare officer, and teasing Claire about PC Kevin's frequent visits to the surgery are not matters that hold any interest for him.

We'll talk about some of our patients, but most of our interaction is confined to the monthly practice meetings.

'Have you got two minutes?' Ben is looking cool and in control in a white shirt and fawn trousers, and he carries his car keys in one hand and a floral bag in the other. He has a crooked nose and his dark hair is thinning on top. I smile to myself. I'm not sure the image of modern metrosexual man suits him.

'I was just going to make a coffee. Would you like one?' I ask him. I was riding at seven and I could do with a pick-me-up before surgery begins.

'Thank you.' He yawns. 'I can't remember if I had coffee this morning or not. I hardly slept last night. The twins are insomniacs. They stay up all night and sleep all day. I don't know what to do with them. Emma's at the end of her tether.' He glances down at the bag. 'Oh no, I should have left this with them at the nursery. I'll have to go back. Don't worry about that coffee.'

'What was it you wanted?' I say as he turns away.

'I wanted to let you know that I've agreed to take on one of your patients. I should have spoken to you first. I hope you're not offended, but it sounded to me as though you're better off without him on your list. It's the vet, Matt Warren. He says he wants to see a male doctor from now on. He sounded a bit of a misogynist to me. I was shocked actually.'

'Oh?' I say. 'I hope you told him I was an excellent doctor – for a woman.' I'm joking, but Ben doesn't get it.

'I don't think we should be seen to condone any kind of prejudice,' Ben says seriously. 'It's completely unacceptable and inappropriate.'

'I know. I'm sorry for being flippant.' I feel as if I've been told off. 'Thanks, Ben.' I can forgive him his lack of humour. As a doctor and dad to the terrible twins – they are really sweet, but a handful – I wonder how he copes. 'I'll see you later.'

'Once more unto the breach, dear friends, once more,' he says. 'I notice you're seeing Fifi.'

'I hope you don't mind. She's rather latched on . . .'

Ben gives me a broad smile. 'No, Nicci. I don't mind at all. I think exchanging Fifi for Matt Warren, even though he comes across as a woman-hater, is a result. I've had to put up with Fifi's bunions and her offerings of chicken soup and cranberry jelly for years. I wish you the best of luck.'

'Thanks for that.' I smile back. 'I'd better get going.'

'So had I.' Ben yawns again. 'I must shoot back to the nursery. Lydia won't survive a whole day without Slinky. Slinky's her teddy bear,' he adds in explanation.

I grab a coffee and scrounge a biscuit from the tin in the staffroom. I didn't have time for breakfast because Shane made me keep riding until he was happy with how Willow and I were jumping the grid of fences he'd set up in the school. I think he'd have kept us there all day if I hadn't had to be at work. I take five minutes outside on the bench along the wall at the back of the surgery to mull over what Ben has told me.

It's a lovely day, and even better now that I know Matt is no longer my patient. The church bells are pealing brightly and the light breeze ruffles the petals on the petunias in the hanging baskets. We can be together. We don't have to hold back any more.

I dunk the biscuit, a crumbly digestive, into my coffee. I need to talk to him, but there's no time. Above the sound of the bells I hear a car turning into the surgery car park and the sound of a horn. I tip the dregs of the coffee into the nearest planter, a tub with a bay tree. I have a job to do.

Fifi is my first appointment. She is a vision in Country Casuals, her outfit, as ever, completed with co-ordinating accessories.

'We meet again, Dr Chieveley,' she says, sitting down stiffly on the chair beside the desk. 'Thank you for your advice the other evening. I'm sorry if I interrupted anything. Matt is a handsome young man and if I were a younger woman, and not married, you would have some stiff competition.'

'Fifi, Matt and I are friends, nothing more.' I look her straight in the eyes. 'Is that perfectly clear?'

'Absolutely. So I'm still in with a chance,' she adds with a giggle. 'I apologise. This is supposed to be about me.'

I don't comment.

'I've had the report back from the lab regarding your blood test,' I begin.

'There's something wrong,' Fifi cuts in.

'Unfortunately, there is, but not with you. There was a problem with the blood samples and I'm afraid we need to repeat them. I've booked you ten minutes with Claire after this appointment for her to take some more.'

'Oh, I don't mind. Claire is good fun. Isn't she supposed to be going out with Kevin?' Kevin is one of Talyton St George's police constables, friendly and somewhat ineffectual. 'I did ask her if she was forging a particularly close relationship with the local force, but she denied everything.' Fifi changes the subject. 'Dr Mackie is my doctor, but you and I get along so well, I'd rather see you for now. It's all right, Dr Chieveley—' she smiles wryly '—I, of all people, know what I'm like. I hope you don't mind but I feel that you believe me, and that's reassuring. You take me seriously, whereas others in this town do not.' She shakes her head sadly. 'Sometimes I wonder why I bother, committing myself to all the things that I do, the WI, Talyton Animal Rescue and acting on the council, but it's my duty.' She smoothes down her skirt. 'It's all about having a social conscience.'

With emphasis on the 'social', I think, smiling to myself. Fifi loves the social aspect.

'Anyway, Dr Mackie has, as I've said before, done wonders for my bunions, but he seems to be struggling with my other aches and pains. My wrists are killing me.' She holds out her arms, resting the backs of her hands on the desk.

I don't know what to say. I don't want to encourage her by criticising Ben. I don't want that all over town.

'Have you been examined recently?'

'Do you mean poked and prodded, Dr Chieveley?'

I nod.

'No.'

'Let's get you undressed and on the couch. I'd like to check your back and joints properly.'

'Oh, thank you. That would be marvellous.'

I close the blinds, shutting out the sunshine, and pull the screen in front of the couch to give Fifi privacy. She takes some time to undress and I wonder if she's struggling to unfasten her buttons. Then I watch when she gets dressed again after I've examined her. It isn't easy.

'I'm going to refer you to a rheumatologist at the hospital. Your aches and pains suggest you might have arthritis.'

'Am I going to seize up like the tin man?'

'Once we know what's going on, we can start you on some treatment and a course of physio.'

'Thank you,' Fifi breathes.

109

I don't think she could be happier at having something really wrong with her, a genuine diagnosis, even if I'd told her she'd won the lottery, as she gushes on about how marvellous I am and how Dr Mackie got it wrong about her pains being all in her mind.

'These things happen,' I say. 'No one can get it right all the time. And I might be wrong.'

'Oh no, I think you're right. I can feel it in my bones.' She smiles. 'Literally.'

Fifi leaves for her blood test in a state of high excitement.

The last thing I hear is her calling down the corridor to Janet, saying, 'I told you I was ill.'

I see several more patients, including three children with various childhood ailments: eczema, tonsillitis and impetigo. My last patient of the morning is Bridget, who owns Petals the florist's on Market Square. She's in her early fifties and was diagnosed with diabetes about a year ago, soon after the vets at Otter House diagnosed her dog – the bulldog I see her walking in the church-yard – with the same condition.

They say that dogs often look like their owners and Bridget and her pet are a prime example, apart from the hair. The bulldog has a smooth tan and white coat, whereas Bridget has a frizzy, blonde, shoulder-length bob. They share the same jawline and set of the eyes, and not only look similar but share the same dogged determination to keep going in adversity. Bridget's a single mum and works long hours. She's also lost a lot of weight since her diagnosis, but she's still quite dumpy. Her tatty green sweatshirt with the Petals logo and her jeans two sizes too big don't exactly flatter her apple-shaped figure. 'How are you, Bridget?' I ask.

'I feel fine, but have you seen the results of my last blood test?' I call them up on the screen, as she continues, 'Claire said I needed to see you to decide if I should make an appointment with my consultant. I'm not due to see her for another six weeks.'

The sample shows evidence that Bridget's blood sugar levels have not been well controlled with her medication. 'You haven't changed how you store the insulin, or anything like that?'

'Daisy – that's my dog – doesn't have the same problem. She has exactly the same number of units every day.'

'I can't really comment on a dog.'

'Maz, the vet, says diabetes is similar in other animals.'

I refrain from suggesting she book an appointment at the vet's for herself if she has more faith in them, but I do confess I'm at a bit of a loss as to what's going on with her. I tell her I'll talk to her consultant and be in touch.

'That would be useful,' she says. 'I can't keep taking time off to go to the hospital. I've had to leave a note on the door of the shop as it is, and I've had a delivery this morning that I need to see to. Cut flowers need nurturing, especially on warm days like today.'

'If you think of anything in the meantime that might be significant, let me know.'

'I haven't been smuggling extra cake and chocolate into the shop, I promise you. My daughter would go ballistic. She's a vet nurse and she's very strict with me and Daisy. Every calorie has to be accounted for.'

Once Bridget has gone, I lock the consulting room door and call Matt. I can hardly speak I'm so nervous.

'Matt Warren here.' He pauses. 'Ah, it's you, Nicci. Is this about the horse or is it a social call?'

'Social,' I say. 'I wonder if you'd like to come round to my place for dinner one night?' I purposely don't include the dog in the invitation because it gives a reason for him not to stay over, which means I won't have to go through the awkward conversation where, if he asks to stay, I have to tell him I'm not ready to sleep with him. It's far too soon for me.

'I'd love to,' he says.

It takes a couple of minutes for us to synchronise our diaries and set the date.

'I'll see you then,' I say, aware that I'm grinning from ear to ear. 'Goodbye, boyfriend.'

Chapter Seven

If Wishes Were Horses

'Did I mention I've invited Matt round for a romantic meal tomorrow night?' I say to Claire as she removes the paper towel from the exam couch in the consulting room after the last patient.

'Nicci, you know that's the first I've heard of it,' she says with irony. 'I don't understand why you haven't raised the subject before.' She gazes at me as I type up a letter of referral. 'Have you decided what you're going to give him?'

'I was hoping you might be able to help me out. I need something really easy that I can do in the slow cooker, perhaps.'

'Oh no, it's impossible to make a stew look sexy,' Claire says. 'What about a meaty meal, steak and thick-cut chips?'

'I wouldn't feel as if I'd put enough effort in to that.' Inside, my inner goddess suggests that there isn't much point in putting in lots of effort when I won't be able to eat a thing. Matt makes me feel sick to the pit of my stomach in the nicest possible way.

'How about oysters?'

'I don't think we're in need of any aphrodisiacs,' I say, smiling.

'How about a chilli? Don't give him fish – I gave my last boyfriend prawns and it turned out he was allergic to them.' Claire chuckles ruefully. 'It turned out he had a bad reaction to me as well.'

'Prawns aren't classed as fish,' I point out.

'I can't believe you're so wound up about this. It must be very serious, Nicci. You don't offer to cook for a man if it's just a date.'

'For goodness sake, I thought I'd cook for him, in a friendly kind of way.'

'Since when have you cooked for your friends? The only time you've invited me over was for scrambled eggs on toast.' She pauses. 'Dress in something hot, give Matt a glass of wine and he won't care what he's eating. Don't give him garlic though. Avoid it at all costs. You don't want garlic breath in the morning.'

'Who says he's staying over?'

'He will be, won't he?' she says, sounding surprised.

'I'm not ready for all that yet,' I say. 'It's early days.' I rushed in with Henry and look where it left me. 'I want to take it slowly. I want to enjoy going out on dates and being treated like a princess.'

'That doesn't have to stop when you go to bed with someone,' Claire says, appalled.

'Well, it kind of did with Henry. Once I slept with him, he seemed to think he didn't have to bother any more.'

'I think you're frightened of emotional commitment, Nicci. If I were you, I wouldn't be worrying about dinner at all. I'd be concentrating on breakfast.' Claire giggles. Her humour is infectious and I find myself giggling along with her. 'Steve's here,' she says eventually. 'Do you want me to send him in?'

'I need five minutes to finish this letter – I want to do it while it's fresh in my mind. You go and get on with whatever you're doing. I'll call him in when I'm ready.' It doesn't take long.

'Am I glad to see you again, Doc,' Steve says when I fetch him from reception. He walks along the corridor to the consulting room, dressed in a baggy Hawaiian-style shirt, blue cargo shorts that stop below the knee, white socks and brown sandals. 'I really thought I was a goner.' He takes both my hands and gives them a powerful squeeze. 'You saved my life.'

'Steve's brought us chocolates,' Claire calls from where she's helping Mr Brown manoeuvre his wife's wheelchair out of a tight corner between the door to the nurses' room and a trolley-load of paper towels and various containers of surgical scrub and hand gel.

'I didn't manage the turn, did I?' I overhear Mr Brown say while his wife is haranguing him about his steering.

'It's a jolly good job you aren't driving. In my opinion, you should be banned,' she says, and I smile to myself. Mr Brown is her long-suffering carer, and although she sounds terribly ungrateful they seem to love each other in an odd sort of way.

'Come on in, Steve,' I say, extricating myself from his grasp. 'Take a seat. How are you?'

'I'm well enough. I'm here for my MOT.'

'Well enough?' I ask, wondering what he means by that.

He shrugs. 'I'm a bit down, but they say that's normal for someone who's gone through what I have.'

'Don't be too hard on yourself. Give it time.' I glance through Steve's notes on the computer and read the latest letter from the consultant. 'Have you managed to make any changes yet? Have you started an exercise regime?'

'What are you trying to do? Make me feel guilty?' Steve smiles. 'It's all right, Doc. I know you're trying to help. To be honest, this attack has shocked me to my senses. My daughter's just announced her engagement and I want to be here to walk her down the aisle.' A tear springs to his eye. 'I want to be around to see my grandchildren. I have so much to live for, but I'm finding it really hard. I've fooled myself into believing I'm an active kind of man because I'm out and about every day but I've never done enough exercise. I've always been aerobically challenged.' He forces a grin – he isn't acting as if he's on the stage today. 'I'm challenged by the thought of doing anything aerobic, anything that involves wearing a leotard and breaking into a sweat, basically. I've tried dieting. I start every New Year's day, without fail, but my efforts never last much after midnight on the second of January.'

'You've been to see Dr Mackie before for cholesterol tests and lifestyle advice.'

'I know, but I haven't taken any notice. I'm afraid to say that I'm a bit of an ostrich when it comes to my health,' he says. 'It's too late to say I wish I'd done things differently, isn't it?'

'It's never too late to make changes,' I counter. 'How is the drinking?'

'I don't drink that much—' he pauses '—I expect all your patients are in denial about the amount they drink.'

'Do you drink alcohol once, twice or three times a week, or every day?'

'I have my five a day.' When I frown at him, he smiles. 'Not really. I do get confuzzled between my drink and my fruit and veg. No, it depends. I only drink on high days and holidays, and for me, because I'm a lucky man, every day is a high day. I'd like to think that I have at least two alcohol-free days each week, and I do tend to take a couple of weeks off before Christmas to allow for the seasonal excess.' He hesitates. 'Do you think garlic would help?'

'It might keep the vampires away, but it won't do much for your arteries unless you address your weight, diet and alcohol consumption,' I say. 'This is serious.'

'I know.' He rests his pudgy hands in his lap. 'I want to be serious, but I'm not all that good at it. When will I be able to return to the stage? Will I be fit in time for the panto season?'

'I'd hope so. You can do whatever you like, as long as you don't overdo it.' I pause. 'Steve, make sure you take advantage of all the support that's on offer. Don't try to muddle through.' I feel keenly for him – I'd like his life to end up like the traditional pantomime, happily ever after.

It's far too soon for me to be entertaining thoughts of the happily ever after for me and Matt Warren, but I'd be lying if I claimed it hasn't crossed my mind. I suppress the idea, blaming my overactive imagination.

I ride Willow before work on Friday morning, having made sure the house is tidy and the food is ready in the fridge. I had a brainwave and ordered fish pie, along with pre-prepared vegetables from the WI in return for a donation to one of the local charities. Mindful of Claire's comment about unwanted reactions to eating fish, I did check with Matt and he has no allergies. All I have to do is pop it into the oven and, as Gordon Ramsay would say, 'Done.'

Everything is going to plan, the second to last patient of the day is booking another appointment at reception and I've signed the last repeat prescription from the request box. I've arranged to visit one of my housebound patients on Monday and asked Claire to order in some vaccines for someone travelling to South Africa in the near future. I smile to myself as I pull up the waiting list on the computer. There is only one more to see, Matt is coming over for dinner and I couldn't be happier.

You might well accuse me of paranoia, but I pick up my mobile and check for messages, just in case there's a problem.

'Can't wait xMatt'

I smile to myself for being such a fool as to doubt him. Nothing is going to get in the way and ruin our first real date tonight. I glance at the clock. There are less than two hours to go.

I head out to reception to call in my last patient, but Fifi accosts me on the way.

'I'm sorry,' Claire says. 'I tried to stop her, but she wouldn't listen.'

'This can't wait,' Fifi says. 'This is an emergency. Oh, Dr Chieveley, there's been a break-in at your home. I've reported it to the police, but I thought you'd want to come straight down to have a look.'

It takes a few seconds for Fifi's news to sink in.

'Broken into? Oh no, that's the last thing I need.' I feel sick. 'There must be some mistake. It's probably Frances,' I go on, hoping that my neighbour has finally succumbed to temptation and had a good snoop around.

'Frances wouldn't do a thing like that,' Fifi says in her defence.

'All right, I'm sorry.' I feel violated at the thought of a stranger entering my house and going through my possessions.

'What can I do to help?' Claire looks at me, her eyes wide with concern.

'Could you let Ben know I've had to pop out? I'll be back as soon as I can.'

'Don't worry about getting back. I can cancel your last appointment or transfer them to Ben. He won't mind.'

'What won't Ben mind?' Ben says, interrupting as he walks out of his room, a urine sample half hidden under a piece of paper towel in his hand. 'Claire, can you deal with this, please?'

'Nicci's been burgled. I said she should go.'

'You must go, Nicci.' Ben turns to me. 'I'll hold the fort.'

'Are you sure?'

'Yes, but one of us should come with you,' Claire says, relieving Ben of the sample pot.

'There's no need. I'm here,' Fifi interrupts. 'The police are on their way, and they can walk from the police station in the time it takes to start a car.'

'Well, don't go inside until they get there. No heroics,' Ben says.

I go back and grab my bag, my heart pounding with apprehension at what I'm going to find. I've been burgled once before, when I was a student in London, and it was a nightmare, but I had less to lose back then, just my bank cards, some cash and a couple of pieces of jewellery.

'I can't believe this is happening.'

'Nor can I,' says Fifi, taking the lead in her heels and flowing skirt. 'This is the first criminal offence to be committed in Talyton St George since those boys from the new estate were caught scrumping apples from the orchard over at Uphill Farm. Never in all my time as Lady Mayoress can I remember there being a domestic burglary.'

I'm not too happy about the idea that I'm making history.

'There was the curious case of the missing gnomes a few years ago,' Fifi goes on. 'They disappeared en masse from residents' gardens, and a few weeks later those people received postcards from all over the world, purporting to be from their gnomes, who were allegedly taking a gap year together.'

'Did they return from their travels?' I say rather abruptly. I'm more worried about the fate of my home than that of a few garden ornaments, but Fifi is already onto the next topic of conversation.

'So much for the Neighbourhood Watch scheme!' she exclaims. 'Why was no one watching?'

I trot along, trying to keep up with her, crossing the road to find a small crowd gathered on the pavement outside the churchyard opposite my house. There's also a police car slewed across the middle of the road with its blue light flashing and one of Talyton's police constables, or Kevin as he's better known, is standing behind the driver's door, looking up at the front of the house, as if he's ready to make a rapid getaway.

Meanwhile, Fifi holds my arm and guides me towards the house, handbag at the ready – for attack or defence, I'm not sure which. There are no signs of forced entry. In fact, the front door is wide open. My heart sinks.

'I've started leaving it unlocked. What an idiot.'

'Everyone leaves their doors unlocked,' Fifi says. 'It's part of the charm of the place.'

'Fifi,' Kevin calls. 'You can't cross the cordon.'

'What cordon?' she says sharply. 'I can't see any cordon.'

'I'm waiting for someone to fetch some tape from the

station.' He moves around the car and joins us. 'We believe they're still inside.'

'Why don't you get in there and arrest them then?' Fifi totters forwards, at which the policeman intercepts her.

'Because we don't know who they are. They might be dangerous.'

'Oh dear. What is the world coming to?' I assume Fifi is talking about the prospect of there being dangerous criminals in this sleepy Devon country town, but she continues, 'What are you, Kevin? Man or mouse?'

'It's the rules, Fifi,' he says, colour rising to his cheeks. 'I'm awaiting reinforcements.'

'Well, where are they?' she says hotly.

'On their way from a traffic incident. They're just rounding up a loose horse in Talyford and putting it back in the field. They won't be long.'

'It's a farce, if you ask me,' Fifi says, brandishing her handbag. 'Nicci, you get round to the back door. I'll take the front. You, Kevin, follow me.'

It's daytime, but there's a light on in the front bedroom and the sound of pop music coming from the depths of the house.

'Fifi, if you enter the house I'll have to arrest you.' Kevin pulls out his truncheon. It doesn't make him appear any more impressive and Fifi seems flummoxed when he suddenly changes his mind and continues, 'Let me go first.'

A child's voice rings out as Kevin heads inside the house. I follow close behind. It's my home and these are my burglars, after all.

'Mummy, Mummy! It's a policeman. Are we in trouble?'

Another voice, the voice of an irresponsible adult, yells out, 'Tell him to go away, Mummy's having a nap.'

A girl of eleven or twelve, dressed in a striped sundress and glittery jelly sandals, appears in the hallway with a boy of about three on her hip. The boy, a flame-haired redhead, dressed in a grubby T-shirt, shorts and Crocs, is eating a slice of toast. His cheeks are smeared with raspberry jam.

'Good grief, is that you, Sage?' I step past Kevin. 'It is you. And Gabriel too.'

'Do you know these people, Dr Chieveley?' Kevin is frowning while Fifi falls uncharacteristically silent.

'Mummy's having a nap,' Sage says. 'Hello, Auntie Nicci. We didn't have a key, but the door was open so we let ourselves in. Hope you don't mind.' She smiles, and I see my sister in her – long honey-blonde hair, freckles, captivating blue eyes and heart-shaped face. Suddenly I'm overwhelmed with tears of relief and joy at seeing my niece and nephew again. I hold out my arms as Sage continues, 'I did try to phone you on Mummy's mobile the other day.'

'It's all right. I'm sorry to have inadvertently caused all this bother, Kevin. They're family.' I hug them tight, not wanting to let them go. 'Am I glad to see you!'

'Do you want to press charges?' Kevin asks.

'No, of course not.' I do want to have a word with my sister though. What was she thinking of? All she had to do was call me to let me know she was dropping by. 'Where is Mummy?'

'Upstairs, having a nap, as I said,' Sage responds, deadpan, and I don't believe her. I wonder how many times she's had to lie on behalf of my sister.

'Let's get the kettle on,' Fifi says, taking over. 'Kevin, you go back to chasing horses or whatever it is that you do best.'

'It's all right, Fifi,' I protest. 'I can deal with this now.'

'Oh no, you need some support. You've had a terrible shock.'

'Come on, Sage and Gabriel. Let's go out to the kitchen, away from all these prying eyes.' I walk through ahead of the children and Fifi, who appears to have attached herself to my family. I'm too confounded to argue with her.

The kitchen door is shut. I push it open, releasing the aroma of fish pie. There are empty plates on the breakfast bar, along with half-filled glasses of blackcurrant squash, the washing machine is in full spin and my sister is sitting on a stool, with her blonde curls tumbling down her back, just like Goldilocks in the house of the three bears, reading my magazines and drinking my coffee.

'Cheska, what on earth are you doing here?' I exclaim, moving across to touch her shoulder and kiss her cheek. 'What's going on?'

My sister looks up and flashes me an apologetic smile. 'Can we leave the inquest until later?'

I know what she's getting at, not in front of the children, or Fifi.

'Cheska, it's lovely to meet you.' Fifi moves in to

greet her. 'Welcome to Talyton St George.'

'Excuse me, Fifi, this is private,' I say. Cheska looks thin and drawn, her freckles standing out against her pale skin. She's wearing a faded green sundress and flip-flops. Usually she cares about her appearance, in a bohemian kind of way, but today she looks as if she couldn't be bothered. She reminds me of a stray dog desperately seeking someone to love them. A lump catches in my throat because I do love her, always have done and always will, because no matter how much grief she's caused, especially to Mum, she's still my sister.

'I'll be discreet. You won't know I'm here.' Fifi puts her handbag down on the worktop and takes the kettle to the tap to fill it. 'Where do you keep your teapot?'

'I don't have a teapot. I use teabags.'

'They'll do.' Fifi makes tea for me, Cheska and herself.

'Sage, there are some yoghurts in the fridge – get one for your brother,' says Cheska when Gabriel is pestering her for something to eat.

Sage turns to me. 'Is that all right, Nicci?'

'Go on,' I say.

'You remember Auntie Nicci, don't you, Gabriel?' Cheska says. Gabriel responds by grabbing the yoghurt and a spoon from his sister, and hiding behind his mum's legs, pulling her skirt up around her long limbs. 'She's Mummy's sister.'

'I think he was too young to remember me,' I say.

'He knows all about you though. Mummy, you told us about when you and Nicci were little,' Sage cuts in.

Cheska smiles at me fondly. 'I told them the story about when you took the wrong medicine because you didn't read the label. You took syrup of figs instead of cough mixture and ended up with an upset tummy.'

'I thought you said she had a dire ear,' Sage says, clearly confused.

'Yes, diarrhoea – that's the same as an upset tummy,' Cheska says.

'Great,' I say, 'you used me as an example of a cautionary tale and then embarrassed me with it.'

'I want them to know who you are,' she says with a flicker of a smile.

'Mummy says you're very clever because you're a doctor, but when I had tonsillitis I had to see another doctor and she wasn't very good because she sent me away with the wrong medicine, and we had to go back and see her again.'

'These things happen,' I say, amused and relieved that they didn't happen to me, so I still have my reputation intact as far as my niece is concerned.

'Nicci will be able to have a look at you next time, because you're bound to get it again.'

I register alarm, but try not to show it in front of the children. The next time? How long is my sister intending to stay?

'Can I ride your horse?' Sage asks, changing the subject. I recall that Cheska brought her along to see Willow at the yard when they were staying in a caravan on the coast one summer with her current boy-friend, Alan. At least, I assume he's current. Maybe, they've fallen out and that's why she's here.

'We'll see,' I say. 'Willow's in training at the moment.'

'I wish I had a horse,' says Sage, confirming my suspicion that horses run in the blood, that equestrianism is an inherited disorder.

'A rabbit would be easier to manage,' I point out as the church bells chime six o'clock, which triggers Fifi's decision to make a move.

'I must love you and leave you,' she says. 'I have a meeting of the Parish Council.'

And I have a date. I start to panic. Matt will be over in an hour, and I haven't showered, and I haven't got any food, and the house looks like a tip, and I have company. So much for our romantic meal!

I see Fifi out, making a path for her through the shoes, books and soft toys scattered across the hall floor, and I wonder what to do.

I can't bear the thought of putting him off, but I can't see that I have a choice. I don't think he'll be angry, just disappointed. I call him, but there's no reply, so I leave a message on his voicemail, warning him of a change of plan before having a quick word with Cheska.

'I'm going to have a shower before we talk about your plans,' I tell her.

'I haven't really planned anything beyond this moment,' she says ominously, and any hope I have that she is en route to a B&B or hotel or an old friend's house for the night is dashed.

'That's so typical of you.' My sister is impulsive, reckless even. 'You never think ahead. What if I hadn't been here? What would you have done if you'd found I was on holiday or something?'

'You are here,' she says, frowning, 'so it isn't an issue.'

'Don't you dare go anywhere,' I say, exasperated with her already and concerned that she might move on as soon as she's arrived, whether or not she has anywhere to go. 'Promise?'

'Promise,' she says.

'Good. We'll continue this conversation later.'

'Have you got a hot date, or something?'

'I'll reveal all, I promise. Give me five.' I rush upstairs, grab my dressing gown and turn the water on in the shower. It runs for a while before I realise that it's freezing. There is no hot water. On further inspection of the room, I discover that my towel is on the floor, covered in dark handprints. Cursing under my breath, I throw on some clean clothes, jeans and a white vest top, not the ones I was planning to wear later for my date with Matt. My sister and her kids have used all the hot water.

I run back downstairs.

'Cheska, we need to talk.' At the same time, there's a knock at the door. 'I'll go,' I say. It's Matt.

'I'm early – I hope you don't mind.' He smiles. 'My last patient came out of recovery sooner than expected, so I thought why not surprise you?'

This is the least of the surprises today. I'm pleased to see him, but wish I'd had time to have the conversation with my sister about where she's spending the evening while I'm spending it with Matt.

'Didn't you get my message?' I ask.

'My mobile's out of battery.' He steps up close so I

can see the pulse at the base of his neck and the hint of dark stubble on his chin. 'To be honest, I couldn't wait to see you, Nicci.' He hesitates. 'Aren't you going to invite me in?'

'Come on in,' I say, smiling, and he walks into the hallway, handing me a huge bouquet of flowers from Petals, wrapped and tied with a bow, and with the same pale blue and purple theme as my cross-country colours.

'For you,' he says, kissing my cheek.

'Thank you,' I say, touched. I can't remember the last time anyone but a patient gave me flowers. I catch hold of Matt's arm and lean up to kiss him full on the lips.

'Something smells good,' he observes when I draw away, my heart pounding and heat flooding through my body. 'You've been cooking.'

'Ah yes, the food . . . There's been a bit of a hitch.'

'There was some food in the kitchen and we've eaten it all up,' Sage pipes up from behind us. 'It was very nice. On the packet it said, "made in Talyton by the WI".'

I groan inwardly. 'Thanks for that.'

'That's all right.'

Matt chuckles. 'I thought you women valued honesty in a relationship.'

'I wanted to impress you.'

He takes my hand and squeezes it. 'You come across as the perfect woman with the perfect life, but I'm very relieved to find out that you are human after all.'

'Is that your boyfriend?' Sage goes on.

'I hope you're going to answer that,' Matt says,

raising his eyebrows at me as if to say, what on earth's going on?

'Yes, I suppose he is.'

'I didn't know you—' he goes on, staring at Sage as if she's a ghost.

'I don't. This is Sage, my niece.'

'Hello, Sage. Nice to meet you,' Matt says politely.

'Niece to meet you.' Sage bursts out into peals of laughter.

'I'm so sorry, Matt.' I usher him through to the kitchen and out of the back door. 'Sit down. I'll get you a drink, then I'll explain. Wine?'

'Yes, thank you,' he says, bemused.

'I don't know whether the wine is any good, but I spent a while choosing it with old Mr Lacey in Lacey's Fine Wines, and it came at a rather fine price, so it should be drinkable at least.' I fetch the bottle and a glass from the kitchen.

'We'll go,' Cheska says, standing up. 'I can see we're in your way.'

'But where will we go, Mummy?' says Sage, her voice tremulous. Poor girl. She's exhausted – and scared. 'You said, we haven't got anywhere, except Nicci's house.'

'Cheska,' I say wearily, 'sit down. You and the kids aren't going anywhere tonight. Give me a few minutes. I'll sort this. Sage, I promise that you, Gabriel and your mum are not in my way. Everything is going to be fine. Just stay where you are.' I run my hands through my hair. 'Please!'

In the garden, I pour Matt a glass of wine and sit on the chair opposite him at the table. I explain about Fifi and the police and it all comes out in a jumble, and to my chagrin I find myself close to tears. In response, Matt moves his chair next to me, slides his arm around my shoulder and pulls me close.

'Hey, it doesn't matter about tonight. I'm cool with it.' He touches my nose, his glass still in his hand. 'Why don't I take you out instead? My treat?'

'I'd love to,' I say, 'but I can't. Not tonight.'

'All right, I understand,' he says mournfully.

'I haven't seen my sister for a very long time, over a year, and she's turned up not merely on my doorstep but inside my house and I need to find out why.' I'm torn between catching up with my sister, who is clearly in a bit of a state, and a romantic evening with Matt.

'Family is family,' Matt says. 'We'll get together again soon. How about tomorrow? Oh no, I'm giving a presentation to some other equine vets at an area meeting. It's just an update on my research, but I don't think I can cancel. I'm on call on Sunday. How about Monday?'

'I've got a cross-country clinic with Shane.'

'Shane again? Is there anything I should know about you and him? You're always with him . . .'

I can't help laughing.

'He's very familiar with you. In fact, I keep meaning to ask you, why does he call you Phoebe? Delphi says he calls you Phoebe,' Matt goes on as I'm trying to work out what he's talking about.

'You mean VB. It's short for Velcro Bum because I stick to the saddle, most of the time anyway.'

Matt grins. 'Okay, that's weird, but I can deal with it. How about Tuesday night? Don't tell me – it's dressage night.'

'It's a late night surgery,' I smile.

'We're going to have to co-ordinate our diaries, otherwise we'll never see each other.' Matt looks disconsolate.

I can empathise with him. It's frustrating.

'Come over to my house next Saturday after morning surgery. I'll show you around.' He grins. 'I'm not expecting visitors.'

'That's the point. Neither was I.'

'Hey, no one's looking,' Matt says, glancing towards the house. 'Kiss?'

'I wouldn't say no . . .' I don't say no. I lean into him as he holds me close, and touches his mouth to mine, sending shocks of electricity darting up my spine. The kiss deepens. He tastes of hot coffee and mint. My pulse thrills. I reach out, one arm behind his back, my other hand spread across his thigh, feeling the taut spring of his muscles beneath my fingertips. Matt stills.

'Now, we're being watched,' he murmurs.

I groan with frustration as we pull apart and sit up.

Sage is peering out of the kitchen, half hidden by the partially open back door, and in spite of hearing my sister telling her to leave us alone, it's somehow stolen the moment.

'Everything else I want to do with you, girlfriend, needs to be done in private,' Matt says, his cheeks flushed with colour, as he stands and holds out his hand to help me up. 'I'm sorely tempted to kiss you again, but we'll wait. It's going to seem a very long time until Saturday.' He squeezes my hand. 'I hope all goes well with your sister. She seems to be in a bit of a state.'

'I'm sorry,' I repeat.

'Don't be. These things happen.' He tips his head to one side. 'The Bobster dog will be pleased. I shall go and spend the rest of the evening with her.'

I see Matt out, only to find Frances from next door ringing the bell. She uses her free hand to put her specs on – the frames are elaborate, like bejewelled butterflies – and readjust her hair. I believe she wears a wig because the colour changes from day to day. Tonight it appears the colour of pink grapefruit and clashes with her blue Paisley print tunic.

'Oh, hello,' she says, addressing Matt rather than me.

'I'll be off.' He rolls his eyes at me as he sidles past her. 'I'll text you.'

'Make it soon,' I say, fending off Frances's attempted invasion of the house by blocking her way. 'Hi, Frances. Before you ask, everything's fine.'

'I know. Fifi dropped by to tell me when I was at work. Is there anything I can do, anything you need for your unexpected visitors? I have blankets, pillows and spare towels.'

'Thank you, but I think they've found everything they could possibly need,' I say wryly.

'Oh? All right then. I'll leave you in peace.' She pauses. 'By the way, I brought you this.' She holds out a plastic tub. 'I imagine you're ready to make another friendship cake by now.'

'Oh no, Frances, I haven't the time.'

'Of course you have, dear. Besides, I'd be most grateful if you could take this one on, only I've exhausted my friends at the practice and the WI, and it isn't right to let the yeast die. This very same yeast has been making the rounds of Talyton St George for the past three years – to break the chain would be a bad omen, like neglecting to deal with a chain letter.'

Thanking her again, I take it from her. She's given me two tubs of the stuff before, but anything for peace and quiet, I think, both of which are distinctly lacking when I return to the kitchen, having made sure the front door is securely shut.

'Will we see Granma while we're here?' Sage asks.

'I hope so,' I say at the same time as Cheska says, 'No.'

'I remember Granma,' says Sage, but Gabriel has never met her, although he claims to have done.

'Describe her then.' Sage, now half dressed in a vest and pyjama bottoms, challenges her brother. 'What colour is her hair?'

'Black,' says Gabriel. 'She looks like a witch.' He cackles with laughter.

'No, she doesn't.'

'That's enough,' Cheska says, breaking them up before World War Three erupts. 'I don't want to hear any more about Granma.'

'Auntie Nicci, I was wondering where we're all going to sleep,' Sage says, changing the subject.

'Let me think,' I say, my mind drifting back to the kiss. It's hard to concentrate on anything, but eventually, I sort out the sleeping arrangements. Cheska and Gabriel are to share my double bed, while Sage has the single bed in the spare room and I have the futon in the attic. I imagined that Sage and Gabriel would play up about going to bed in a strange place, but they are both sound asleep within ten minutes of Cheska tucking them in.

My sister rejoins me in the kitchen where I've made myself a tuna sandwich, not quite what I was planning for dinner.

'I would say make yourself at home, but it seems you already have.' I put the kettle on. 'More tea?'

'I could do with something stronger.'

I fetch the rest of the bottle of wine. She drinks the first glass in one go.

'Cheska, aren't you going to tell me what you're doing here? I've been trying to get in touch with you for ages, I hardly ever manage to speak to you and suddenly you turn up at my house.'

'I thought we'd come and see you, Sis,' she says.

'You could have called, or even texted me to let me know you were coming.'

'Don't you want us here?'

'Of course I do. You're always welcome. How many times have I told you that?' I say, dropping a dirty knife into the dishwasher and slamming the door shut with some annoyance at my sister's inability to see my point of view.

'You could have fooled me,' she says. 'You've been a little off with me since we arrived.'

'That's unfair. I had to leave work early because the police were outside my house with a suspected burglar inside.'

'I've told you, we let ourselves in. The door was open.'

'You should have come round to the surgery first.' I'm aware that Cheska is staring at me the way she used to when we were children.

'Should have, could have, would have,' she says, tipping her head to one side. 'You're as bossy as ever.'

'It's a big sister's prerogative,' I say, smiling as my mind fills with memories of how we used to spend time together and how I imposed my wish to play horses on her.

'That's your opinion,' she says, her expression softening. 'I suppose it wasn't all that convenient us turning up this evening. The boyfriend seems nice.'

'Hands off,' I say, more cheerfully. 'How's Alan?' Alan is Gabriel's father. Sage calls Alan her dad, although her real father isn't around any more. He left my sister when Sage was small.

'Oh, we're on a break.'

'I should have guessed. I'm so sorry . . .' I try to get my sister to look on the bright side. 'If you're on a break, it isn't irretrievable.'

Cheska stares into her wineglass. Her lip trembles and a tear rolls down her cheek. She puts her shades on, but I tell her to take them off because she doesn't have to hide anything from me. She's always been like this, either upbeat and positive, or down in the depths of despair. The problem with my sister is that she feels far too much.

'I love him, but it isn't working,' she sobs. 'We're at each other's throats all the time. There's no one else. It's all about money, or the lack of it.'

'Are you in debt again?'

'Who isn't?'

'How much?' I ask, but, like a chancellor struggling to stay in power, she isn't going to reveal the extent of the deficit. 'You should have told me this sooner. I can pay off your debts and you can repay me when you're in a position to do so.'

'Nicci, I can't keep running to you for help. I have to do this on my own.' She grabs a piece of kitchen roll and blows her nose.

'You don't have to though,' I say, reaching out for her shoulder and giving her the slightest shake. 'We're always here for you.'

'We?' she says, her voice suddenly laced with suspicion.

'Me—' I hesitate before going on '—and Mum.'

Cheska falls silent.

'Does she know you're here?' I lean closer. 'Haven't you told her?'

'Why should I? She hates me.'

'She doesn't. I've seen her in tears, devastated because she doesn't know if you're safe.'

'If her grandchildren are safe, you mean? She doesn't care about me. You were always the golden daughter.'

'What happened is in the past.' It's almost fourteen

years ago now since Cheska disappeared for the first time.

'Try telling her that. I'll never forgive her for the way she treated me.'

'You weren't very kind to her, running away from home like that, pregnant and with a complete stranger.'

'He wasn't a complete stranger. He was Sage's father.'

'He was old enough to know better than to take advantage of a sixteen-year-old girl and isolate her from her family.'

'What family?' Cheska growls. 'You were away at uni, Dad had moved in with the scarlet harlot – and I don't know how you can go on about the age gap between me and Ewan when that woman was less than half Dad's age.'

'What about Mum?' I cut in. 'She was there for you.'

'She treated me like I was six. She followed me when I went out. She even locked me in once.'

'Because she was petrified you were going to get yourself into some kind of trouble, which you did.'

'She hated Ewan. She wouldn't let him anywhere near the house.'

'Because he was a thief.'

'That's what she thought. He wasn't a thief, Nicci.'

'Why did he end up in prison then?'

'That was after. He was set up.'

I take a deep breath. I don't want to argue but, 'I'm going to have to tell her,' I say.

'Don't, because she'll be straight round. Nicci, give me a chance to get myself together. I'm not up to a fight right now.'

She's very calm now and I can see I'm not going to get through to her tonight. I pour her a second and then a third glass of the wine I bought for Matt. By midnight, the bottle is drained and so am I.

'I'm going to bed,' I say eventually. 'I have a riding lesson in the morning, so I might not see you before I go.'

'The kids will be up at the crack of dawn. Gabriel is an early bird, not a night owl.' Cheska smiles weakly. 'I hope we don't disturb you.' She is grateful and contrite. We hug.

'Everything will be all right,' I tell her.

I retire to the futon, which is so lumpy it makes me feel like the girl in 'The Princess and the Pea.' I check my mobile and find that I've missed a text from Matt. 'Hope all well XXX.' I text him back. 'XXXX.'

Chapter Eight

Only the Horses

'Hello, Nicci. Cup of tea for you.' The early dawn light sears the back of my eyes – there are no blinds on the attic windows – and the figure of my niece gradually forms in front of me, a good fairy in tatty blue pyjamas, holding out a mug.

'What time is it?' I ask.

'I don't know. Mummy said you had to get up early because it's Monday morning. It's early.'

I look for the alarm clock, but remember I'm in the wrong room. I squint at my mobile. Five a.m.

'Please don't be cross.'

'I'm not cross.' I pull myself up and take the mug from her. 'Thank you very much for the wake-up call.' As she perches on the edge of the futon, I refrain from pointing out that five o'clock is early even for me. I was hoping for a lie-in. 'Did you sleep all right?'

She nods. 'I slept with Mummy and Gabriel in the end.'

Smiling at the thought that I may well join them, having spent three uncomfortable nights on the futon, I take a sip of the watery, sweet fluid in the mug.

'That is a lovely cup of tea,' I say. 'Have you found yourself some breakfast?' I go on, noticing the cornflake stuck to her sleeve. This is a girl who knows her way around a cupboard.

'Mummy says she'll give you some money.'

'She does, does she? Well, you're my guests. You don't have to pay your way while you're staying here.' I place the mug on the floor at the same time as a loud crash reverberates through the house from downstairs.

'What is that?' Sage says, wide-eyed at the distinct tinkling sound of breaking glass.

'I think you mean what *was* that?' I sigh. Pulling my duvet around me, I head downstairs with Sage running ahead to find Gabriel sitting on the kitchen floor surrounded by the remains of at least three glasses. He's crying his eyes out and holding up his finger which is dripping blood.

'I hurt myself.'

'Nicci, he's bleeding,' Sage says, squatting down beside him.

'Sage, be careful. You haven't got any shoes on and there's glass everywhere. Everyone, keep still.' I check Gabriel's wound, and having ascertained that he isn't going to bleed to death I grab a dustpan and brush and sweep up as much of the glass as I can before I fetch the first aid kit.

It isn't the best stocked of kits, considering I'm a doctor, and there's a muddle of horsey and human equipment in the box. I end up applying a dressing followed by a veterinary bandage to hold it on. It's overkill really, but Gabriel loves the fact that it's purple.

Sage finds him some breakfast while I clear up, but within minutes he's off again and before I know it, he's making a den in the living room with the cushions from the sofa and a boat from the coffee table turned upside down. I don't know whether to laugh or cry. The house is a mess, and Gabriel is giggling and shouting, 'Auntie Nicci, ahoy there!'

'Ahoy there to you,' I call back with a chuckle before turning away to gaze out of the window. Bridget, the florist, gives me a wave as she takes her dogs into the churchyard for a stroll. I wave back.

'Have you got some rope?' Sage asks. 'We're going to get a sheet and make a sail.'

'There's some string in the kitchen,' Cheska says, joining us. 'Morning, Nicci. I hope you don't mind – I've borrowed your dressing gown.'

'Do I mind?' I start to laugh. 'Cheska, it's like my home's been taken over by an alien race, but no . . . I don't mind in the slightest.' I was craving company and now I have it. The house has come alive.

Having told my sister and the kids to make themselves at home, I get ready for work. I'm itching to call Mum, but decide to give Cheska a couple more days to get herself together and call her herself, hoping that the gossips don't get to Mum first.

'Nicci, a word,' Ben says quietly from the doorway of his consulting room when I arrive at the surgery just in time for my first appointment a few days later. 'In here,' he adds.

'What's wrong?' I ask. It's ridiculous, but my heart is beating hard. Has someone made a complaint of some kind? It does happen occasionally.

'Oh, nothing's wrong,' he says, smiling as he sits down at his desk, his fingers forming a steeple under his chin. 'I didn't want to ask you about a rather delicate situation in front of the others, but are you and Matt Warren an item?' Ben's cheeks grow pink. 'I overheard the others talking.'

'Yes, I think I can say that now.' I find myself blushing too. 'It's all right though, he's no longer a patient.'

'And you let me call him a misogynist,' Ben says, teasing me. 'Really, Nicci.'

'What else could I do? I said we couldn't go out together unless he changed doctors and he had to make up an excuse. I did the right thing, didn't I?'

Ben nods.

'I'll treat him gently,' he says. 'He said you were rough with him.'

'Did he?'

'Yes, when he was denigrating your medical skills. He said you hurt him, your hands were cold and you refused to listen.' Ben's brow furrows briefly. He tips his head back and rolls his eyes. 'How could I have been so stupid? I should have guessed something was up.' He grins – he's in an unusually good mood. 'He's a great actor – he should have been on the stage.'

143

Having talked with Ben, I see my first couple of appointments before running into Claire, who calls me aside into the nurses' room.

'Can I have a word?' she says quietly, closing the door behind us. 'This might be nothing, but I think you should hear it and make up your own mind.'

'That sounds ominous,' I say, trying to guess what this is about.

'I'm not sure.' She falters. 'I'll present it as a hypothetical situation. Let's say, hypothetically, that someone, let's call them A—' She gazes at me, eyes wide. 'That's you.'

'Me?'

'Is going out with someone, B—'

'Matt?'

'That's right. But someone else, C, has categorically stated to the practice nurse that they are in a relationship with B, even though the aforesaid nurse was under the impression that A has just started going out with B.' Claire pauses and I start to feel slightly sick when she continues, 'I hate these kinds of situations, but I don't want to see A get hurt.'

I bite my lip. What is going on here?

'There's probably no truth in it at all,' Claire adds.

'Then why did Mel say it?' The hairs on the back of my neck prickle with unease. Someone is lying, but who? Matt or Mel? 'When did she talk to you?'

'You mean, when did C say this to the practice nurse?' Claire gives a small smile. 'About ten minutes ago, when C came in for a tetanus booster. C was full

144

of her plans to go and work away from here for a couple of years to gain more experience before coming back to Westleigh as B's partner – in the veterinary sense at least. She's very ambitious.'

'She does give that impression,' I say calmly, but inside I'm all churned up because this conversation suggests that either Mel has designs on a partnership at the hospital, or she has designs on Matt, or he's stringing both of us along.

'Have I said too much?' Claire says quietly. 'I'm sorry if I've overstepped the mark, but I thought you'd prefer to know.'

'It's fine,' I say, raising my hand.

'Is it?'

'Well, no, it isn't. I feel like I'm on a rollercoaster, up one minute and down the next.'

'Don't do anything rash,' Claire says. 'Give Matt the chance to give his side of the story.'

'Why would Mel make something like that up?'

'A woman scorned and all that. Speak to him.'

'How will I know if he's telling me the truth? He told me they'd split up three months ago, but what if they're still together and he's been lying all along?'

'Do you believe that?'

'I don't know what to believe.' I shake my head, swallowing back the tears that are perilously close to spilling over and rolling down my cheeks. 'I do know one thing though. I'm not going to let Matt make a fool of me.'

'You aren't having the best time, are you?' Claire says. 'The gossips are out in force. Fifi has been in to drop a request for a repeat prescription in the box at reception.'

'That's ridiculous, she has at least a month's supply of her tablets and creams. I should know because I prescribed them.'

'Frances turned up with a poster advertising a WI event, a cake sale to raise funds for Talyton Animal Rescue, but all she wanted to talk about was your sister turning up out of the blue. And, although it's probably a complete coincidence, your other neighbour has arrived,' Claire says. 'Be careful what you say. She's the reporter for the local newspaper, the *Chronicle*, and she's roving around the waiting room, looking out for a story.'

'How do you know?'

'She's always looking for a story.'

'You mean Eternally Frazzled Mum?' I begin to pull myself together, forcing a small smile. 'That's what I call her, but not to her face,' I add quickly.

'I'm not surprised she's frazzled – she has three sons and a touch of acopia.'

Acopia is our informal term for someone who is unable to cope with everyday life. It affects most of us from time to time, but not me, not today. My patients come first.

I call my neighbour Ally Jackson in with one of her sons, eleven-year-old James, who she shoves along in front of her. She's dressed in a pale pink trouser suit and big white beads, while her son – a slightly overweight boy with a pudding-basin haircut, striped shirt and long trousers – holds out his hand, showing

off a finger wrapped in an enormous bandage, suggesting partial severance if not complete amputation.
I'm tempted to send him straight to A&E, but decide to
unwrap it first to assess the injury. I ask him to lie on
the exam couch because he's looking pale and sweaty
and I'm worried he might faint. I insist that his mum
sits down for the same reason. I have one patient on my
hands – I don't need another.

'So, James, you better tell me what happened to you,'
I say, talking calmly to reassure him. 'I'm going to take
this dressing off.' I pick up the scissors, noticing how
he winces when he sees them as if he's afraid I'm going
to cut off a second finger.

'He got bitten,' Ally says.

'Mum, I can speak,' James says with the confidence
of a boy who has had to grow up quickly.

'What was it?' I say, assuming it was a dog at least.

'It was Nathan.'

'You mean another person did this?'

'Nathan's our pet rat,' Ally says.

Very gently, I unwrap the outer layers of bandage
until I can peel off the cotton wool padding underneath, which reveals a tiny indentation in the boy's
finger and an almost invisible streak of blood.

'It's pretty bad, isn't it?' he says, admiring the
damage.

'Oh, I can't look.' Ally hides her face in her hands.

'It's going to be all right.' I bite my lip to stifle a
chuckle. I love my job. 'Tell me again, this Nathan, why
has he taken against you, James?'

'We adopted him from the Sanctuary, the rescue

centre where Buttercross Cottage used to be. Do you know it?' Ally says.

'I know where it is.'

'Anyway, we took Nathan on a few months ago.'

'It was ten months ago. Get your facts right, as you keep telling me, Mum.'

'Is he a healthy rat?'

'He's yellow, like the colour of custard.'

'Why did he bite you, do you think?'

'I was giving him a treat, and unfortunately, he thought the end of my finger was a yoghurt drop.'

'He's one spoiled rat,' Ally says proudly. 'James looks after him very well.'

'It's never a good idea to bite the hand that feeds you though,' I point out lightly. 'Now, what do we need to do, do you think? Have you cleaned the wound?' It's so small I can hardly call it that, but it could do with a flush with antibacterial wash. To make an occasion of it, I move across to grab a kidney dish from under the sink.

'I want to be a doctor,' James says.

'Not an ordinary GP though,' Ally says, apparently oblivious to her put-down remark. If only she knew how important a GP's role is in the community, supported, of course, by practice nurses like Claire and receptionists like Janet. I wonder what she would do without us, I think, as she continues to sing her son's praises. 'He's doing well at school. He's in the top set for maths and his tutor praised him for his art project.'

'Mum, do you have to?' James groans.

'That's great though,' I say. 'You'll need good grades in your exams.'

'What does a doctor do all day?' he asks me.

'I see patients like you, ones who've been hurt, and I decide when someone needs to go to hospital. Basically, I make people's lives better, I hope.'

'He needs antibiotics,' Ally says officiously. 'You *are* going to give him some.'

'Not this time. We don't give out antibiotics like sweets. If he develops an infection, we'll use them, but not before.'

'I'd prefer the wound not to get infected in the first place,' she says.

'Just keep an eye on it and come back if there's any redness, heat or swelling.' I turn to check James's records onscreen. 'You're up to date with your tetanus injections – that's great.' Except that it reminds me of what Claire told me about Mel this morning.

'What about Weil's disease?' Ally interjects. 'I've been looking it up on the web.'

'It's nothing to worry about in this situation. It's highly unlikely.' Not only is Ally Eternally Frazzled, she's also the archetypal pushy mother and completely neurotic.

'Is that you on the horse?' she asks, spotting the photos on the wall.

'It is. I take her to competitions. She's an eventer.'

'You see, when you're a consultant, James, you'll be able to afford the luxuries in life,' Ally says.

I suppose it's true that horses are considered luxuries.

'I see my lovely horse as an essential,' I say, smiling.

'Well, it's all right for some,' Ally says, rather

sharply, and I think how she must struggle as a single parent on a reporter's wages. She can't earn very much and she has three sons. I have only one horse.

She softens a little. 'I should run an article about you and your horse. It would be wonderful, Talyton's galloping GP. Oh, Dr Chieveley—'

'It's Nicci.'

'Nicci, I could run it in our Tuesday edition – it's always quiet news-wise on a Tuesday.'

'It's quiet every day of the week round here – that's what you're always saying, Mum. Nothing ever happens in Talyton St George, except hatches, matches and despatches. Did you know,' James goes on, turning to me, 'there's never been a murder in this town? The most exciting thing that's ever happened is when we had the great flood and the bridge got washed away.'

'Please don't create any more dramas, James,' Ally says. 'Just be careful when you're feeding Nathan in future. Thank you, Nicci. I'll be in touch about the article.'

'I'm always happy to help.' I type up the notes and leave Matt a message on his voicemail saying I need to talk to him, before wandering into reception.

'Crisis over?' Janet asks, looking over the top of her monitor at reception.

'I hope so. Boy mauled by rat.'

'Oh dear,' she says. 'There's a message for you from Mr Brown. He's requesting a home visit for his wife. You know, it isn't my place to say, but I really think he should be getting some respite care. He's exhausted.'

'In an ideal world,' I begin. It's been difficult for us as a surgery to provide support for carers since the cottage hospital closed a few years ago. Mr Brown does need a break. In fact, I've become more worried about his state of health than his wife's. He looks unkempt in his old nylon shirts and trousers and squeaky shoes.

'He looks after that old dog of theirs too, the one with the dodgy tummy. I know it's on a special diet, but it's never quite right.'

I admire Mr Brown for his dedication. He never complains.

'I don't think you realise how hard it is being a full-time carer,' Janet goes on.

I thank my lucky stars that I don't. I have an inkling now as to how tough it is, seeing my sister with Sage and Gabriel. Keeping Gabriel out of mischief is a full-time occupation. It's relentless, which is one of the reasons why I'm grateful for the excuse that I have to go straight to the yard after work to ride Willow – it's Friday so it's my early finish. The other reason is that it gives me time to think about Matt, who hasn't responded to my message yet.

Hiding behind the screen in the consulting room, I change into my jodhs and polo top, waiting until I reach the yard to put my boots on – short ones with half-length chaps which are cooler in the summer than long boots.

I grab Willow's head-collar and head down to the paddocks to find her. As I approach, I notice a fence is down and there are two horses in Willow's field instead of one, and the interloper looks like Dark Star.

What has he done to my horse? Has he kicked her, or bitten her?

With a sense of foreboding, I start to run.

Dark Star walks over to greet me while Willow hangs back, but it isn't Willow that's hurt. Dark Star has come off worst. He's scraped his shoulder galloping through the fence and has a gash across his knee. It isn't bleeding much but the flies are already settling on the wound. I catch Dark Star first. Although he's keen to see me, he isn't so impressed by the idea of wearing Willow's head-collar, but I have mints in my pocket and he's a quick learner – the head-collar goes on before he gets a mint, not the other way round.

'Walk on,' I say, and he moves forward, his head level with my shoulder but nodding with each stride. He's lame. My heart sinks. Delphi won't be happy, but then it's her problem if the fences aren't secure. Someone must have forgotten to switch the energiser on to electrify the section between Willow and Dark Star, and Dark Star took advantage of it to go visiting. He's a gelding, and what Delphi would describe as a bit 'studdy' and keen on the mares. When I reach the stables I call Delphi to come and have a look at her horse.

'I found him with Willow,' I say, somewhat annoyed. 'She could have broken her leg. I can't risk this happening again.'

She apologises and promises to fix the fence.

'What do you think, Nicci?' she goes on. 'Does that need stitching?'

'Delphi, I'm a doctor, not a vet. Horses and humans are different. Aren't you going to call one of the vets?'

'Couldn't you ask Matt to have a look? On a casual basis, I mean?' she adds. 'He'd do it for you as a favour, wouldn't he? He seems rather keen on you.'

'He probably would, but Dark Star isn't my horse, Delphi.' I'm hoping not to encourage her pursuit of a free consultation because I know that's what she's after. Anyway, until I've spoken to Matt I'm not sure whether I have a relationship with him or not.

'He could check Willow over at the same time. She was galloping about earlier in the wind. I nearly brought her in because I thought she was going to do herself an injury. I wish I had now.'

'I'll go and get her,' I decide. I trot Willow up in the yard and Delphi pronounces her sound. She has years of experience, but she isn't a vet, and she's worried me with all this talk of Willow belting up and down in the field, and I decide I'll give Matt a call anyway.

This time I get straight through to him.

'Matt, I was wondering if you could come up to the yard and have a look at a couple of horses.'

'Willow?'

'Yes, and one of Delphi's, the big brown horse, Dark Star.' There's a moment's hesitation. 'We'll share the call-out fee between us, if that's all right with you.'

'Forget the bill, girlfriend.'

'I don't want to take advantage,' I say flatly.

'You can take advantage of me any time,' he chuckles, apparently oblivious to the tone of my voice. 'Are you at the yard right now?'

'Yes.'

'Ask a silly question . . . I should have guessed. I'll be on my way then. I can come to you en route to a partners' meeting at the pub. I shouldn't be more than ten or fifteen minutes. You can thank me later,' he says and I cut the call, feeling confused. I wish I could tell whether his tone was genuine or whether he's just putting it on. I'm dreading the conversation we're going to have, but for the sake of my sanity I have to be sure this time.

When he arrives, bringing his car onto the yard and parking it right outside Willow's stable, he opens the door and a small tan and white Jack Russell terrier comes flying out.

Matt whistles her to heel when he gets out after her. She stays with him for two seconds before she's off again, racing across the yard to the feed room.

'She's looking for rats. She's a great ratter.' Matt moves up close to me and makes to reach for my hand. The terrier comes flying back and interrupts with a flurry of barking. I step back, crossing my arms.

'Get down!' Matt says. 'Off.'

This time she listens and sits down on his foot, gazing up at us, her head cocked to one side, her lips drawn back to reveal her teeth.

'I think she's saying "paws off the master",' Matt says, grinning.

'Can you tell her to go away? She's making me nervous.'

'She's jealous. Bobster, hop it.' She moves a few paces away before immediately returning, her eyes fixed on mine.

Don't stare back, I tell myself. I don't know why I know that. I must have read it somewhere in an article about how to avoid dog attacks.

'Are you and the Bobster in a long-term relationship?'

'We haven't been together for very long. She was a client's dog and she kept jumping in my car and coming home with me. I didn't realise she was there the first time, which was really awkward because I was accused of dog-napping.' He smiles at the memory. 'When she did it the fourth or fifth time, she ended up staying. Her previous owner felt rejected.'

'It's a strange way to pick a dog.'

'I didn't pick her though. She picked me.'

'Why's she so possessive?'

'Because she loves me. I'm flattered. If she didn't feel so strongly, she wouldn't care.'

Like me, I think ruefully, and I'm ready to open my mouth and ask him about what's going on between him and Mel when Delphi interrupts, hoofing across the yard in heavy boots.

'Okay, vet to the rescue. Tell me what's happened.'

'Does it need a stitch?' she asks.

'He hasn't had a chance to look yet, Delphi,' I say, scolding her because Matt is doing us a favour, dropping in at short notice. I go into the stable and lead Dark Star outside to make the most of the light.

'This could do with a single suture here on the knee, but otherwise it's good news,' Matt says. 'There's no damage to the joint itself.'

'Pity,' Delphi says. 'I was hoping to try for loss of use with the insurance company.'

'You aren't fond of this one, are you?'

'He's trouble. Will he be scarred?'

'It will hardly be noticeable. I'm going to sedate him again. It won't take long, then I'll have a look at Willow.'

Matt injects Dark Star with sedative into the vein in his neck, then puts on blue, latex-free gloves to cleanse the wound and close it with a single stitch.

Delphi offers to trot Willow up for us. The horse is anxious, throwing her head in the air, which makes it more difficult to assess her paces. I note how Matt is frowning, standing there with one arm across his chest, resting his chin on the other hand. She looks sound to me, but I'm not sure he feels the same.

'What do you think?' I say apprehensively.

'Can we lunge her in the school for a few minutes?'

'Of course,' Delphi says, and we pick up a lunge-line and whip on the way.

'I think she's okay,' Matt says to reassure me, 'but I just want to be sure. She's a rather special patient because she belongs to my girlfriend.'

'Are you two . . . How marvellous.' I can see Delphi's thinking how convenient it will be and how she can install Matt as yard vet.

I believe she might be disappointed very shortly, although no one will feel more let down than me.

'I always thought I'd marry a vet,' Delphi says wistfully.

Who said anything about marriage? I want to say, but I'm too embarrassed.

'Did you have a particular vet in mind?' Matt asks.

'Alexander Fox-Gifford. I adored him. I still do, and I'd have taken him like a shot, but he didn't feel the same. I was always good old Delphi, she's a brick, someone to confide in.'

'I thought you'd fallen out with him,' Matt says.

'With his father. Oh, Matt, don't worry. I'm not planning on changing practices. He's married now with a young family.'

'There'll be other men, other vets,' Matt says brightly.

'It's too late for me now.' Delphi glances down at her filthy nails. 'The horses are my family.'

I open the gate to the outdoor school and move a coloured pole and a couple of blocks out of the way so Delphi can put Willow on a circle at walk and trot in both directions.

'What do you think?' I ask Matt again, but he doesn't answer. He seems lost in thought, so I leave him alone.

'Pull her up now, Delphi. That's enough.' He moves in and runs his hands down Willow's foreleg, picks it up and examines each part, prodding and squeezing the joints and tendons. 'When you thought she was sore after the one-day event, which leg did you think it was, Nicci?'

'That one, the off fore.'

'I can't see anything obvious, but I'll just do a flexion test on the concrete before we put her back.'

By the end of his investigation, Matt advises me he can find nothing wrong, but there is something niggling him, that she might be a little uneven on the right rein in trot. At the first sign of anything, I'm to let him know immediately.

'You bet I will.'

'That horse is the most important creature in Nicci's life,' Delphi observes when we return Willow to her stable and check on Dark Star, who is sleeping off the effects of the sedative. 'You're going to find it hard to compete with Willow for her attention.'

Matt looks across at me and smiles, but I can't smile back.

'Are you all right, Nicci?' he asks once Delphi has gone.

I shake my head.

'I got your message, but I haven't had a spare minute—'

'I have a question for you,' I interrupt. 'Why would Mel tell my nurse that she's going out with you when I was under the impression that you're going out with me?'

'I've told you, we were an item for a while, but we finished ages ago.' Matt frowns. 'I've been honest with you, Nicci. I can't see there's a problem.'

'Well, there is because she told Claire this today.' I watch his face, fighting to control the tremors of anger, disappointment and distress that shudder through my body.

'What the . . .' Matt swears. 'Either she's lying, or your nurse got the wrong end of the stick.'

'Claire wouldn't get something like that wrong.'

'Okay, so it's Mel.'

'Why would she do such a thing?'

'It's obvious, isn't it?'

'To you, maybe,' I say sharply.

'She's still in love with me.' A smile crosses his lips. 'Or she hates me so much she wants to wreck my relationship with you.' Matt takes a couple of steps towards me. 'Mel's completely mad – that's one of the reasons I couldn't stay with her. She's just too much.' He lowers his voice to a husky whisper. 'Please, Nicci, don't let my ex-girlfriend poison what we have.'

A pulse begins to beat inside my head, a throb of hope, because I do believe him and although what we have so far really isn't very much, I sense that it's a solid enough foundation on which to build.

'I'm sorry I doubted you,' I say, reaching for his hand.

'That's all right.' He squeezes my fingers. 'I'd have jumped to the same conclusion if I'd been in your position. I'll speak to her at work.'

'Will she listen though?'

'I think she'll see sense. She'll probably be really embarrassed.' Matt leans in and kisses my cheek. 'Are you still all right for tomorrow?'

'I am now,' I say, more cheerfully.

'I'll see you sometime after one,' he says, releasing my hand. 'How are your visitors? Are they staying for much longer?'

'At the moment it feels like they're here on holiday, but I can't help thinking from what my sister's told me that they could be around for a while.'

'Oh well, you can always come to my place if you need to escape. You're more than welcome. Any time.'

Any time. Those words, more than anything, reassure me that there is nothing going on between Matt and his ex. He wouldn't invite me over if he thought I was going to find Mel there.

Back at my house Cheska is cooking dinner. Having recovered my appetite after my conversation with Matt, I'm so hungry I could eat anything, so I'm happy to sit down with fish fingers, oven chips and lashings of tomato ketchup.

'I hope you don't mind,' Cheska says, 'I borrowed a few pound coins from the pot.'

'That's fine.' I keep my change in a pot by the phone in the hall. 'Help yourself to anything you want.' I mean it. I want her and the children to feel welcome because I've realised over the past few days that they need some stability in their lives while Cheska and Alan decide whether or not they can make amends. She's still in contact with him by text at least, making me think that all is not lost between them. Sage and Gabriel are happy here, even if they're causing havoc in the house – last night I found one of the wardrobes emptied of clothes because they were looking for the way in to Narnia.

I don't want them to move on in a hurry and risk losing contact with them again, not just for my sake and theirs, but for Mum's too, which is why I tackle Cheska again once the children are in bed asleep.

'I told you, I don't want to have anything to do with her,' Cheska says.

'She'll find out by herself,' I say. 'The next time she's

in Talyton, someone will ask her how you and the children are, and then how will you feel?'

'The same as I do now.'

'I wish you'd just speak to her,' I say sadly as I watch her pour herself a glass of wine as if she's dismissing the subject. 'Where's the harm in that?' My sister doesn't respond. I think she's scared that if she sees her she'll break down, and she's too proud or too stubborn to acknowledge there has been wrong on both sides.

'I'm going for a shower,' I say, but on my way I call Mum.

'Where are you?' I ask when I finally get through to her. 'I tried you at home and there was no reply.'

'I'm out and about with Robert, actually,' she says. 'I didn't realise I had to keep you in the loop once he'd been vetted and passed sound, so to speak. I thought we were beyond that.'

'You seem pretty serious about Robert. You're seeing rather a lot of him. Is he the one?'

'Nicci, you young people are so idealistic. I'm not looking for a soulmate, just someone nice and without too many bad habits. I don't want to be lonely any more.'

'You can be lonely when you're with someone – that's what you used to say about you and Dad.'

'It was a long time ago and that's enough about me. How are you, darling?'

'I'm in a state of shock. Cheska has turned up.' I was going to add 'on my doorstep', but 'in my house' would be more accurate. 'With Sage and Gabriel.'

'Oh!' My mother utters a cry, much like the baby I

gave an injection to today. 'How are they? No, don't tell me now. I'll be straight round. Robert! Don't put the pony away.'

'No, Mum, you're not to come round. I don't want a scene.' But it's too late, Mum has already put the phone down. I decide not to shower after all, and within ten minutes, the clip-clop of hooves, moving at a spanking trot, announces my mother's arrival. Robert must have driven like a demon. The hooves fall silent. The doorbell rings.

'Nicci, let me in. Where are my grandchildren?'

'Please, not in front of the neighbours,' I say, letting her into the hallway, but no further. 'For goodness sake, I asked you not to come.'

'I thought I'd never see them again.' She looks past me. 'Cheska!'

I turn to find my sister in the kitchen doorway, her arms folded and her face a thundercloud of anger, bitterness and regret.

'I should have known you'd invite her round.'

'I didn't. I let her know you were safe—'

'That's right. Wave a red rag at a bull, why don't you? You can never rely on family.' Cheska turns and slams the kitchen door, the sound reverberating through the house.

'The children are in bed!' I exclaim. 'Mum, I'm sorry, but you have to let me handle this.'

'She'll never come round,' she sobs. 'She hates me.'

'Give it time. You know what Cheska's like – rush in and you'll spook her like a horse. You will see your grandchildren.'

'I wish I could believe you, Nicci.'

'Have faith.' I give her a hug, thinking everything might have been different if she'd had faith in Cheska in the past, trusting my sister's judgement about what was best for her, rather than imposing her own views.

I lead her back outside where Robert, standing at the pony's head, comforts her.

'There, there, my lover,' he says. 'Come along with me.'

I watch them leave in the trap, amazed that Frances hasn't turned up to see what's going on, and that the children are still asleep. I check on my sister, who has taken herself off to bed, and call Mum later to make sure she's all right.

I'm so tired of being the grown-up, responsible sister all the time. I wish I could kick over the traces just for once, but I can't. It isn't me.

Chapter Nine

Love Me, Love My Dog

With Matt, it isn't a case of out of sight, out of mind, because firstly, I can't stop thinking about him and secondly, he's constantly reminding me by phone call and text that he's keen to see me.

'N E time after 1pm, don't 4get Mattxx'

'As if   x', I text back.

On the day of our date, with butterflies dancing in my stomach, I park on the driveway in front of the brick and tile building that is part way through its transformation from a pair of semi-derelict farm-workers' cottages to one house, as evidenced by the presence of two separate front doors, one red and one green, that open onto a path that borders a single lawn. The grass has been mown, but the flowerbeds are overgrown with a mixture of shrubs, roses and pink mallows.

When I get out of the car, Matt comes marching up with the Bobster at his heels giving me a bark and a growl.

164

'Hey, that's enough,' Matt says sternly.

'She really doesn't like me,' I say, feeling a little threatened. 'She's snarling. I can see her teeth.'

'She's smiling,' Matt insists.

'I don't believe you. She's sucked you in completely. Love me, love my dog.'

'She's a great dog.' He reaches for my hand, pulls me round and kisses me on the lips, and I'm buzzing with joy and happiness and anticipation. He's amazing.

'Thanks for the invite.' Much as I enjoy their company, I need a break from my sister and her children. It's been a shock to my system, having been used to living alone and pleasing myself. 'If I talk in a funny voice today, Matt, it's because I've overdosed on children's TV – *Peppa Pig*, *Postman Pat* and endless repeats of *Bob the Builder*.'

'You can talk however you like. Welcome to my humble abode.' Matt grins as he guides me to the rear of the house, his hand on the small of my back while the Bobster runs back and forth barking. 'Do come in.'

I follow him through the open door into the kitchen where there is a dish of strawberries and a jug of clotted cream on the oak table and a kettle whistling on the range. I look around at the beams that run across the high ceiling, the rustic dresser and the colourful plates arranged on it. There are postcards on the walls, sent from all over the world.

'I can't bear to throw any of them away,' Matt says. 'This is my favourite room in the house,' he goes on.

'It's lovely.' I gaze out of the double doors and across the garden, where the lawn, big enough to require a ride-on mower, sweeps down to two fruit and vegetable plots. Along the edges of the grass are borders of shrubs and flowers: hollyhocks and lavender, and in the centre, a pear tree. Beyond the end of the garden are green fields with grazing sheep and a distant farmhouse.

'Help yourself to strawberries, then I'll show you around.' Matt leans his head to one side. 'I could show you the bedroom, if you're interested.'

'Matt!' I blush in spite of, or maybe because of, the fact that I was thinking along the same lines. It's a dilemma for me, though, because in my heart I want to leap straight into bed, but my head is telling me it's too soon.

'I've been looking forward to having you to myself, just the two of us.'

'Don't forget the Bobster,' I add.

'She won't let me,' he says, picking out a strawberry and holding it to my lips. 'Taste this. I picked them from the garden less than an hour ago.'

It's sweet, succulent and fragrant with summer sun - shine, and I laugh when Matt leans up close and kisses away the juice that trickles down my chin. He holds me closer until I can feel the growing heat between us. 'Let me show you around,' he whispers, releasing me slowly, and taking hold of my hand, but before we can go anywhere, a buzzer sounds from the range.

'That's my cake,' Matt says. 'It's ready.'

'You bake cakes!'

'One variety only – fruit cake.' He moves away and I watch him grab what looks like a tatty old T-shirt, using it to take the cake out of the oven.

'Haven't you heard of oven gloves?' I say, horrified.

'It's all right,' he says sheepishly. 'It's clean.'

'Yes, but . . .' I bite my lip. I expect the oven's hot enough to have killed any bugs.

'We'll let it cool down for a bit. I don't want it to crumble when I cut it.' Matt rests the tin on a wire rack. 'Let me show you the rest of the house. The living room's next door. I haven't lit the fire for a while . . .' He kicks a dog bed to one side.

'Where does the Bobster sleep?' I ask.

'Down here at night.'

'That's good. I thought you might have let her sleep on the bed.'

I accompany Matt on a tour of the house. He's understandably proud of his home and what he's managed to do to it so far. It's warmer and more personal than the house where I live, although it's chaotic with coats hung over the dining room chairs and photos of his family propped up on the piles of vet journals that overwhelm the bookshelves.

I can't help it but I find myself on the lookout for signs of the ex-girlfriend. All I find is a bottle of pink shower gel in the bathroom, which is a good sign that whatever they had together it wasn't all that much. I reckon the length and depth of a relationship can be measured by the number of shared possessions and the extent of the mingling of belongings.

It didn't take me long to disentangle my things from Henry's, which in retrospect should have told me something long before we split up. Even when I stayed over, he didn't like me to leave anything behind. Every hairbrush, spare toothbrush and sock was handed back to me pronto, and vice versa. The only item Henry left at my place was a DVD of *Twilight* that someone – another ex-girlfriend, I suspect – had left with him and he didn't want.

Even so, I find it surprising that there's nothing of the ex-girlfriend's here. Unlike the Bobster, either Matt didn't let her get her paws under the table or he made sure every reminder was removed. There is another alternative, I tell myself, that he didn't invite her here, which confirms what he's told me, that it was nothing more than a fling, and lends weight to the argument that Mel was lying to Claire for reasons known only to herself.

Matt shows me his bedroom. I walk over to look out of the window at the hills beyond the garden, keeping my eyes on the sheep in the fields as Matt moves up beside me, his hand on my waist. My heart is pounding.

'It's a fantastic view,' I murmur, unable to frame anything more interesting to say while he's standing right next to me.

'It is,' he says in a hoarse whisper.

I take the tiniest step aside, afraid of the intensity of my attraction to him and his to me, because I know he's gazing intently at me.

'It's all right, Nicci,' he sighs. 'I'm not going to grab you and throw you down on the bed, although there's nothing I'd like to do more.'

'I don't want to rush into—'

'It's fine with me. I understand, and I respect you for that. When I make love to you, I want it to be special.'

'Thanks . . .'

'I'm very fortunate living here,' he says, abruptly changing the subject. 'If I have trouble sleeping, I can always count sheep.'

'Very funny,' I say drily as his mobile rings. He pulls it out of his pocket and checks the screen.

'I'm sorry. I'll have to take this.' From the way he's frowning, I can tell it's bad news, for our date at least.

'I've got to dash off to the hospital. There's a colic on its way in.'

'That's all right.' My heart plummets with disappointment and some confusion because I didn't think Matt was on call today.

'It isn't really,' he says, echoing my thoughts. 'I can't believe how the fates seem to be conspiring against us.'

'Why do you have to go?'

'I'll explain later. I need to shift.'

'We'll have to organise another date and make it third time lucky.'

'Why don't you come with me and see what we get up to?' Matt hesitates. 'That's if you don't think you'll be bored.' He grins. 'It does involve horses though, if that helps to persuade you.'

'Well, yes, if you're sure. That would be great.'

'I can show you around the hospital, and depending on how long it takes, we can come back here later.'

'I'd hate to miss out on the cake.' I giggle because I can see the funny side of the situation.

On the way to the hospital, he explains why he's been called in.

'I'm doing a series of studies for a paper, and this

colic fits the bill,' he says. 'It's sod's law – these cases always turn up on my days off.'

'Perhaps you could write a paper on that,' I say flippantly.

'Yeah,' he says, but I don't think he's listening to me now. His mind is elsewhere as he drives us straight around the back of the hospital and parks the car.

'This way,' he says, and I follow him, trying to keep up as he marches into the building. We head along an indoor walkway laid with a rubberised floor and painted white with five looseboxes along one side. Three of the boxes are occupied. Matt nods towards a big bay horse. 'That one's stable-blocking, so to speak. He needs to go home.'

'Do the horses mind being here?' I ask.

'They get used to it. We don't keep them longer than necessary. Like people, they do better at home.' We turn the corner into a high-ceilinged room occupied by a chunky black pony standing in the stocks, trapping it in a small space where it can be safely restrained for a thorough examination. The pony is surrounded by a crowd of people, including another vet, nurses and the pony's owner.

'Robert? And Mum,' I exclaim, when I catch sight of my mother standing beside her man-friend.

'Nicci,' she says, walking over to me and bursting into tears. 'It's Beauty. Robert's driving pony,' she adds in explanation.

'Why didn't you let me know you were here?' I say, hugging her.

'Because I knew you were going to Matt's today.'

'You should have called.' I change the subject. 'How is she? What happened?'

'Robert took me out for lunch, and when we came back to the farm, we found her lying down in the field. The poor thing, she's in so much pain.' Mum steps back and wipes her eyes, smudging her mascara. 'We're afraid she'll have to have an operation.'

'And that will cost me a bloody fortune,' Robert grumbles, taking over comforting my mother.

'But you will have it done?' Mum says anxiously. 'You won't have her put down?' Robert doesn't answer. He strokes my mother's back and gazes towards the pony, his mouth set in a grim straight line as the vets work on her. There are two – Matt and Mel, one of the last people I wanted to see.

She is preoccupied with fixing an intravenous cannula in the pony's neck with a stitch. Although her long wavy locks are tousled, she doesn't look as if she's been on her feet all day and probably the previous night too.

Matt picks up the probe on a small ultrasound scanner mounted on a trolley and runs it over the pony's belly as Mel gives him Beauty's temperature, respiration and pulse. Having scanned the pony, Matt sticks a great big needle into the lowest point of her belly and drains off some fluid into a tube which he hands to one of the vet nurses.

'It's surgical,' he says. 'Let's get her prepped asap. Mel, you make a start while I talk to the owner, Mr—'

'Robert Ash.' Robert steps up to shake Matt's hand and holds onto it as if he's clinging to Matt as his only hope. Matt calmly disengages himself and explains the surgery and the possible outcomes.

'Worst case scenario is that we put the pony through the surgery, it doesn't work out and you're left with no pony and a bill of several thousand pounds,' he says. 'Is she insured for vets' fees?'

'I've never believed in insuring everything. I'm a farmer and you know what farming's like. There's no money in it.' He shrugs. 'The pony's of little monetary value.'

Mum gasps at this comment.

'It's your decision,' Matt says. 'Would you like five minutes to talk it over?'

'Robert, you have to give Beauty a chance,' Mum interrupts. 'She works hard for you. She's saved you an awful lot of diesel.'

'I don't know.' Robert scratches at his sideburns. 'I'm very fond of her.'

I join Matt while they deliberate.

'Let's give it a go, Matt,' Robert says, as Mum puts her arm through his. 'I don't want to lose her.'

'Would you like to wait at the hospital while she's in surgery?' Matt asks.

'I've got stock back at the farm that need looking after,' Robert says. 'What about you, Kathryn? Do you want to stay?'

'Not really. I don't think I can bear it.' She looks towards me.

'I'll be here,' I say, watching Robert walking up to the pony standing with her head down and eyes half closed, swaying slightly with the effect of the sedative she's been given. He slides his hand under her long mane and gives her a pat.

'Take care, Beauty,' he mutters. 'Best of luck.' With my mother following along behind him he turns and walks straight out through the double doors into the yard, where an ancient Land Rover with a battered trailer is parked.

He might pretend he doesn't care, but he's gutted. I can't imagine how I'd feel if it was Willow.

'Let's get her into prep,' Matt says. 'Nicci, you can come along too.'

'Aren't you going to introduce us?' Mel says when we join her and the rest of the team in the prep area.

'Of course.' Matt sounds cool, but I detect some tension in his voice. 'Mel, this is Nicci. We were at my house when I got the call. Nicci, this is Mel, our houseman.'

She stares at me, and now I know why Matt's feeling uncomfortable. It can't be easy having to introduce your girlfriend to your ex, particularly such a critical ex. I'm aware that I'm being inspected, like one of the horsey patients, picked apart and dissected under Mel's cutting gaze. She really doesn't like me and it crosses my mind that she suspects I know about her strange behaviour with Claire, pretending she's still with Matt.

'Matt,' she goes on, dismissing me. 'I need to speak to you about the horse that came in last night.'

'Let's get this one sorted first. Nicci, you can wait upstairs – there's a viewing gallery and a coffee machine.' He hands me his keys. 'You might want these. It's going to be a long afternoon.' He touches my shoulder, a brief but telling gesture for Mel's benefit, I suspect. 'I'll catch up with you later. Oh, the car's insured for any driver, in case you're wondering.'

'Thank you,' I say. 'Good luck.'

I don't know what I was expecting, but it's a proper, full-scale operation, not delicate and bloodless keyhole surgery. The pony lies anaesthetised on her back on a hydraulic table under the bright theatre lights, her feathery feet wrapped in plastic bags and most of her body covered with green drapes to reduce the risk of contamination. Matt, Mel, two vet nurses and a couple of technicians – scrubbed up and dressed in gowns, masks, hats and gloves – stand around the patient.

Matt and Mel are side by side, gazing down at the coils of gut they've pulled out of the pony's belly and spread across the drapes.

'Here we go.' Matt uses forceps to point to a dark purple length of gut that appears to have lost its blood supply. 'Let's resect this section from here . . . to here. Do you agree?'

'Do I dare disagree, you mean?' Mel says. 'No, it's fine. This is one decision I can respect, even if I don't agree with you on very much else.'

I thought she might have been off with him, considering what he said about her reaction when he ended their relationship, but she seems fairly cheerful, flirty even.

I can't help feeling horribly jealous. I know they have to work well together as part of a team. It's the way it has to be, but I wish they wouldn't stand so close together, passing meaningful looks and touching hands as they manipulate the surgical instruments glinting beneath the theatre lights.

Matt's entire focus is on the pony and the team.

'Mel, you're supposed to be resecting that.' He points to a healthy part of the gut beyond the piece that's damaged beyond repair. 'Not my arm, thank you, or anything else for that matter.'

'Will you stop hovering and move your arm out of my way? I do know what I'm doing.' Mel holds up the scalpel and flutters her eyelashes at Matt. 'You've taught me well.'

'Thank you,' he says, with mock solemnity, and I feel slightly nauseous. I don't like seeing my boyfriend flirting with his ex. I don't think he's even aware he's doing it. It's the way some surgical teams work and I've seen it many times before when I was a junior doctor.

'Nicci,' Matt calls up. 'Could you do us a favour, come down here, slip some covers over your shoes and take some piccies of this? The camera's on the shelf in the room on the way into theatre. You can't miss it.'

I pick up the camera and start snapping, following Matt's instructions.

'I hope you aren't going to faint,' Mel says. 'We haven't got the staff to pick you up.'

'Nicci won't faint,' Matt says. 'She's a doctor. She's one of us.'

Mel gives me a sour look, then turns to Matt. 'Oh, Nicci, of course, I remember now,' Mel says. 'You'd

175

been over at Nicci's before you came round to pick up the Bobster from the flat the other night.'

The flash goes off on the camera. Immediately, my brain homes in on her comment. Matt collected the dog from Mel? On which night?

'You said you were meant to be having dinner at Nicci's house, but something came up.' Mel grins. 'As it always does with you, Matt, without fail.'

I notice the slight scowl crossing Matt's face in response, as if Mel is overstepping the mark, or is he afraid she's going to reveal more than she should?

'Do you need me any more?' I ask abruptly.

'No, that's great, Nicci. Thank you.'

I switch the camera off and stick it back in its case. Why didn't Matt mention that he'd left the dog with Mel? Why did he give me the impression he was going straight home to see the Bobster? Did he stop for coffee and a chat when he collected the dog, or – my suspicious mind is racing – did he stay overnight?

'All we have to do now is make sure there are no leaks and then we can close her up,' Matt says. 'The signs are positive and the surgery's gone well. We'll have to see how she wakes up.' He looks at me, not quite meeting my eye. 'One step at a time.'

This is mad, I tell myself as I return the camera and head back up to the gallery. Did Matt not mention Mel because he didn't think it was important, or because he did think it was important and wanted to hide it from me? Maybe Mel is the one telling the truth. Maybe the ex-girlfriend isn't quite so ex as Matt's made out. My palms grow damp and my heart hammers like the hooves of a bolting horse. Now I don't know what or who to believe. I wait until Matt's finished operating, and then I join Mel in a padded recovery box as she watches the pony struggling to get back up after her operation. Matt phones Robert and writes up his notes in his office.

'Do you think she'll be all right?' I ask Mel. I hate to see her getting onto her front feet before falling down again. She's sweating and confused, but she's fighting.

'It'll be a few days until we can be certain.' Mel turns to face me. 'How did you meet him?'

'Matt?'

'Well, of course, Matt.'

'Oh, we happened to run into each other and got talking.' I really don't want to discuss it.

'Has he made you listen to live jazz on the quay yet?'

'It's none of your business,' I say.

'So he has.' Mel smirks.

'He has what?' Matt reappears, out of his scrubs now, his hair ruffled and a spatter of blood on his arm.

'I was just saying, you took Nicci to the same place we went to for our first date.'

'Mel!' he exclaims, his complexion darkening with suppressed fury. 'Do you mind?'

'It's all right, darling,' she goes on smoothly. 'You're so predictable.' She turns back to me. 'I expect he ordered the profiteroles too.'

'Mel, how's the pony?' Matt snaps.

'She's doing okay, but I still need to talk to you about the horse. In private,' she adds, glaring at me.

'There's no need. I've put my head over the door and looked at your treatment plan, and it's fine. Keep it on the penicillin and I'll check it again in the morning.' Matt gazes at me. 'I'm taking Nicci home.'

To his home or mine, I wonder? On the way back towards Talyton, I'm not sure where we're going, in more ways than one. 'It was a bit of a coincidence your mother showing up at the hospital,' he says, breaking the silence.

'Yes, I was surprised to see her.' I bite my lip, tasting metallic blood. It's only a small thing, but considering everything else, it niggles. 'Matt, why didn't you tell me you'd left the Bobster with Mel the other night?'

'I didn't think.' The gearbox grates as he changes down a gear.

'I want everything in the open,' and I want him to know how I feel. 'I want us to be honest with each other from the start.'

'I know, and you're right, but I didn't mean to—' he clears his throat '—I didn't intend to deceive you. I was going to leave the dog with Mel all night – she has a dog too – but your family arrived and I thought I'd rather have the Bobster at home with me.'

'It wasn't that you saw the opportunity to spend time with Mel?'

'Nicci, all I wanted was to spend the evening with you. I know what you said about her telling your nurse that she was still involved with me—'

'You did speak to her?' I interrupt.

'She said there was a misunderstanding. She said she was talking in the past tense. Your nurse misinterpreted what she said. It seems reasonable – Claire would be keen to look out for you.'

'But why on earth would Mel raise the subject in the first place?'

'Perhaps Claire did.' Matt smiles softly at me. 'You mustn't be jealous of Mel. I work with her, but it won't be for much longer. She's only with us for a couple more months, then she's off to another practice. She'll probably become a partner pretty soon. She's very good.'

I don't want to know that Mel is good at anything.

As we continue along the lane, he rests his hand on my thigh, sending tiny shocks of electricity across my skin.

'I'll never do anything to hurt you, Nicci, I promise. I do have some standards. And Mel is a nightmare. I would never take her back.'

I glance at the shadowy profile of his face. Do I believe him? I have to if we're going to survive as a couple, but can I see my way through this? There are still two months to go until Mel pushes off, giving her plenty of time and opportunity to try to seduce Matt back into her bed, and although I believe him when he says he wouldn't be tempted, there's a part of me that can't bear for a moment longer to think of them continuing to work together.

'I don't want to take you back to your house,' Matt says gruffly as we get close to his home. He pulls in at the side of the lane beside a five-bar gate, leaving the engine running. 'Stay over tonight,' he whispers, his breath warm against my ear. 'Please . . .'

It's enough to melt the heart of an iceberg, but not me.

'I want to go home,' I say, fighting the impulse to throw my arms around his shoulders and bury my face in his neck. 'Another time.'

'Another time,' Matt echoes.

'I've got to be up to ride Willow in the morning,' I say, knowing it sounds like a lame excuse. What I really mean is that I need some time to think.

Chapter Ten

Only Fools and Horses

'Delphi,' I ask when I'm up at the yard the next day.
'Could I book a lesson for my niece on one of your
ponies?'

'Whenever you like. I've got a group lesson of child
beginners next Saturday at ten. I should be able to find
another pony.' She smiles. 'I have more than enough to
choose from. In fact, I ought to get around to advertis -
ing another one for sale.'

'Delphi, I said Sage would like a riding lesson, not
that she wants to buy a pony. Please don't let that idea
even enter her head. She isn't staying with me for ever
and the last thing my sister needs is a pet of any kind.'
I sigh. 'She can barely look after herself sometimes.'

Delphi chuckles. 'It was worth a try. But I do have
that rather nice chestnut pony, Tizzy. She's rather too
good for the riding school.'

'Isn't she the nutty one?' I have to ask. 'Sage needs
one of the quiet, ploddy ones, like Harry.'

'I'll get her on one of the old kick-alongs.' Delphi pauses. 'Are you sure you're all right?'

'Quite sure,' I say, biting hard on my lip.

'Are you up for a dressage lesson later today? Only I'm going to see a horse tomorrow and I'm not sure I'll be back in time.'

'How about now?'

'In twenty minutes. The indoor school will be free at ten.'

'That'll give me time to get Willow tacked up.'

Riding takes my mind off Matt, for a while at least. Delphi is a hard taskmaster, tramping around the centre of the indoor arena, yelling instructions, many criticisms and a few compliments. She has one tone of voice: loud. I ride straight and tall with a long whip for dressage, touching it against Willow's sides now and then to reinforce the signal from my leg. She doesn't need much encouragement because she likes to work, and at the end of half an hour her neck is damp with sweat and my head feels prickly under my hat.

'That'll do,' Delphi shouts. 'We'll work on the half-passes again next time. Orf you go – unless you want me to wash Willow down.'

'I'll do it,' I say. 'Thanks, Delphi.'

'In that case, I'll go and grab Dark Star. He really needs working every day.'

As I walk to cool the horse down, thoughts of Matt flood back into my head. I hope I haven't put him off by going on about Mel and the dog, and what it appears that Mel said to Claire. I grab my mobile and call him while I'm walking Willow, partly to find out how he is, partly to hear news of Beauty – assuming it's best to hear news straight from the horse's mouth, so to speak – and partly to see if we can arrange to meet up again.

He's well, and Beauty is up and about and on intravenous fluids until she's ready to be offered food and water by mouth.

'Have you forgiven me?' he asks.

'As you suggested, there was nothing to forgive,' I say.

'I should have thought about how it would look.' He pauses. 'Shall we try again?'

'That's what I was calling you about. And I didn't have a chance to try any of your cake.'

'Ah, and you won't now,' he says, his tone teasing again, 'because I've eaten it.'

'You'll have to bake another one.'

'I'll do that. When are you free?'

When Matt is free, I'm not and the earliest we can meet is next Saturday, which is almost a week away.

'I do want to spend some time with you, Nicci, because what with my work and your riding, we don't have much opportunity.'

'Are you putting in a complaint?'

'Yes, I am.' He's joking, but there's an edge to his tone. I think he's beginning to resent my all-consuming hobby already, even though he's too cool to admit it.

'You can join me at the yard whenever you like. You can help me, mucking out and cleaning tack.'

'I'd hate to do anything that makes my shoulder worse,' he says cheekily.

'Why don't you meet me at the yard next Saturday afternoon? My niece is having her first riding lesson and the Bobster can have a run around. I can drop Sage back home and we can go out for a pizza, or something.'

'Or you can come back and have cake at my place.'

'I can't wait.' Saying goodbye, I jump off Willow and lead her back to her stable, making the most of the brief respite from my overcrowded house. Occasionally, I wonder if I could bed down in one of the foaling boxes Delphi keeps free for emergencies.

Willow stands quietly. I whip off the saddle and place it on the lower half of the stable door, then swap the bridle for a head-collar and leave her with the rope slung over her neck. I don't bother to tie her up – she isn't going far. I give her a wash down, concentrating on the sweaty bits behind her ears, her chest and saddle patch. She shakes her head and flicks her skin when the cold water from the hose touches her, but eventually she relaxes, standing with her head low, her eyes closed and her lower lip hanging down.

'Willow, Henry might have had a point when he said you looked like a donkey.' I stroke her and scratch her withers and she utters a sigh of deep contentment. I love this horse. She appreciates my company and she loves to work. I wish I could write a prescription for every patient I saw to spend half an hour once or twice a day with a horse like Willow, not one like Dark Star, though, I think as I catch sight of him sidling around the outdoor school. Unlike Willow, his presence raises the blood pressure rather than lowering it. Prescribing a session with Dark Star when he's in a bad mood could be fatal.

Delphi is hauling back on the reins, keeping his neck tightly arched so his chin almost touches his chest. He looks as if he's about to explode with tension, spattering white foam from his mouth, his coat dark with sweat, and snorting as he trots along, pounding his feet and sending up showers of grit that seem to wind him up more than ever.

'Steady,' Delphi says, her voice run through with desperation, 'steady there. Nicci,' she calls, 'would you come and open the gate?'

I abandon Willow to let Delphi out of the school. She dismounts and gives the horse a jab in the mouth.

'He's a bit of a headcase,' I say, recalling the pony I had on loan when I was thirteen, a New Forester called Pepper. I lost count of how many times I fell off.

'I'm going to school this creature to within an inch of his life and then I'm going to sell him. He's no use to me.'

'It's a shame.' Dark Star is a charismatic horse and I've grown to admire his fighting spirit as I've got to know him better as Willow's stable-mate, although I still don't trust him.

'I thought he'd make a fantastic dressage horse, but he hasn't the temperament,' Delphi continues. 'Why don't you have a ride on him sometime and see what you think?'

'Er, no thanks,' I say quickly. I'm just too busy, and besides, I want to stay in one piece.

'You can't rely on Willow being around for ever. You

could do with a second string to your bow, and Dark Star fits the bill.'

'On paper, maybe.' His breeding is perfect. 'I'm not looking for another horse. I'm concentrating on Willow – she's all the horse I need.'

'Can you say the same for Matt?' she says wickedly in that crystal-cut accent of hers. 'Is he all the man you need?'

'Delphi,' I exclaim as she throws me Dark Star's reins and I hang onto him while she drags his saddle off, hangs it over the stable door and sponges him down with cool water from a bucket. If this was an attempt to endear him to me, it doesn't work because he's on his toes, fidgeting, switching his tail and scraping his front foot on the concrete.

'Have you thought about changing his feed?' I ask Delphi.

'I've stopped his oats.' She hesitates. 'Are you seeing Matt later?'

'No, and I'm not talking shop when I do see him, if that's what you're asking.'

'It's only a tiny thing, Nicci, just to ask him if he can get me some bromide to calm the horse down.'

'Delphi . . .' I don't want to hassle Matt with veterinary questions when he isn't at work. It's happened more than once and I don't want him to feel I'm taking advantage.

'I can pick it up from the hospital one morning. I'll send you a text to remind you.' She throws a light rug over the horse's back and takes the reins from me, leading him into his stable.

'I can't wait,' Sage says, jumping up and down on our way to Tack n Hack the following Saturday afternoon. 'I'm going to ride a pony.'

And I can't wait, I think, smiling to myself, because I'm going to see Matt again at last. He's meeting us in the car park at the yard so we can spend time together. The Bobster comes too and the four of us walk inside the shop, which is filled with all kinds of horsey gear: gleaming bits and stirrups, hand-crafted leatherwork, bridles, saddles and brushes. I buy various beauty products for Willow – specialist shampoos for grey horses, mane and tail conditioners and hoof oil to make her feet shine. The last thing I bought her was a pink browband inset with crystals.

The bell rings, calling one of Delphi's army of horse-mad girls to the front.

'Hi, Nicci. Can I help you?'

'I'd have thought you'd know exactly where everything is,' Matt teases. The scent of his aftershave mingles with the aromas of wax and saddle soap.

'Sage here needs a hat, jodhpurs and boots.'

The girl looks at Sage. 'I hear you're riding Harry today. I learned to ride on him too. He's lovely.'

Sage blushes and smiles.

'I'll go and find a couple of hats for you to try on,' the girl goes on. 'The jodhpurs are all on the rack over there.'

'Shouldn't you borrow the kit for a while to make sure she likes it?' Matt says.

'What do you mean "Make sure"? Of course she's

going to like it. It's in her genes,' I say, grinning. 'Lighten up, Matt.'

'I'm afraid horses do tend to run in families, usually down the female line,' he agrees. 'Wouldn't you prefer to take up something like chess or tiddlywinks?'

'Tiddlywinks?' Sage starts giggling. 'What's that?'

'In the days before computers, all we had to play with were plastic counters,' Matt says gravely.

'If it doesn't involve ponies I'm not interested,' Sage says. She puts her fingers in her ears. 'La la la la la.'

'I can't imagine you playing tiddlywinks,' I say, amused at the idea of Matt flicking counters across the floor for fun.

I stop to pick out two pairs of jodhpurs from the children's rail. 'Here, try these on, Sage.'

Matt and I wait outside the refurbished changing room while Sage changes into a grown-up beige pair, followed by a fun pair in pink and navy.

'Aren't you worried she'll hurt herself? What does her mum think?' Matt says quietly.

'Matt, you're being a spoilsport. What's got into you today?' I reach my arm around him to give him a hug for being a great big softie.

He shrugs. 'I don't know. I'm sorry. I don't want to ruin Sage's big day when she's been looking forward to it.'

'I like these best.' Sage appears in the beige jodhs. 'They're like your best ones, Nicci.' She does a quick canter around the shop, hanging onto imaginary reins, and pulls up at the till with a snort and a stamp of a hoof.

Matt looks at me, one eyebrow raised.

'Of course, I never used to do anything like that,' I say, but he knows I'm fibbing. 'Although I did once perform a complete dressage test in the dentist's waiting room.'

I offer to buy Sage a stick, but she doesn't want one because she swears she will never hit a pony.

'I think it's cruel,' she says.

'Sometimes ponies need a reminder of who is the boss,' I point out. 'A good rider uses a stick as a guide, and never in anger.'

I can see that she remains to be convinced. I set her up with a hat and boots and she's ready for her first lesson with Harry, one of the little grey Welsh ponies who looks like a miniature version of Willow.

Harry is a good pony. He knows Sage is a beginner and ambles around on the lead rein with his nose level with his knees. If he was any more relaxed he'd fall over.

Delphi asks Sage to give him a kick and she gives him a very half-hearted flap of her legs.

'Harder,' shouts Delphi. 'Give him a smack. Oh, you haven't got a stick.'

'I don't want one,' Sage yells back.

'Your niece is a feisty one,' Delphi observes lightly. 'I can see I'm going to have to whip her into shape.'

I'm sure Delphi will have plenty of time to teach her how to ride because, when the lesson is over, Sage is determined to come back for a second one the following weekend. Sage and Matt feed mints to Harry, Willow and Dark Star while I join Delphi in the office, where she writes the time of Sage's next lesson in the diary.

'Have you heard the rumours?' she asks. 'I wondered if Matt had said anything to you. I didn't want to ask him in case they weren't true – I don't want to make a fool of myself.'

'What rumours?'

'The one about the houseman being pregnant. According to Neil, the farrier who was at Westleigh doing some corrective shoeing the other day, Mel is almost three months' gone.'

'I would have heard if Mel was pregnant,' I say. 'Matt wouldn't have been able to keep that to himself – it would cause a certain amount of disruption at the hospital as she wouldn't be able to take any X-rays because of the risk to the baby. He would be grumbling like mad.' A dark thought enters my head. 'Unless . . .' No, if she *is* pregnant and the dates are right, it can't possibly be Matt's baby because he split with her back in March. She would have conceived at the beginning of May.

'Oh well,' Delphi shrugs before staring at me expectantly.

'No,' I say, holding up my hands. 'I'm not asking him.'

'You haven't seen her at the surgery then?'

'She'd hardly book in to see me, would she?'

'You're a doctor.'

'I'm Matt's current girlfriend and Mel doesn't like me one little bit.' I pause. 'Delphi, I'd let sleeping dogs lie if I were you. It's no one's business, but Mel's.'

'Have you heard that one of Henry Belton-Smith's

grooms is taking him to an industrial tribunal for unfair dismissal?' Delphi continues. 'I thought you'd be interested.'

Smiling, I shake my head. 'I'm not interested in anything Henry does.'

'You used to be.'

'I'm going out with Matt now. I've dealt with the Henry episode and moved on.' I change the subject. 'I'd better go and put Willow's rug on.'

Matt has left when I get back, so I make sure my horse is tucked in for the night before taking Sage home. I grab a shower and head out to Matt's.

We have pizza from the Co-op and a freshly-baked fruit cake for dinner. I notice how Matt picks off a couple of slices of pepperoni and surreptitiously slips them to the Bobster, who sits drooling underneath his chair at the kitchen table.

'I hope I'm not going to bore you with horse talk,' I say, 'but it is my specialist subject.'

'I realise that.' Matt shakes his head. 'You'll never bore me, Nicci.'

'Do you ride?' I go on.

'I don't.'

'You're a horse vet, and you don't ride?' I say, surprised.

'I'm not the only one around here. You're harking back to the olden days when vets rode to check for broken wind and bridle lameness. I started to learn at vet school. One of the other students . . .' He pauses. 'It wasn't for me.' He smiles, but the smile is forced. 'I guess I didn't like the breeches that much.'

'We could ride together sometime,' I suggest.

'No thanks. I'd rather keep my feet on the ground.'

It's a shame, I think. We could have spent some time in the yard together.

'What about mucking out? Didn't you have to do that at vet school?'

'I worked at a yard one summer, but the girls used to do the stables for me in return for favours, the occasional kiss, if they were lucky. I'm teasing. I wasn't overly confident with girls back then.'

Later, when we're ready to cuddle up on the sofa, Matt puts the Bobster in the dog bed – it's pristine, I notice, without a single hair or muddy pawprint on the cover.

'Stay,' he says and we retreat to the living room that runs the width of the two former cottages. It's unfinished. There are patches of bare plaster on the walls and no curtains, but you can see its potential with its brick chimneypiece and log burner ready for use in the winter. We sink down into the soft green sofa and Matt puts his arm around my shoulder and pulls me towards him for a kiss. Suddenly, a small tan and white dog appears between us, standing on Matt's thigh and bouncing up and down trying to lick his nose.

'Get off!' I say. 'I thought you said you'd put her to bed.'

'I had.' He chuckles at my expression of horror. 'You saw me.'

'Why won't she stay there?'

'Because she's afraid she's missing out.' He tips the

Bobster off his lap, gets up and calls her back to the kitchen. 'I'll shut the door this time.'

'Good idea.'

The Bobster has an alternative plan though, which consists of howling as loud as she can. It's incessant and a highly effective passion killer. Matt sweet talks her, gives her a biscuit and a chew, and leaves the radio on, changing the station twice in case she has a preference for classical music over pop. But nothing works.

'If I were you I'd send her back,' I say caustically. 'What about seeing a psychologist?'

'For me or the dog?' He smiles ruefully. 'I think I might need counselling if she keeps on like this.'

'I'm glad you feel the same way I do. That racket is driving me mad.' I put my arms up as he stands in front of me, having returned from the dog for the umpteenth time.

'What's this?' he asks.

'Pull me up. I must go home – I have a long day tomorrow. I'm training at seven.'

'With Shane?' I watch a frown flit across Matt's face.

'You aren't jealous, are you?' I tease as he pulls me up and into his arms.

'Just a little, maybe. Don't you ever give your poor horse a day off?'

'She has one day a week when she has a bran mash for breakfast and time out in the paddock, just chillaxing, but it's usually a Wednesday.'

'Why don't you stay?'

'Another time.'

Matt pulls me closer and kisses me passionately until, eventually, I brace my palms against his chest.

'You're making me want to stay,' I murmur. 'I want to stay.'

'Stay then. The dog's gone quiet at last.'

'I haven't got any clothes.'

'You don't need any. Come to bed . . .' His final word on the matter, uttered in a husky whisper, explodes any resistance I have left. 'Please . . .'

I take his hand and we climb the stairs together.

I lie in bed with Matt's arms around me and a big smile on my face, warm with the afterglow of making love with him for the very first time. It was perfect. He is perfect and I could stay like this for ever, listening to his breathing as dawn approaches.

'Go back to sleep, darling,' he murmurs.

'I'm not sure I can,' I say as the cockerel starts to crow and a hen starts clucking frantically as she lays an egg, a large one if the number of decibels is related to the size.

'Do you have to keep a cockerel?'

'I like the old rooster – he has a purpose, to keep the hens happy and provide the next generation of chicks. I got them from Hen Welfare and some of them are getting on a bit. The fox got one the other day, the rotten bastard!' Matt sits up, pulling the duvet from my shoulders. Shivering, I tug it back from him. The dog has joined us and is curled up between mine and Matt's legs.

'I thought she slept downstairs.'

'I was trying to impress you,' he grins. 'I told a little white lie because I didn't want to put you off.'

'It doesn't seem very hygienic.' I wrinkle my nose at the sight of a few tan and white hairs on the bed.

'She's all right, aren't you Bobster?' Matt reaches down the bed and strokes her head. 'She's probably just as concerned she'll catch something from you.' He chuckles and although I'm minded to flip him over the head with a pillow, his humour is infectious and I find myself laughing with him.

'I'd better get up,' I say.

'Stay . . . I don't have to be at the hospital until nine.'

'It's tempting, but I've got to go. Shane's expecting me.'

'Not Shane again.' Matt groans. He's only half joking. He met Shane earlier in the week when he dropped by at the yard to see one of Delphi's horses and I was having a training session on Willow. 'I've seen the way he looks at your legs, as if he's caressing them with his eyes.'

'That's his job,' I smile. 'He makes me work on my position. In the saddle,' I add, so there's no mis - understanding.

'I've seen him groping your thigh. I think that's my area.'

'Oh Matt.' I'm laughing. I really don't see it that way, and neither does Shane. 'We've been doing this on and off for years.'

'And it shows. You're like an old married couple, arguing the tiniest detail.'

'I guess Shane and I do know a lot about each other,

but if we were going to be more than friends it would have happened by now. Anyway, he's happily married.'

'Whatever,' Matt says as I get out of bed and give him a kiss before gathering up my clothes from the night before. 'I don't like the idea of another man making you sweat.'

'I'll see you later. Do you mind if I grab some toast on the way out?'

'Help yourself,' he says with a sigh. 'Have a good day.'

'And you. See you later.'

When I arrive at the yard, having diverted to the house to change into my riding gear, I drop my stick and fumble with the girth straps as I tack Willow up. Shane is on my case straight away.

'You mustn't let that boyfriend of yours distract you. It isn't fair on the horse if you're just a passenger. Have you taken up drinking, or something?'

'I have few, if any, vices. You know that. No, it's my nephew and niece who are keeping me awake,' I say, but I don't think Shane believes me.

'No excuses,' he says sternly. 'You really need to make sure you get a good night's sleep. There's no point in me turning up at some unearthly hour of the morning if you're in no fit state to train.'

'Shane, please, can't we be friends today?'

He chuckles when he responds, 'I need to maintain my authority. We are not friends. I am your trainer. Go on. Stop dreaming about lover boy and get on your horse.'

Blushing, I lead Willow out of the stable. Shane gives me a leg up, the momentum almost throwing me over the other side as Willow takes a couple of steps forwards before I can catch up the reins and bring her back to a halt.

'What have you planned for today?' I ask.

Shane walks with me to the jumping field where the ground is good, in spite of a day's rain.

'I thought we'd do some grid-work. That way, we can work on Willow's obedience and suppleness and not bore her before the weekend.' Shane moves a couple of poles, one in each hand, taking them to the centre of the field to start building his grid of fences. 'Now, stop chattering and get moving. Warm her up.'

I don't know about Willow but Shane certainly warms me up, making me canter on the lunge without stirrups before the grid-work, an exercise requiring precision steering.

'Legs!' he yells. 'More legs!'

'You're killing me,' I call back.

'What did you have for breakfast?'

'Toast.'

'One slice or two?'

'One.'

'It's all very well feeding your horse on the best competition mix but you need to eat properly too. A full English breakfast. Eggs, bacon, sausage and beans. That's what I had this morning.' Shane folds his arms across his chest. 'I'm beginning to question your commitment. You don't deserve this lovely horse.'

'You know how to make me feel guilty.'

'You pay me to make you feel bad about yourself. With a bit of luck it'll give you the kick up the pants you need.' He grinds some grass down with the toe of his boot. 'You have no chance when you're flabby and unfit, Nicci.'

'We'll see about that,' I say, smiling.

'That's what I like to hear, a bit of fire.'

Afterwards, I wash Willow down and let her dry off as she munches on some hay, wondering how busy Matt is at the hospital and realising that after last night, I don't feel I have to worry about Mel any more. She is well and truly the ex-girlfriend now. I clean and check through the tack, drinking tea and sharing more yard gossip, and then turn her out for a couple of hours. Delphi will bring her in again later and put her to bed.

Chapter Eleven

Hold your Horses

Another week and a half passes. I stay over with Matt twice more and meet him for Sunday lunch at the Barnscote Hotel. My boyfriend is far from serious at times, treating most of life as a joke, but our relationship is growing stronger and deeper, and every day I learn more about him and love him a little more.

Cheska, Sage and Gabriel continue as my house guests, and although my sister appears to have no intention of moving on in the near future, I worry that she'll suddenly decide to leave. It would be the best news if she went back to Alan, but not before she and Mum have had time to reconcile over the past. How am I going to get them together? I have a plan.

Beauty does well after her operation, but she ends up staying at Westleigh much longer than expected because an infection develops in the wound in her belly, so Matt keeps her in for intense treatment with antibiotics.

Partly to thank him for looking after Beauty, and partly to introduce us all properly to each other, Mum and Robert invite me and Matt for lunch on the Saturday of the last weekend in July. She suggests inviting Cheska and the children too, but when I broach this with my sister, she is adamant she still wants nothing to do with her.

'I don't understand why you can't at least talk to her,' I say, frustrated. 'I know she hurt your feelings, but she was under pressure too. She thought she was doing the right thing, what was best for you.'

'She was trying to control me.'

'Because you were only sixteen. She was responsible for you.' I pause. 'Think about it. You were pregnant by a man twice your age who ended up in prison. How would you feel if Sage was in that situation? Would you be so keen to let her have her freedom and make her own choices?'

My sister falls silent.

'So, will you come to Mum's for lunch?'

Her answer remains an emphatic no.

However, Matt is keen to join us, but on the day, an hour before he's due to pick me up and drive me over to Mum's in Talymouth, he has to cancel.

'I'm really sorry, Nicci,' he says. 'I'll try to catch up with you later. Have fun.'

I would have more fun if Matt was there, I think regretfully, but as it turns out my mother and Robert are celebrating their engagement and their joy is infectious.

'I'm sorry Matt couldn't be here,' Mum says when

we're enjoying coffee on the balcony overlooking the sea and Robert has gone out for a stroll along the front.

'He was called in to the hospital.' While I'm saying this, I realise that he didn't say exactly why he couldn't make it, but I'm assuming there's been an emergency.

'I think he's wonderful,' Mum sighs dreamily. 'If only I was twenty years younger.'

'He is lovely. He's like a puppy dog who wants to spend all his time with me. It's weird because I'm not used to that. I was lucky if I saw Henry every couple of weeks, but Matt texts and calls me all the time.'

'Make the most of it, Nicci. Go with the flow.'

I lean back in the chair and gaze out to sea. 'Sometimes I worry that he might dump me because I spend too much time at the yard.'

'There's an obvious answer to that.'

'I've already suggested that he learns to muck out, but he isn't too keen. He says not only is it bad for his shoulder, it's too much like being at work, not that he does any mucking out at the hospital. They have grooms to do that.' I hesitate. Matt Warren makes me feel as if I'm flying. I never felt this way about Lawrence or Henry, or any of the other less serious boyfriends I've met along the way. I didn't feel this adored or this spoiled. 'It's a little scary, actually, Mum. It's like a dream and I'm afraid I'm going to wake up and he'll be gone.'

'Don't be silly. Matt isn't going anywhere,' she says with confidence.

'What if I can't do it? What if I can't live up to

his expectations? What if I can't make the same commitment?'

'I'm glad I'm not a doctor,' Mum says with a smile. 'You overanalyse everything. This is a relationship, not a patient. You don't have to pick it apart to find something wrong with it. Matt wanting to be with you all the time seems really healthy and normal to me.'

'Thank you for that diagnosis,' I say wryly. I change the subject. 'What will you do when you're married? Will you sell the house?'

'What would I want to do that for, darling?'

'I assumed you'd move onto the farm with Robert.' If – and it's a big if – Matt and I ever got married, I'd want to be with him. 'That's the whole point of getting married, isn't it? To be together.'

Mum smiles. 'We're getting married because we want to be together and commit to each other. I love him, but I don't want to live with him. We'd drive each other mad.'

I scratch my head. I don't understand.

'Let me explain,' she says, clearly amused. 'I like listening to the news and current affairs on Radio Four. Robert likes pop and rap.'

'Does he? I can't imagine that somehow.'

'He says it's good for the cows, that it helps them relax and let down their milk, but he plays it in the house too. It's agonising to listen to. I can't stand it and we've agreed that we're both too set in our ways to compro - mise. This way, we can each have our own space.'

'It seems rather extreme having separate houses. Couldn't you just have separate rooms?'

'No, Nicci, this will work very well for us.' She fetches a cafetière of fresh coffee and pours two more cups. 'How are the children?'

'Gabriel's fine. Sage has been riding.'

'What does your sister think of that?'

'She's okay about it as long as she doesn't have to have anything to do with it.'

'Will Sage follow in your footsteps?'

'She's a natural,' I say, smiling.

'I wish I could see her ride,' Mum says wistfully. 'Do you think there's any chance that your sister would agree to meet with me? Can't I come to the house again?'

'I'll see what I can do, but you might have to accept that it's too late, Mum.'

'I'll never give up hope,' she says. 'I wish I'd handled things differently back then, but I wasn't in a good place at the time.'

Soon, I return home, expecting Matt to contact me at any time to let me know how the horse is doing. I text him, but he doesn't text back.

On Sunday morning, I text Matt again to make sure he's okay. Either he's still at the hospital or he's tucked up in bed asleep. I smile ruefully. I'm not sure I'll ever get used to his irregular working hours.

'Do u want to meet me 4 ur first lesson in mucking out? XXX'

'Cya there, 30 mins. XXXXXXXX,' he texts back.

I feed Willow and I've just turned her out in the paddock for a while when Matt turns up at the yard with the Bobster, who runs around the empty stable, searching out mice and chasing them into their holes in the walls. Wagging her tail, she snuffles and pounces through the shavings, making me laugh. Matt smiles, but he seems preoccupied.

'You'd better show me how to muck out,' he says, rallying a little. 'What class of implement do I need?'

'You need a wheelbarrow – there's a pink one over there. And a shavings fork, shovel and broom. The shavings fork has teeth that are close together,' I explain as he frowns at me.

'Are you all right?' I ask him when he returns with the tools rattling in the wheelbarrow.

'I'm fine, Nicci. Really. I've just been extremely busy at work.'

'And your shoulder? How is that?'

'Not too bad.' He picks the shavings fork out of the wheelbarrow with one hand.

'I'm glad to hear it.'

'By the way, your barrow's got a wobbly wheel.' He tries to hand me the fork.

'I don't want that.'

'You're going to show me what to do.'

'Oh no, I'm not. You have to learn by doing. Nice try.' I park the wheelbarrow outside the stable door and let Matt make a start.

'Don't throw away too many shavings – I don't want to give Delphi an excuse to increase my livery charges.'

'I'd be all right if I didn't have an audience.' Matt looks past me.

Delphi, one of the grooms and a couple of the teenage girls who help out at weekends are standing behind me, peering into the box.

'Do a good job and I'll take you on,' Delphi says, smiling as Matt pitches the first forkful of dirty shavings into the barrow, sending at least half of it back onto the floor. 'You're going to have to get a lot of practice in first though. I've got at least ten more boxes to muck out if you want to perfect your technique.'

'No, Delphi. My strategy is to prove how rubbish I am at this so I don't have to do it again.' He leans on the fork.

'Now, Matt, no slacking,' she scolds, staring at the groom and the teenagers. 'That goes for all of you too.'

They rush off with Delphi following them, brandishing an imaginary whip, while Matt continues to lean on the fork.

'You heard what Delphi said,' I say lightly.

'Nicci,' he says. 'I need to talk to you about something.'

'Don't tell me – you've had enough of being here already.'

He shakes his head, his expression sombre. 'It isn't that. I wanted to say I'm sorry about having to pull out of lunch with your mother and Robert.'

'That's all right. These things happen. Horses – and humans – don't choose when they're sick.'

Matt frowns. 'It wasn't about a horse. It's about Mel. I saw Mel.'

'Mel? What for?' My heart stops beating and my throat floods with bile. Why can't she stop stirring up trouble? Why doesn't she just leave us alone?

'She asked me to meet her. Oh, Nicci—' he makes to

move towards me, dropping the fork into the shavings '—it's a nightmare.'

'Well, if you're prepared to drop everything for her, then so be it.' I can feel anger and jealousy building up inside me. Because of what Henry did to me? Because I can't help thinking, why does this always happen to me? 'Why? Why did you agree to meet her?'

'I'm sorry.' Matt reaches out for me, but I step back. I can't bear the idea of him touching me when he's been with her. 'I'm very, very sorry, but she's pregnant.'

'Pregnant? So the rumours are true?' I pause. 'Are you sure she's having a baby?'

'My baby,' he confirms quietly.

'How? How come?'

'The usual way, I guess,' he says, his tone flat and without life. He runs his hands through his hair.

I lean back against the wall and sink down onto my heels. Matt kneels before me in the mucky shavings, his complexion the same shade as Willow's tail.

'Is she keeping it?' My voice sounds harsh to my ears.

'Yes, but this won't make any difference to us, I swear.'

'But it will,' I say, breaking down. 'You know it will.'

He takes my hands in a firm grasp and I try to pull away, but I can't – he's too strong.

'Nicci, you're a doctor. You must see this sort of thing all the time.'

'When? I mean, how pregnant is she? Are you sure it's yours?'

'I have no reason to doubt her.'

'Except that she wants to trap you into going back to her,' I say, angry now.

'It happened before we split up and before I met you. That'll teach me to rush from one relationship to the next—'

'You said it wasn't much of a relationship,' I cut in. 'You said it was a fling.'

'I don't want to argue about the definition of a relationship.'

'I do, seeing as we seem to have a difference of opinion.'

'I knew you'd be upset . . .' Matt tilts his head to one side '. . . but I thought you'd be more realistic. I want to play a part in my child's life, but not Mel's.' He hesitates, close to tears. 'I didn't want this. I don't want it any more than you do. It's a bloody mess.'

'You can say that again,' I murmur.

'She said she didn't tell me before because she wasn't sure. She thought she was stressed from work and from us breaking up. Nicci, she says she was in love with me. I've treated her abominably.' His voice trails off. 'I didn't realise . . .'

My heart sinks to the soles of my wellington boots. 'You still have feelings for her?'

He's too honest. 'I do, but not in the way you're thinking. I don't feel anything for her in a boyfriend-girlfriend kind of way. I mean, I feel sorry for hurting her feelings, and for making her pregnant.'

'It takes two,' I say, sniffing back tears. I wish I could say I'm cool about this, we'll work something out, but I can't because there's that little niggle, like a toothache, that won't go away. 'There's no chance that this pregnancy arose from a recent occasion when you were dropping off the dog, or waiting for a horse to come round at the hospital?'

Matt frowns. 'A comfort shag, you mean?'

I nod.

'Nicci, no! She's ten weeks gone, so it didn't happen while we've been together,' Matt continues miserably.

'You said you split up with her in March, three months before you asked me out. I'm not a mathematician, but if she's ten weeks now, you must have slept with her at the beginning of May.'

'I'm sorry, I told a little white lie to make me look better. Three months sounded so much better than six weeks. I didn't think it would come back to haunt me . . .'

'So you lied because you thought you wouldn't get found out. How can I trust you? You didn't tell me about Mel looking after the Bobster, she's still working at the hospital and it's taken you a while to raise the subject of her being pregnant.' I silence him with a glare. 'You've been acting weirdly since you cancelled lunch at my mum's. You've hardly been in touch. I'd say it looks more than a bit shifty.'

'It's because I was afraid—'

'Of hurting my feelings, or of me finding out you've been lying to me all along?' I get up, furiously brushing the shavings off my jodhpurs.

'I'm so sorry, I never wanted to hurt you.'

'Well it's a bit late for apologies, and I can't go out with someone who is so . . . so shady.'

'Nicci—' Matt starts to scramble up. I push him back

to keep him away from me, not hard but forcefully enough to make him overbalance and fall into a pile of droppings. He swears as I look down at him. He's in the proverbial in more ways than one and I don't care.

'That serves you right,' I snap.

'Do you want me to go?' he asks quietly, getting up.

'Yeah,' I stammer.

'I'll call round later?'

'I'll get in touch with you.'

'Nicci, please . . .'

'Go!' I cry. 'I can't bear to look at you any more!'

'Okay . . .' I hear the catch in his throat. 'I'm sorry.'

'I'm sorry too.'

Staring at the toe of my boot, I wait until he's gone, listening for his footsteps followed by the sound of running water as he rinses his hands under the tap outside the stable. Eventually, I hear the roar of an engine and scream of tyres. Like a robot, not feeling anything, I pick up the shavings fork and start muck - ing out furiously, separating the soiled shavings from the clean ones and filling the wheelbarrow. As I turn to push the barrow across to the muck heap, Delphi appears at my side.

'Is everything all right?' she asks. 'Only I noticed Matt had to dash orf in rather a hurry.'

I turn away, not wanting her to see I've been crying.

'He found he didn't like mucking out as much as he'd expected,' I say, my voice cracking. I have no desire to discuss my love life with her, with anyone for that matter, especially when I don't understand what's going on myself. I love Matt and I think he loves me, but right now I don't think I can believe a word he says.

On Monday, I arrive home to the sound of a culture clash – the church bells are in competition with the dance music pulsating from the wide open windows of my house. There's yet another tub of yeast on the doorstep with a note from Fifi this time, telling me she thinks I'd like to make a friendship cake. It's the last thing I feel like doing.

I push the door open, stepping over the post, scattered shoes and a teddy bear, to reach the kitchen. It looks as though twenty trainee chefs have been cooking at the same time, downed spatulas and wooden spoons and left. The back door is open and a couple of flies hover lazily over the butter left out on the breakfast bar. The sink is full of dirty dishes while the dishwasher remains empty. And there's a load of washing that isn't mine in the machine, a pink wash.

I look a little more closely. 'Nooo,' I groan. Someone has washed my best pair of jodhpurs with a pair of red socks and everything has gone pink. I could almost turn to drink.

My heart sinks as I search for the tea bags. There are no tea bags. There is no coffee either. Outside on the lawn, Sage and Gabriel are playing with suds in the washing-up bowl, the bottle lying on its side, almost empty.

'Where's your mum?' I call, making them jump.

'Sh,' says Sage. 'She's having a sleep.'

Keep calm and carry on, I tell myself as my heart

pounds with suppressed fury. I've been at work all day while my sister has been lying in my bed with the duvet pulled over her and the curtains closed.

'Cheska, wake up. I need to talk to you.'

She peers over the duvet, her hair stuck to her face as if she's been crying.

'Now! This minute. I have had enough.'

'So have I,' she whimpers. 'I've made such a mess of everything.'

I don't think she's referring to the house somehow.

'Cheska, you have to pull yourself together. What have you been doing all day?'

'I'm tired,' she says, her voice thick with tears and sleep.

'You're so ungrateful.' My eyes drift from my sister's face to the wall opposite where there's a huge scribble of black felt-tip pen like a ragged spider's web. 'What the hell is that?'

'What?' says Cheska.

'That over there. That's new.'

'Oh, that was Gabriel,' she sighs. 'I told him not to . . .'

'Look, I rent this house. I've put down a deposit and I'd really like it back at the end of the tenancy. And I might want to stay on here for another year.'

'He's only three years old – you have to cut him some slack,' she says in Gabriel's defence. 'Anyway,' she adds flippantly – because she's embarrassed, I hope – 'that scribble might be worth something in the future when he's a famous graffiti artist.'

'Dream on, Cheska. From the evidence, Gabriel isn't

211

going to be the next Banksy.' I pause, the anger and stress of the day building inside me. I can't help it. I snap. 'Get up, you lazy cow! What the hell do you think you're doing? I've let you stay here and supported you and your kids and all you can do is slob about, making a mess and never cleaning up after yourself.'

'It won't be for long, just until I get myself back on my feet.'

'How are you going to do that by lying around in my bed?' Furious, I pull a curtain too hard and the end of the pole falls. 'Now, look what you've made me do.'

'You did it yourself.'

'I wouldn't have if you hadn't—' I realise I sound like I'm about ten and arguing with my sister just the way we used to, blaming each other for our misfortunes.

Suddenly, there's a snort. I look at Cheska, stuffing the corner of the duvet in her mouth, trying but failing to stifle a giggle.

'You never change, big sister.'

'Neither do you, little sis.' Despite myself, I can't stay angry with her for long. Anyway, I'm aware that I'm taking out my anger with Matt on her, and that's not fair. I jump onto the bed. 'Shove up.' We sit side by side, looking at the sloping curtain pole and Gabriel's scribbles. 'That one,' I say, pointing, 'resembles a skateboard in a rather abstract, postmodernist kind of way.'

'I don't know what you're talking about,' she smiles.

'To be honest, Cheska,' I smirk back, 'neither do I. I'm blagging it.'

'I'm sorry for being a pain.'

'It isn't you. It's me. Yes, that's a bit of a mess, but it can be sorted. No, I've had a bad day.'

'A couple of bad days?' My sister raises one eyebrow. 'It's man trouble, isn't it? Matt's let you down?'

'I'm not sure. His ex-girlfriend's just announced that she's pregnant with his baby.' My sister's lips form an O as I go on, 'I don't know what to think.'

'It isn't ideal, but it might not be so bad. Matt still wants to be with you, doesn't he?'

'I don't know if he's telling the truth—'

'Why shouldn't he be?' she interrupts. 'I thought he was Mr Perfect.'

'Or Mr Too Good To Be True.' I pick some dirt out from under my nails – I dropped in to see Willow and give her a carrot on the way home. 'What if he's lying and he's slept with her while he's been with me?'

'Is there anything that leads you to believe that's the case?'

I tell her about the odd claim Mel apparently made to Claire about how she was Matt's girlfriend when he was going out with me, about Matt's economies of truth over the Bobster and about the problems thrown up by Mel's due date.

'I don't think any of those things are relevant, Nicci.'

'Of course they are. I need to know if he's been cheating on me.'

'You're always round at his house – when you're not at the yard. I can't imagine he'd risk what you have for a trip down memory lane, so to speak.' Cheska shakes her head. 'It's more important to ask yourself if you want to remain involved with a man who has a child. He might be the best guy in the world, but once the baby comes along, who's to say he won't change his mind and decide that he wants to shack up with the ex and play happy families? You could end up feeling like the mistress of a man who's having an affair.'

'I know.' I feel like howling. 'What am I going to do? Love him, or leave him?'

'Shoot, shag or marry? You decide.' She pauses. 'Is he going to all the scans and check-ups with her?'

'I'm sure he will. He'll feel responsible. He'll want to support her.'

'And then there's the money,' Cheska says.

'That doesn't matter, does it? I'm perfectly able to pay my own way. I don't need to rely on a man to support me.'

'You see, from what you're saying, Nicci, Matt is a good man and there aren't many of those around, so I reckon you shouldn't be too hasty in making your mind up. Give him a chance. Talk to him.' Cheska reaches out her hand. 'I'm truly, madly and deeply sorry,' she adds quietly, and I'm not sure if she's sorry about the house or Matt or both.

'Mummy, Gabriel's got washing-up liquid in his eyes,' Sage calls up the stairs. Gabriel starts bawling as though to emphasise the point.

Cheska looks at me. 'I think that's one for you. You're the doctor, Nicci.'

'Thanks.' I chuck a cushion at her.

Sage and I take Gabriel into the bathroom.

'Shouldn't we take him to the surgery?' Sage asks.

'I don't think there's any need. I have an eye bath here somewhere. Let's have a look, Gabriel.'

'I can't see,' he cries. 'It's hurting me.'

'How did it happen?' I ask Sage when I'm bathing Gabriel's eye.

'We were making the mixture for blowing bubbles and Gabriel took the bottle and squirted it in his eye. I told him not to.'

'Never mind.'

'I'd like to be a doctor,' Sage says.

Having rinsed the detergent out of Gabriel's streaming eye with a lot of fuss and cooing from Sage, I pronounce no lasting injury. But can I say the same about me and Matt?

Chapter Twelve

Vet to the Rescue

There is only one way to find out and that is, as Cheska suggested, to speak to Matt – which is a little ironic considering she refuses to have anything to do with Mum.

I struggle through a day at the surgery before driving over to Matt's, but he isn't there. I call him to discover he's tied up in surgery and is likely to remain so into the night. Mindful of disturbing me at three in the morning, he texts me instead of calling to arrange to meet the following evening.

Arriving at the surgery on Wednesday morning, I find Claire in reception, talking to Kevin, the police - man.

'Hi,' I say, 'is everything all right?'

'Kevin's dropped by to check our security arrange-ments.' Claire blushes.

'Are they satisfactory?' I say lightly, not believing her because Kevin colours up too. 'You need to talk to

Ben,' I say. 'He's responsible for the locks and alarm.'

'I'll do that,' Kevin says. 'I'd better get going for now though. I'm giving a talk on stranger danger at the school in half an hour.' He clears his throat. 'Will I see you later, Claire?'

She glances up at him. 'Seven o'clock at the Dog and Duck.'

I smile to myself. I tease her mercilessly in the staffroom at coffee time about her falling into the long arms of the law.

'Don't you dare make any truncheon jokes,' she says, trying to force her mouth into a prim and proper pout while eating a cream doughnut and ending up in a fit of giggles. 'I've known Kev for years,' she says eventually. 'It's only recently that I've noticed how good he looks in uniform.'

'I believe he'd say the same about you,' I point out, getting up and resting my hand briefly on her shoulder. 'I hope you have a great time.'

'And I hope you and Matt sort things out between you,' she says. 'I'm sorry, Nicci. I think everyone knows that Mel's pregnant and the baby's Matt's.'

'How?' I say.

'Fifi says that your sister told Frances, talking over the garden fence while they were hanging out the washing, and Frances told Fifi.'

'My sister? I'll kill her,' I exclaim. 'What was she thinking of? It's a private matter.' It isn't fair.

Claire hesitates. 'Mel came in to see Ben the other day – I had to sort out a pregnancy test and book her in to see the midwife.'

My heart constricts with pain – the fact that Mel has made the pregnancy official and public makes it feel agonisingly real.

'Nicci, I said I have Bridget on line two,' Janet cuts in from the staffroom door. 'She has a query about her diabetes. Can you speak to her now, or should she ring back?'

'I'm sorry, Janet, I was miles away.'

'I can tell,' she says. 'Are you all right? Don't tell me you need to see a doctor too.'

'Or a nurse,' Claire cuts in. 'I can check your ears for wax. Janet's asked you the same question three times.'

'So, do you want to speak to her?'

'Yes, I'll take it in my room. Put her through, Janet, thank you.'

I speak to Bridget while I log on. She's having trouble with her blood sugar levels again and I suggest a slightly increased dose of insulin. She requests a prescription, which I tell her I'll print, sign and leave for her to collect from reception, where Claire catches me once more.

'Nicci, I have Mrs Brown with me. Would you mind coming to have a look at her leg ulcer? I really don't think we're getting anywhere.'

'Of course,' I say, and I spend fifteen minutes chatting to Mr and Mrs Brown and planning a fresh approach to the management of Mrs Brown's ailments. She must take the record for the patient with the most problems in the practice, but she rarely complains. When I compare my troubles with hers, they are nothing.

At the end of the day I head for home. The church bells are ringing, the bell-ringers practising their peals, and somewhere a dog is barking. I've forgotten my key and the front door is locked. I tap on the window, trying to attract Gabriel's attention, but he's completely involved with *Peppa Pig* on the television.

'Gabriel,' I call. I catch sight of my reflection in the window, my face is shiny with sweat and my hair flat and sticky.

'There, I said you should let me have a spare key.' I turn at the sound of my neighbour's voice.

'Hello Frances.'

'I have a pot of old keys – one of those might fit the lock.'

'Please don't worry. I'm sure someone will hear me in a minute.'

'Well, if you need anything, anything at all, cup of tea while you wait—' Frances gazes at me, her eyes filled with sympathy '—or a shoulder to cry on, you know where I am.'

'Thank you,' I say stiffly. I knock at the window again rather harder than I intended. This time, Gabriel turns and stares. Recognising me, he smiles and waves and turns back to *Peppa Pig*. 'Gabriel, you're supposed to run to the door and let me in.'

I move around to the door and yell through the letter box. 'Yoo hoo. Anyone else at home?'

'It's you, Auntie Nicci,' says Sage when she opens the door a couple of minutes later. 'Mummy told me to check, so I went upstairs and looked out of the window and there you were.' She grabs my arm, jumping up

219

and down. 'Have you seen the paper?' Without waiting for me to respond, she rushes off to fetch a copy of the *Chronicle* and thrusts it into my hands. 'You're on page three. You're famous.'

I open the newspaper and there I am in a photo with Willow under the headline: 'Talyton's Galloping GP'.

'What do you think?' Sage says.

My neck grows hot as I read Ally Jackson's purple prose. It's embarrassing, but also flattering.

'I'm going to cut it out and keep it,' Sage goes on, and my heart melts when I realise how proud she is of her aunt.

'Nicci, you're back earlier than I expected.' Cheska emerges from the kitchen. 'I've made a lasagne – it's in the oven.'

'Is this some kind of peace offering?' I say, slightly irritated with her.

'What do you mean?'

'You know very well,' I say, reading her expression, 'for telling Frances about me and Matt.'

'I'm sorry about that. It kind of slipped out.'

'What did you tell Frances, Mummy?' Sage interrupts. 'Nicci, are you having a baby?' she goes on excitedly.

'Sage!' Cheska warns.

'It's all right. No, Sage, I am not pregnant. Matt's having a baby with someone else,' I add bitterly.

'Don't you love him any more?' Sage says sorrow - fully. 'Doesn't he love you?'

'I don't know.' I turn back to Cheska. 'Forget dinner. I'm not hungry. I'm going out.'

I drive to Matt's – for the first time since we met, he's cleared his diary and is home at six, waiting for me. The Bobster greets me with a riot of barking when I enter the kitchen at the back of the house.

'Hello,' I say as Matt stands up from the table, moves across to me and brushes his lips against my cheek. I kiss him back, wanting, aching for him to hold me and tell me that Mel isn't actually pregnant and everything will be all right, but he looks tired and anxious. I want to comfort him in turn because I can see that this situation with Mel has affected him deeply. Life isn't one big joke any more. It's serious.

'I'm glad you're here,' he says, offering me a hot drink and a piece of cake. 'I baked it specially.'

'No, thank you. Tea would be good, but I couldn't eat a thing.'

'Why don't you go and sit down? I'll be right behind you.'

I settle on one of the armchairs in the living room, waiting for him to appear. He passes me a mug of tea before sitting on the sofa, the Bobster jumping up beside him.

'What kind of day have you had?' he asks, breaking the silence.

'Okay.' I shrug. 'How about you?'

'I've been out on my rounds all day. While I've been driving around the countryside, I've been doing a lot of thinking.'

'You've had a lot on your mind,' I say, gripping tightly on the mug of hot tea until my fingers burn.

'I know. I'm so sorry.'

'So am I. But Matt, I do understand why you stretched the truth about when your relationship with Mel ended. It's one of those things.'

'Can you forgive me, though?' he asks gruffly. 'I mean, I've broken your trust and I know how important that is to you.'

I rest the mug on the carpet, get up and walk across to him. I sit down on the edge of the sofa, beside the Bobster, aware of a cold, wet nose nudging my hand as I gaze into his eyes, my heart beating loud and hard.

'I forgive you,' I say, a sob catching in my throat. 'I don't want to lose you. The last couple of days have been unbearable.'

'I'm sorry,' he repeats. 'I wish I'd never met the woman.'

'So do I.' More than he will ever know, I think.

'Does that mean . . .' Matt leans towards me. 'Bobster, get down.' As if aware of the enormity of the moment, for once the dog takes notice of her master, jumping down and rooting around in the fireplace, finding one of her smelly old bones to gnaw on.

I shake my head.

'I assume you'll be spending time with Mel and the baby,' I go on quietly. 'And that Mel will not be moving away in the foreseeable future. I don't know if I can deal with that. Who's to say you won't get back with her in the end?'

'I've already said, never again. I'm going to do the right thing by Mel because she's the mother of my child, no other reason. I want to be part of the baby's life. I want to be a proper dad.'

At the word 'dad' a tear spills over and trickles down my cheek. I can taste salt on my lips.

'Nicci . . .'

The room blurs in front of my eyes. The thought of seeing my boyfriend with another woman's baby cuts me to pieces. Wouldn't I always be thinking that it should have been our child, our firstborn?

'If I could turn the clock back . . .' Tentatively, Matt reaches out and strokes a lock of my hair from my cheek with a tender caress. I turn and lean into him, burying my face in his chest, breathing in his familiar scent of horse, surgical spirit and musk. He wraps his arms around me, pulling me close as he strokes my back.

'Oh Matt.'

'It's going to be all right,' he says.

'Is it? I'm not sure.' I'm not sure I can go through with it.

Matt's breath is warm against my ear and his hearts thudding under my fingertips. 'Stay over,' he whispers.

I could forgive him almost anything, but can I deal with his involvement in Mel's and the baby's lives? Can I see myself making a commitment to Mel's child because, as Matt's partner, I would have to be prepared to care for it too? Call me selfish, or just plain scared, but I'm afraid that it would be too much of a struggle, that I would end up loving Matt less.

I stiffen. 'I can't do it,' I mutter, pulling away and looking into his face.

'Is this it?' he says, his eyes shimmering with tears.

'Please don't say it's over. Don't let Mel come between us.'

'It isn't just Mel though, is it?' I say, standing up.

'Nicci,' he says, his voice breaking, 'I think I love you.'

'I think I love you too, but it isn't enough,' I say, crying. 'Let me go. It's better this way.' I walk out, not daring to look behind me in case the sight of him makes me weaken. Outside, I stare up at the sky and I feel completely alone. My heart is broken.

I'm not so alone when I return home and I'm glad of my family's company over the next few days. Without them I might well have curled up in a ball and given up, but I can't do that in front of Sage and Gabriel. Work helps me too, and Willow, of course.

And what about Matt? He's called and texted every day to tell me that he'll always be there for me, if I should change my mind.

Mum calls me too to let me know that Beauty has had to return to the hospital at Westleigh for another operation to repair a hernia which formed as a result of her colic surgery, and to find out if the rumours are true that Matt and I are no longer an item.

'I'm so sorry, darling,' she says when I confirm that it is indeed the case and explain the reasons for the split. 'How are you? Is there anything I can do?'

'Thanks for the offer, Mum, but, no.'

'Are you keeping busy?' She pauses. 'Of course you are. Is your sister still with you?'

'She is. And I want to ask you something while we're

on the subject. It's her birthday on Friday and I'm planning a small celebration with her and the children. I'd like you to be there too.'

'Does she want me there?'

'I'm not going to give her the choice.'

'Is that wise, after the way she lost it last time?'

'If I could just get you together in the same room with the kids and a glass of wine, Cheska might see how things could be if she could bring herself to forgive and forget the past. Please, Mum.'

'It sounds so simple, but I suspect this rift between me and your sister runs far deeper than you imagine, Nicci.'

'What do you mean?'

'I'll be there,' she says without responding to my question.

'Can you do me a favour though?' I ask. 'Let yourself into the house round the back. It's at seven o'clock on Friday.'

I think a party will cheer us all up.

On Friday morning, I get up extra early to ride Willow before work because it's only a few weeks until the last one-day event I've entered for this season. She's fit and well-muscled and I'm maintaining her stamina with plenty of hacking, trotting and cantering up steep hills. Having washed her down, I turn her out so she can have a good roll in the paddock. I watch her choose her patch beside the gate where she's grazed the grass down to a few blades, sink down to her knees, rub her face against the bare earth and roll. She rubs her back,

225

her legs in the air, her expression one of ecstasy, before rolling right over to her other side. She repeats the exercise twice then stands up, shakes, and wanders away to graze.

'See you later, Willow,' I call, but she isn't listening. Her flanks are reddish-orange with mud stains. I don't know why I bothered to run the hose over her.

That afternoon after work, I send Cheska to chill out in the living room while I enlist the children to help with the preparations. Sage makes the card and Gabriel helps me blow up balloons. I buy a cake from Jennie's Cakes, flowers from Bridget at Petals, wine from Mr Lacey and party food from the Co-op.

'Who is coming to the party?' Sage asks.

'You, me and Gabriel.'

'What about Matt?'

I shake my head, suppressing a wave of regret. I don't know how long it will be before I stop missing him. 'I thought we'd keep it close family only.'

'Will Alan come for Mummy's birthday?'

'Daddy?' says Gabriel.

'No,' I say, registering their disappointment. I can see them thinking that this isn't going to be much of a party, and I wish that Cheska, who was clearly badly hurt by our parents' divorce, had been more careful about putting her children in a similar position where their father figure is absent from their lives.

Sage spears cocktail sausages on sticks and puts them onto a plate from which Gabriel promptly helps himself.

'Gabriel, stop it. They're for later,' Sage says.

'Okay,' he says, taking another one.

'It's time to get this party started,' I say, trying to divert them.

'We'll go and get Mummy,' says Sage. 'She's going to have a big surprise.'

'She certainly is,' I agree. Little does Cheska know exactly how big a surprise it is.

Sage and Gabriel lead her into the kitchen.

'For me?' Cheska looks from me to the balloons and flowers, and back.

'Happy birthday,' I say, moving up to give her a hug.

'Sis, you shouldn't have.'

'I wanted to,' I say, feeling a fraction uncomfortable at having to deceive her. 'Wine?'

'Please,' she says.

'Sausage,' says Sage, picking up the plate. When Cheska declines, Gabriel offers to eat her share. 'You've had twelve already – I counted the sticks.'

I pour her a glass of wine, a large one. I think she's going to need it.

'Cheers,' I say, handing it over.

'Aren't you going to have one?' she says. 'I dare you to break the habit of a lifetime.'

'It's all right. I'll stick with apple juice.'

'You are so predictable, Nicci.'

I glance down the garden, catching sight of Mum walking up towards the patio. 'There is one more surprise for you,' I say, moving past Cheska to open the back door. 'Come in, Mum.'

'It's Granma,' says Sage.

'Granma,' echoes Gabriel, wide-eyed.

Mum steps inside. I close the door behind her and quietly turn the key in the lock.

'Happy birthday, Cheska,' Mum says.

Cheska loosens her grip on the wine glass, which drops to the floor, smashing into tiny pieces.

'Oops,' says Gabriel.

Cheska glares at me. 'Nicci, what is she doing here?'

'I invited her. Mum, grab yourself some wine.' I get another glass out of the cupboard for my sister.

'How could you do this to me on my birthday, of all times? I'm not staying.'

'Oh yes you are,' I say fiercely. 'You are going to sit down and talk.'

'What about the mess?' Sage asks.

'I'll clear it up later. Now, can you and Gabriel go up to my room and make a pass the parcel? I've left the prize for you to cover in as many layers as you can. The sticky tape's on the bed and you can take the rest of the *Chronicle* to add to the wrapping paper that's already up there.' I grab the wine bottle and carry it into the living room, ushering my mother and sister along in front of me. 'Sit!' I tell them.

Cheska drains her fresh glass of wine in one go before perching her bottom on the windowsill. Mum sits on the sofa, sipping at her wine. I sit on the arm - chair in between them like a referee.

'I'll start then,' I say, watching them staring at each other. 'I'm not here to take sides, nor do I expect you to become best friends. What I would like is for you to be on speaking terms – for Sage and Gabriel's sake.

They're lovely kids and they deserve the chance to get to know their grandmother.'

'If they knew what she's like, they'd run a mile,' Cheska says snappily.

'Darling, no,' Mum murmurs.

'Don't you "darling" me,' Cheska says, standing up straight. 'I am not and have never been your "darling".'

'That isn't true,' Mum argues. 'I've always loved you.'

'You have the strangest way of showing it. If you'd loved me, you would have respected my decisions, like you did for Nicci.'

'Well, she always makes the right choices.'

'Mum,' I cut in. I wish she hadn't said that. She's antagonising Cheska further with her implied criticism.

'Let's go back, shall we?' Cheska says. 'When Nicci went off to uni, you couldn't wait for me to leave home too.'

'That isn't true.' Mum gazes down into her glass. 'I admit, I wasn't the most fun person to be with when Nicci left. I missed her.' She looks up at me. 'We used to spend so much time together with the horses.'

I can sense my sister bristling with anger and resentment.

'Yes, so much that you didn't have time for me,' she spits. 'You never had time for me.'

'I tried,' Mum says, 'but you pushed me away. And then you fell pregnant. At sixteen!'

'And you were so ashamed, you could hardly bear to look at me,' Cheska says.

'It wasn't that. I was upset that you'd thrown everything away on that bastard—'

'You didn't know him from Adam,' Cheska cuts in.

'I knew he was no good.'

'I don't believe you're still arguing over a man all these years later,' I say. 'Why can't you both agree to get over it and move on?'

'She gave me the money for a private abortion,' Cheska says, her voice like ice. 'You see, Nicci, if our precious mother had had her way, Sage wouldn't be here. She's here wanting to see her grandchildren, yet if she'd got her own way, she wouldn't have any. She doesn't deserve them!'

'I didn't know this. Why didn't I know about this?' I mutter as Cheska makes for the door. 'Hey, where are you going?'

'Out,' she says, collecting up her bag and shoes from the hall. The muscles in her arm are taut and sharply defined as she yanks the front door open.

'What about the children? What do I tell Sage and Gabriel?'

'I'm sure you'll think of something, you deceitful cow,' she snaps. She stumbles outside and slams the door in my face, the sound vibrating throughout the house and bringing the children downstairs, Sage clutching the pass the parcel.

'Where's Mummy gone?' she asks.

'Oh, she's popped out for a while,' I say, forcing myself to maintain a brave front when inside my emotions are in turmoil – disbelief at my mother's behaviour, compassion and resentment towards my sister for keeping the secret of their falling out from me, and worry for Sage and Gabriel at their mother walking out in the middle of her surprise birthday party. 'She's being a bit of a party pooper.'

'I think I should go as well,' Mum says, joining us. 'I'm sorry, Nicci.'

'I'm sorry too...' I pause. 'Why did you never say anything?' I feel betrayed, left out.

'I felt so guilty afterwards,' she says. 'I tried to forget it. Cheska never did and I don't suppose she ever will.' Mum looks towards Sage, tears in her eyes. 'I'll never forgive myself.'

I throw my arms around her. 'You can't blame yourself for the rest of your life,' I say. 'You did what you thought was the right thing at the time.'

'I know,' she says, more calmly now, stepping back and taking a tissue out of her sleeve. 'Hindsight is a wonderful thing.' She forces a smile. 'Goodbye, Sage. Goodbye, Gabriel. You'd better go and put some music on for the pass the parcel. I'm sure Auntie Nicci will join in.'

So I'm left with two kids who are concerned about the whereabouts of their mother, a glut of party food, a pass the parcel with an unbelievable number of layers to get through, a couple of bottles of wine and an awful lot to think about.

Sage puts the radio on, and I take control of the volume while she and her brother play pass the parcel, arguing about ownership every single time the music stops. Completely stressed out, I do what I have never done before. I pour myself a glass of wine and another and then another, until I am sitting on the floor, surrounded by shredded paper with Sage feeding me jelly babies and Gabriel asleep on the sofa.

I try to get up, but the room is spinning and I feel terribly sick.

'Are you okay?' Sage asks me. 'Mummy gets drunk sometimes,' she adds matter-of-factly.

'I'm not drunk,' I protest, slumping back down on the carpet, my back against the coffee table.

'You should be. You've had a bottle of wine all to yourself.'

'Thank you, Sage.'

'Do you think Mummy will be back soon?'

'I expect so.' I'm slurring. I've been such an idiot. How am I going to manage, drunk in charge of two kids? 'Sage, would you mind fetching my mobile? I think I left it in the kitchen by the sink.'

She brings it to me and I try calling Cheska, but her mobile is off, so I ring Matt instead.

'Nicci, how are you?'

My heart leaps at the sound of his voice. 'Matt, I'm sorry to bother you, but I couldn't think of anyone else.' I don't want anyone else. 'I feel really unwell,' I mumble.

'I'll be straight round,' he says. 'Don't move.'

Don't move? I stare at the screen on my mobile. I can't move. I feel as though I've been anaesthetised.

Fifteen minutes or so later, I hear Sage letting Matt in and their voices in the hall. I must have drifted off for a while because when I wake, the children have disappeared and Matt is virtually carrying me up the two flights of stairs to the attic, where he gives me sips of water before undressing me very gently and tucking me into bed.

'Would you like me to tell you a story?' he says, smiling. 'I've already read *Postman Pat* twice, but I reckon I could manage it once more for you.'

I try to smile back, but my lips are numb and out of control.

'I don't know what came over me. I'm sorry,' I mumble.

'You will be tomorrow. You're going to have one hell of a hangover.'

'I shouldn't have called you.'

'Hey, let's have none of that.' Matt sits on the edge of the futon, holding my hand. 'Get some sleep, darling. It's all right,' he goes on. 'I'll stay over.'

'Are you sure?'

'Of course I'm sure. Can I sleep here? With you?' He pauses. 'Someone should be with you when you're in this state.'

I nod weakly. Still fully clothed, he slides into bed alongside me and holds me close as I drift into a deep, alcohol-induced slumber.

Chapter Thirteen

White Horses

I wake with the sun burning into my eyes, a throbbing headache and severe nausea. Groaning, I roll over, only to find Matt lying alongside me. I stare at him. He opens one eye.

'Hi,' he says, a smile playing on his lips. 'How are we this morning?'

'Bad,' I say, closing my eyes to quell the sensation of giddiness that threatens to overwhelm me. 'I knew there was a good reason why I don't drink. Remind me never to touch the stuff again.'

'Let me get you some breakfast,' he says, getting up.

'No, I couldn't—'

'You'll feel better with something inside you.'

Matt returns from downstairs with tea, paracetamol and fried eggs on toast – and Sage and Gabriel, who are curious to find out how I am and if there is any news of their mum.

'Let Nicci eat her breakfast in peace,' Matt says,

dismissing them. 'We need time to decide what we're doing today. I thought we might go on a bit of an adventure.'

We? I wonder what's going on. Sage and Gabriel are excited though and they're happy to take themselves off for a while to watch the television while Matt plans a trip out.

'Matt, what are you doing?' I say, forcing down a mouthful of toast. I really can't face the eggs.

'They're having a rough time. I thought it would be easier for them to cope with their mum's absence if we took them out for the day.'

'What about work? I thought you were supposed to be at the hospital this morning.'

'I've had a word with Jimmy. He's going to cover for me. I've done enough favours for him recently. He owes me.'

'I don't want you to do this, thinking you can make it right between us,' I begin.

'I have no expectations,' he says gravely. 'I'm not going to make any secret of the fact that there's nothing I want more than for us to get back together, but if you can't deal with it, then c'est la vie. I'll have to be content with being friends, if you're willing.'

I watch him picking imaginary pieces of fluff from his trousers and a lump forms in my throat. He is beautiful inside and out, and I can't feel indifferent about him.

'I'm not sure I can be just friends with you, Matt,' I say hoarsely.

'That's going to make life difficult then.' He hesitates. 'Do you want me to go?'

I shake my head. 'You've been so kind. Last night . . . there aren't many ex-boyfriends who would have come over to rescue me.'

'To be honest, I'm glad you got raving drunk, Nicci.' Recognising that I've had enough and that the sight of congealing cold eggs isn't going to help me, Matt takes my plate and puts it on the floor. He clears his throat and reaches his hand across the duvet until the tips of his fingers are inches from mine. 'Is there any chance . . . No, I shouldn't have said anything. You've made up your mind. I'm sorry.'

I slide my fingers closer to his until they make contact.

'Matt, you've shown me what I'm missing.' I look up and meet his gaze. 'I don't know how things will work out between us. I'm scared I won't be able to deal with you seeing Mel and the baby, but I'm willing to take the risk, if you are.' I wait, my chest tight, unable to breathe, until he answers me, inter-linking his fingers through mine then curling his fist around my hand.

He leans towards me and kisses me on the cheek.

'Let's see how it goes,' he murmurs. 'Now, where shall we go today? I thought the beach as the weather's okay, or we could go to the farm the other side of Talysands, the one where you can drive a tractor and stroke the donkeys and the goats.'

'Have you got buckets and spades?' I ask, amused at Matt's enthusiasm.

'You know, I think there are some in the shed in my garden. If not, I'll invest in some. We can buy a crabbing line and bait at the same time.' He pauses. 'I'll have a look when I pop back to fetch the Bobster.'

I'm still in the shower, trying to wash away the alcohol that seems to ooze from every pore on my skin, when Matt arrives back with the Bobster. I clean my teeth, towel dry my hair, leaving it loose, throw on shorts and a vest top and run downstairs to find Matt in the living room with Sage and Gabriel. Gabriel is trying to pack clothes for the beach – all of his clothes – into a shopping bag while Sage is sitting on the sofa with the dog on her lap.

'Get off,' I say, but the Bobster is oblivious, as is her owner. 'There are some establishments where dogs aren't allowed on the furniture, and this is one of them.'

'She isn't doing any harm, is she, Sage?' Matt grabs me around the waist and pulls me close.

'She's all right.' Sage puts her arms around the Bobster's neck, and the dog licks the tip of her nose, making her giggle, and I can see there's no point in pursuing the point. I'm not going to win this one.

'Thanks again for last night,' I whisper to Matt. 'I don't know what I'd have done without you.'

Our eyes and lips lock in a lingering kiss, making me wish for a brief moment that it was just the two of us.

'Oh, please, no PDAs,' I hear Sage sigh.

'What's a PDA?' Matt asks, turning to her.

'A public display of affection.'

'Is that text speak? I don't speak text.'

'That's because you're so old,' Sage says.

'I can learn,' Matt says, grinning.

'I'll teach you when we're on the beach,' Sage says. 'Nicci, have you packed your swimming costume?'

'I've put it in the bag, but I'm not sure I'll wear it.'

Matt's grin broadens. 'This isn't a nudist beach, Nicci. We're going to the far end of Talysands so the dog can come with us.' He lowers his voice. 'Not so you can parade naked across the sand, although I wouldn't have any objections . . .' He stops abruptly. 'I apologise. I shouldn't have said that, not yet. We've only just agreed to make a fresh start.'

'It's all right, Matt,' I say. 'I want you to be you, not on edge, pretending to be someone you aren't.'

'Did you know I can lip read?' Sage cuts in.

Matt blushes. 'I do now.'

'I'm ready,' says Gabriel, dragging his bag that's as big as he is across the floor.

'I don't think you'll need your pyjamas,' I say, catching sight of them hanging out of the top. 'We'll be home by teatime.' But no matter how much I try to convince him, Gabriel will not leave his pyjamas or anything else behind, so it all goes into the boot of my car.

'It's lucky I couldn't find any buckets and spades,' Matt says, putting another holdall in the back. 'They would never have fitted. We'll have to buy them from one of the shops along the front.'

A strange odour of rotting meat accompanies us on the journey to the coast, and at first I wonder if the Bobster, sitting in the footwell at Matt's feet, has a problem with wind.

'What's that smell?' says Gabriel, who has no concern for social niceties.

238

'It's you,' says Sage with sisterly fondness. 'You stink, little brother.'

'I don't. Mummy, I don't stink.'

'Mummy isn't here, silly.'

'I want my mummy.' Gabriel kicks and screams perched on his car seat behind me. It's most distracting.

'It's bacon,' Matt says.

Gabriel stops kicking. 'Bacon? I like bacon. That smell is like poo.'

'It's bait for the crabs,' Matt goes on to explain quickly. 'It was past its use by date so I stuck it in my bag. It seemed a shame to waste it.'

'Yuck,' Sage says, chuckling.

'I hope you didn't put it anywhere near the picnic,' I say.

'I don't think we'll catch any crabs with that,' Sage says, her mouth turned down at the corners. 'They won't like it – it's disgusting.'

'That's the whole point,' Matt says. 'The more revolting it is, the more the crabs will like it. We'll catch loads of the little buggers.'

'Matt!'

'I mean creatures,' he says with a grin.

'Buggers,' says Gabriel. 'Buggers, buggers, buggers.'

'You are a bad influence,' I tell him.

When we arrive, our first stop is at one of the shops along the beachfront to buy buckets, spades and crab lines. Gabriel isn't happy with any old bucket. Oh no. He chooses a purple one shaped like a castle and a bright yellow spade. Sage goes for a blue bucket and a matching spade.

'Do you want one, Matt?' she asks.

'I don't think so. I don't think the doctors will approve of me doing any digging because of my shoulder.' He glances at me. 'Mind you, my doctor isn't here.'

'I'll tell,' I say. I'm teasing. 'How is it anyway?'

Matt swings his arm back and forth and over his head.

'Not too bad,' he says, sounding surprised. 'The steroid Ben gave me must have had an effect. It was bloody painful for the first couple of days.'

'Matt.' I give him a nudge. 'No swearing.'

'Does she always nag people like this?' he says, turning to Sage.

'No, just you,' she says, shielding the sun from her eyes.

'I wanna catch a crab,' Gabriel complains. 'I'm bored.'

'Let's go,' Matt says, and we carry various bits and pieces along to the end of the beachfront where we join the path that continues on top of the wall running alongside the estuary. We stop just beyond the moorings for the fishing boats and the small yachts and set up the crabbing lines over the edge of the wall.

While Matt unpacks the stinking bacon, I point out the colourful houses and hotels of Talymouth on the opposite side of the estuary, and the rocky sandstone cliffs.

'That's where Mummy and I used to live with Granma when we were kids,' I say, but neither Sage nor Gabriel is impressed. They're too busy listening to Matt's instructions.

Sage lowers the first line into the water with Matt's assistance, while I hang onto Gabriel who is in danger of throwing himself over the edge in his enthusiasm to catch a crab.

'How can you tell there are any down there?' Sage asks, looking at the muddy brown water.

'Just wait and feel for the tug at the end of your line.' Matt squats down beside her. 'Give it a little pull.'

'I've got something.'

'Pull it up.'

'Yes!' she says in triumph as she brings up a good-sized crab out of the water, at which it promptly detaches itself and drops back in with the bait firmly between its pincers. 'Bother.'

'I reckon that one's done this before,' Matt says. 'Let's try again with some more bacon. Watch out for seagulls.'

It's Gabriel who lands the first crab, a small one with a green carapace and barnacles.

'Drop it in the bucket,' I say, but he doesn't like the crab as much as he thought he was going to. He screams, drops the line and runs for the bushes behind us as the crab lifts itself onto its back legs and makes a break for freedom, scuttling sideways to the edge of the wall and dropping back into the water with a plop.

Sage laughs.

'I don't like it. I don't like it!' Gabriel wails.

'What do we do?' Matt says rather helplessly. 'Shall we go and get an ice cream?'

'I wanna catch a crab,' says Sage. 'It isn't fair if Gabriel catches one and he doesn't want to, and I want to but I don't get a chance because he's being a cry baby.'

'All right,' I say, intervening. 'Gabriel and I will get an ice cream. You can catch up with us. There's a café over there where we can watch from a safe distance.'

Later, the crab incident apparently long forgotten, we head back towards the seafront to spend some time on the beach. I stake our claim to a small territory above the tideline, arranging the towels and unpacking the cool-box while Matt strips off his shirt and jeans – and I'm mightily relieved to see that he's wearing shorts rather than Speedos. The wearing of Speedos could very well be a deal-breaker. Matt jogs down to the sea with Sage and Gabriel, where they scream and splash about in the waves, Sage in a strappy summer dress and Gabriel in shorts because they don't have swimming costumes with them. Matt's making a good job of distracting them – they've only mentioned Cheska's absence three times so far. I settle down to make the most of the sun on my skin and watch the 'white horses' dancing on top of the water, soothing away the remnants of my hangover.

Matt picks something up and walks up to the smooth dark sand, still wet where the tide has fallen away. He bends down and starts writing in the sand.

'What does that say?' Sage says, joining him, her face

flushed, her hair damp and her legs dripping with water.

Matt pauses, keeping what I can see now is the end of a cuttlefish bone in the sand. 'Be patient, Sage. You'll see in a minute.'

'That's a love heart,' she cries out and comes running up to tell me, even though you can hear her joyful cries from one end of the beach to the other. 'Nicci, Nicci, Matt's drawn you a love heart.' She holds out her hand. 'Come and see.'

'Pull me up,' I say, and we jog down the beach to join Matt, who is standing with his hands on his hips, admiring his handiwork.

M 4 N 4 Ever.

'No one's drawn a love heart in the sand for me before,' I say, going over to kiss him full on the lips. 'Thank you.'

'I'm hungry,' Gabriel interrupts, and we go back to eat our picnic. There is sand everywhere, in the drinks and the food. The Bobster sits drooling, waiting for crumbs.

'That must be why they're called sandwiches,' Sage says.

'I think it has more to do with a man called the Earl of Sandwich who decided it was a good idea to put a filling between two slices of bread,' Matt says.

'My explanation's better than yours.'

'I want ice cream,' Gabriel says, throwing his bread onto the sand, where a young seagull with speckled plumage swoops down and grabs it.

'You've had one already,' I observe.

'Can't we have another?' Matt says. 'Is there a rule that states a daily dose of one ice cream only?' His eyes light up with humour. 'It can't have anything to do with healthy eating. Look at the picnic you've brought, Nicci. It's all cake and chocolate and fizzy drinks.'

I give him a lightly mocking look. He's far too soft.

'Oh go on,' I say.

'I'm buying.' Matt touches his back pocket, remembers he's wearing shorts and digs around for his jeans under the spare towels to find his wallet. 'Come on, Gabriel, let's go. What do you girls want?'

'I'm all right thanks,' I say after Sage has put in an order for a cornet with raspberry ripple ice cream and two flakes.

'Why don't you two go, Sage?' Matt says. 'I can give you my wallet. Don't lose it though.'

I watch them go, Gabriel trotting alongside Sage to keep up with her.

'Peace at last,' Matt grins. 'At least we can watch them from here.' He lies back with a towel strategically placed across his midriff to his knees.

'Where's the dog?' I ask.

'She's gone with them.'

'I meant to ask you how Beauty is doing. Mum said she was back in hospital.'

'Yes, I was really hoping I wouldn't see her again – not your mum, the pony. I repaired the hernia on Friday, and she's up and about again. I won't let her go home until we're sure there's no infection in the wound like last time.'

'I bet Robert isn't happy, having to pay out yet more money.'

'You know these mad owners. They'll do anything to save their horses.'

'We're back,' Sage announces happily soon after. She drops Matt's wallet into the cool-box. 'Thank you, Matt.'

'Thank you, Matt,' Gabriel echoes.

Matt gazes at me and I give him a rueful smile. I know what he means, that it would be good to have some time together, just the two of us, but it isn't to be.

Back at the house we have fish and chips, and Sage has a shower and Gabriel a bath. There are sticky fingerprints and tiny heaps of sand all over the house.

Sage reads her brother a story and Matt and I are trying to persuade them both to go to bed, but they're concerned because their mum isn't home.

'Where is Mummy? Hasn't she texted you, Auntie Nicci?' Sage asks.

'She hasn't, but maybe she's on a train and hasn't got a signal, or she's run out of battery.'

Sage's lip wobbles and my heart melts.

'Listen, Sage,' I say, tucking a lock of her hair behind her ear. 'She will be back.' I pause. 'Now, go to bed. Goodnight.' I give her a hug. 'You never know – Mummy might be here when you get up in the morning.'

I hope she is anyway. I'll be livid with her if she doesn't turn up or at least let me know where she is. I'm also concerned though. Surely even my irrespon-sible sister wouldn't abandon her children like this, knowing they'll be worried, and I can't help wonder - ing if she's met with an accident.

I check that both the children are in bed before I rejoin Matt in the living room. I'm exhausted. My hangover is catching up with me.

'I know you're concerned about Cheska, but I enjoyed today. It was great.' He leans back, puts his feet on the coffee table and pats the sofa alongside him. At first I assume it's a gesture meant for me, but it's for the dog. I smile to myself as the Bobster sits herself beside him. I give up. What are a few hairs between friends? Matt holds out a treat from his pocket. Oh, and a bit of drool, I think, as the string of saliva dangling from the Bobster's chin drips slowly onto the fabric. Rather sheepishly, Matt scrubs at it with a piece of tissue.

'I saw that,' I say sternly.

'I'm sorry.'

'Perhaps we're incompatible.'

'I can change.'

'I don't want you to change.' I lean across to kiss him, aware that the Bobster is giving me one of her looks, showing the whites of her eyes and setting her mouth in a squiggly line like a Snoopy dog, an expression that means I really want to growl at you, but I know I'll get told off if I do. 'I like you just the way you are.' I do. I touch my lips to his stubbly cheek. He smells of the sea and when I kiss his lips he tastes of salt and sweet toffee ice cream.

'I wish I could take you upstairs, but I don't suppose they're asleep.'

'And there's no way of guaranteeing that they'll remain asleep either.' I sit down beside him, the opposite side from the Bobster. 'I've texted Cheska again.'

I stroke Matt's hair, curling it through my fingers, but I can't settle. 'I'm going to call the police.'

'I don't think you can count her as a missing person yet,' he says.

'I've left at least five messages on her voicemail,' I go on.

'Hey, don't panic, Nicci.'

'What am I going to do? What if she's not back by Monday? I was going to ride first thing and I've got to be at work at nine.'

'So have I,' he says, 'otherwise I'd offer to have the kids for a while.'

'They aren't your problem, not that they are a problem,' I add quickly as Sage appears, crying in the doorway.

'I can't get to sleep.'

When a cuddle doesn't help, I end up giving her ice cream that drips off the spoon and onto the sofa. The Bobster licks it clean.

'Never mind,' Matt says.

'I'll go to bed now,' Sage says eventually.

'Cheska isn't much like you,' Matt observes. 'She seems pretty thoughtless.'

'I've always been the sensible one,' I say. 'Does that make me sound boring?'

'Cautious. Which is weird when you're more than happy to risk your neck on a horse.'

I'd love Matt to stay, but together we decide he should go home because it would feel awkward if Gabriel should turn up in my bed and find Matt there as well.

'I'm sorry.'

'Another time soon,' he says, rubbing noses as we embrace at the front door.

'Soon,' I echo.

'I hope you have a peaceful night,' he smiles.

It is not peaceful. Sage has nightmares about giant crabs and tidal waves, crying out several times during the night, and at some unearthly hour of the morning, Gabriel crawls under my duvet, snuggles up and falls asleep.

Sunday passes in a blur, and somehow I manage to keep the children occupied and my growing anxiety hidden. But on Monday morning I sleep through my alarm, which means I don't get to the yard to ride Willow and, more worryingly, there is still no sign of Cheska. At seven, I slide out of bed, trying not to disturb Gabriel, who once again lies with his head on my pillow, his flaming curls falling across his face, his thumb in his mouth.

I've got to be at work before nine. I can't leave the children home alone. What am I going to do? I notify the police – they can make enquiries when they decide it's appropriate. I grab a quick shower before waking Sage.

'Where are your clothes?' I ask her, as she stretches and stares at me, bleary-eyed. 'It's time to get dressed and have breakfast.'

'Where's Mummy?' she asks, and my heart sinks because I'd hoped to avoid that conversation until later. 'Have you heard from her?'

'Not yet,' I say brightly. 'I imagine she's on her way though. She should be back very soon.'

'I worry that Mummy will do something bad to herself and we won't know where she is,' Sage says in a small voice.

I touch her back. 'Has she ever suggested she'd do anything bad?'

'Sometimes when she's really sad, she says she'll walk out and disappear, or she'll hurt herself.'

I'm torn between compassion for my niece and anger towards my sister. It's all very well harbouring dark thoughts, but you can't express them in front of your children. It isn't fair.

'I keep asking her to go to the doctor,' Sage goes on, sounding like she's twenty-one, not eleven. 'Could you speak to her, Nicci?'

'Certainly,' I say. I'll be having words with her when she turns up. Sage is right – my sister needs profes - sional help.

I ask Sage for their home address, but when I try to trace the phone number the landline has been disconnected.

'Is there anyone Mummy might go and stay with? Has she got a best friend?' She's mentioned a couple of people, but I haven't a clue who they are. It crosses my mind that I should drive up to London and look for her, but if she isn't at the flat where she lives with Alan, it will be a wasted journey. When I ask Sage where

Alan works, she says he's a plumber and he goes out and about in an unmarked, unidentifiable white van, which is no help at all.

'Are you going to look after us today?' Sage goes on bravely.

'Yes, I suppose I am.' I'll have to.

'What are you going to do about work?'

'I haven't figured that out yet. Don't worry though. I'll think of something.' What can I do? I can't possibly take them to the surgery. There's the nursery in Talyton, but I don't like the idea of leaving Gabriel with complete strangers, not without preparing him in advance, and Sage is far too old.

I call the surgery to see if I can negotiate a later start with Ben, but Claire says he's out on an urgent house call and there are two patients waiting for me already. There is only one thing for it – I call my mother.

She's over the moon.

'Of course, I'll have them for you.' She pauses. 'Nicci, I'm so sorry about the other night. I wish I'd talked to you about it, the abortion . . .'

'Mum, there's no time for that right now, and I know you would have done what you thought was best at the time. Just come over to the house asap.'

'I'm on my way, poor little mites. Oh, I can't wait to see them.'

'Mummy doesn't mind us seeing Granma?' Sage asks.

'She isn't here to ask, so we'll assume it's okay. Now, hurry up and get dressed. I've got to go to work. I have patients waiting for me.' I can tell it's going to be one of those days.

Mum's on my doorstep within fifteen minutes.

'I'll have to leave you to it, I'm afraid,' I say, throwing on a cardigan. 'Sage, you know where everything is.'

'I do, Nicci,' she says.

'Don't worry about us,' Mum says with a smile. 'We're going to have a lovely day.'

When I return from work, they appear, from the state of the kitchen, to have had far too much fun together. For once, Mum's clothes are rather the worse for wear, spattered with what could be cake mix and tomato ketchup, but she's still smiling – for the children's benefit anyway. She's extremely anxious about Cheska.

'She hasn't been in touch with you, Nicci?' she says, taking me aside.

I shake my head. I've tried calling her several times throughout the day.

'I spoke to that daft police constable on the phone – I didn't like to go down to the station with the children.'

'What did he say?' I ask quickly.

'He said he's making some enquiries and he'll let us know when he has any news, but he wasn't terribly optimistic. Cheska's an adult and she left voluntarily. And she has a habit of disappearing.'

'I know,' I say, forcing optimism. 'I just wish she wasn't so thoughtless. All she has to do is text me to let me know she's safe.' I change the subject, finding it too painful to think of the alternative, that she's done something really stupid and hurt herself. 'How have the children coped?'

'They've been wonderful. You know, I've loved having my grandchildren for the day. Sage is such a clever girl – she reminds me of you. And Gabriel – well, he's cheeky and happy-go-lucky, much like Cheska used to be at his age.' She lowers her voice. 'Do you think she'll let me have them another time now she knows I'm not going to snatch them away from her?'

'Sage and Gabriel, would you like another day with Granma sometime?' I ask them when they return to the kitchen to show me the drawings they've done, a rainbow and a 'Please come home, Mummy' card, the sight of which makes me want to cry.

'Can we do some more cooking?' Sage says. 'We made gingerbread men and iced them.'

'Didn't you save me one?'

'We ate them all,' Sage giggles. 'I had two and Gabriel had three.'

'They didn't want any tea,' Mum says.

'Hardly surprising,' I say quietly.

'Let me spoil them a little. I have to make up for a lot of lost time.'

I keep my thoughts to myself, that she might have to make the most of this precious day, in case Cheska throws a wobbly when she does come back and refuses to let her see them again. I can only hope that this is progress, and that Sage and Gabriel will be able to put pressure on their mother themselves.

I notice a rosette lying among the post and other debris on the kitchen worktop and wistfully I picture Willow in my head. How I wish I could be riding instead.

*

It's three days in all before my sister comes home. She calls me from the train.

'Hi, sis. You couldn't give us a lift, could you?'

'Actually, I couldn't.' Although I'm relieved to hear her voice and know she's safe, I'm furious with her for not getting in touch before, and I'm in the middle of morning surgery. 'I can't just drop everything. You'll have to get a bus.'

'There isn't one for another two hours. Buses to Talyton St George are as rare as hen's teeth, you know that. What about Matt? Could he pick me up?'

'I'm not asking Matt. How much is a taxi?'

'I can ask,' she says brightly.

'I'm not paying for it. Cheska, you've brought this on yourself. You'll have to bloody well walk.'

'Nicci, you swore!' she exclaims. 'You never swear.'

'You've driven me to it,' I tell her sharply. 'You have one hell of a lot of explaining to do.' I cut the call and immediately phone Mum at the house to let her and the children know Cheska is safe and well and on her way. Then I turn my attention back to Fifi Green's blood test results, mulling over the possible causes of her anaemia before I call her up to give her the news and a plan of action to return her red blood cell count to normal.

Cheska arrives at the surgery two hours later when I'm sitting in the staffroom eating lunch with Claire.

'Nicci, would you mind? The taxi driver's waiting outside,' she says as if nothing has happened.

'Yes, I do mind. Tell me why I should bail you out again? You're a liability, Cheska. You're thoughtless, cruel—'

'But the driver needs paying. What am I going to do?' she goes on helplessly.

'Oh, for goodness sake. Will he take a card? I haven't got any cash on me,' I say, fuming inwardly as I get up to fetch my purse out of the locked drawer in my desk in the consulting room. Luckily he does take cards. When I return, I find my little sister eating the remains of my sandwich.

'Hey, that's mine.'

'I'm sorry. I thought you'd finished with it.' She smiles. 'I wish you wouldn't get so stressy.'

My fingers tighten around my purse. 'I take it that you've been having a good time while putting the rest of us through hell.'

'That's rather melodramatic,' she counters.

'Hardly,' I say. 'Where have you been?' I take her aside into the consulting room where we continue our conversation in private.

'Where do you think? I went to see Alan,' she goes on without waiting for my response.

'You and Alan? Are you back together?'

'Not. We had some fun trying, but it's time to accept it and move on.' Her eyes begin to water, but they're only crocodile tears, I think crossly.

'You could have texted to let me know where you were, or left your address. We've all been worried sick. Sage thought you'd come to harm. We've even alerted the police.' I stamp my foot. 'How could you?'

It's as if a lightbulb is suddenly switched on in my sister's brain. 'I'm sorry. I was angry with you, so I went to see Alan, and I kind of got swept up with seeing him again, and I thought everything would be fine because Nicci will look after Sage and Gabriel,' she says, turning to face the window. 'I thought you'd enjoy getting to know the children.'

'I did, but you forget that some of us work for a living, and I have a horse to ride. I can't drop everything to babysit for three whole days.'

'Where are the children?' She turns abruptly to face me.

'With Mum,' I say simply.

'How could you? They're *my* children.'

'Why don't you treat them properly then? I love them too, Cheska, which is why I made that call. You left me with no choice. It was Mum or Social Services. You're completely irresponsible.' I take a step towards her. 'Sage and Gabriel have loved every minute they've spent with their grandmother. Whether you like it or not, they should continue to have a relationship with her.'

'What about me? What about what I want?'

'Right at this moment, I really don't care. You're so bloody selfish.'

'At least I'm happy,' she sobs, despite the fact that clearly she isn't

I fall silent, I'm out of my depth and unable to deal with her. She is a slave to her emotions, taking life's highs and lows to extremes. She knows better than I do how to have fun and perhaps if I'd been able to let myself go in the same way as Cheska, I would have had more fun too. Or maybe my life would have ended up in a similar mess.

Not only does she exhibit extreme emotions, she inspires them in others – I am both livid and supremely sorry for her. My heart goes out to my confused and lost little sister.

'Cheska, come here.' I hold out my arms and she lets me give her a hug. 'I'll take you to Mum's to collect Sage and Gabriel. I bet they can't wait to see you.'

'They're at Mum's house?'

'Don't start again, Cheska,' I say, upset at her attitude after I've done my best to cope. I pick up my bag and keys and drive to Talymouth.

'I'll wait in the car,' she says when I park outside our old family home, a three-storey terrace painted the palest cornflower blue and facing out to sea.

'You're coming in with me,' I say, getting out and tapping on the roof of the car. 'Move!'

'What are you trying to do, Nicci? Make me play happy families?'

'I'm not forcing you to do anything. You're going to go in there and give your children the biggest hug ever. I'll look after Mum,' I add because I know she's going to be devastated.

As I anticipated, Sage and Gabriel almost fall out of the front door into Cheska's arms when we ring on the bell. Gabriel looks as if he's been making mud pies, while Sage clutches a pink trowel.

'Mummy!' Gabriel squeals. Cheska squats down and holds him tight. 'Mummy, Mummy, where have you been?'

'Mummy went on a little holiday. I'm sorry, darlings—' Cheska looks up at Sage '—I should have kept in touch.'

'We had a holiday too, in a way,' Sage says, giving her mother a kiss. 'Matt and Nicci took us to the beach and Gabriel was scared of a crab.'

'I was not,' Gabriel says.

'You were. You cried. You're always crying.'

'What else did you do?' Cheska asks quickly.

'We've been shopping and gardening with Granma.' Sage glances behind her where Mum is standing in the shadows of the hall beyond, her arms folded and her lips pressed together.

'Let's go.' Cheska gets up and takes the children by the hand.

'We haven't finished planting the new rose bushes yet,' Sage protests. 'We can't go yet, can we, Granma?'

'Let them stay, Cheska.' Mum takes a step towards my sister.

'Please, Mummy,' Sage says.

'Nicci needs to get back to work.'

'I can bring them back to Nicci's later.'

'No,' Cheska says. 'I'm here now. They're my kids.' She glares at Mum. 'You can stop playing the doting granny now.'

'I'm sorry, Mum,' I say as I hang back for a moment, watching Cheska helping Sage and Gabriel into the car.

'Although I've been worried sick about Cheska, I've loved having Sage and Gabriel, but I always knew it wasn't going to last.' Mum shakes her head sadly. 'At least I have you and Robert, and a wedding to organise.'

I look out to sea where the sailing boats are racing from one end of the bay to the other. A seagull perching on the chimney pots cries mournfully. I wish I knew how to bring two of the people I love the most together and make everything right between them.

Chapter Fourteen

Horse Whisperer

Cheska is back, reunited with Sage and Gabriel, and Matt and I are rebuilding our relationship, and it's a relief when life settles down to something approaching normal, for a couple of weeks at least.

At work, I refresh the waiting list. There are three for me. I smile wryly. There is a visitor to the area with an ear infection and one of Eternally Frazzled Mum's boys with a suspected appendicitis – not just a tummy ache, but a suggested diagnosis. Ally has been on the internet and when I call her in, she brings what looks like a ream of notes printed from Wikipedia and various other websites where you can check your symptoms, but I soon set her straight.

Fifi comes in for a check-up next.

'I wonder if you can help me,' I begin. 'I was wondering if you had any jobs going at your garden centre.'

'Any vacancies?' Her brow forms papery crinkles.

Although well preserved, she's beginning to show her age. 'Are you thinking of throwing in the towel already, Dr Chieveley? Are you going to give up medicine after all that training?' She raises her hands. 'Who will look after us? You are such a wonderful doctor. Irreplaceable.'

'It's very kind of you to say so and I'm flattered, but it isn't for me. It's for my sister.'

'Oh?' Fifi leans closer, as if to exact a confidence.

'Her visit's turning out to be a bit more than a holiday.'

'There is a temporary position, filling shelves and manning the tills. Would that appeal to her?'

'Is there an application form or anything?'

'Oh, tell her to come in for a chat at midday on Friday.' Fifi taps her nose. 'Keep it under your hat though – I don't want to be accused of favouritism.'

'Thank you. That's really good of you.'

'It's a pleasure,' she says, her cheeks growing pink. 'So, is she staying permanently?'

'You'll be able to ask her that question. Fifi, I'm very busy.'

'Of course you are, Dr Chieveley. Ed Pike is waiting to see you. It's such a terrible to-do for his family. We don't usually have those sort of goings-on around here.'

'What on earth are you talking about?'

'The sex change,' Fifi says in a hushed whisper. 'Haven't you heard the rumours?'

'I don't normally listen to gossip,' I say, amused at my attempt at self-delusion. Of course I do. 'I prefer to get my information straight from the horse's mouth.'

'It's been said that Ed has been taking extracts of wild yam for its feminising properties.'

'I really don't know what you're talking about,' I cut in.

'You must do. It's to help him through his transition from Ed to Edwina.'

I shake my head. 'You really mustn't believe everything you hear. Surely you know that by now. Go on. Off you go.'

When I get home, Cheska and I take the children down to the green by the river for a walk. We stop just beyond the stile and sit down in the long grass. Gabriel toddles around, his red curls coppery in the sunlight, as he plays with a ball I bought from the newsagents to allay his distress at having to return a football that came over the fence from next door the other day. I say 'plays', but I don't think he's going to be the next David Beckham because he misses the ball more often than he makes contact with it. In the meantime, Sage is read - ing, sitting down cross-legged with her hair falling over her eyes.

'Would Sage like her hair cut when the hairdresser comes?' I ask my sister.

'What's wrong with her hair?' Cheska says defensively.

'Nothing. I just thought Maria's coming next week and I'd ask her to do Sage and Gabriel as well, if you're happy.' I don't want my sister to think I'm taking over, but I do like to get things done.

'I thought you'd go to some top salon.'

261

'I like to keep local people employed. It's called being part of a community.'

'I still don't understand why you came back. You could have gone anywhere.'

'I came back because this is home. I love this area, I have friends here, and most importantly, it's close to Mum.' I smile. 'Going back to the hairdresser—'

'If you want to keep her busy, then go ahead. Let her cut the kids' hair.'

'It isn't that exactly. As I said, it's more about keeping local people employed . . .'

My sister closes her eyes.

I give her a nudge. 'You can't keep dodging the issue. You said you were going to look for work and I've found a vacancy up at the garden centre.'

My sister wrinkles her nose.

'You can't afford to be picky. It's part-time, mainly on the tills, and you get a uniform so you won't have to splash out on work clothes.'

'What, a saggy green sweatshirt or a tabard?'

'They wear polo-shirts, yellow, pink or lilac, I think, with the centre's logo. They're quite tasteful, considering the owner's style of dress.' I think of Fifi turning up at the surgery like the mother of the bride all the time. I dig around in my bag and pull out a Post-it note and drop it onto my sister's lap. 'You have an interview on Friday at lunchtime.'

She sits up abruptly. 'A what?'

'It's at twelve-thirty.'

'How could you?'

'It's a special favour from Fifi. Cheska, you need to

do something. It isn't just the money, although that would come in useful when you start looking for your own place. It will give you a chance to get out and meet people.'

'I don't need to meet people,' she says, pursing her lips. 'Anyway, what will I do with the kids when I'm at work? It's impossible.'

'I'll have them. The garden centre is open for late-night shopping on Thursdays and Fridays throughout the summer, and you can do alternate Saturdays and every Sunday. It's perfect.'

'What about your horsey events?'

'Ah . . .' I look down and fiddle with the fastener on my bag, popping it open and shut.

'Don't even think about it.'

'Cheska, it's common sense, something of which you appear to possess very little.' I should have bitten my tongue because I can feel this discussion flaring into a full-blown sisterly row. 'Mum adored having them when you were away and she'd love to have them for a few hours now and then. I'd be there too and you wouldn't have to see her. All she wants is to be part of their lives, and yours, if you'd only give her a chance.' I am cut to the core by my sister's attitude. 'I'm trying to help you out here.'

'Oh yes, my perfect sister. Well, I don't want you to put yourself out on my behalf. I can look after myself. I'm not a bloody charity.'

'Prove it then,' I say, standing my ground. 'Go to the interview and give it your best shot.'

*

263

'Show me,' I say, when Mum turns up to take me to the yard the following evening after work, Robert sitting in the lorry waiting.

She tips her head to one side, pretending to be embarrassed, before holding up her left hand to reveal a beautiful antique diamond ring. At first I'm afraid she's going to tell me it belonged to the dead wife.

'It's beautiful,' I say. 'I'm jealous.'

'We went to an antiques market to choose it. And no, it isn't that he's a tightwad, or whatever you now call people who are prudent with their money. It was my choice. This is my second time round and I wanted something with history.'

'You've got that in Robert, haven't you?' I giggle.

'You can mock, Nicci. It's good to have a partner who has plenty of life experience to talk about and interests you can share. I have great hopes for you and Matt. There was a time when I thought you were going to beat us down the aisle.'

'Mum, it isn't a race.'

'I know. I'm so glad you're back together.'

'I'm surprised you've rushed in like you have.'

'The first time I met Robert face to face, I knew he was more than "just a friend". It's all right, I know that's what you called them,' she adds, smiling. 'Come on. Let's go and fetch this pony.'

'This is a day I didn't think we would see,' Mum says when we head out of Talyton in the lorry. 'I won't forget the look in Beauty's eyes when we found her in the field. She was begging us to help her.'

'Which I did, against my better judgement, dearest

Kathryn,' Robert says gruffly. 'I did it for you, not the pony. You would never have agreed to marry me if I hadn't.'

'It's very appealing when a man is fond of children and animals,' says Mum, stroking his thigh. We both know Robert's bluffing. He loves that pony.

'You're making me feel like a gooseberry here,' I say.

I'm driving with Robert sitting beside me and Mum next to him, but I really wish they'd chosen to sit with Robert beside the passenger door, because I am finding it hard to cope with him stinking of cows and pressed up against me, taking up a lot of space in his enormous sheepskin coat.

At the hospital I reverse the lorry into the parking area. 'Do you need travel boots and a tail guard?' I ask. 'The boots might be a bit big, but you can borrow Willow's.'

'Thanks for the offer,' Robert says.

'We should put boots on her,' Mum says. 'The last thing we need is for Beauty to hurt herself on the way home. I'm sorry if this is spoiling your evening,' she goes on. 'I expect you'd rather be out with Matt.'

'I'm not sure what he's up to tonight.'

'I was hoping he might be at the hospital. I spoke to him on the phone and he said we could pick her up whenever we like, one of the benefits of him being my daughter's boyfriend.'

I don't enlighten her as to how close it came to us splitting up for good over Mel and the baby.

'One of the vets will be there,' I say, 'but I'm not sure which.' I'm actually hoping that it's Mel.

265

It is Mel, her hair tied back, a slash of bright lippy across her mouth and her eyes ringed with black eyeliner. She's wearing a blue sweatshirt over green scrubs and short black wellington boots, and even in that get-up she manages to look sexy. It isn't fair.

'Isn't Matt here?' Mum says, sounding disappointed.

'He's at a partners' meeting,' Mel says, looking at me superciliously as if to say, you didn't know that, did you? And it's true, I didn't, but she can't make me feel bad about it because Matt and I are secure in our relationship.

'I'd like to pay my bill,' Robert says. 'I don't like to be beholden to anyone.'

'You can settle by card if you like, or wait until we invoice you like last time,' Mel says.

'I've got the cash here now. I'd rather give it to you than carry it around with me.' Robert fishes around in the deep pockets of his sheepskin coat and pulls out wads of notes held together with elastic bands. 'It's all here,' he says, but he insists on counting it out in front of Mel, not once, but twice. She's fine about it, which surprises me. I thought she'd be irritated and impatient to get the pony out of here, but she's gracious.

'Here she is,' Mel says when we walk through the yard. Beauty pokes her nose over the stable door and whickers. Her forelock has been twisted into a plait incorporating a yellow tag with her hospital details, name and number.

'Hello, girl,' Robert says gruffly. He strokes Beauty's

face and a lump catches in my throat at the sight of the man and his pony.

'She's a fiery little thing,' Mel says. 'She's done well this time round.'

'When can I drive her again?'

'Don't rush it,' Mel says. 'Give her a full six months from the surgery. We don't want to risk another hernia because she's overdone it. Do you need a hand to load her, or can you manage?'

'We'll be fine,' Robert says. 'It's three against one and she walked straight into the trailer the last couple of times.'

'She wasn't well then,' Mum points out. 'She didn't care.'

'She always loads first time.'

'You said you'd never loaded her before she started coming over to the hospital.'

'Hey,' I cut in. 'It's too soon to be arguing like an old married couple. Save it for a few more weeks.'

Mum and Robert smile fondly at each other.

'I'll get on then,' Mel says.

It's a really awkward situation, but I need to speak to her to make it clear where I stand as far as Matt's baby is concerned.

'Mel,' I say quickly. 'Can I have a quick word?'

'What's this about?' she asks, but I'm pretty sure she knows already because she's taking a rapid guilt trip back to reception as if she's trying to shake me off.

'Congratulations,' I begin. 'Matt's told me about the baby.'

'Oh?' Under the light at the entrance to the building, I can see the flush on her cheeks and the glint of irritation in her eyes. 'Thanks, but it has nothing to do with you. It's between me and Matt.'

'It *is* my business.'

'I really don't see how it can be, now that you and Matt aren't together any more. The way he went on about you – I knew you were too good to be true. No one could possibly be that perfect.'

'I'm flattered he thinks of me that way,' I say icily.

'Thought,' Mel says. 'It's in the past. Matt's promised to commit to me and the baby.' She strokes the slight swell of her stomach.

'I know. He's told me and I wouldn't expect anything less of him.'

'Of course, I'll be staying around now,' Mel goes on, and I think she doesn't know, does she?

'That's cool with me,' I say. 'Matt and I aren't planning on moving anywhere.' She stares at me. 'We're actually back together. He must have forgotten to mention it to you.'

Mel opens and closes her mouth like a dying fish.

'I do feel sorry for you,' I say, moving close to her, 'with the prospect of being a single mum ahead of you, but whether you like it or not, Matt is my boyfriend. There is absolutely no chance of him coming back to you, so you can stop playing games. You're beginning to make your - self look like a stalker. Do I make myself clear?'

'I believe so,' she says.

'Good.' All I want to do is get out of here. The confrontation with Mel has left me feeling stressed out, but if I was hoping for a quick getaway in the lorry, I am disappointed.

'Beauty's enjoyed her stay at the hospital so much, she doesn't want to go home,' Mum says when I return to the car park. She's standing beside the ramp while Robert leads the pony – with Willow's boots up to her elbows – towards the lorry. Beauty puts one hoof then another on the bottom of the ramp and stops dead, baulking at the idea of going any further.

'Get on,' Robert growls, but Beauty merely reverses, tosses her head, yanking the lead-rope from his hand before trotting off to the neat lawn nearby where she puts her head down to graze.

'The little bugger,' Robert says, examining the silvery rope burns on his palms. 'She took me by surprise.'

He catches her, wraps the rope around her nose and tries again, but Beauty isn't having any of it. One of the grooms appears with the offer of lunge-lines and whip. After two hours of trying both the carrot and the stick approach, there are six of us against one pony.

'How long can she keep this up without hurting herself and opening up the wound?' Mum asks eventually.

'She's going to have to stay here,' one of the grooms says.

'No way,' Robert says. 'She's cost me a fortune – cleaned me out already.'

'Can I have one last go?' I interrupt.

'What are you, some kind of horse whisperer?' Robert says wearily. 'Oh, go on.' He throws me the end of the lead-rope and I walk the pony away.

'Whoah,' I say when we're a little way from the lorry. I let Beauty sniff my hands and check me out. She tries to nudge me out of her space, but I send her back with a flick of the rope. 'What's your problem, pony?' I murmur. I scratch her neck, which she loves, stretching out with her top lip quivering. 'Let's go.' I turn her to face the lorry, quickly so she hasn't got time to think about it, and walk her smartly towards it. She's going in. I keep walking, and the power of positive thinking, or the fact that she's decided, like the rest of us, she's had enough, carries us up the ramp and into the box where I wait for Robert to shut the gates behind us so she can't run out again.

'Good girl,' I tell her, giving her a mint from my pocket.

'How did you do that?' Robert asks when we're driving back to the farm.

'I asked her nicely,' I say, grinning.

When we arrive at the farm it's dark. Robert leads Beauty into her stable, a pen more suitable for a sheep than a pony, in one end of a barn. In fact, her sole companion is a lame old ewe. Robert gives her a flake of sweet-scented hay and a bucket of fresh water. It's a far cry from the luxury Willow lives in.

'Let's have a drink to celebrate Beauty's return,' Robert says, his arm around my mother's waist.

'I'm going home,' I say. 'I'll drop the lorry back to Delphi's. She'll drive me home.'

'I can do that,' says Robert.

'There's no need.'

'Thanks for this evening,' he says.

I smile. 'It's no problem. I expect Beauty would have preferred to travel in your trailer as it turns out.'

'Yes, I think she does prefer second class over first,' Robert says. 'She's a funny old bird.'

I wish Mum and Robert goodnight and head back to the yard. I don't mind. Any excuse to see Willow. I park the lorry and wander over to see my horse. The lights are on and Delphi is doing her last routine checks on the horses, swapping Dark Star's stable rug for a lighter fleece. She maintains that nine-thirty is her last visit to see them, but I wouldn't be surprised if she turns up at midnight too. I don't know how she does it. Like looking after Gabriel, it's relentless.

On hearing me, Willow whinnies and my heart lifts. I stroke her and she nibbles at my hair, and my troubles evaporate. When I'm with my horse, nothing else matters.

Chapter Fifteen

Give a Dog a Bone

It's going to be a difficult day, I think. It's Friday, a couple of days after I helped collect Beauty from the hospital, and Matt is taking Mel for a scan. I know it's important to him, I know it's something he has to do, but even though I fight it I'm wracked with pain and jealousy at the thought of him sharing such an intimate moment with his ex-lover, bonding over their baby.

During the first part of the morning, I struggle to concentrate, knowing that Matt is with her, but when I receive a text from him to say he's back at Westleigh and, apart from being slightly small for its dates, the baby is fine, I relax a little.

At coffee time, I head for the staffroom for a drink, but decline the cream slice Claire offers me.

'I can't. I'm in training.'

'That's a first,' Janet says. 'That means we can share the extra one, Claire.'

'Shane's giving me grief. I'm going to the gym three times a week as well as riding, and living on tuna and pasta.'

'He won't know,' Claire says.

'He'll force me into a confession, then make me trot on the lunge for hours without stirrups as penance.' I finish a glass of water. 'I'll see you later. Just eat that—' I point at the slice, oozing cream from its puff pastry layers and gleaming with sugary icing '—before I come back.' On the way back to the consulting room, I call Bridget through from reception.

'How are you?' I say, ushering her to the chair beside the desk. 'Is this about the hand?'

'You should have been a detective,' she says with irony.

'I am and my powers of deduction are amazing,' I say with equal sarcasm. There are some patients who appreciate it and some who don't. Bridget is someone you can have a banter with without it causing offence. 'If I am not very much mistaken, you are here about your hand, the one with the bandage.'

She chuckles as she starts to remove the dressing.

'I stabbed myself with my scissors – not deliberately, I hasten to add. I'm always doing it.' She sighs. 'I think it's my age.'

'Let's have a look,' I say, finding a shallow wound with swelling and heat around it. 'When did it happen?'

'Last week. It should have healed by now.'

'There's some infection there. I'll clean it up.' I fetch

273

a kidney dish, gloves and cleaning materials. 'How is the diabetes? Have you seen the consultant?'

'Ah, I don't know how to say this, but I have a confession to make.'

'Bridget, you must take this seriously. How many times have I told you?'

'I've been to see her, but I couldn't bring myself to admit that I do know why I haven't been under control.' She shakes her head, her frizzy curls bouncing about. 'I was hoping to keep it quiet, but I can see it's a stupid thing to do. I'm playing Russian roulette with my health.' She holds up her hand. 'And here's the evidence. It won't heal because of the diabetes.'

'You'd better tell me . . .' I dab at the wound, making her wince. 'I'm sorry.'

'You really need to learn to be more gentle, Dr Chieveley,' she says lightly. 'They say you make grown men cry.'

'Do they? That's the first I've heard of it.'

'And small children.'

I smile to myself. 'Tell me about your theory on the diabetes.'

'Remember I told you the vet said that the disease was exactly the same in dogs as it is in humans? Well, it turns out that it isn't. I ran out of insulin a couple of times and I thought I could use Daisy's doggy version.'

'Bridget, that's so dangerous. You could end up killing yourself!'

'Shannon, my daughter, caught me out one day. I didn't realise that although I was injecting the same amount from the syringe, it was more dilute than my own insulin, so I wasn't using enough.' She pauses. 'I thought the vet knew more about it than you.'

'So it won't happen again?'

'Shannon's made sure I never run out by organising a regular delivery from the pharmacist.' She hesitates. 'You won't tell anyone, will you?'

'Your secret is safe with me,' I say, chuckling. 'Have you started barking yet?'

'Not yet, although Shannon might say otherwise when I'm yelling at her to get out of bed some mornings.'

I send Bridget away with a prescription for antibiotics and an appointment for a week's time before calling in my next patient, James from next door with Eternally Frazzled Mum, who has good reason to appear frazzled today.

'I've had to take time off work again,' she says, bustling in. 'I can't afford to keep doing this.'

James walks in behind her, his shoulders slumped, his T-shirt stretched across his chubby frame and his jeans slung low around his hips, revealing a pair of pink and white striped pants. He has the beginnings of a black eye and something is wrong with his nose.

'What can I do for you?' I ask.

'Mum's been duffing me up,' he says.

'Oh, don't be silly, although it's tempting consid - ering what you boys put me through.'

A tear of blood trickles from James's left nostril. I hand him a box of tissues. He sits with it on his lap and the blood drips into the box – not quite what I was intending.

'Take a tissue.' Ally nudges him in the shoulder. 'Tell the doctor what you've been doing.'

'I was on the trampoline and I bumped into one of the poles,' he mutters.

'Go on,' Ally says. 'Why did you bump into one of the poles?'

'It was last night,' he goes on reluctantly. 'I was trampolining in the dark.'

'Ah, I see . . .'

'But *he* couldn't see. That was the problem,' Ally says, lightening up. 'I'm worried he's broken his nose. It looks crooked to me and he has such handsome features.'

'Oh, Mum,' James sighs. 'Do you have to?'

I make much of examining his nose to prove to Ally, if nothing else, that there is absolutely nothing to worry about. The nose isn't broken. It only looks broken because it's distorted by the bruising from where he came into contact with the metal pole.

'This isn't going to affect your good looks in the future,' I assure James. 'It will not stop all the girls chasing after you.'

He grimaces, still too young to be interested in the opposite sex, unlike some of us, I think wryly to myself.

'I would suggest that you abandon this extreme sport of yours in order to prevent any further incidents,' I add with a grin.

'Thank you, Nicci. You've put my mind at rest.' Ally

fishes her bra strap out from under her top. 'Let's get you home, James. I must get back to work.'

Another hour passes and I'm finished for the day. I'm just about to leave for the yard when Fifi phones to ask where Cheska is because she hasn't turned up at the garden centre.

'I've been waiting for her,' Fifi complains.

'I'm sorry,' I say. 'I'll see if I can get hold of her and find out what's happened.'

'If she can't get herself organised to turn up for the interview or let me know she isn't coming, I don't think this is going to work,' Fifi goes on.

Infuriated at my sister's behaviour, I apologise profusely on her behalf and drop by the house to have a word with her on my way to ride Willow.

Cheska is sitting on the lawn in the garden, sunning herself.

'Hey, don't you know you'll get skin cancer,' I say snappily.

She shades her eyes and looks in my direction.

'Oh, it's you, Nicci. I wasn't expecting you back until this evening.'

'Why aren't you at Fifi's?' I ask her. 'She was expecting you.'

'I didn't see any point,' she responds. 'It'll never work out. You haven't got time to look after the children and I can't afford to pay for childcare.'

'For goodness sake, Cheska. You haven't even tried. And it isn't all about the money. You need to get out and meet people. You need to get a life.' I gaze at her. 'If you want to sit around moping, you're welcome.' I won't interfere again. There isn't any point going for an interview if you don't want the job – Fifi would have seen straight through her immediately.

I turn to go back inside the house.

'Where are you going?' Cheska asks.

'To the yard. Where do you think?'

I return home later, having taken Willow for a good gallop and had a session at the gym en route. I'm coming downstairs in my bath robe after a shower when Matt turns up.

Sage offers to switch off the television and leave us alone.

'There's no need, Sage,' I say. 'It's all right. We'll go out.'

'I've got some food at my place,' Matt says as though he's reading my mind.

'Pasta?' I ask.

'Remember, Auntie Nicci's only allowed to eat healthy food, because she's in serious training,' Sage says.

'Let me get dressed and find my keys,' I say, hanging back to avoid any possibility of a hug or kiss, because all I can see when I look at him is a vision of him with Mel, driving her to the hospital and sitting with her as she lies on a bed, with her belly exposed, and their faces as they gaze at their baby on a screen. 'I'll catch up with you.'

When I get to Matt's house, the Bobster gives me a cautious greeting, coming in for a pat before heading off outside with a bone.

'She likes to bury them for a while,' Matt says, putting a saucepan of water on the top of the range and sprinkling a pinch of salt and a splash of oil. 'When they're really smelly, she digs them up and brings them back in.'

'Matt, that's vile.' I stand by the dresser where a black and white photo catches my eye. My heart misses a beat because I know exactly what it is. It's the scan of the baby.

'I know.' Matt takes a bag of pasta out of one of the cupboards and puts it on the kitchen table. 'Are you all right, Nicci?'

Shaking my head, I pick up the photo.

'Do you know if it's a boy or a girl?' I ask.

'We decided we didn't want to know.'

'We?' Matt and Mel making decisions together. My fingers tremble and the baby's features blur in front of my eyes. 'I told you – I'm not sure I can deal with this,' I choke. I put it back down and turn to leave. 'It's too much . . .'

'Come here,' Matt says, his footsteps right behind me as I rush outside, trying to put some distance between us. 'Nicci, please don't go.' He catches my arm and pulls me up short.

I turn to face him. His eyes are filled with pain and regret, and something else, fear, maybe.

'I can't bear to lose you,' he begins. 'I wish I'd never met Mel, but I did. It was a fling and I thought she understood that. It was never going to go anywhere. Oh dear, like the Bobster, I believe I'm digging myself into a hole here. What I mean is, when I said I wasn't looking for a relationship as such, she made out that it was fine because she wasn't either. I accepted what she said at face value.'

'It's different for girls.' I'm not being sexist, but it's what I believe, that it's impossible to have a no-strings attached fling. Being a doctor, I know all that cuddle hormone released during sex plays havoc with the female brain.

'I think she trapped me with this pregnancy. She thought I'd commit to her because of the baby, but I can't do that, Nicci, because I'm committed to you. You have to believe that.' He pauses. 'Please don't walk away from this. It will get better, I promise.'

'I can't see how,' I sob. 'You'll be with her when the baby's born.'

'I won't be far away, but Mel's mother is going to be her birth partner,' Matt says. 'I thought it might help . . . I don't know what else I can do.' He releases my arm. 'I want to be with you, not Mel. I'm done with the one-night stands and the single life. I want to go to bed with you every night and wake up with you every morning.' He takes a deep breath and continues, his voice breaking. 'We can get through this, you know. I love you, Nicci.'

'Oh, Matt.' There are no words to describe the way I feel. My heart lurches and my stomach is tied up in knots. 'I love you too . . .'

He sweeps me into his arms and holds me close, planting kisses down my neck, and I melt into his embrace.

*

Later, I can't stop smiling in the darkness as I lie in Matt's arms, warm and secure, listening to the rise and fall of his chest, the gurgle in his belly and the beat of his heart.

Matt wakes me with tea, toast, butter, and honey from the hive. The sun is shining through the curtains, the pigeons cooing in the oak tree at the end of the garden, and the hens clucking in their coop. I stretch and yawn. It's idyllic.

'I wish I could come back to bed.' Matt leans down in his white bathrobe to kiss me, and I put my arms around his neck.

'Come back then,' I say, smiling.

'I can't,' he says, stroking my shoulder. 'I've got rounds to do at eight.'

'What time is it now?'

'Seven-fifteen. I'm going in the shower then I'll be off. You stay there – there's no rush.'

I sit back against the headboard of the bed. He's right. There isn't. It's Saturday, Delphi's doing Willow for me and I'm not riding until mid-afternoon.

'When are you home?' I ask. Now we're back on track, I want to spend as much time with him as possible.

'Lunchtime, I hope,' he says. 'Will I see you then?'

'I'll pop into Talyton and pick something up.'

'You can take the Bobster, if you like. It would do us both a favour. I wouldn't have to take her to work with me. She doesn't enjoy it that much.' He sighs. 'For once, I'd rather stay here too. I'll see you later.' He hesitates as he leaves, freshly shaven and bearing the scent of mint toothpaste, tea and honey. 'Please don't

281

let the dog off the lead down by the river, or she'll bugger off.'

'I haven't agreed to walk her yet.' The Bobster might be Matt's idea of a best friend, but she certainly isn't mine. She looks cute enough, but although Matt and I are reconciled, the dog and I still treat each other with an air of suspicion.

'You will. You'll get into her good books, and I know how you're itching to get back to your sister and her kids . . . not,' he adds, grinning. 'Make yourself at home. And don't feel you have to muck out here.'

'I won't,' I say. I do though. I stack the dishwasher and tidy up the kitchen a little before heading into Talyton St George, following the path along the brook down into Talyford and along the lanes into the top end of town with the Bobster on the lead and a bag slung over my shoulder. In town, I buy bread and cheese, leaving the dog tied to the ring embedded in the wall outside the baker's shop.

The Bobster and I walk on down to the green, where a group of men, overseen by a pair of swans, are putting up a tent for the annual Beer Festival. The Bobster utters a couple of good-humoured yaps before flirting with Mr Brown's dog, Muffin, who is pottering along with his owner in the sunshine.

'Um, sorry,' I say, pulling her away.

'It's no problem,' Mr Brown says. 'How are you, Dr Chieveley?'

I'm sure it's me who should be asking him that question, but I reply that I'm well. I'm very well, in fact, thanks to getting back with Matt.

'And you?' I ask him.

'We are as well as can be expected.' Locks of thin grey hair fall forward over his forehead. 'No better, no worse, and Mrs Brown is about the same.'

His wife has been about the same since I arrived in Talyton, but Mr Brown seems diminished. His tan coat hangs from his bony frame and his shoes are falling apart. He's so busy looking after everyone else he doesn't have time to care for himself.

'Have you had any help recently?' I ask him. Somehow it seems easier to talk on the green, away from the surgery and with the dogs as icebreakers. 'Do you get any respite at all?'

'The WI come to sit with my wife once a week so I can go shopping, and Fifi usually drops in with a cooked meal on a Tuesday, but I keep having to remind them that we are not a charity. I can manage, you know. I don't want her taken away and put in a home.' He's almost in tears. 'She'd hate that.'

'Do you have any other assistance at home?'

He shakes his head. 'I don't need it. When my wife first fell ill, I had to learn quickly. I found out how to cook and clean.' He smiles with a rare flash of humour. 'And shop for ladies' smalls.' Then he looks somewhat shamefaced as if he's touched on a subject he shouldn't.

'You're a man of many talents. You're a hero, Mr Brown, but even superheroes need helpers.' I make a mental note to see if I can arrange for the Browns to be assessed for extra support when I'm next at work. 'Remember to drop by if you need us, even if it's just for a cup of tea.'

'That's a lovely dog.' Mr Brown leans down to stroke the Bobster's head. 'Is it yours?'

'She's my boyfriend's dog.'

'Mrs Brown and I were married by the time we were your age,' he comments. 'We were teenage sweethearts. Anyway, Doctor, I'd better not keep you any longer. Have a lovely day.'

I wish him goodbye and he continues back across the green to the footbridge over the river, while I head the other way along the path until I reach the stile. I climb over and post the Bobster through the gap at the bottom, having checked there are no sheep around before I unclip her lead. I decide, in spite of Matt's warning, to leave her running free. She doesn't stray far from my heels until she spots a fisherman on the riverbank, sitting under a parasol with his paraphernalia – including a cool-box for storing his catch, I guess. She races across and dives into a plastic tub, emerging with her nose caked in bran and live mealworms writhing as they drop out of her mouth.

I rush up and try to grab her by the collar, but she dodges away to snatch another mouthful of what is apparently a delectable snack.

'I'm so sorry,' I gasp. Although I'm working out at the gym regularly now, I'm not as fit as I thought I was.

'That dog of your'm's a thief,' the fisherman complains, taking the end of a smoking pipe from between his lips. The smell of tobacco rises into the air. In spite of the warm day, he's wearing a hat and cape. 'Why don't you keep her on the lead?'

'I will do.'

'When you catch up with her, you mean. I bet I catch a fish before you catch that dog.'

'Can I pay you compensation for what she's eaten?'

'It's all right. They don't cost me anything. You're the doctor, aren't you?'

'It's Nobby, isn't it? I didn't recognise you with the hat.' I don't bother to ask him how his detox is going – I can see the beer cans in the cool-box, which isn't for storing his catch at all. He realises I've spotted them.

'I like to have a little drink while I'm out fishing,' he explains. 'It's thirsty work and there's hardly any alcohol in them cans. If I'd wanted to drink proper-like, I'd have bought a bottle of cider. You'd better go after that dog,' he goes on. 'She can run faster than you, my lover.'

I jog along the riverbank, looking among the bushes by the old railway line. 'Bobster,' I call. 'Bobster!' I realise what a ridiculous name it is. It doesn't exactly roll off the tongue and I'm getting odd looks from a pair of teenagers sitting in the grass and smoking roll-ups. My palms are pricking with sweat at the thought of having to face Matt at some stage to admit that I didn't listen to him.

I don't know much about dogs, but I was under the illusion they were supposed to be faithful companions. The Bobster appears to be the exception to the rule. I thought she liked me better now too, having shared a bed with each other, but I was mistaken.

I march along the line of trees bordering the old

railway line, checking through the undergrowth with a stick.

'Bobster, I'd like to go home.' Recalling how Matt bribes her to come to him, I try a different approach. 'Biscuits!'

Something moves in the bushes. Two rabbits fly out and scuttle through the grass, disappearing into a hole in the bank further down. Frantically, I shout louder.

'Biscuits!' I strain my ears for an answering yap while I probe the bank with the stick. It's soft and sandy and full of holes and there's an area that's recently been dug over. Squatting down, I take a closer look. There's a yap from deep inside the bank. My heart sinks. What if she's stuck down there? How am I going to get her out? What if I can't get her out? Matt will never forgive me.

'Bobster,' I call again. 'It's going to be all right. You hang in there.'

She answers with a whine.

'Good girl.'

I enlarge one of the holes with the end of the stick, but the tunnel beyond starts to cave in so I stop. How long can a dog survive without food and water?

'You'll never find um, Doctor.' It's Nobby Warwick again, his rod slung over his back and the cool-box in his hand. 'It's like a rabbit warren down there.'

'That's because it *is* a rabbit warren,' I say, angry at myself and worried sick for the Bobster's safety. There was a time when I wouldn't have minded if she'd made herself scarce, but things are different

286

now. She's important to Matt, so she's important to me.

'I can give you a hand. The Dog and Duck doesn't open for another half an hour. Officially, like. I only goes in there for a pint now and again.'

How can he be thinking about drinking at a time like this? I want to scream at him. 'I thought I'd better stop digging in case the earth falls in on her.'

'Why don't you give it a bit of time? Go home, have a cuppa then come back with a shovel. It's no use digging with a stick. She'll be out the other side of them bushes somewhere. If you're lucky, she'll dig herself out. That's what terriers do, unless she'm been crushed by a load of earth.'

'Thanks for the reassurance, Nobby,' I say with irony.

'Think nothing of it, Doctor.'

'Did you catch anything?'

'Them otters have been here before me again.'

'Have you seen otters down here?'

'They're back this year. It's natural, I suppose, but they don't like sharing.' Nobby shrugs ruefully. 'I'll have to go and tickle some trout on the north side of the Fox-Gifford estate.' He grins, revealing missing teeth. 'Don't go dobbing me in though. Cheers, Dr Chieveley.'

'Goodbye.' I frown as I watch him walk back along the path through the field beside the river. He moves with a shuffling gait, a consequence of the alcohol perhaps, but he covers the ground quickly now he's heading in the direction of the Dog and Duck, just like

Willow does when we're out on a hack and we turn for home.

Eventually I decide to take his advice and walk back in the same direction too, but without the Bobster. I debate whether or not I should contact Matt at work, but decide this is something I need to do face to face. I check my mobile. He's texted to say he'll be back by one, so I have half an hour to worry about what he's going to say.

I walk back through town, picking up a marrowbone from the butcher's, which I take back and stick in front of the hole in the bank, hoping it might tempt the Bobster out. But she doesn't appear and I realise time is running out. I'm going to have to go and fess up to Matt.

At Matt's house, hot and sweating, I take a deep breath and head around the back. He keeps the doors locked but there's a key under the brick beside the water butt. The back door is already open and Matt is lying on the hammock with a glass in his hand.

'Cheers, Nicci,' he says. 'Did you have a good walk?'

'Oh, God, Matt, I'm so sorry. Something terrible's happened.' I stare down at the Bobster's lead. 'I've lost her. I'm soooo sorry. I've been calling her for ages.'

Matt grins.

'It isn't funny. I'm not joking.'

Matt whistles through his teeth and with a yap, the Bobster comes racing up the garden through the rhubarb and forget-me-nots with a fresh marrowbone between her jaws.

'Oh, thank goodness.' I start to cry with relief. 'I didn't think I'd ever say this, but I'm actually pleased to see her.' What's more, she seems pleased to see me, running in circles around my feet with the bone in her mouth, squeaking and whining. The gift of a marrowbone seems to have won the way to her heart.

'She must have made her own way home,' Matt explains. 'She was here when I got back ten minutes ago. I told you she'd do a runner if you let her off.'

'I know and I'm sorry. It won't happen again, I promise.' I pause. 'Don't you have to train her, or something?'

'The Bobster knows her own mind. She does her own thing. I don't want to change her.' Matt grins. 'Okay, that's me being lazy. I probably should, but I don't have the time or inclination. What's that old saying?'

'You can't teach an old dog new tricks.' Wiping my eyes, I smile back. 'Matt, are you free tonight? I could come back after I've been to the yard.'

'Oh, I don't know . . .' He's teasing and I sit down hard beside him on the hammock, making it swing. He slides his arm around my shoulders and kisses me. 'I've got a better idea. Why don't you forget about the horse and the yard and stay here with me?'

'You know why,' I say brightly. 'It's the last one-day event of the season in two weeks' time.'

'And?' he says.

'I want to win it, of course.'

'I wish you didn't.'

'I'm sorry? What did you say?'

'Don't you ever worry? Eventing's a dangerous sport. I don't like you taking part.'

'So you've said, but you won't put me off.'

'I'd really rather you didn't do it.'

'Matt! Don't be silly.'

'I mean it,' he says quietly.

I hold his gaze as he looks into my eyes.

'Last night, you said you loved me, that you loved everything about me, so how can you suddenly change your mind? Eventing is part of my life.'

'Would you give it up for me?' He looks away. 'No, I'm sorry. I can't ask you to do that. Forget I said anything about it.'

I lean back and push my feet against the ground to make the hammock swing again. I'm not sure I can forget. It seems more than a little controlling.

When I go home to change into my riding gear, I find a fat trout left in foil on the doorstep.

'That's a funny present!' Sage exclaims when we unwrap it in the kitchen. 'It's a bit like one of those strange stories about fish falling from the sky.'

I smile to myself. I think it's a bribe from Nobby Warwick in return for my silence. It crosses my mind that I could be accused of handling stolen goods, but no one will find out because we're going to cook and eat the evidence.

'Did you stay with Matt last night?' Sage asks.

'I did, not that it's any of your business,' I say sternly, but Sage clearly thinks it is, because she goes on, 'Are you in love, Nicci?'

'I think so,' I say, not wanting to explain the intricacies of what being 'in love' can mean because it would take too long.

'Good,' she says. 'I like Matt.'

'So do I,' I say. 'So do I.'

Chapter Sixteen

Pride Comes before a Fall

The next two weeks are devoted to preparing for the one-day event at the end of September. Summer gives way to early autumn and the leaves are turning from green to orange, yellow and brown.

Finally the day of the event arrives. I think Willow knows we're running late because she's decided to rub three of the plaits in her mane out on the partition in the lorry on the journey. It's being held at East Hill again, having been moved from another venue because the heavy rain over the past couple of weeks has affected the ground.

I lead her out of the lorry.

'Willow, what have you done, you naughty girl?' I say, when I see the curls in her mane. 'She can't go into the ring like that and we haven't got time to redo them.'

'Don't panic.' Mum is with Sage, who is joining us today to watch me and Willow perform. 'I'll see to Willow.'

'I'll help,' Sage offers. She's dressed in leggings and pink wellies and wearing her hoodie over her head to keep the rain off. It's drizzling at the moment and it looks as if it's set in for the rest of the day.

'You can hold the pot of plaiting bands for me,' Mum says. 'You get changed, Nicci. Hurry up.'

'How long have I got?'

'Half an hour to warm up before your test.'

I shake my head. It isn't long enough. Some horses are ready to compete after ten minutes and some need an hour to settle. Willow needs forty minutes to warm up and get her head straight. Any less and she isn't ready to listen. To make things worse, I don't feel terribly well turned out, because Cheska washed my white jodhpurs with a pair of red socks and I'm wearing my second best pair with the stain on the knee. I tried to buy another pair in Tack n Hack, but they didn't have my size in stock and because I left it too late for Delphi to put the order in, they haven't turned up in time.

I spring up the ladder and through the door into the living quarters of the lorry, which is sparsely furnished with a bench seat with stowaway storage underneath, a sink, microwave and kettle, and toilet cubicle in which there isn't enough room to swing a proverbial cat. I strip off my waterproof trousers and exchange my T-shirt for a shirt and stock. I tie it carefully before securing it with a pin, which I manage to stab into my finger.

I swear under my breath when I notice the blood staining the immaculate white fabric. I run my finger under the tap and grab the last plaster, which is really too small, from the first aid kit. It's going to be one of those days.

'Granma's done the plaits,' Sage says when I emerge from the lorry. 'Willow looks really cool.'

'That's great,' I say.

'What can I do now?' she asks.

'Where are the studs?' Mum interrupts.

'They should be in the spares box.'

'I can't find them.'

'I can't jump without studs,' I say, panicking.

'Sage and I will look for them while you're warming up.'

'The ground's going to be pretty slippery if this rain carries on.' I check the local forecast on my phone. 'Heavy showers with longer spells of rain later.' I look at the sky, at the grey clouds scudding above the hills. I hope the worst of it holds off until after the event.

'Nicci, you have blood on your collar,' Sage observes.

'I had a bit of an accident with the stock-pin.'

'There's another shirt somewhere in the lorry,' Mum says.

'I'll get it,' says Sage.

'No, don't worry. I need to get going.' The butter - flies are having a field day in my stomach, lurching rather than fluttering, because it suddenly occurs to me that I can't remember the dressage test. Sage tested me and I knew it backwards last night, but now . . . ?

'Have you seen the test sheets?' We have a folder of laminated sheets for all the different dressage tests.

'I'll find that too, and bring it over to you.' Mum sighs. 'What would you do without me and Sage?'

'Thanks.' I unbuckle Willow's head-collar that Mum has left over her bridle to keep her tied to the lorry, and lead her across to the ramp, where I check the girth and stirrups before mounting, then I ride her over to the warm-up area. There's no sign of Henry or Shane so far, although I know they're both competing today, and I haven't seen Matt. I tell myself that's a good thing – it means I can concentrate.

Willow is lively, spooking at blades of grass.

'Do you mind?' I sigh. 'I have no wish to end up down there in the mud.'

She isn't listening. She trots an oval when I'm asking her for a circle and sticks her nose in the air when I ask her to flex her neck and come onto the bit. I don't know about her looking like a donkey – at the moment, she feels like one.

'I'm not sure what planet you're on today,' I grumble when she goes from donkey to racehorse in an instant, taking a sideways leap at the sight of a big brown leaf. 'Come on, Willow. Pull yourself together.'

'Having fun, Nicci?' I turn to find Shane riding up beside us on a long-striding bay mare with a coppery sheen to her coat. 'Remember to breathe,' he adds with an encouraging smile. 'Good luck.'

'Same to you,' I say as he passes by.

In spite of an initial hiccup when Willow makes the unilateral decision to head away from the dressage arena instead of towards it when we're first called, the test goes reasonably well. We have a bit of a wobble along the centre line and an early break into canter, but we're back on track. Shane catches up with us again when we head towards the lorry.

'Not bad,' he says.

'It could have been better,' I say, patting Willow's muscular neck.

I walk her around for a few minutes, letting the reins through my fingers to the buckle so she can stretch and relax, while I watch Shane's test from a distance. It isn't often that I get the chance to see him ride, and it's an education.

I return to the lorry where Sage greets Willow with a mint and Mum throws a rug over her back to keep her warm.

'Matt's here,' Sage says.

'He's made himself at home in the lorry – I told him to help himself to coffee.'

'Hi, Nicci.' Matt waves a mug at me. 'Can I get you one?'

'Thanks, but no, I can't face eating or drinking anything.'

'You can see why I don't understand your passion for the sport, if you can call it a sport,' he says. 'What fun is there in being that nervous?'

'I live for the adrenaline rush.'

'Nicci depends on it,' Mum cuts in, then she adds, to my embarrassment, 'mind you, it isn't the only thing that makes her heart beat faster.'

'Mum! Do you have to?' I say as Matt blushes.

'I'm trying to help you relax, love,' she says. 'You seem very tense today. Now, let me look after Willow.

I've found the studs so I'll put them in, and as soon as Shane's done, you can go and walk the course with him.'

Matt jumps down to the ground.

'I'd better be off. Thanks for the coffee.' He moves round and touches my back. 'Good luck, Nicci. I'll catch up with you later.'

I change into a waterproof jacket with 'Team Willow' embroidered across the back, and join Shane to walk the showjumping course.

'It's a tight course,' says Shane. 'You'll have to make sure you keep the rhythm on the corners. And it's kick, kick, kick at the double. It's a bit of a stretch.'

'If she jumps like she did last time, she'll make it with feet to spare.'

'Don't get too cocky. How does it go? Pride comes before a fall.'

'And pain comes after.' I smile at his look of consternation before adding, 'I made that bit up.'

The sun comes out, catching the gleaming coloured poles of the show-jumps. There are a variety of fillers at the base of the fences, cat's eyes, stars and flags, and a skinny – an ultra narrow fence of orange and black flames.

'Be careful at the flames of desire.' Shane is pleased with himself for making that description up. 'You don't want a run out towards the collecting ring. I see lover boy's here – I hope he isn't too much of a distraction.'

'Ha ha,' I say drily.

'Good luck, VB.'

Considering my state of mind, the jumping goes well. Both Shane and I jump clear, and we're first and second with Henry in third place. I'm lying ahead of Shane, but there's less than a penalty between us. No one can afford to make a mistake out on the cross-country course if they're going to maintain their position.

I ride back to the lorry park. Henry's box is parked three down from mine.

'I don't believe it,' Henry says, riding up beside me. 'A jumping donkey!' He backs his horse up, jabbing it in the mouth with one hand on the reins. Willow puts her ears back and swishes her tail. I'm glad I'm not his girlfriend any more, and even happier I'm not one of his horses. 'Behave!' he says, digging it in the ribs with his spurs.

'How's Matt?' he goes on.

'You can ask him. He's about somewhere.'

'You still with him?'

I nod, although it's none of Henry's business.

'Even though Mel's pregnant with his baby, allegedly.'

'There's no "allegedly" about it,' I say, unhappy that Henry has raised a subject that's never far from my mind. I don't need any more reminders.

'Matt's certain then?'

'Henry! You can't help yourself, can you? Stop stirring.' I pause.

'Well, if it ever gets you down and you fancy some fun, no strings attached, you know where I am.'

'Henry, if you were the last man on earth—'

'All right.' He grins. He's weathering badly, his skin is like a fifty-year-old man's. 'It's always worth a try.' He looks past me where Shane is riding up towards us. 'Oh, here's your bit on the side. Hi Shaney, how's it going?'

'Hello, Henry. Good thanks.' Shane asks his horse for a turn on the forehand, effectively pushing Henry out of the conversation.

'I don't know how you managed that dressage score, VB. I reckon the judge is blind.' Shane is ragging me deliberately.

'Ever the graceful loser,' I tease back as Matt turns up too.

'I've just come to wish my girlfriend luck,' he says with a confident smile. He rests his hand briefly on my thigh. 'Take care, Nicci.'

By the time I'm ready to go it's been raining hard for an hour, but the ground is still tolerable, although one or two of the take-offs are getting slippery. I canter Willow over the practice jump. The first time she's hesitant, which isn't like her and I wonder if she's trying to tell me something. I trot her in a couple of circles. Is she sound? I'm not sure. I wonder if I have time to call for Matt – I thought he might have come down to the start to see us off, but he isn't here – but when Willow jumps a second time her blood is up and she flies it with ease.

Deciding that there's nothing to worry about, apart from my overactive imagination, I keep the horse moving while I wait for the starter to call us into the box. I check the fastenings on my air vest and loosen the medic alert band on my arm to allow the blood to circulate, while the rain begins to seep through my jodhpurs and gloves.

'You're next,' calls the starter, and I ride Willow into the start box built from white posts and rails. I wait for the countdown – three, two, one and we're off. I squeeze her sides and she springs forward, taking a confident hold of the bit. I give her a quick pull back to remind her that I'm the one calling the shots and we take up a good steady ground-covering gallop towards the first fence, a big log with advertising sponsor boards on each side, red flag to the right and white to the left, after which we take the broad swing right up the hill between the trees and spectators.

Willow gets into her rhythm and I'm beginning to enjoy it, in spite of the rain in my face and the wind in my ears. Willow makes nothing of the open ditch, the palisade or the bullfinch, jumping bravely through the brush protruding out of the solid base, relying on my assurance that the landing is safe because she can't see it as she approaches.

I pat her neck to thank her before galloping on down the hill, this time to the water jump – a complex of obstacles, arranged around an artificial lake. Remembering my discussions with Shane last night, I take the quicker but trickier line because I'm in this to win it, not to come second or third. I wonder about taking a pull as we're hurtling across the grass towards the log into the water but decide to let Willow go. Unlike some horses, she has no fear of water and she doesn't hesitate.

I count down the strides. 'Three, two—'

Something goes wrong.

Willow loses her footing, sliding towards the base of the log, and for a split second I'm not sure if she's going to stop or go. I hold on tight, throwing her the reins to let her recover herself, which she does, hurling herself over the fence, but she's lost too much momentum and catches one or both hindlegs. I don't know which because we're both falling, me first and Willow second, the horse catching up with me as she topples into the water, so close I can see the flash of iron shoes travel-ling past my eyes as I try to roll myself into a ball, but the air vest's gone off with a pop and I'm like a beached marshmallow.

Willow catches me, crushing my chest and squeezing the breath out of my lungs. Then she's gone and I'm trying to get up and I can see my poor brave horse on her side flailing in the water.

I struggle to grab the reins to help her up, but I'm in agony, hurting all over, my legs are dead and my head is swimming and I just can't get there, but I can see the pain and terror in her eyes and the red flare of her nostrils. I can hear people yelling, and there's someone in the water with me, pulling me out onto the bank.

'I can't breathe,' I gasp.

'Hang on in there, Nicci.' It's Matt's voice, sounding rather distant. 'I'm going to take care of Willow. Don't worry – everything's going to be all right.'

I'm aware of a curtain of rain and tears falling across my eyes.

My beautiful horse hauls herself up with a grunt of

effort onto her feet, but when she moves forward, she can barely touch one of her front feet to the ground. The last thing I remember is her limping away with someone at her side. My cross-country colours are sticking to my limbs and I'm shivering, my teeth chattering uncontrollably, the sound knocking around inside my skull. Someone – I'm not sure who – places a shiny silver survival blanket over me, but I still can't breathe for the pain concentrating in my chest, and the blanket feels so heavy I tear it off.

As soon as I get rid of it, it's back again and my mother's voice, calm but edged with panic, says, 'Keep still, darling. The doctor wants to stabilise your neck before they move you.'

'She's a doctor,' Mum says, 'so she understands what you're saying.'

'I've called for the air ambulance,' someone says. 'It's on its way.'

I feel so stupid and embarrassed, and I can't stop the tears of pain and frustration trickling down my face. They've held the other riders on the course and now everyone has to wait for me because I didn't take a pull on the way into the fence, because I didn't listen to what Willow was saying to me before we set off. I should have withdrawn her from the competition. It wasn't worth risking her neck and mine. I've let Willow down. I've let everyone down.

I overhear anxious voices.

'We need to get the horse out of the way before we can land the helicopter. There isn't time to wait for the horse ambulance and we're worried about its welfare.

We can't force her to walk far on three legs, so we're thinking of getting the screens up.'

My immediate reaction is that they're going to shoot her.

I grab wildly for my mother's arm. Don't let Matt put her down, I try to say, but no sound comes out of my mouth. Mum answers with a weak smile. She doesn't get it, does she? If Willow dies, life will not be worth living.

My heart flutters with panic because I can't communicate with her, with anyone, and I'm beginning to fade from pain and shock and lack of oxygen. I think I'm dying.

I drift in and out of consciousness, high on painkillers, and I have no idea how much time passes until I wake in a bed in a hospital ward with my mother at my side, holding my hand.

'How long?' I mutter.

'Sh, Nicci. You've been here for twenty-four hours.'

'How can that be?' I gaze up at the fluorescent striplights. 'I've lost a whole day.'

'It doesn't matter because you're going to be fine.' Mum purses her mouth. Her face is lined with anxiety and I wish I hadn't put her through this. 'Can you remember what happened?'

'I came off,' I say hesitantly because I'm not sure how much I want to remember. 'Where's Matt?'

'Matt? He's at work, but he'll be here later. I promised I'd let him know as soon as you woke up.'

'I can do that. Where's my mobile?'

'It's in my bag. Just a minute – I'll find it.'

I shift my body to sit myself up, but sharp pain grabs at one side of my chest, making me cry out.

'Here, let me help you.' Mum slides another pillow behind my head and presses a button at the side of my bed, raising the end. I'm, in a ward with three other beds surrounded by grey metal rails from which hang royal blue curtains. To my left is a window with a view of the sky. 'You're going to be all right, darling. You had a knock on the head. You've fractured your collarbone and a couple of ribs, and bruised your spine, but the doctors say you'll make a full recovery.' She gives a small smile.

'How is Willow?'

'Matt's dealing with her.'

'So she's still alive.' I sink back into the pillow. Thank goodness . . . I thought they were going to shoot her.'

Mum reaches for my hand. 'You mustn't worry.'

'I need to know how she is. Is she badly hurt?'

'She's injured her leg, but we don't know how severe the damage is yet.'

'Will she have to be put down?'

'Let's concentrate on getting you better.'

This implies that the horse requires some 'getting better' as well, so there *is* something really wrong. Now I know exactly how frustrating it is when members of the medical profession won't tell you anything.

'Matt will be able to tell you more.' Mum takes my mobile. 'Can I?'

When I nod, another sharp pain sears its way up my

neck. She says she's going to call my sister to let her know how I am.

'You're speaking to Cheska?' I say, surprised.

Mum smiles ruefully. 'I'm speaking to Cheska, but it's all about you. We haven't touched on anything else, but it's a start.' Her voice is filled with an expectation that I hope is not misplaced. 'Maybe there really is a silver lining to every cloud. Perhaps this will bring us together and I'll have my other daughter and my grandchildren back.' She pauses. 'Oh, it's too soon to be dreaming about that. Nicci, you being here is enough.' She nods towards the entrance to the ward where a man is trying to get through the door with an enormous bouquet of flowers. 'I'll leave you two to it.'

'Nicci. Thank God.' Matt leans down and kisses me on the cheek, puts the flowers on one of the chairs beside the bed and sits down on the other. He looks exhausted, his cheeks hollow and dark shadows beneath his eyes, but my heart lifts and my aches and pains diminish – he's more effective than any pain - killer. However, his presence has a side effect – it reminds me of my horse.

'Matt, how's Willow?'

'Hey, first things first. How are you?'

'I'll feel a lot better when someone – i.e. you—' I prod him lightly in the arm '—tells me how my horse is, because I'm really scared that something terrible has happened to her.'

'Well, like you, she's in hospital. Don't worry, I've made sure she has the best stable in the yard, a room with a view.'

'So she's alive?'

'I can categorically state that when I last saw her thirty minutes ago, she was on her feet. I can prove it,' he says. He pulls out his mobile phone and shows me a picture of Willow in a stable with the deepest bed of shavings I've ever seen. She's wearing a stable rug and picking at hay in a net.

'But? There is a but,' I say, gazing at the massive bandage on Willow's front leg.

Matt nods. 'She's torn a tendon, so I've put the Robert Jones dressing on to give her some support and discourage her from using the limb too much while we decide what to do.'

'Which tendon is it?'

'One of the tendons in the back of her lower leg.'

'You don't have to dumb it down for me.'

'All right, it's a significant tear in the DDF, deep digital flexor tendon.'

'Did it happen when she fell, or could she have had the beginnings of a tear before? I thought she was slightly off on the right fore in the warm-up area, but I ignored it.'

'We'll never know for sure, but yes, it is possible. I thought the organisers should have stopped the event. I know they were under pressure, but it's too much of a risk with the ground as it was. They could at least have taken the water jump out – the approach was getting pretty boggy by the time you were on the course.' Matt pauses. 'I didn't want you to set out in the first place, rain or no rain.'

'If I'd listened to what she was telling me and if I

hadn't pushed her, she might have been all right.'

'It's no use beating yourself up. It's a pointless argument.' Matt strokes my hand. 'Anyway, we'll talk about the options for Willow later. You need to rest.'

'I can't rest if I'm worrying about her. I thought you might have—' My lip trembles and I can no longer speak.

Matt smiles softly. 'I can't put her down, can I, not without the owner's permission.'

'Please . . .'

Matt gives in and tells me the options.

'Either we don't treat her at all . . .'

'And she's put down.'

'That's one possibility, unless you turn her out as field companion or potential brood mare.'

'She'd be bored stiff,' I say, trying to imagine my clever horse mooching around a paddock for the rest of her life.

'What I'd suggest is that we try the stem cell route of repair.'

'You'd better tell me a bit more about it before I give you permission to experiment on my horse.'

'It isn't an experiment – this therapy's been used with good results for a while now. We've had three horses at the hospital do very well with it. Anyway, if you let the injury heal naturally, you'll be left with scarring and a weakened tendon. If we intervene we can make the injury heal better, though not necessarily more quickly. I've scanned the leg and put her on box rest.'

'Bed rest for horses,' I say. 'For how long?'

'Full healing takes up to eighteen months.'

'Okay, where do these stem cells come from?'

'I can extract the cells from Willow's bone marrow, under sedation, from her breastbone. It's straightforward but as with everything, there are risks.'

'And then what?'

'I send the sample off to one of the stem cell labs, and they'll grow them before returning them to me to implant into the damaged tendon. Then Willow goes into rehab for twelve months, the aim being to get her back into full work. Simples.'

'You make it sound so easy, but I can't see Willow surviving three months on box rest. She'll hate it, and she'll go ballistic when I turn her out.'

'We'll sedate her for that too,' Matt says.

I can see that he's itching to go ahead with the treatment. It's Willow's best chance of returning to fitness.

'I need to think about her long-term welfare. If it fails, will I have put her through a lot of pain and suffering and confinement in a stable for nothing?'

'That I can't tell you,' he says gravely, stroking his chin. 'As with everything in life, there are no guarantees.'

'So, what does my vet recommend?'

'Willow's your horse. It has to be your decision.'

I think for a moment. When it comes down to it, there is no decision to be made. I'll do anything to get Willow better. I owe it to her. I put her into this situation, so it's up to me to try and make things right.

'Where there's life,' I say. 'Let's go for it.'

'That's great. If you're willing to bear the cost of the therapy, I won't charge you for the investigations and hospitalisation.'

'I can't let you do that. She's my horse.'

'And you're my girlfriend, I hope, unless that fall made you see sense.' He chuckles. He doesn't mean it. 'And it's my practice.'

'Can you stem cell me?' I ask.

'I can give you a hug,' he offers.

It's one of those occasions where a saying rings true: love hurts, but to feel his arms around me, to know I'm alive, is bliss.

'I don't like hospitals even though I have one of my own,' he observes.

'No one does, do they?'

'I said I'd bring your sister and the children in to see you later.'

'That would be nice, but I'm expecting to go home very soon.'

'Hey, there's no rush.'

'I need to get back to work.'

'Ben's organising a locum for as long as it takes, while you concentrate on getting yourself better. I thought you . . . when you were lying there so still . . .' His voice breaks and my chest tightens with guilt and compassion.

He kisses me again and again. 'I thought I'd lost you. I've never been so scared in my life.'

To my surprise I feel tears warm and wet against my cheek, Matt's tears.

'Matt, you're crying. I'm sorry, I didn't realise . . .'

I don't know what to do and I haven't a clue how to console him. Gradually, he regains his self-control and pulls away from me, keeping his hands on mine.

'You remember you once asked me if I'd ever been engaged?'

'Yes . . .'

'The girl I proposed to – I met her at vet school.'

'The one who turned you down?'

He nods and bites his lip.

'And?' I go on.

'She was a brilliant rider, tipped for a place in the British eventing team. Anyway, she was riding her horse cross-country one day. She fell.'

From his expression, I don't need to ask what happened. I reach out my arms to hold him, but the pain is too much. I can't reach him because of my fractured bones, and he is unreachable anyway, in a place long ago and far away.

'It was the worst day of my life.' He grimaces as he explains what happened to the girl, the love of his life. 'There are times when I never want to see another horse again.'

'I didn't realise. You never talked about it.'

'I thought it would make you feel insecure. You were jealous of Mel.'

'It's only because I feel so strongly about you, Matt. I'm so sorry for what I've put you through.' I reach out gingerly for his hand and stroke his fingers. 'It won't happen again. It was a combination of circumstances – the weather, the ground, the horse and most of all, my riding . . .'

'Let's look forward, not back,' Matt says.

'Thank you for the flowers. They're beautiful.'

'Just like you,' he says gently.

Over the next forty-eight hours, I have a constant stream of visitors bearing cards and gifts. The nurses are always asking with ironic smiles if anyone can read the sign detailing visiting hours and the limit on the number of visitors per bed at any one time, but they bend the rules for Matt because he's a vet, he's charming and he's hot, depending on which nurse you talk to.

It does make me feel better, knowing people are thinking of me, even if their sentiments are rather confusing. For example, Steve seems to think he's cheering me up when he tells me in a sombre tone, as if I'm not out of the woods yet, that you never know when your number's up.

'Thanks for the gift,' I say, staring at a bunch of grapes so shiny and perfect they look like stage props. 'Are you sure those are real?'

'Of course they are. Only the best for my doctor,' he says.

Claire drops by with a cider cake from Jennie's and tells me not to worry about work because they have a lovely locum.

'You won't need me any more,' I say.

'The locum doesn't eat cake. You should hear her going on at us about healthy eating. There's only so much we can take. We can't wait to have you back.'

'It's going to be at least a couple of weeks.'

'Ben says six.'

'I'm negotiating. It depends how I feel and how quickly my bones heal.'

'What does Matt think about that? I bet he isn't happy.'

'He'd rather lock me up in a box – he's very protective.' Why did I say that? It dawns on me that it's something I feel uncomfortable about. He's fun and strong-willed, and I know he wants what's best for me, but I'm starting to wonder if what he thinks is best is quite different from what I think is best. It's a tiny niggle, like the twinge of a sensitive tooth. I try to forget about it.

'Hey, Nicci, your boyfriend's back,' one of the nurses calls from the ward entrance.

'I'll go,' says Claire.

'You can stay.'

'Two's company. See you soon, Nicci.'

'Thanks, Claire.'

'By the way, I forgot to tell you – the Browns have been assessed as eligible for a carer to pop in twice daily to help get Mrs Brown bathed and dressed, and to put her to bed.'

'That's great. When does that start?'

'Next week, I think.'

There is an awful lot of simpering from the nurses whenever Matt makes an appearance. He always arrives bearing gifts, a bouquet of flowers from Petals or boxes of clotted cream fudge, which I surreptitiously share with the nurses, so I don't end up with a rump like a horse.

Wincing, I haul myself up to a sitting position and run my fingers through my hair to make myself half decent. It doesn't work. I feel wrecked. Matt pulls a chair close to the bed.

'You don't have to do that for my benefit.' He's teasing and my reaction is to laugh, but the pain cuts me short.

'Please don't.' I breathe. Laughter is supposed to be the best medicine, but it really hurts.

'How are you today?' Matt asks.

'Not so bad. In fact, I'm ready to go home. They've said tomorrow.'

'That's great. I'll take you home – you can come to mine and I'll look after you. Please, Nicci, it's perfect,' he goes on when I hesitate. 'I can help you out—' my skin tingles at the sound of his husky whisper '—do the things you can't, like scrub your back.'

'Matt, it's a lovely offer, especially the back scrub, and I'd love to show you my bruises in return,' I tell him, 'but seriously, I don't want you to see me in the mornings all grumpy because I'm incapacitated and unable to ride. I get a bit cranky if I can't get out on the horse.'

'Well, you won't be riding for a while.'

'I know,' I sigh. 'But as soon as my injuries heal, or maybe a bit before, I'll be back in the saddle.'

'Now who's disobeying doctor's orders? Really, Nicci.'

I'm chuckling, but sober up quickly when I realise Matt's serious.

'Matt, I'm not stupid. You know, Delphi rode when her arm was in plaster.'

313

'I hope you told her off.'

'It was way before I qualified as a doctor. She's amazing. She can ride most horses without reins or a saddle.'

'Delphi's mad,' Matt says, 'and you're as bad. Promise me you won't get back in the saddle too soon. Promise,' he repeats.

'I promise,' I say eventually, more to shut him up than anything.

He kisses me. 'I'll see you later. I can sneak back in after hours. You don't mind, do you, Carly?' he says to one of the nurses passing by with a tray of medications.

'I didn't hear any of that, Matt,' she says, her face glowing.

He leaves as Mum turns up with Sage.

'This is for you,' Sage says handing me a card with a drawing of me – I can tell because she's dressed me in my cross-country colours – and Willow jumping a fence.

It reads, 'To Nicci and Willow, get well soon. Lots of love from Sage x'

I turn away, choked up and put it on the shelf behind me, wincing as I turn back. 'I shouldn't have done that.'

'Does it hurt a lot?'

'It's getting better. That card is lovely, Sage. Thank you.'

'Granma says that seven falls make a rider.'

'That's what they say. I must have come off more like seventy times since I started riding.'

Sage's eyebrows shoot upwards. 'Then it isn't right,' she says.

'Possibly not,' I agree.

'You've fallen off a lot.'

'It isn't entirely surprising – I've spent many hours in the saddle.'

'And a lot of time out of it,' Sage says chuckling. 'Auntie Nicci, are you a good rider or not?'

'I'm okay, but there's always room for improvement.' I pause. 'I hope it hasn't put you off riding.'

'No way,' she exclaims. 'I want to go cross-country one day.' She changes the subject. 'When do you come out of hospital?'

'Tomorrow, I hope,' I say, at which Mum also offers to collect me and take me home.

'It's all right,' I say. 'Matt's coming to get me.'

'Oh? Is he taking you home with him?'

'He's dropping me back to the house.' I notice I don't refer to it as my house any more. Matt can't look after me because he's at work. Cheska's going to help me out. I don't want to become too dependent on Matt and I don't think drifting into living with someone is a great idea. I want to move in when we both choose, not because of circumstances, even if Matt does see it as a great opportunity to try and persuade me to live with him.

Chapter Seventeen

Bits and Pieces

A few days later Delphi drives the lorry to collect Willow from the hospital. I'm not allowed to drive yet, which is ridiculous because I'm sure I can manage, even with a fractured collarbone. The lorry has power steering, after all. And Ben is happy for me to start work again soon with some half days, proving that my condition isn't that bad.

Delphi parks the lorry, saying she'll wait while I go and fetch the horse.

When I look over the stable door, Willow whinnies in recognition. Matt is in there too, running his hands down her legs while Mel holds her on a head-collar. Mel's padded jacket fails to hide her pregnancy.

'Hello,' I say, over the moon to see my horse again, but a little unnerved to see Matt and Mel together.

'Hi, darling,' Matt says, looking up. 'She's ready to go.' He walks across and kisses me, and I'm aware of Mel's sharp intake of breath. I glance past his shoulder. Mel's eyes glint from the shadows as she bites her lip.

Matt turns. 'Would you mind taking her over to the lorry while I have a word with Nicci about aftercare?'

'Yes, I do mind,' Mel says. 'I'm not here to look after your girlfriend's horse.' She throws down the end of the lead-rope, making Willow start. 'Do it yourself.'

'Mel!' Matt exclaims. 'Don't get upset. Think about the baby.'

'What about the baby?' she says bitterly.

'Our child,' Matt continues, frowning.

'Oh for goodness sake, it isn't your baby, Matt.'

He steps back, his eyes wide with shock.

'It isn't yours,' she repeats.

'How?' His fists curl with anger and distress and I open the door, wanting to comfort him, but he pushes me away. 'Tell me how that can be.'

He doesn't believe her, I think, but I recall what Henry said about the baby allegedly being Matt's, a statement which, looking back, implied an element of doubt, and I remember how Matt said the baby was small for its dates at the scan.

'I made a mistake.'

'There was someone else? After all you've said about the way you feel about me?'

'When you ended it, I was shattered,' she sobs. 'I had a stupid one-night stand and I slept with somebody else.'

'Who?' Matt growls. 'No, don't tell me. It doesn't matter. I don't want or need to know.' He pauses. 'Why did you do it?'

317

'I hoped you'd come back to me,' she stammers. 'I love you, Matt.'

'This isn't love. It's bloody madness.'

Mel's face loses all its colour, she looks devastated. Then pushes past him and makes her way across the stable yard. I stand, gazing at my poor boyfriend, who looks pale and confused.

'Are you okay?' I ask him gently.

'I'm not sure.' The muscle in his cheek tautens and relaxes. 'I've just got used to the idea that I'm going to be a dad. I've been dreaming about the child, imagining how he or she would grow up, who they were going to look like . . .' He swears. 'I can't believe she carried the pretence on for so long.'

I hear a door slam.

'Do you think someone should be with her?' I say tentatively.

He sighs. 'I'll get one of the nurses to make sure she's all right.' He touches my back and I turn to give him a hug. 'I'm sorry.'

So am I, I think. I feel sorry for Matt and although I'm furious with her, there is a small part of me that feels some sympathy for Mel. She needs help and support, not blame.

'I've got a couple of visits to make,' he says eventually. 'Can I come over later?'

'Course you can,' I say. 'Whenever you like.'

He says goodbye, and I rescue Willow, who's standing at the end of the stable, flicking her ears back and forth and showing the whites of her eyes. She doesn't like confrontation. It makes her nervous.

318

'Come on, girl.' I pick up the end of the lead-rope. 'Let's get you home.'

I'm so pleased to see Willow back at the yard that I spend the rest of the afternoon and long into the evening with her, fortifying myself with hot chocolate and crisps, and promising myself I will return to a healthy diet when I'm better. After I left the hospital I visited her every day at Westleigh, and I cried every time to see her being so stoic about her situation, confined to a loosebox, and the treatment that caused her some distress, in spite of the painkillers Matt gave her.

Once everyone has disappeared home, fog drifts in from the sea as dusk falls. I redo Willow's stable bandages – I'm not sure how much they aid healing, but it makes me feel better. I pick out her feet, remove the droppings from her stable and refill her hay net, and then I sit in the corner on an upturned bucket, watching and listening to her munching contentedly on her hay.

I hear the sound of a car and Dark Star next door shifts around his box as Matt appears at the stable door.

'I guessed I'd find you here,' he says smiling ruefully. 'There was no one at home.'

'My sister was taking the kids out for tea to an old schoolfriend of hers she met at Sage's new school.' I pause. 'How are you?'

'After Mel's revelation, you mean?' He runs his hands through his hair. 'It's a weight off my mind. How about you?'

'The same. I can't forgive her for what she did, but I'm relieved she came clean in the end.' I move over to the door as Matt opens it for me.

'I wish I was your horse,' he says. 'You can scratch my withers any time.'

'Thank you for saving her life,' I say.

He takes me by the hand and pulls me to him for a kiss and a bear hug.

'Your nose is cold,' I giggle. He's dressed for the weather in boots, a big coat, and cords, and smells of musk and horse and surgical scrub.

'We could go and get passionate in the barn,' he suggests.

'We can't,' I say, relieved that it's impossible. 'It's filled top to bottom with hay and straw for the winter.'

'Come back to mine then.'

'Aren't you on call? I don't want to wake up and find a cold empty space in the bed, like the other night . . .'

'Not tonight,' he says.

Willow nudges him in the elbow.

'You aren't invited.' Matt laughs. 'I don't want to snog a horse, thanks.'

'At least she likes you,' I say, thinking of the Bobster.

I interlink my fingers at the back of Matt's neck.

'When do you think I'll be able to ride her again?'

He shrugs. 'I've told you before, darling, I don't know.'

'And there I was, under the illusion you'd have an informed opinion.'

'Don't rush it.' He strokes the side of my face, and I

feel the slight catch of roughened skin against my cheek. 'Nicci, you do understand that she might . . .'

'Never come sound,' I finish for him. 'I don't want to think about that until it happens. It might not, after all, so there's no point in fretting about it.'

'That's true,' he says, deep in thought, 'but you have to be prepared. Have you trotted her up since you got her home?'

'I'm too scared to.'

'Let's run her up now – I'll give you a free consultation.'

I put a bridle on Willow, in case she's too feisty to hold in a head-collar, and trot her up under the yard lights outside.

'Nice haunches,' he says brightly.

'Hey, keep your eyes on the horse,' I say. 'What do you think?'

'She's two tenths lame, which is pretty amazing, considering. We might see a deterioration when we turn her out.'

'I wonder if I shouldn't start looking for another horse.'

Matt takes a half step back. 'You can't replace Willow.'

'I'm not talking about replacing her. I'm suggesting bringing a younger horse on while I'm waiting to see if she can come back into work. I can't afford an eventer that's already fit and ready to go, but I could buy a youngster or a horse that needs some work.'

'That's crazy,' he says. 'You'll have two horses on livery and I'll never see you. And what will you do if

Willow does go sound? You wouldn't be able to let one of them go.'

'You could hack out with me.'

'No way. I've told you before, you'll never get me into the saddle.' Matt is serious, his expression dark in the shadows cast by the dim yard lights. 'I will never ride,' Matt repeats, 'and I would really prefer you not to,' he adds very quietly.

'Are you saying you don't want me to ride again?' I'm shocked. I've been worrying about whether I'll be able to ride at all, and the effect of any psychological scars, and expecting Matt to support me through the challenges of getting back in the saddle, yet here he is saying he wants me to stop. He's hinted at it before, but he's never said it outright like this.

'I don't mean altogether,' he says. 'I mean, I'd be happier if you didn't compete again.'

'That makes me feel really uncomfortable.'

'I'm thinking of your safety.'

'But it comes across as if you're trying to control me,' I argue. 'Eventing is part of who I am. If I didn't compete, I wouldn't be me any more.' A lump of emotion catches in my throat. 'If you're trying to change someone, it means you don't want them the way they are.'

'I want you the way you are – just without this obsession you have with the eventing.'

'I'm not obsessed,' I cut in. 'It's perfectly normal for people to have interests and hobbies. You have your bees, and they aren't exactly the safest things to deal with, are they?'

'It's different,' he says, but I can't see how. 'You must

promise me that you won't ride until you're fully recovered from the fall, and then you'll think about whether or not you go on to compete again in the future.'

'I won't ride until I'm better,' I say grudgingly, 'but I can't promise to stop eventing. I can't do that.'

'Nicci, let's forget it for now. I'm shattered and you look completely exhausted,' he says, changing the subject. 'Let me drive you home.'

'Thanks, Matt. I was going to ask Delphi.'

I put Willow to bed, then Matt takes me by the hand and we walk to his car through sweeping waves of fog, and I wonder if the conversation is closed for good, or whether it will resurface in the future.

'Can I get you a cup of tea?' Sage asks a few days later when I'm curled up on the sofa with my arm in a sling – Matt was right about slings being a nuisance – and my Kindle in my free hand. I also have a stack of books on the coffee table alongside me, a packet of pain - killers and a glass of water. It's frustrating not being able to do very much, apart from stare at daytime TV or read.

'That would be lovely, thank you.'

'Would you like a biscuit too? If there are any left,' she adds with a sparkle of humour.

'Yes please.'

'Jammie Dodger or Jaffa Cake?'

'You choose.'

'I'll bring one of each.'

I watch her heading out of the door. I love the idea of being nursed, but Sage takes it to extremes. She's like a little mother rather than a child, while my sister . . . she's immature, like a teenager. For weeks, she's been hanging around the house like a wet weekend. I'm sure she's depressed, but she won't admit it, not to me, or more importantly, to herself.

'Haven't you got homework?' I call after Sage, who has been at the local school for half a term now.

'Yes,' she calls back.

'Don't put off the evil moment for too long.'

Cheska joins me briefly.

'Can I ask you a favour?' I say. I'm not sure why when it's my house. 'Two favours actually.'

'What's the third?' she says, looking out of the window – I sometimes wonder if the sight of the graves makes her depressed. 'There's bound to be a third one.'

'I don't want to come across as a nag, but I'd prefer it if you didn't leave your underwear all over the house.'

'It isn't hurting anyone,' she says.

'I don't like Matt seeing it.'

'It isn't as nice as yours.'

'Exactly, so he might think it's mine and I really don't want that.'

'What's wrong with that? Everyone wears under - wear,' Cheska giggles suddenly, 'except when they go commando.'

'It's all skanky and old,' I say, being mean.

'We can't all afford Ultimo and Victoria's Secret.'

'Yes, because some of us have jobs,' I say, rounding on her crossly. 'Just don't leave your pants all over the house when Matt comes over, and promise me you won't go commando. Talyton St George isn't ready for that.'

'You're such a prude, Nicci.'

'Am I?' I touch my throat.

'You really need to learn to let yourself go.'

She's making me feel insecure. Am I really that inhibited?

'Is Matt coming round this evening?' She turns and smiles at me. 'That's the other favour, isn't it – you want me to make myself scarce?'

'For a couple of hours, that's all. He'll be round at seven-thirty and I'd appreciate being able to sit here with him and enjoy a quiet meal, just the two of us.' My mood lifts at the thought. 'This is like living in a student house, having to negotiate arrangements for guests. By the way, have you seen my top, the White Stuff one with the tie at the front?'

'Oh?' Cheska touches her lip. 'I might have put it in the washing basket. I borrowed it the other day, but I knew you wouldn't mind because you said to help myself to anything I need.'

'I was going to wear it tonight.' I want him to hold me close, ribs and collarbone permitting, and kiss me and make me forget the rest of the world.

Matt arrives early because he had to put his last patient to sleep.

'It was too late. By the time the horse arrived at the hospital, it had a strangulated bowel and raging peritonitis.' He frowns and then says, 'I've got the Bobster in the car. Do you mind?'

325

'Bring her in,' I say.

Matt and I settle on the sofa with cold drinks and nibbles of chopped peppers, sun-dried tomatoes, hummus and pitta bread. The Bobster sits at the coffee table, drooling and inhaling deeply as if imagining she could suck the food across the table and into her mouth.

'We need to talk about Christmas,' I say.

'Do we?' Matt gazes at his mobile, clearly hoping it will ring and save him from this discussion. 'Now?'

'Matt, if we don't discuss it now, it'll be the New Year before you know it.'

'You aren't one of those ghastly control freaks who wants to plan everything down to the very last detail?'

'You've seen my "to do" lists. What do you think? At least I'm organised, unlike someone else around here I could mention.'

'Spontaneity is good,' he says, moving so close I can sense the thrilling caress of his breath against my neck and his hands finding the curve of my waist. 'Life would be pretty dull if you had it all planned.' He pulls me against him. 'Do you fancy doing something spontaneous right now? After we've talked about our plans for Christmas, that is . . .'

'Of course I do, but my sister . . .' I glance up at the ceiling.

'Shame,' he murmurs.

'I'm off over Christmas and working for much of the New Year. How about you?'

'The same,' he says. 'We could spend Christmas Day together, unless you have plans to be with your family.'

'I think I can do a bit of both.' It's going to be a

difficult time unless my mother and sister can bury the hatchet before the festive season. Is there any chance that they will? 'When will you see your family?' I ask.

'I'll drive across to see them on Boxing Day for a second Christmas dinner. Come with me – if you want to, that is. They'd love to meet you.'

'I'd love to meet them,' I say.

'Have you seen—' Cheska stops abruptly in the doorway, dressed only in a bra and tiny pants. 'I'm sorry, I didn't hear you come in. I thought you were coming at seven-thirty.' She carries on oblivious to both my embarrassment and Matt's discomfort. Being a gentleman, he looks studiously at my sister's face, rather than the obvious attributes she's parading in front of him. 'I can't find my pink top.'

'It will be on a radiator somewhere,' I say.

'Not in here. I'll go and look elsewhere.' Cheska smiles. 'Don't mind me.'

'We won't,' I say, but I do mind. 'She could at least have thrown a towel around her before turning up semi-naked,' I say to Matt when she's gone. 'Cheska says I sound like a prude.'

'I guess you wouldn't feel so insecure if your sister didn't have such a cute body,' he says.

'I'm sorry.' I stare him straight in the eye.

'Your sister has a lovely figure.'

'Matt!'

His lips curve into a smile.

'It's all right. I was trying not to look.' He pulls me close again. 'Have no fear. It isn't a patch on yours. You have the hottest body I've ever laid my hands on,' he continues. 'And no, I'd never consider laying my hands on your sister. And I wish I'd never started on this because I can see your mind is running riot. It's you I want, Nicci. I love you.'

'This is going to cost you. You're going to have to take me out for dinner to make up for it.' I'm teasing now because I do believe him when he says he has no designs on my sister.

I tackle my sister in the morning to check that she has no designs on my boyfriend.

'I hope you weren't coming on to Matt last night,' I say to her over breakfast.

'He isn't my type,' she says. 'He's just too nice.'

'I'm not sure I believe you, Cheska. In fact, I've had enough of you swanning about the house and failing to contribute anything financially or otherwise.' I pick up the carton of orange juice Cheska's left out on the breakfast bar to pour myself a drink, but there's only a small splash left. 'You have two lovely kids, but you won't take any responsibility for them.'

'That isn't fair,' she says, accusingly. 'I love them.'

'Who took Sage to look at the school? Who bought her uniform?'

'You didn't have to do all that. You just took over.'

'Because I see what needs to be done and I get on with it, whereas you – you don't do anything. You won't look for a job. You won't make any attempt to mend bridges with Mum. And when you condescend to do any chores, you make a mess of them.'

'I wish you'd chill a bit, Nicci,' she says, rounding on

me. 'You really should take up drinking and let your hair down. You're so uptight.'

'But I'm in control of my life,' I say, hurt.

'Exactly. You never ever let go of anything. You're like a bloody robot. We're only here because you look at me as some kind of charity case, someone to put right and do the right thing by.'

'That is complete rubbish and you know it.' I'm furious at the injustice of her comment. 'If you don't like it, you know what you can do,' I say, in tears. 'You can pack your things and leave.'

I've calmed down a little by the next morning and I assume that our bust-up will soon blow over. When I leave home for my first half day back at work, Sage is up, pattering barefoot around the kitchen. Cheska is in the shower and I'm assuming Gabriel's still in bed. I'm tempted to go and stand at his bedside, whining and pulling at his covers, as he did to me last night. It's no wonder he's tired.

'I'll see you later,' I say to Sage. 'Have a good day at school.'

'I'm not going. It's an inset day when the teachers have training to remind them how to do their job.'

'I'd better go and do mine.'

'Before you forget how to do it,' Sage says with a cheeky grin.

Realising that they'll all be home at lunchtime, I call in bringing fresh bread, cheese and some apples, but to my confusion, I open the front door to find my sister sitting astride a suitcase, squashing the lid down while she instructs Sage on how to fasten it so it stays shut, a feat that involves a length of rope and some baling twine from the yard. Gabriel is watching, his teddy bear hanging upside down from his hand.

'Where are you going?' I ask.

'Nicci?' My sister looks up, her face flushed. 'I thought you were at work—'

'I thought I'd join you for lunch.'

'Oh?'

'You're leaving?'

'That's what you want, isn't it?'

'And you were going to sneak away without letting me know.' A sharp pain cuts across my heart like a knife. 'How could you? How could you just disappear without telling me where you're going, or giving me the chance to say goodbye?'

'But Mum, you said—' Sage cuts in.

'I know what I said, thank you.'

'You can't go today. I've booked another riding lesson for Sage.' I'm not sure which of us is looking forward to it the most, and Matt's going to drop us at the yard and Delphi's offered to give us a lift back. 'It's all organised.'

I hand the bag of food to Sage, telling her to take it into the kitchen.

'Gabriel, you help Sage with the lunch. Mummy and I need to talk.' My sister follows me meekly into the garden and down to the end. 'After all I've done for you this had better be good.'

'You're right,' she begins. 'I'm perfectly able to

stand on my own two feet, and you and Matt don't need us getting in the way. I feel like a bloody gooseberry living in this house, so what I've decided is to move out and find somewhere else to live with the kids.'

'Yes, but where?'

'I don't know yet,' she responds, smiling as if she doesn't have a care in the world.

'I don't understand. How can you leave with the children if you have nowhere to go?'

'I'll find somewhere. There are rooms to rent advertised in the newsagent's window, and there's the B&B at Barton Farm, or if we get really stuck, I can ask at the caravan park.' She sounds rational, yet there is a hint of mania in her responses.

'It's the end of the season – the caravan park is closing.'

'I'm going to ask about the rooms first.'

'You can't have three of you in one room.'

'Why are you being so negative?'

'I'm not. It's you, being over-optimistic.' I pause. 'You can't move out without finding somewhere to go first.'

'That isn't the way I operate.'

'I realise that. What about staying at Mum's? She has loads of spare room.'

'You are joking?'

'This might not be the right time to mention it, but that stuff about the abortion. Mum's really sorry.'

'I don't care.'

'Well, you should,' I say bluntly. 'She loves Sage and

Gabriel, and she regrets trying to force you into having a termination. It isn't because she hated you. It's because she thought it was best for you, her daughter.'

Cheska opens her mouth to argue, but I flash her a warning look.

'Let me finish. She didn't see how you could cope alone with a baby at sixteen.'

'I wasn't alone. I was with Sage's dad.' Cheska's lips tremble at the memory. 'Mum always hated him. She's so bloody prejudiced.'

'With good reason. He left you.'

'That was a long time after Sage was born. We were together for three years before everything fell apart.'

'He went to prison for theft and GBH.'

'He was set up,' Cheska insists.

I'm beginning to lose patience with my crazy little sister, but I keep my cool because I don't want to drive her away.

'Look, let's forget the past and concentrate on now. For the children's sake, unpack your bags and wait here until I get back tonight. I'll have a chat with one or two people who might know of a house to rent around here, and then we can talk again. I'm not having you living in a single room. Promise me you'll wait. Don't go and do one of your disappearing acts.' I pause. 'Cheska, I need you to promise?'

She starts rambling, talking as if she's invincible. I recognise her mood, the excitement in her voice, the glint in her eyes and the mania.

'I don't need you to help me out, Nicci. I don't need anyone.'

I wonder now if Alan couldn't cope with Cheska's behaviour, her ups and downs. To be honest, she's like a hand grenade – you never know when she's going to blow up.

'Listen, I've got to get back to work in half an hour. Make sure you're here when I get home. Even if you're still intent on leaving, give it one more day. Don't rush off without saying goodbye.' I can feel my face crumple. 'I thought you were going to stay.'

'I really don't want to hang around now I've made my mind up,' she says.

Sage joins us in the garden. I'm sure she's listened to every word. She has the ears of a bat and the memory of an elephant.

'I wanna stay another night, Mummy, because I have to say goodbye to Harry and Willow,' she says quietly, her voice wavering. 'Do we have to go? Only I'm going to miss them sooooo much. And Auntie Nicci,' she puts her hand into mine. 'And school. And Granma. I like it here.'

My heart is breaking for her and myself. I'll miss them too. I'll miss the chaos and the noise, *Peppa Pig* and the graffiti on the walls.

'Please, Mummy. Can we stay just one more day?'

'I'll see, darling.' Cheska glances wildly around at the luggage as if she's looking at it but not registering it in her brain. 'We really should go.'

Sage folds her arms across her chest. Her chin juts forwards.

'I'm not going with you,' she says icily. 'I'm staying with Auntie Nicci.'

'You can't.'

'I want Nicci to be my Mummy from now on.' Sage stamps her foot. 'You can do what you like. You're fired.'

Cheska looks at me and I look at her, and suddenly the mood lifts.

'Who do you think I am, your apprentice?' She giggles. 'You can't fire your mother. It's impossible. Whether you like it or not, Sage, you're stuck with me.'

Cheska's words sober me. If I let her run off, it's Sage and Gabriel who will suffer. It's past time that I spoke to my sister about her erratic behaviour. I send the children out to buy milk and sweets, and sit her down for one of the most – no, *the* most difficult consultation of my life. I've thought about how I should broach the subject and whether I should act with tact or go for the blunt approach, but when it comes down to it, I just blurt it out.

'Cheska, have you ever considered that you might be bipolar?'

'What do you mean? That I'm mad?'

'What I'm saying is that you have all the signs of bipolar disorder.' She's frowning as I continue, 'You've always been impulsive, and sometimes you're sociable and upbeat, and other times you hide away and I don't hear from you for months. I'm not criticising or attacking you. I want to help. It's important for you and the children that you're well.'

'I'm not ill.' She swears. 'Really, Nicci, you've been reading too many medical textbooks.'

'I'm a doctor. That's what I do.'

334

'Well, there's no need to use me as a guinea pig. Go and practise on someone else.'

'I can't diagnose or treat you because I'm family. What I'm suggesting is that you register with Ben, the other doctor at the practice. He can talk you through it and refer you on to the right people, if it's necessary.'

'Are you doing this because you want me to be seen leading a normal, respectable, boring middle-class life?'

'Of course not, although I'm pretty sure that's the sort of life you are leading right at this moment, seeing as you're living with me, your normal, vaguely respectable, boring middle-class sister.'

'You aren't normal,' she says, sitting on the lawn plucking at the grass.

'Thanks a lot.'

'I don't mean you're mad,' she says. 'You're extraordinary.' She pauses, biting her lip. 'Nicci, there are times when I think I'm losing my mind.'

'So, you will see Ben?'

'Don't push it.' She stands up and brushes grass from her skirt.

'It's nothing to be ashamed of, Cheska.'

'I don't want to be labelled. I won't be able to get a job.'

'If you are bipolar, you can have treatment—'

'I'm not taking mind-altering drugs,' she interrupts. 'And I don't want talking therapy. I want to be me.'

'It won't change you. All it will do is smooth out the ups and the downs and make everything easier to cope with.'

'I shan't take anything, so there's no point in going to the doctor.'

'You are a very stubborn patient.' I start picking up half-empty glasses of squash, tipping out the wasps taking advantage of the unseasonable October weather. 'I'll leave it with you then.'

Cheska is cool with me for a few days and I wonder if I should have said anything, but I know I'm right. My diagnosis is correct. It isn't something I could have kept to myself. If she doesn't want to accept help, that's up to her, I've done what I can.

Chapter Eighteen

Feeling Down? Saddle Up.

'Hello, Nicci.' Delphi looks over the stable door where I'm changing Willow's rugs. It's a cold day in late November, and she needs an extra layer. 'All mine are having their pyjamas on too,' she observes. 'It's going to go down to minus one overnight.'

'I'm glad I'm not one of your riding school ponies.' They stay out full-time all year round.

'That's how they're supposed to live – out 24/7. It's better for their heads – it's bad for business when they gallop orf with the small children. Delphi snorts with disapproval. Willow snorts as if in agreement with her. 'Shane and I were wondering if you wanted to have a ride.'

'Is Shane here?'

'He's dropped by because he had a cancellation. Go on, Nicci. Dark Star is tacked up ready. You know you want to . . .'

I disentangle a small knot at the base of Willow's

mane. 'I don't know . . .' I want to, but I also know how strongly Matt doesn't want me to, and the fact it's on a horse he considers a bit of a nutter doesn't make it any better.

'Seeing as Shane's here, I thought it would be nice for you to work with him again, for old times' sake.'

I sigh inwardly. Delphi can be very pushy, or am I blaming her for my lack of resistance to the idea of a ride? I'll be riding in an enclosed arena with Shane present. What can go wrong? Matt can't tell me what to do – it isn't right.

'I'm not supposed to ride for another couple of weeks. My ribs are taking longer to heal than my consultant anticipated.'

'You're a doctor. You can give yourself the all-clear, and Matt need never know,' Delphi goes on. 'Shane and I won't breathe a word.'

'Oh, all right then,' I say, with a frisson of excitement at the thought of being back on a horse again, a challenging, fiery horse with potential, like Dark Star. 'I'll grab my hat.'

Delphi and Shane have been plotting this moment, I think to myself as he gives me a leg-up onto Dark Star in the chilly confines of the indoor school. I swear it's warmer outside in the yard.

I stroke Dark Star's neck, which is slightly bristly where his clip is growing out. I slip my feet in the stirrups and take up the reins, and I'm back in the saddle. Although I have butterflies in my stomach because it's the first time since I came off Willow, I forget the odd twinge in my ribs and tighten my calves sending Dark Star forwards. He breaks pace into a jog. I pull him back, but he doesn't respond until Shane calls, 'Whoah there, big boy,' and he slows to a bouncy walk.

'VB, don't forget to breathe,' Shane says. 'You're tense and you're transmitting that tension to the horse. He's picking up on how you're feeling. He's one of those sensitive kind of guys that you ladies say don't exist.' An image of Matt briefly crosses my mind as I recall him crying when he visited me in hospital after the fall – he's a sensitive guy too – and I'm risking everything we have by giving in to temptation and riding Dark Star, but I'm still miffed with him for not being strong enough, I suppose, to overcome his opposition to my desire to compete. I know it isn't something I can agree to because it's such a big part of my life.

'VB, listen up!' Shane yells, laughing at the same time. 'Book yourself an appointment to syringe out your ears. I said change the rein at marker K then, when you hit the track again, into working trot.'

I relax my fingers on the reins, sit deep into the saddle, squeeze my calves against Dark Star's sides and he springs forward like a cat, taking me by surprise, so instead of trotting when we hit the track, we're in canter. I stay with him though, which is possibly a surprise for him in return.

'He usually manages to part with his rider doing that trick of his,' Shane says. 'Keep him going forward, that's it, a twenty-metre circle at A. You remember which marker that is, the one at the end of the school?' He's being sarcastic.

'I haven't been out of action that long,' I say, smiling.

'No backchat. No cheek,' Shane says with mock sternness. 'Now bring him back to trot and ask for a canter at X.'

At X, I tentatively give Dark Star the aids for canter, at which he shies at either the sound of sand flicking up against the side of the arena or some imagined monster.

'Well sat, VB,' Shane chuckles. 'Don't look down – if you do, that's where you'll end up.'

The next time I'm not so lucky. When I ask Dark Star to canter at the corner, he strikes off on the correct lead, then puts in a sneaky buck – I hold on but he catches me by surprise, entering rodeo mode, bucking repeatedly along the long side of the school. I cling on, trying to keep his head up and pushing him forward at the same time, but I'm too tense and tight, and with a twist of his body, he tips me off, sending me flying through the air and into the sand, where I land with a gasp and a splat.

The pain . . . I let go of the reins. I have no choice as Dark Star gallops to the end of the arena and waits by the door for Shane to catch him and lead him back.

'Are you okay, VB?'

'I think so.' Gingerly, I stand up. No bones broken this time, although I've jarred my collarbone again. There's a sandy orange stain and sand stuck to my buttocks, but my ego is more bruised than my bum. 'Give us a leg-up, will you?'

'Are you sure?'

'Quite sure.'

'You don't have to. Perhaps the other doctors were right after all, and you need more time before you start riding again.'

I can't resist getting back in the saddle and I feel ready. It's my choice – as I've heard my patients say: 'I felt fine, doctor, so I went ahead and did what you told me not to do.'

'Shane! As you know, I am a doctor, so please get on with it.' Before I lose my nerve altogether . . . 'I'm not going to let Dark Star think he's won.'

Back in the saddle, I give him a stern telling-off, making sure he doesn't get away with anything. I move him on, making him trot circles, leg yield and perform perfect serpentines before asking him to canter once more, prepared this time for the bucking, keeping a firm hold on his mouth and my legs close to his sides. He moves beautifully. He looks and feels amazing. It's his brain that's the problem.

'He needs more work,' I say at the end of the session as I give him a pat and dismount. 'He's an intelligent horse. Some of this naughtiness is down to boredom.'

'He needs plenty to think about,' Shane agrees as I walk the horse around for a few minutes to cool down. Dark Star looks at me askance at first then settles and lowers his head, walking alongside me. 'When are you up here next?' I ask.

'Whenever you want me,' Shane replies. 'I need the work, VB. Does that mean—?'

'I'll ride him. He's great.' I remind Shane that he mustn't mention to Matt that I've been riding again, let

alone on Dark Star. If he finds out, he'll kill me –
metaphorically speaking – and it will be the end of a
beautiful relationship.

'How will you convince him it's all right?' Shane
asks. 'I'm not sure how I'd feel if my other half went
behind my back.'

'I'll find a way. Once I've ridden a few times and I
can prove he's safe, Matt will come round.' I smile
wryly. 'I can only hope.'

Dark Star is so different from Willow. I don't feel like
I'm in partnership with him. For now, we feel more
like two lovers at odds with each other, but will there
be passion at the end of the day?

I am back from the yard later than I said I would be,
and when I get home, Matt's car is outside. Swearing
under my breath, I glance down at the evidence of my
fall. This is not good. What can I do? Can I blag it? Can
I avoid being caught out?

I leave the car a little way along the road, pull a cap
over my particularly bad case of hat hair, and go
around to the rear of the house so I can walk up the
garden path to the back door and sneak in that way,
leaving my muddy boots on the patio. As I enter the
kitchen, I'm greeted by the aroma of just-baked fairy
cakes and – my heart sinks – Sage and Gabriel sitting at
the breakfast bar, scraping out the pink sponge
mixture from the bowl. I think they're supposed to be
eating it but it's all over their faces.

'Auntie Nicci!' Sage exclaims.

'Sh!' I say. 'I'm not here.'

She frowns, but Gabriel doesn't get the subtleties of

the message. He'll never make it in the diplomatic service.

'Why? Are you playing hide and seek?'

I hold my breath then groan when I hear Cheska's voice.

'Nicci, is that you? I didn't hear you come in.'

'She came in the back door,' says Sage.

Here we go, I think, as Matt and Cheska join us in the kitchen. Matt smiles at me as he folds a used fairy cake case and drops it into the pedal bin, making me smile back in spite of my situation. He's gradually becoming more domesticated – there was a time when he'd have left it lying around for the Bobster to chew into soggy pieces and spit out on the floor.

'I couldn't wait for the icing,' he says.

'We're going as quickly as we can,' Sage says. 'Anyway, I thought you were going to buy some more sprinkles.'

'I will do.'

I'm just beginning to think there's a chance that Matt is going to push off to the shops and I'll get away with it but he moves to the breakfast bar and takes another undecorated fairy cake from the batch cooling on the rack.

'I'll go as soon as I've had another one of these.'

Like a naughty child, I sidle into the corner, hoping to hide the evidence of my fall. My pulse is racing and my palms are damp. Even now I could come clean, but I can't bring myself to because I know how strongly Matt feels about me riding again, especially so soon and on Dark Star.

'Hi, darling,' Matt says, coming over to join me. 'I drop in to see how you are and find that you're up at the yard with Willow.' He kisses me, his forehead bumping into the peak of my cap. I want to laugh but the renewed force of the pain in my ribs is too much to bear. I bite my lip.

'I think you've overdone it,' he says. 'Go and sit down. I'll bring you tea and a cake.'

'She can't sit down in those dirty jodhpurs,' Sage chuckles, repeating my words back to me. How many times have I told her that she can't come into the living room to watch television until she's changed out of her riding gear?

'That's me been told,' I say brightly. 'I'll be a few minutes.' I start to edge my way around the kitchen, but I can't quite make it to the door without either revealing my rear or looking like a freak.

'Did you fall over in the muck heap, Auntie Nicci?' Sage sings out. 'Turn round and show everyone your bottom.' Sage is too sharp for me. 'That's sand – you've been riding, you lucky thing!'

I am mortified. I can't lie.

'Nicci?' says Matt, the muscle in his cheek taut.

'I fell off Dark Star,' I say in a tiny voice.

'You what?' A veil of disappointment falls across his eyes.

'How did it happen?' says Sage, oblivious to the tension between us. 'Did he buck you off?'

'More importantly, what the hell were you doing on that horse in the first place?' he growls. 'You promised me . . .'

'I'm sorry,' I say, close to tears. 'I can explain.'

'Don't bother.' He pushes past me.

'Where are you going?'

'Home to see the dog. I can rely on the Bobster.'

'Matt! Wait!' I follow him down the hallway. I grab for his arm, but he shakes me off.

'I've got to get out of here. I need some air.'

'Bye, Matt,' Sage calls after him.

Matt hesitates, as if he's just remembered we're not alone.

'Goodbye Sage, and thanks for all the cakes.'

'So what did happen?' Sage says, tugging at my sleeve as I watch Matt drive away and the rain fall from a grey sky. It pours from the gargoyles' mouths and drips down the stonework of the church on what is turning out to be a miserable evening.

'Matt and I have had a falling-out,' I say quietly.

Sage slips her hand through mine.

'He'll be back,' she says. 'He loves you and he's going to buy us some sprinkles for the fairy cakes.'

I appreciate her conviction, even if it is misplaced, and I realise that this doesn't affect me in isolation. The children have grown fond of Matt – he's become a part of their lives as well as mine.

'Come on, Sage. Make me a cup of tea and I'll tell you all about how I fell off Dark Star.' I throw myself down on the sofa in my filthy jodhpurs. On the outside, I'm calm, normal Nicci, as I am when there's a crisis at work. On the inside, I'm in turmoil as I regale Sage with my horsey tale, embellishing it with gory details before wondering if I've gone too far. 'I hope I haven't put you off.'

'Oh no,' she says.

'Sage, can you think about having a bath or shower before we eat, please,' Cheska says, interrupting. 'Dinner's in the oven.'

'Mummy, do I have to?' she moans.

'Yes, you do. Give Gabriel a hand to tidy up the toys in the bedroom too.' She waits, leaning against the doorframe, arms folded until Sage leaves the room, when she takes her place on the sofa.

'Have you been doing something you shouldn't?' she asks. 'I thought you weren't allowed to ride for another week.'

'What's a week?' I shrug. 'What difference will seven days make?'

'How do I know? I'm not a doctor,' Cheska says dryly as I bury my face in my hands.

'I've been so bloody stupid.'

'That's the first time I've ever heard you say that, you being the perfect sister. Come on.' She puts her arm around me. 'Matt will come round.'

'I don't think he will,' I sob. Not this time. Not when I've kept on at him about how much I value honesty and trust . . . 'I lied to him. I promised I wouldn't ride again until I got the all-clear.'

'It's nothing,' Cheska says. 'He's over-reacting.'

'He can just about deal with me riding when I'm fit, the schooling and hacking side of it, but he hates me competing.'

'It's ridiculous, though, when he works with horses and his clients ride.'

'He has good reason,' I say. 'He lost someone

346

important to him, a girl he was at vet school with. She came off her horse when she was eventing. The horse hit a fence, took a rotational fall – that's how he described it – she took the weight of the horse full on . . .' My voice trails off.

'Poor Matt. Was he in love with her?'

'He loved her but she didn't feel the same way about him.'

'And he loves you?'

I nod.

'And you love him, so you mustn't let something like this come between you.' Cheska smiles. 'Like me and Alan, you two need your heads knocking together.'

'What's this about Alan? You haven't mentioned him for ages.'

'I've been texting him.'

'You aren't planning to go back?'

'We're settled here now. I'm really grateful that you sat me down for that talk. You were right about my state of mind, Nicci. I've registered with Dr Mackie, who's prescribed some medication and organised some support for me, and Sage is happy at school. I'm not going to uproot the children again, but Alan might come and visit us sometime.'

'I'm glad.' I make to stand up, but Cheska pulls me back down.

'Don't go after him now. Leave it until tomorrow when you've both had time to calm down.'

'Since when have you become an agony aunt?'

'I didn't know I had it in me. Perhaps I can make a

career out of it.' She pats my knee, reminding me of our mother. 'Come on. Cheer up.'

'I need to grab my bag out of the car,' I say, remembering I've left it there. When I leave the house, I notice a pot of sprinkles on the doorstep with a note scribbled on a Post-it advertising horse worming products. I read it through a sudden blur of tears.

'To Sage and Gabriel. I'm sorry I had to rush off. Hope these will do. Matt.'

I pop it indoors before returning for my bag, when I notice Matt's car is still parked down the road in exactly the same place. Has he been waiting for me all this time? My heart lifts slightly. Does he want to talk? Is he prepared to forgive me? It was only a minor fall after all, nothing serious.

In spite of the driving rain and the dark, and the sense of foreboding I always feel in the presence of the shadowy headstones lurking behind the railings of the churchyard, I jog along to Matt's car and bang on the window. He looks up, his face pale beneath the light from the streetlamp.

'Open up,' I mouth and he opens the passenger door. I go around the other side and clamber in. We both sit facing the windscreen watching the rain pour down the glass. 'Thanks for the sprinkles,' I say eventually.

'I promised the kids—' He breaks off and runs his fingers roughly through his hair. 'I'm sorry, Nicci. You were right about all that honesty stuff being important. It's essential.' He grips the steering wheel and turns to face me. 'I don't feel I can trust you any more.'

'Only about the riding,' I say.

'It's the thin end of the wedge,' he cuts in.

'Can't you see, I wouldn't have felt I had to keep it quiet if you hadn't gone on about it? I knew you'd be upset and angry with me if you found out, and if I'd told you beforehand that I was going to ride Dark Star you would have tried to persuade me not to.'

'And quite right too as it turns out. You weren't ready to get back into the saddle.'

'I was in the school with Shane. It was a soft landing. For goodness sake, Matt, I wasn't at full gallop out on a cross-country course.'

'Why can't you see it from my perspective? You're so consumed with the idea of getting Willow to Badminton you can't see the dangers.' He pauses. 'You're like a horse in blinkers.'

'This girl,' I begin. 'The vet student . . . it's eight or nine years since it happened?' I'm hazarding a guess.

He nods.

'So why do you still let it get to you?'

Matt leans closer to me and rests one hand lightly on my shoulder.

'She was like you, Nicci. Clever, fun to be with and a talented horsewoman. And I was in love with her, as I am completely in love with you. Can't you see? Each and every time you set out on a cross-country round, I'm tortured by the thought you might not come back.' He bites his lip to control his voice before continuing, 'I know it sounds over the top and you'll probably suggest I get some counselling, but I really can't stand it. The thought of losing you in such a way is too much to bear.'

349

A single bell tolls – the bell-ringers are practising for a funeral.

'I can't take the risk of losing someone again. I'm sorry, Nic—' he chokes. 'It's over.' He almost pushes me out of the car. 'Goodbye.'

I stand in the cold and wet, watching him drive away and I feel as if he's ripped my heart out and taken it with him. The rain seeps through my clothes. I don't care. I close my eyes and open my arms to its icy assault, but within seconds I hear the clunk of a window-catch and Frances's voice.

'Nicci, get yourself indoors and into a hot bath this minute, or you'll catch your death and they'll be tolling the bells for you. I'm bringing round the bath salts.'

What can I say? I want to die. Matt has dumped me and I think it might well be final.

Chapter Nineteen

Star Quality

When I arrive at the yard on my way to work, Delphi has left Willow tied to the ring outside her stable while she's mucking out. When Willow sees me parking the car she pricks her ears, and as I approach she whickers to greet me. I give her a mint from my pocket, offering it to her in the palm of my outstretched hand, and she takes it very gently, her breath warm against my skin and her whiskers tickling.

'How is she, Delphi?'

'She's well. But it was so cold I had to put an extra layer on her overnight – it might be worth investing in a new fleece. We've just had a batch of new arrivals in the shop. There's a mint-green combo that would suit her down to the ground.'

'Are you spending my money again?' I grumble lightly. 'I can't afford to keep buying presents for you, Willow, when all you do is stand around.'

She nudges me with her muzzle, asking for another mint.

'You spoil her,' Delphi says.

'I know, but she's worth it.' I rub Willow's ears before moving on to give Dark Star a mint too because he's looking out of his stable at me with his ears pricked. 'I'll drop into the shop later. I'm in the mood for a bit of retail therapy, but in the meantime, I've got to get to work.'

'Think of us freezing our fingers to the bone while you're sitting in a nice warm surgery.'

'You'd hate it,' I smile.

'I would indeed.'

Later, I sit at my desk at the surgery, reaching past a giant poinsettia Fifi insisted on giving me as a gift from the garden centre, and switch the computer on. I wait for it to load, and for my mind to fill with thoughts of the day ahead, reviewing the patients I've asked to see again. There's Ruby, Frances's eight-year-old grand-daughter, who has eczema and asthma, Ed Pike, who is due back to see me to discuss the results of his latest blood tests, and Mrs Brown who is booked in for one of her regular check-ups.

Try as I might, I can't get Matt out of my head. I grab a tissue and blow my nose. What am I going to do about him? It sounds pathetic for the strong, independent woman that I am to spend her time inwardly – and outwardly – weeping over an ex-boyfriend, but I really don't think I can live without him.

I'm beginning to feel I'm being too stubborn, too

intransigent over making a compromise. I gaze up at the photo of me and Willow flying over the cross-country fence. Yes, I will miss eventing if I give it up for good, but I won't miss it in the same heart-wrenching way that I miss Matt. If he missed the girl who died half as much as I miss him, then I can understand where he's coming from.

I pick up my mobile and call him, leaving a message on his voicemail and hoping it isn't too late. I check the time. I'm running behind, which isn't the best start to a busy morning surgery, but I manage to catch up.

Mr Brown brings his wife in her wheelchair, crashing along the corridor from reception to the consulting room.

'His driving's no better,' Mrs Brown says with a smile.

He looks better though, I think. He's put on some weight and had his hair cut.

'How are you both?' I ask them.

'The same as ever, Dr Chieveley,' Mr Brown says.

'Oh, don't talk nonsense.' His wife nudges him. 'You've had a new lease of life since Tina came. She's the carer. He didn't want her at first, but now he says he couldn't live without her.'

'We don't really need her help,' Mr Brown says, 'but she's a very nice woman.'

'I'm glad it's working out,' I say. At least, this way, the Browns can stay together in their own home.

By lunchtime, I'm seeing my last patient.

'Come on in.' I show Ed Pike through to the con-sulting room.

'Look at me. I'm a free man. No children. No dog,' he says brightly.

No vest either, I notice. He's looking well, having put on some muscle, and he's wearing a shirt, tweed tie and cord trousers.

'How's it going?' I ask as he takes a seat.

'I feel so much better. I can't believe how bad I felt, but I didn't realise it. I kept putting the tiredness and lack of energy down to running around after the kids. I'm on top form now.' His expression grows serious. 'What about the blood results though, Nicci? Are they okay?'

'They're good,' I say. 'Your hormone levels are within normal limits, so we've got the dosage right. All you have to do is carry on taking the medication and come in for regular blood tests for monitoring.'

'That's brilliant.' Ed pauses. 'Do you want to see my . . . um, chest at all? I've been working out.' He's no longer the shy, awkward patient I saw at the beginning when he could hardly bring himself to mention his problem, and I can tell I'm going to see his chest however I respond because he's taken off his tie and is unfastening the buttons on his shirt. He stands up and slips his shirt off, revealing his pectorals. 'What do you think?'

'That's very impressive,' I say, before wondering if my observation could be considered inappropriate. 'It's a dramatic change from how you were before.'

'Yep, no one makes jokes about my moobs any more, apart from one of the estate workers who asked me if I'd had a reduction and then if I'd burned my bra.'

'Oh dear.'

'It's all right. I had him beating for Lord Underbrooke, one of our regular visitors, when he turned up with his shooting party. That's a risky business if ever there was one.' Ed smiles.

'How is your job?' I ask.

'My boss has confirmed I'll be all right there for another couple of years at least.'

'That's great.'

'It's a massive relief, and it's thanks to you, Nicci, because I couldn't have pulled myself back together if I'd still felt so bad about my appearance.' He sighs. 'That makes me sound like such a girl.'

'Lots of men have problems with their body image,' I say. 'They just don't like to talk about it in the same way as women.'

'I've left something at the desk for you. It's nothing much, just a token.' With that, he dresses and leaves with a repeat prescription to take to the chemist's for more medication for his thyroid, which is what caused his problems in the first place. Curious, I go and see what he's left for me, thinking it might be chocolates or biscuits that I can share with the rest of the staff.

'I've put them in a bin bag in the fridge,' Janet says when I ask her. 'They're in the drawer at the bottom, well away from the milk. It's disgusting if you ask me.'

'What are they?'

'Go and see.' Janet wrinkles her nose. 'You're in for a nasty shock.'

It's a brace of pheasants! I feel quite the country GP now.

'What do I do with them?'

'Don't ask me,' Janet says. 'The sight of them is enough to turn me vegetarian. Ugh. They're foul.'

'You're right, Janet,' I chuckle. 'They are indeed fowl. As in F-O-W-L. Oh, never mind.'

'I get it,' she says. 'If I were you, I'd get your boyfriend to pluck them and take their entrails out – he'll know which bit's which.'

I don't enlighten Janet, as she answers the phone, to the fact that I'm not sure where I am with Matt at the moment.

'Nicci, don't go away.' Holding the phone to her ear, she looks in my direction, her expression one of concern. 'It's Steve Wilde.'

I'm not sure what condition Steve's heart is in at the moment, but mine stops. 'Where is he?'

'On the way here. His daughter's bringing him. He's having chest pains.' She returns to the call. 'Tessa, don't worry about the parking. Come straight in.'

'I'll grab the trolley,' I say as Janet puts the phone down. 'Call an ambulance just in case, and if Ben or Claire are around, I could use reinforcements.'

'Claire's at lunch and Ben's with a patient. I'll fetch him.'

I open the door to the nurse's room, grab the wheelchair from inside and push it out to the front of the surgery where Steve is getting out of a car, his hands pressed to his chest, his eyes rolling with pain and anxiety, but he's able to walk to the wheelchair without gasping for breath or turning blue.

Joining him, I take hold of his wrist to check his

pulse, which is fast but regular.

'Sit down, Steve,' I tell him.

'I can walk,' he says.

'Sit down, Dad,' his daughter says, her voice threaded with panic, which doesn't help when someone's having a heart attack. However, it works and Steve responds by sinking into the wheelchair so I can push him into the treatment room – with difficulty, because he's still a large man in spite of his attempts at dieting.

'Watch your driving, Doc,' he mutters as I steer him into the trolley with a clash of metal against metal.

'I'm sorry,' I say before asking him to lie on the couch.

'I'm having another one,' he gasps. 'I know I am. The pain . . .'

'Didn't I tell you to call an ambulance last time?' I scold as I rig up the ECG machine to get a trace of the electrical activity in his heart.

'Yes,' he says sheepishly.

'Well, there's one on its way now. Hold still,' I say as the trace jumps. 'Tell me what's been going on? When did these pains start?'

'I had a couple of twinges overnight.'

'So you thought it would be a good idea to see how you felt in the morning? How many times do I have to tell you, Steve?'

'She's such a nag.' He looks towards his daughter, who's standing out of the way in the corner of the room, clutching a bag and keys. 'She's worse than your mother, isn't she, Tess?'

'Dad,' she sighs. 'We're only trying to help you.'

'I know, love.'

I watch the trace. His pulse is slowing down, approaching a normal rate.

'You know, I don't think this is a heart attack,' I say, calling Janet through to ask her to cancel the ambulance.

'I told you so, Dad,' says Tessa. 'He was drinking beer and eating pickled eggs last night.'

'I wasn't.'

'You were.'

'Oh no, I wasn't,' Steve says in the manner of a panto dame.

'Oh, yes you were.'

'Oh no, I wasn't.'

'He was, Dr Chieveley.'

I listen to Steve's chest for a moment to give me a chance to collect my thoughts and make sure I'm not making a potentially fatal mistake.

'So, what's the verdict?'

'Indigestion. I'm going to prescribe you antacids and a sensible diet.'

Steve rolls his eyes in that theatrical way of his. 'Don't you ever have any fun, Nicci?'

'I have more than enough fun, thank you,' I say.

'You know, you should come along to the panto. We're holding it at the school this year. I'll let you have a couple of tickets.'

'I thought they were sold out – I saw the posters.'

'Oh no,' he touches the side of his nose, 'I have some reserved for special guests like you and Claire. It's the dame's prerogative.'

'I'm not sure it's my scene,' I say, although it would be right up Sage and Gabriel's street, if they're still living here at Christmas.

'You're never too old for panto.'

Life goes on and I hear nothing from Matt. Although I try to convince Cheska to speak to Mum again, she stubbornly refuses to acknowledge her existence, let alone agree to see her. A week later and I'm at the yard with Sage for her riding lesson.

Having had a stern word with Willow about not trashing her new winter-weight fleece, I watch from the side of the outdoor school, my hands in my pockets and wrapped up in several layers of clothing – including some particularly unalluring pale pink thermals – against the cold. I respect my mother more than ever, standing out in the elements like this. She did the same for me through rain, wind and snow.

Sage is riding Harry, or rather Harry is taking advantage of her and tanking around the school at a fast trot with Sage trying to keep in rhythm with his manic pace.

'Whoah, Harry,' Delphi calls from the middle. At the sound of her voice, he slows to a walk. 'That's better. He's got the wind under his tail today.'

'Yes, Delphi,' Sage shouts back.

'How are you going to keep him calm?'

'Remember to breathe! And relax!' Sage replies.

I feel for her. I've ridden any number of naughty ponies.

She walks him in a small circle, but Harry soon

decides he's done his fair share of small circles. He takes hold of the bit, sticks his head in the air and trots off in the opposite direction. In the corner, he strikes off into canter which would have been a great move if that was what Sage was asking him for. She pulls on the reins, her hands up near her face because she's left them too long, but Harry swishes his tail, does a cheeky buck and flies into a gallop.

'Whoah, Harry,' Delphi calls again, but he's well away, bolting round and round the school with Sage clinging onto the saddle now, her face as white as a freshly washed numnah. 'Hold on, Sage.'

'Delphi, do something,' I yell. I can't bear to watch. She's going to come off. She's going to hurt herself.

Delphi ambushes Harry, holding out her arms and standing in his path, but he's too quick, changing direction to avoid her, at which Sage loses her stirrups and her seat, flying into the sand and landing on her back with an audible thump. Delphi goes for the pony – typical! – while I run to Sage.

'Keep still,' I tell her. 'Don't move.' There are tears in her eyes and she's trying not to cry. 'Where does it hurt?'

'Um, all over . . .' She touches her side.

'There?' I ask.

'A bit.'

'What about your neck? Your back? Your head?'

'A bit,' is her response to every question, and it's a while before I decide that it's safe to let her sit up.

Delphi brings Harry across. 'On you jump, Sage,' she says.

'Just a minute, Delphi. She's had a hard fall.'

'It wasn't that bad, was it?'

'It wasn't the best thing that's ever happened to me,' Sage says bravely.

'Well, it's lucky we have our yard doctor here to give you the all-clear,' Delphi goes on. 'Let me give you a leg-up.'

Before I can argue that Sage should take a break, she's back on Harry and Delphi is walking around the school beside her, not holding the pony but close enough that she can grab him if he gives any trouble.

'Delphi, was that cantering?' Sage says.

'That was a bit faster – it was a good gallop.'

'That's brilliant – I've always wanted to gallop like Auntie Nicci does.'

Delphi turns to me as they walk past. 'Harry's getting too big for his boots. He does this sometimes. He's lovely with the complete beginners but as soon as they can start telling him where to go and what to do, he starts to assert himself. He can be a very naughty pony.'

I don't say anything. He gave me more of a fright than I care to admit. I touch my chest – somewhere in the depths of my clothing my heartbeat is beginning to return to normal. It's been an eventful lesson for Sage, and an important lesson for me. I can see where Matt is coming from when he says he's scared to watch me event. I can watch my fellow competitors ride cross-country – Henry, in particular – with equanimity, but it's much harder to watch someone I care deeply about falling off a pony.

'Can I ride Willow one day?' Sage says, beaming from ear to ear at the end of the lesson.

'One day, when she gets better,' I say, because she's going to get better eventually. I'm determined that she'll be sound enough to be a hack. 'But you'll have to have a few more lessons on Harry before you're ready for a bigger horse.'

'Your turn, Auntie Nicci,' Sage says when she dismounts in the lower yard. 'You're riding Dark Star. Shane says I can watch.'

Why have I chosen to ride again? Because, as Shane says, I have nothing to lose. I'm clear to ride and I'm not competing, not that it matters because I haven't seen Matt since that cold rain-swept night a week ago.

'You know what VB stands for now?' Shane says as I lower myself gingerly into the saddle onto a soft, padded seat saver that Delphi has kindly added to my ever growing list of horsey must-haves – and added to my livery bill, of course.

'Go on. You're going to have to tell me.' I lean down and check the girth.

'It means Visibly Bruised.' Shane chuckles.

'Oh, shut up,' I say lightly.

We work in the indoor school this time, under the floodlights, one of the advantages of being a grown-up, I tell Sage. I don't have to prove anything to Delphi or Shane any more.

I don't fall off this time and I don't carry a whip.

'Are you sure that's wise?' Delphi asks.

'He doesn't like it.' I trot past, flicking sand up

against the boards at the side of the school. 'He's going much better without it. Put a jump up for us, Shane?'

'Are you sure? It's always better not to run before you can walk, VB.'

I don't respond. I relax my fingers on the reins and squeeze lightly with my calves, sending Dark Star forward into canter. He moves beautifully and jumps one metre, then one metre twenty without hesitation.

'Good boy,' I tell him, stroking his neck.

'Do you want me to put it up again?' Shane shouts across the school.

'I'm going to stop there.' I bring the horse back to walk, giving him another pat as he blows softly through his nostrils and stretches his neck. 'He isn't nasty, Delphi. He's just a sensitive soul.'

'Oh, you'll be telling me he's finding himself in a minute, Nicci. You do talk nonsense sometimes. He's lulling you into a false sense of security. You wait – he'll soon try you out again.'

I smile as I walk him around on the end of the buckle, but my good humour gradually wanes as thoughts of Matt flit into my head, like the small birds that fly from rafter to rafter above.

I miss him. I miss his smile. I miss waking up with him in the morning with the Bobster at our feet, something that happened regularly in the weeks before my accident.

'Nicci, can I have a word?' Shane says, interrupting my chain of thought. 'In private.'

'If you have a medical problem, you'll have to make an appointment.' I'm teasing him now and he knows it.

'It's about Dark Star.'

'Sage, you come and help me put the horse away,' Delphi says tactfully, which makes me suspect that she's in on this too.

Shane waits until Dark Star's clattering hooves fall silent.

'I've been thinking about what happens now that Matt's confirmed Willow is definitely out of action for the long term.' He starts making patterns in the sand with the toe of his boot. 'You need another horse and Delphi's keen to sell, so I thought you should make her an offer.'

'I'm not sure.'

'Why not? I know it's a huge financial commitment taking on a second horse, but you don't have any other vices. It's the perfect solution.'

'If I decide not to compete any more, there's no point in me having a horse like Dark Star. He'd be wasted.'

'You won't be happy not competing. I know you, and if you're saying this because you think you'll get back with Matt and live happily ever after, you're making a terrible mistake. You'll hate him for it.'

'What if I have to compromise? I miss him.'

Shane takes me by the shoulders and gives me a gentle shake.

'VB, what's got into you? Where is your fire?' He ducks to meet my eyes. 'You might not remember, but when I was fourteen or fifteen, I was bullied mercilessly for being a horse-mad boy. People told me I was gay, that I was a girl, that I had a sexual fetish for horses like the teenager in *Equus*, that I was a pony boy . . .' His voice fades. 'Don't look that one up on the internet by the way.'

'I do remember how people talked about you.'

'I got through it and now look at me. I have the life I've always dreamed of because I didn't compromise or give up. Nicci, you are a brilliant rider – you can't just walk away. It would be such a waste of talent.' Shane releases me and takes a step back. 'Lecture almost over. Most of all, on a selfish and personal level, I'd miss you . . .'

I'd miss Shane too. I'm missing the eventing, the dressage series and the showjumping competitions that run through the winter months, but ultimately, I can live without them, whereas I can't survive without Matt. Well, I can. That's a bit of an exaggeration, but nothing is the same without him.

I collect Sage from the tack room where she's washing Dark Star's bit in a bucket of water.

'Hi there,' I say. 'We must go.'

'Do we have to?'

'We'll be back.'

'Maybe sooner than you think,' Delphi says. 'Have you remembered that Matt's coming tomorrow at ten to scan Willow's tendon?'

'But it's Saturday.'

'He says he hasn't got anything better to do now that—' Delphi stops short. 'Listen to me and my big mouth. I can deal with it, if you don't want to be here, Nicci.'

'Thanks, but I'll be here.' Willow's my horse and I need to know what the prognosis is for her return to work – and for any reconciliation with Matt.

Chapter Twenty

Hold your Horses

I try not to raise my hopes when Matt arrives at the yard, parking outside Willow's stable. The passenger door of his four-by-four opens and a blur of tan and white dog flies out straight towards me. The Bobster is delighted to see me, squeaking and snuffling and running in and out of my legs.

'Hello, Bobster,' I say, a lump catching in my throat at the realisation that the dog has missed me like I've missed her and her master.

At Willow's stable, Matt greets me with a gentle but hesitant smile that serves as a painful reminder of better times. He's lost some weight and the line of his jaw is more sharply defined, suggesting he's been under stress. Breathing his familiar scent of aftershave and antibiotics with a hint of horse makes me feel slightly dizzy. My pulse flutters and all I want to do is throw myself into his arms and say I'm sorry.

'I'm here to scan your horse,' he says. 'Would you mind hanging onto her?'

'No, of course.' I catch Willow, slip the bit into her mouth, slide the bridle over her ears and fasten the throatlatch and noseband, fumbling with the buckles. I'm nervous, but it has less to do with my concerns for Willow and more to do with trying to behave normally – as if Matt and I are merely common acquaintances. Part of me wishes I'd taken up Delphi's offer and let her deal with the vet's visit.

'Have you got her?' I blush, aware now that Matt has been watching me over the stable door. He brings the ultrasound machine and a bottle of gel inside and asks me to back Willow into the corner. He squats down and removes her stable bandage, something I should have done beforehand. As he passes me the bandage our fingers touch. He pulls away quickly, as if he too is aware of the electricity that passes between us, confirming that whatever we had, it isn't over.

'How are you?' I ask him, making small talk.

'Good, thanks. The shoulder's better.' He drips some clear gel onto the end of the ultrasound probe and places it against the back of Willow's front leg, angling and sliding the probe and adjusting the focus on the screen of the machine.

'What do you think?' I say anxiously.

'It's looking as I'd expect at this stage. There's the usual amount of heat and swelling. Nicci, I haven't got a crystal ball. I don't know for sure that she'll ever be completely sound, but I think, all things considered, that she'll come sound enough to be a happy hacker, which is what you want, isn't it?'

Matt looks up at me, holding my gaze and my chest tightens with desire and yearning. It's a relief that Willow's on track to make a return to light work at least, but what I really want more than anything is to have him back in my life, not merely as my vet, but as my best friend and lover.

'When did you say I can turn her out?' I ask.

'Not for another couple of months.'

'She hates being in all the time.' I stroke her shoulder.

His lips curve into a rueful smile. 'I think it's you who hates the idea of your horse being in. Willow doesn't look as if she could care less.'

'That's your opinion,' I say stiffly, convinced that I know my horse better than anyone.

'How's Willow's next-door neighbour? Still as mad as ever?'

'He might be a bit hot-headed, but he has loads of potential. Someone is going to end up with a fantastic horse, if they're prepared to do the work with him.'

'Have you heard about Mel?' Matt asks.

I shake my head.

'She's left Westleigh. We've taken on a locum until we can recruit a new houseman.'

'I see . . . where has she gone?'

'She's shacked up with Henry Belton-Smith.'

'Henry! I should have guessed. It was something he said.'

Matt stands up and starts packing the ultrasound machine away, loading it into the boot of his four-by-four and slamming the tailgate while I put Willow's bandage back on and remove the bridle, secretly pleased that Mel and Henry have got their come-uppance. They deserve each other.

'I could do with a coffee,' he says as I emerge from the stable and close the door. 'Do you fancy keeping me company?'

'I'd love to, but I'm going shopping with my mother. She wants me to vet her choice of wedding dress.'

'I see . . .'

'We could meet later,' I say. I have nothing to lose and everything to gain. 'Matt, I've missed you.'

He moves up close to me and takes my hands. 'I've missed you too.'

'Is there any chance we could start again?' I whisper.

'It was a stupid argument,' Matt says.

'I don't think we can just forget about it when it's clear how important it is to you,' I say as he strokes my fingers. 'You need to know that I regret the episode with Dark Star.' I'm blushing as I recall my behaviour that day, creeping around to avoid being found out. 'You also need to know that I've decided to give up competing. I'm not going to event any more.'

'Can you really commit to that?' Matt frowns. 'You've said before that it's an integral part of your life. How can you give it up?'

'I'm not going to stop riding altogether. I couldn't do that, but I've had time to weigh up what is important to me. I can live without eventing, but I wouldn't choose to live without you.' I bite my lip as I gauge his reaction.

'I can't ask you to stop competing,' he says. 'Not so long ago you accused me of being controlling.'

'I know you can't help how you feel. I know you've tried to change.'

'I haven't tried anywhere near hard enough.'

'Matt, you don't have to ask me anything, or try to deal with your demons.' I squeeze his hands tight. 'Now, will you please listen to me? I have hung up my cross-country colours. I am not going to event any more. It's my decision and mine alone. There's no reason for you to feel guilty. And I haven't done this for you. I've done it for us.' Tears prick my eyelids. 'I would far rather stop competing than live without you.'

I gaze into his eyes. Does he still want me? Uncertain, I start to take a step back, but Matt stops me, pulling me into his arms.

'I can't live without you either,' he murmurs, running his hand through my hair and stroking the side of my face. 'I can honestly say that this has been the worst week of my life. I don't know how I got through it.' He kisses my cheek, planting more kisses in a line to the corner of my mouth. 'I'd like to book an appointment with you tonight, Dr Chieveley.'

'And tomorrow night?' I whisper.

'And the night after that,' he says, holding me close, and over the next few days and nights, we make up for lost time.

On the evening of the panto, Matt and I take Sage and Gabriel to the school where the show is being performed on stage in the assembly hall by Talyton's

Am Dram group. My sister, having said that she wasn't interested in watching an amateurish rural production (her words), has agreed to see Mum while we're out with the children. Will they reconcile before the wedding? I'm not sure, but I wish I could write them a prescription to make it right.

Sage, wearing a sparkly dress, jodhpur boots and winter coat, holds my hand on the way in.

'Do you think they'll have found a pumpkin big enough for a coach?' she asks.

'It won't be a real one. Have you got the sweets?'

Smiling, she shows me the bag.

'I wanna sweet,' Gabriel says.

Sage clutches the bag to her chest. 'No, little brother, they'll make you go hyper.'

'He's hyper already,' Matt says, joining in.

'You should see him after he's had a few Skittles,' Sage says.

'I'd rather not,' I say, smiling wryly as I check our tickets. We have seats in the front row so close to the stage that, as Matt points out, we'll be able to see right up the ugly sisters' skirts. Before I can sit down though, Fifi joins us.

'Nicci and Matt, how wonderful. You're so good with those children. Soon, you'll have a lovely family of your own.'

'Fifi, hold your horses on that one.' My awkwardness turns to horror when I find her sitting down in the seat next to mine.

'The front row is always reserved for the guests of honour,' she says. 'Aren't we lucky?'

'Indeed,' I say. 'Is Mr Green with you?'

'No, I'm here to support my niece – she's playing Cinderella.' Fifi places her handbag on her lap and clasps her hands across the top. 'Dr Chieveley, could you tell me if the cold might be affecting my arthritis, only since the weather turned it's been very much worse. My husband suggested some winter sunshine might help.'

I don't really want to get involved in a full-scale consultation, but it seems like a sensible question.

'I think it would be a great idea if you and your husband could afford a holiday in the sun.'

'Oh no, he wasn't saying we'd both go,' Fifi says. 'He meant for me to go alone.'

'You sound like you have a very considerate husband,' I say brightly.

'I suspect he was considering himself, not my precarious state of health. Anyway, if you think it's a good idea, I'll book some time away with my sister, that's if everyone can manage without me.'

Sage gives me a nudge. 'The Eternally Frazzled Mum is here with those naughty boys.'

'Are they?' I look around, worried that Ally might have overheard our nickname for her. 'Where?'

'They're behind yooou,' Sage sings out. 'Get it!'

'You are very funny,' I say, relieved to see that although they are indeed behind us they're a few rows further back, as are Claire and Kevin, who appear to have eyes only for each other. 'You should be a stand-up comic.'

'It's starting,' Sage says, as music comes blaring out

of the speaker to our left and the curtains part, revealing a magnificent set of a pastoral scene with a distant castle, and at the front of the stage, Cinderella, in tattered clothing, sweeping the path up to the door of a cottage, made to look as though it's built from cob and thatch.

I look at Sage's face. She's entranced by the magic of the tale of rags to riches, which could also be described as the story of the rise of a nonentity to a celebrity because the group have given the panto a modern twist. The ugly sisters, one of whom is Steve, come tottering onto the stage in skimpy gowns and ultra-high heels. Their blonde wigs, enormous cleavages, false lashes and fake tan make them look like exiles from TOWIE.

The prince, wearing a cloak, crown and hose and holding a bow and arrow, comes skipping out from the wings. He takes a potshot and a soft toy – a toucan – drops down to the floor with an arrow stuck through it.

'What did he do that for?' says Sage, on the edge of her seat. 'I wouldn't want to marry a prince who kills birds.'

'It's just to show that he enjoys princely pursuits like hunting,' Matt says, letting Gabriel scramble onto his knee.

'He's wearing tights.' Sage maintains an expression of disapproval. 'What does Cinderella see in him?'

I can't help laughing. 'I think he's supposed to be very handsome.'

'And have a good sense of humour,' Matt adds.

'Sh,' says Fifi.

'The prince is a girl,' Gabriel announces. 'Nicci, that man is a lady.'

'Be quiet,' says Sage, embarrassed by her brother.

'You're allowed to shout. Nicci said so,' Gabriel says fiercely.

'The prince is a boy,' Sage says, her tone definitive.

'He isn't.'

'Yes, he is.'

'Oh no, he isn't.' Gabriel leans forward with Matt catching him by the arms to stop him tipping off his lap.

'Hey, that's enough,' I hiss. 'You're confusing the issue.'

I sit back as Sage and Gabriel fall silent for five minutes. As Cinderella sweeps, various small children dressed as leaves roll across the stage, thwarting her attempts to clear the path. When the ugly sisters call the wicked stepmother to punish Cinderella, there are flashes of lightning and crashing of cymbals. Gabriel throws himself into Matt's arms and covers his eyes.

'You aren't scared, are you?' Matt says, giving me a wink.

'No,' Gabriel says, his voice trembling. 'I'm not scared.'

As the wicked stepmother scolds Cinderella and the ugly sisters drag her away into the cottage to chain her to the kitchen sink with only gruel to eat, Gabriel bursts into tears.

'I don't like it. I don't like it,' he repeats.

Matt looks at me. 'I'll take him out. You stay here.'

'Are you sure?'

He nods.

'Don't worry about Matt, Nicci,' Fifi says. 'I expect he's glad to have an excuse to go to the bar.'

'Are you all right, Sage?' I whisper.

She nods, her eyes fixed on Cinderella, her mind miles away in the faraway land of political incorrectness where the poor girl marries a handsome and financially secure prince. The fairy godmother is on stage, waving her wand to bring Cinderella a ballgown, glass slippers and a carriage for the ball. In a puff of smoke, a little grey pony appears pulling a tiny carriage in the shape of a pumpkin.

'It's Harry,' shrieks Sage. 'I didn't know Harry was an actor.'

It brings a tear to my eye to see Delphi dressed in white breeches, black jacket and boots leading the much-loved Harry onto the stage with a plume of feathers in his bridle.

'Cinderella,' says the fairy godmother, 'you *will* go to the ball. Let us cheer you on your way. Hip hip!'

To cheers and applause, Cinderella puts on her glass slippers and starts to make her way to the carriage, but she trips on the hem of her dress and falls forward onto her hands. There's a gasp from the audience followed by silence.

'Nicci, I don't think she's acting,' Sage says, concerned.

If she is, she's extraordinarily talented, I think as Steve dashes across from the wings to help Cinderella up, but she sinks back to the floor, grimacing and holding her ankle.

'Is there a doctor in the house?' Steve shouts.

'Dr Chieveley's right here,' Fifi calls.

I join them on stage, to applause, and have a quick word with Cinderella while Steve ad libs to the audience.

'Cinderella's journey to the ball hasn't started out too well. That fairy godmother isn't up to the job. She forgot to cast the "don't trip over on the way to the carriage" spell.'

'I'm sorry,' I say to Cinderella. 'You aren't going to get through the rest of the performance. We need to get you to A&E for X-rays – I'm pretty sure you've broken it.'

'Oh no,' she wails, touching the back of her hand to her forehead. 'I can't let everyone down. Can't you strap it up for the last half an hour?'

'We can try, but it's against doctor's orders,' I say lightly. 'Fairy godmother, can you magic up a first aid kit from somewhere?'

'There's one in the dressing room,' she says.

'I'm not sure that the prince will get your glass slipper to fit,' I say once I've strapped Cinderella's ankle.

'We'll improvise,' she says. 'The show must go on.'

Somehow she struggles through, carried on a litter for the ball and the finale, when she marries her prince and lives happily ever after. Briefly, I wonder if Matt and I will live happily ever after.

Sage cries at the end. I give her a hug.

'I didn't want it to finish,' she sobs.

'It will always be in your memory. And we have Granma's wedding to look forward to.'

'Mummy says we can't go. She says I can't be bridesmaid.'

'We'll see.' I give Sage a tissue, smiling to myself. Unlike panto, real life is not bad or good or black and white. 'Let's go and find the boys. I expect they'll be at the bar.'

'Gabriel's too young to drink beer.'

'Sage, everyone can see he's underage,' I chuckle.

We join them at the bar, where they're eating choc ices. Matt offers us the same, but we decline.

'I don't know about the children, but it's way past my bedtime,' I say. 'Thanks for looking after Gabriel.'

'We heard that Cinderella called on your expertise,' Matt says.

'She's broken her ankle – Steve's taking her to hospital.'

'The staff are in for a treat if he's still in character.'

'Oh, he is. He'll make the most of it.' I smile. 'He looks so well.'

'I thought he looked a little overheated.'

'That was the spots of rouge on his cheeks.'

'And somewhat overweight.'

'That's padding. I can't believe he almost died of a heart attack in the summer. He seems fitter than ever now.'

'Can we go home?' Sage asks, and I'm touched that she considers my home as hers. I know it's been hard on both sides but, on balance, I love having them around, particularly my niece with her fondness for horses. Although Matt and my sister might accuse me of indoctrination, Sage has a natural empathy with four-legged creatures, dogs included.

'Are you coming back with us?' I ask Matt.

'Try and stop me,' he says. 'I'll drop you off, pick up the Bobster and come back, if that's okay.'

However, his plans soon change when we find my mother's car parked outside my house, which can mean only one thing, I hope – as long as they haven't killed each other.

'I won't stop – you have company.' Matt leans across and kisses me.

'They're kissing,' exclaims Gabriel.

'Oh, grow up,' says Sage, but she pauses. Something's bothering her. 'Is Cinderella a lesbian? She kissed the prince, but if the prince is really a girl . . . Does Cinderella know she married a girl?'

Matt snorts with laughter. 'If she didn't know before, she'll know by now.'

'Matt!' I try to be stern with him, but I can't help joining in, and soon we're all rocking Matt's car with laughter until none of us have a clue what we're laughing about.

'You sound like you've enjoyed yourselves,' Mum says from the living room. She's sitting in the chair opposite Cheska, who's on the sofa, an empty bottle of wine on the coffee table between them.

'Gabriel was a baby – he was too scared to watch.'

'No, I wasn't.'

'Oh yes, you were.'

'Sage, the panto's finished,' I say.

'Oh no, it hasn't. Auntie Nicci, you said it never ends in here.' She points to her head. 'Anyway, that dreadful Fifi woman—'

'Sage, please don't call her that,' I cut in.

379

'She asked Nicci about her arthuritis and Cinderella broke her ankle, but the best bit was that Harry the pony was there.'

'That is one eventful night,' Mum says as I look from her to my sister and back. 'Cheska, why don't you get the children to bed? Nicci and I will make tea.'

'I'd prefer another glass of wine, if there's one going,' Cheska says.

'I'll see if I can squeeze another one out of the bottle,' Mum giggles, and I realise they've both been drinking and Mum will be staying overnight.

'So, you are speaking?' I say when Mum and I are in the kitchen.

'We aren't there yet, but I think I can safely say that we're on the road,' she responds, her eyes bright with tears of joy as she tries to shake the last few drops from the wine bottle.

'Oh, Mum, that's wonderful.' I hesitate. 'Hang on a minute. I think I have another bottle in the cupboard.'

'Cheska's agreed to come to the wedding.'

'What changed her mind?' I ask, taking the cork out of a fresh bottle of wine.

'I've been rather a fool.' I turn to find Cheska leaning against the door, her arms folded.

'You were very young and in love,' Mum says protectively. 'There's no way you were going to listen to me. I used to wish Nicci was at home with us, not at uni – you might have taken notice of her. I'm so sorry I upset you when I offered to pay for a termination.'

'I know,' Cheska says. 'I wish you'd told me about

380

your jewellery going missing though.'

'What was that about?' I ask. 'I haven't heard that one before.'

'My rings and my mother's brooch disappeared when Cheska's boyfriend—' Mum shudders at the memory of him '—came to the house one afternoon. I knew it was him. I knew he was a thief. But after you ran off with him, Cheska, I didn't think there was any point in pursuing it.' Mum struggles to control the tremor in her voice as she continues, 'I didn't care about the jewellery. All I wanted was for you to come back, safe and sound.'

Cheska walks across and touches Mum's arm.

'I'm back now,' she says. 'Thank you, Nicci,' she adds, turning to me. 'You've been the best sister anyone could have.'

'It's nothing,' I say, touched. 'I've loved having you here.'

'We won't be staying for ever,' Cheska says.

'I'm going to look after the children so Cheska can work and find somewhere to live. You can't all live on top of each other for ever,' Mum says.

'There's no hurry.'

'You've changed your tune, Nicci.'

'I'll miss you.'

'You need to think about you and Matt. It can't be easy to find time for him with all your other commitments.' Mum pauses. 'Don't let him go, Nicci. He's a diamond.'

Chapter Twenty One

For the Love of a Horse

Three days before her December wedding, Mum drops a bridesmaid's dress off at the house for Sage. She's so keen to try it on that she strips off in the middle of the living room. She gives me, my mother and Cheska a twirl, showing off the long red dress with the locally made cream lace at the yoke. It fits perfectly, which is a bit of luck because we don't have much time.

'It's the same as the ones Robert's granddaughters will be wearing,' Mum says.

'How many are there?' Sage asks.

'Five.'

'Sage, like Cinderella,' I say, 'you *will* go to the ball.'

'You mean the wedding, Auntie Nicci. You know Mummy says marriage is an—' she frowns '—outdated institution, an anti-feminist—'

'Not now, Sage,' Cheska says, and I breathe a small sigh of relief because I'm sure Mum doesn't want to hear her daughter's colourful views when she's just

382

about to marry Robert. 'What are you wearing, Nicci?' she goes on, changing the subject.

'The blue peplum dress. I bought it the other weekend.'

'Good. That means I can borrow the green maxi dress you have in your wardrobe. I've had my eye on it.'

'Cheska!'

'Please?' she begs and eventually, after much negotiation, I give in.

'Why do you two argue so much?' Sage asks.

'Because they're sisters,' Mum sighs fondly. 'That's what sisters do.'

'If I move in with Matt, it will stop you going through my clothes,' I go on.

'If? Surely, it's *when* you move in with Matt. You're virtually living with him anyway.'

'Where will we go when that happens?' Sage cuts in.

'Where will we go?' echoes Gabriel, stumbling into the room with a glass of blackcurrant.

'Let me have that,' I say, taking it from him before it gets anywhere near the dress. 'You can stay here until you and Mummy decide where you want to live. It's all right, Sage. There's no hurry.'

'But where are we going to live in the end, Mummy?' she asks. 'I don't want to leave my new school, or Harry and Willow, or the Bobster.' Her lip trembles. 'I'd miss them.'

'I'd miss them too,' Gabriel says, not to be outdone.

'We're not leaving Talyton St George,' says Cheska. 'I'm starting work at the garden centre next week, thanks to Mum, who's offered to help me out once she comes back from her honeymoon.'

'You're what?'

'I went to see Fifi to ask her for a second chance, since I let her down the first time, and she's agreed to take me on part-time so I can go to college and get the qualifications I need to go on to train as a nurse. Ben says there's no reason why I shouldn't as long as I'm on the right medication and mentally stable.'

'That's wonderful,' I say, taken aback.

'I'll prove to you that I can do it, sis,' Cheska says. 'I want to use my insight into the condition to help other people.'

'Tell her the rest,' Mum says, and I realise they've been making up for lost time in a big way.

It isn't until later when the children are in bed that Cheska is able to finish the conversation. Alan wants to come and see her and the children.

I wake up at Matt's house on the morning of the wedding. Later, we're in the kitchen having breakfast, scrambled eggs with smoked salmon on toast, a treat in honour of my mother's big day. When we've finished, Matt collects up the plates and puts them in the sink. He's wearing his white bathrobe and his hair is damp from the shower. I smile to myself. He's the kind of man who can make slippers look sexy, and he doesn't seem to find my rather unconventional outfit of pyjamas, hooded top and three pairs of socks a turn-off. I've tried the gorgeous girlfriend look before, but I was so cold my arms and legs turned blue and I ended up resembling an ancient Briton in a skimpy silk slip.

'Are you sure you don't mind coming along, Matt?' I leave the table and move beside him, looking out of the window at the sun rising through the frosted twigs of the plum trees and the tangled skeletons of the climbing roses. 'I'm worried you'll be bored.'

'Of course I won't. I want to come with you.' He takes my hand and gives me one of his caressing glances. 'It might give us some ideas for the future.'

My heart beats faster and louder as I hold my breath, afraid to express my understanding of what he's proposing, in case I'm making a mistake and this isn't a proposal at all.

'Are you being deliberately obtuse?'

Smiling, he leans forward, brushes his lips against mine and looks into my eyes, his pupils dark and dilated. 'Nicci, I was going to do this properly with a ring and flowers, but it has to be now because it feels right . . . Will you . . . will you marry me?'

'Oh, Matt . . .' My heart leaps with joy, my head says don't rush in, but for once I ignore my head and go with my heart. We haven't been together for long and what we've been through with Mel and my fall from Willow has only made us stronger. 'Yes, yes, yes. I'll marry you.' I throw my arms around his neck and he lifts me off the ground and swings me round and we're both laughing and crying at the same time.

The Bobster jumps onto the table and starts barking too, although whether she's as enamoured of the idea of Matt and me getting hitched as we are, I'm not sure.

'You,' Matt says, holding my body tight against his, 'have made me the happiest man alive. I love you.'

'I love you too.' It's all happened so fast. Who would have thought six months ago, when I first set eyes on Matt Warren, that he would become my husband? It's bizarre, outrageous, and wonderful.

'We'll have to keep this to ourselves today,' he says, and I'm grateful for his forethought. 'I don't think we should overshadow your mother's big day.' He grins. 'I'll find it hard to keep my trap shut though. I want to introduce you to everyone as my fiancée.'

I can feel his heart beating, the life pulsating through his body as he continues to hold me close as if he'll never let me go.

'If you're not careful, I'll have to take those clothes off you again,' he whispers into my ear.

'I have to go. I promised Cheska I'd help her get the kids dressed.'

'I'm surprised you're not rushing off to the yard.'

'Not today. Delphi's friend is bringing a horse and carriage down to the church for the end of the service to take the bride and groom back to the farm, because although Beauty's well, she's out of action for another month. Mum doesn't know about the horse – it's very romantic.'

'You'll be going to see Willow tomorrow then?'

'Of course, but I don't feel quite the same about hanging around up at the yard at the moment.'

'Why on earth is that?' He touches the back of his hand to my forehead. 'Are you sickening for something?'

'No. Delphi told me that Dark Star's been sold. I

know he had to go, but it feels like the end of an era somehow.' I bite my lip. 'He might be a difficult horse, but I can't help thinking he'll be even worse at a different yard. He's very sensitive.'

'He's a horse,' Matt says.

'Exactly,' I agree, warming to my theme. 'That's why he'll be so upset. He'll probably go into a deep depression.' I gaze at Matt, noticing the twisted smile on his lips as he tries to control his laughter. 'I can't understand why you're treating it so lightly when you're supposed to be at the forefront of safeguarding horses' welfare.'

'I'm sorry,' he says, sobering up. 'It's a shame, but life moves on. I'm sure Dark Star will be fine.'

I wish I shared Matt's conviction.

'Cheer up, fiancée. You haven't changed your mind?' he adds anxiously.

'Of course not.' I shrug. 'I guess this talk of horses makes me realise how much I miss competing.'

'I guessed that much,' he says. 'You don't really talk about it.'

I don't tell him it's because each time I think about it it's like reopening an old wound.

'It's taking me some time to get used to it, that's all. It's a bit weird not having to get up early to train with Shane or plan the diary to fit it all in. And the winter dressage series is well under way – I used to look forward to that.' I gaze into Matt's eyes. 'It doesn't matter though. I have you.' I touch his arm. 'I'll meet you at the house.'

Some of Mum's friends are staying at her house, and Mum is staying with my sister for the night, to make sure she stays away from the groom. We don't like to break with any traditions in Talyton St George, including the one where it's the bride's prerogative to be late for the occasion.

On arriving at home, the church bells are ringing, yet I discover that my mother isn't ready. Her hair is not quite to her satisfaction and there's a mark on one of her shoes that requires attention. Bridget is delayed delivering the flowers – one of the dogs has eaten one of the bridesmaid's posies, but she'll be on her way very soon.

'Will you help Sage and Gabriel dress while I help Mum?' Cheska says.

It doesn't take long. Sage, ready in her bridesmaid's dress, is watching out of the window when a muddy Land Rover pulls up outside the church gates and Robert, dressed in a dark suit and red tie, gets out.

'Is that the man Granma's supposed to be marrying?' she asks me as Cheska switches the hairdryer on to tweak Mum's hair one last time.

'Haven't you met him before?' I say.

'Once, I think, when we were round at Granma's house. He's very old. I saw a programme on television where the man got married because he was about to die.'

'Robert's not that ancient,' I say, but I can see from her expression that she isn't convinced.

'Matt's quite old too,' she goes on.

'Well, to Granma, Robert is and always will be a prince.'

'He doesn't look anything like a prince,' she says scathingly.

'This isn't a pantomime, Sage.' I walk over and rest my hand on her shoulder. 'All that matters is that the bride and groom love each other and want to spend the rest of their lives together as man and wife.'

Sage looks up. 'Is that what you and Matt want to do?'

'Maybe.' I wish I could tell her. I wish I could run up to the attic, fling open the window and shout our news to the rooftops of Talyton St George, because this is one piece of gossip I'd love everyone, including Fifi, to know about.

'Here's Bridget with the flowers,' Sage says, returning to her view from the window.

'I'll let her in,' I say, noticing how she's struggling to lift a long box of posies from the back of her van with the Petals logo printed along the side.

'Aren't you going to get dressed, Nicci?' Sage asks.

I glance down at my sweater and jeans.

'I've had a shower. It won't take me more than five minutes.'

'I'll get the door,' Sage says.

'Thank you.' I dash upstairs to change into my blue peplum dress and beaded bolero. I straighten my blonde locks and pin a small fascinator to my hair. I add earrings, a pair of high heels, make-up and I'm done. 'How long was that?' I ask when I return to the living room.

'Seven and a half,' says Sage. 'Too slow. Granma, we really must go.'

'Well, I hope Robert's willing to wait for a few more minutes at least, darling.' Mum is dressed at last, wearing a shift dress in cream with an embroidered jacket and a simple tiara. She's adjusting a blue garter at the top of her stocking. 'It's only eleven-fifteen.'

'That's fifteen minutes later than you said.'

'Sage, that's enough,' Cheska says. 'We don't need any more stress.'

'Here come the rest of the bridesmaids and the pages,' Sage says excitedly as a minibus turns up and disgorges eleven children and several adults outside the church. 'Come on, Granma. You don't want to miss it.'

'What are we having to eat?' asks Gabriel, who's perched on the arm of the sofa in his waistcoat and trousers, picking his nose.

'We won't be eating until we get to the farm,' says Mum. 'If you're hungry, you need to have a snack now.'

'It's too late. He's in his wedding clothes,' says Cheska.

'I'm hungry.'

'You've just had breakfast. Go and help Sage find Granma's bouquet while I get changed.' Cheska rolls her eyes at me then smiles. 'Promise me you won't go and get married, sis.'

I pretend I haven't heard, otherwise I'll give myself away.

When we finally arrive at the church I'm surprised to see how busy it is for what is supposed to be a quiet wedding, but then Robert comes from a particularly fertile family of farmers and Mum has lots of friends. I supervise the bridesmaids and pages as they walk down the aisle past the arrangements of foliage and holly covered with scarlet berries, behind Mum, who has asked Cheska to give her away. I can hear the gasps of surprise at what is clearly a serious break with tradition, but for my family it's the perfect choice, a symbol that the Chieveleys are reconciled.

Nobby Warwick is playing the organ. According to Fifi, who caught me briefly outside the church, he is in his cups. His Wedding March is more like a drunken amble along the aisle, but it doesn't matter. It's a pity I couldn't convince him to take responsibility for his health and come off the alcohol, but – I smile fondly as I think of my patients – you can't win them all.

For the service, I take my place alongside Matt, keeping half an eye on the children and half on the ceremony – for future reference.

'I do love a winter wedding,' says the vicar, looking snug in his robes. He makes the introduction before starting the declaration.

'Robert Lancelot Christi—'

'Lancelot?' whispers my sister, a sob of laughter catching in her throat. I raise one eyebrow at her, but she can't help herself bursting into a fit of giggles.

'Sh,' I whisper frantically, aware of many sets of eyes watching me and Cheska, who turns away to compose herself – I know from experience that we'll be okay if we don't look at each other. Her shoulders are shaking and it's like we're kids again, and none of the intervening years and tears ever happened.

The vicar clears his throat and starts again.

'Robert Lancelot Christian Ash, will you take Kathryn Frances Chieveley to be your wife? Will you love her, comfort her, honour and protect her and forsaking all others be faithful to her for as long as you both shall live?'

'I will.' Robert's voice rings out loud and clear through the church.

The vicar repeats the declaration for my mother to confirm her promise to Robert, at which tears prick my eyes, tears of joy, because I know she has found happiness once more.

After the ceremony, the kiss and the signing of the register, we head outside into the cold for a few photographs.

'We'd better not keep the horse waiting too long. It'll catch a chill,' says Robert, holding out his arm for my mother, and I smile to myself because he's oblivious to the effect of the weather on the rest of us.

'What horse?' she says.

'That one.' Robert points towards the church gate where a smart bay horse and carriage are standing by, ready to whisk them away to the farm for the reception.

'For me?' Mum's hand flies to her mouth. 'Oh, thank you.'

'Only the best will do for my wife.' Robert leads her along the path through cheers and a shower of rose petals and confetti. 'Mrs Ash, your carriage awaits.'

'They look very happy,' Matt says, taking my hand.

'Everyone does. It was a lovely wedding.' I look

around at the smiling faces. Sage and Gabriel are tearing around the graveyard, playing hide and seek among the headstones with the other children, laughing and giggling. And me? Am I happy? Yes, I have everything. I'm engaged to the man I love. I have a lovely family and friends, including patients who have become friends, and thanks to Matt, I still have my beautiful horse. I can relax and look forward to Christmas which is only days away.

I do some last-minute shopping with Cheska and stay at Matt's on Christmas Eve.

'Happy Christmas, darling.' In the morning, Matt brings boiled eggs and toast to the kitchen table while the kettle whistles on the range. We're both dressed, ready to go up to the yard. I'm in my jodhpurs, the ones that went pink in the wash, in case Sage and I have time to take Harry and one of Delphi's steady cobs out for a hack – and Matt is in a sweater and chinos.

'Happy Christmas,' I say as he leans down and kisses me on the cheek. 'Thank you.' I push the gift I've wrapped for him across the table. 'Are you sure you won't open it now?' I've bought him a watch and had the back engraved.

'It's the tradition in my family to open the presents after lunch.'

'It's the tradition in mine to open them before breakfast,' I counter.

'You chose the tree, so I'll choose when we open the presents. Don't argue with me, fiancée of mine. Eat your eggs before they get cold.'

'Excuse me, who wears the trousers in this relationship?'

Chuckling, he glances down at my legs. 'I think you'll find that on this occasion, it's me.'

The dresser is decorated with a string of blue indoor lights, a swag of holly and ivy, and a yule log with a red candle that Sage made for us. Outside, the trees and bushes sparkle with a delicate frost and the spiders' webs look like twisted strands of silver in the pale sunlight.

'Do you have to go to the yard?' Matt says.

'It's Christmas Day.'

'Exactly. Surely, you can have one day off.'

'But everyone goes to the yard to see their horses on Christmas Day. It's special.' I start to protest before realising that Matt is grinning at me. 'All right,' I sigh. 'I really should know by now when you're pulling my leg.'

As soon as he sits down to eat, the Bobster leaps up onto one of the spare chairs, pops her head above the table and begs, reminding me of a meerkat with a piece of purple tinsel wrapped around her collar.

'Aren't you going to tell her to get down?' he asks, raising his eyebrow.

'It's Christmas.' I smile. 'You can sit there, Bobster, for one day only.'

'Should I have cooked eggs for her?'

'I think that's pushing it a step too far.' I pause. 'Hurry up. I don't want Willow to feel left out because we're not there.'

'You don't mean that. She doesn't care as long as she gets her breakfast.'

'You are such an old cynic, Matt,' I tease. 'Come on. Get your wellies on.'

As we're grabbing our coats, his mobile rings and I know immediately from the tone of his voice that it isn't good news. It can only be one of those – I swear under my breath – colics. What timing!

'I'll be right over,' he says, looking at me, his eyes wide and questioning. 'I'm so sorry, Nicci.'

'It's one of those things.' I bite my lip. I could cry. 'It's such a shame when I was so looking forward to spending our first Christmas together. You won't be back in time for lunch at Mum's. Everyone will be there, except you.' I pull on my boots. 'I know. Why don't I come to the hospital?'

Matt is most insistent that I go and see Willow.

'I've got to get going. Can you lock up?' He gives me one of his heart-melting smiles.

'I can't believe you're being so cheerful about this,' I begin.

'I'll catch you later.' The door closes behind him and it's just me and the Bobster.

'Let's go,' I say, picking up my keys. I put the Bobster's travel harness on – I bought it recently from the 'For dogs' section in Tack n Hack – and clip it to the seat belt in the car before driving up to the yard. There are lights strung across the sign outside the equestrian centre and a poster advertising Christmas Pony Parties. When I reach the car park, I spot both Mum's car and Matt's.

'I smell a rat,' I say. 'What do you think is going on, Bobster?'

She yaps three times as if to say, 'I don't know.'

I let her out of the car and she races straight for Willow's stable, throwing herself at Sage, Gabriel, Cheska and Mum, who are waiting there.

'Nicci, I'm over here.'

I turn to find Matt emerging from the cover of the barn.

'Matt? Did the horse not make it?'

His eyes gleam with amusement. 'There was no horse. It was a trick. Here—' he holds out his hand '—I've got something for you, but you have to close your eyes. Promise me you won't peek.'

I screw up my face to make doubly sure, then, realising it isn't a good look, I hesitate.

'Close your eyes,' Matt repeats. 'No, this isn't going to work. I'll have to blindfold you.' He pulls a handkerchief from his pocket, one covered with Santas. 'A client gave it to me. It's clean.'

I stand beside the hay, inhaling its musty scent as Matt stands close behind me, tying the blindfold around my eyes.

'Is that too tight?'

'It's fine,' I say.

'No peeking.' He pinches my bottom before spinning me around until I'm giddy and laughing and falling against him. I catch hold of him by the front of his coat. He takes my hand. 'Right, Nicci. Let's go.'

'This is a test of trust,' I tell him.

'But you do trust me,' he says.

'You have been rather furtive over the last couple of weeks.'

'You know I said it was a tradition in my family to

396

open gifts after lunch? I admit that was a cock and bull story – did you really think I'd be able to wait that long to open my presents?'

'I did wonder.'

'I had to think of a way of getting you to wait without arousing your suspicions.'

'This is an elaborate way of giving me a present. Wouldn't it be easier to have done it the usual way, through Father Christmas?'

'Ah, this present wouldn't fit down the chimney.' Matt's voice bubbles with humour and fun.

'So it's a big present?' I ask, fishing for clues.

'It's the biggest present I've ever bought for anyone.'

'So it isn't a new pair of jodhpurs. Is it a wheel-barrow?'

'A good idea because you need a new one, but it's the wrong answer.'

I can't guess now. My mind is in a spin. I catch the aroma of mince pies and mulled wine coming from the tack room as we pass – Matt is taking me on a round-about route to wherever we're going.

'Stop,' he says and I become aware of people crowding in around me, but no one is saying anything. It's as if they're holding their breath.

'Hi, Auntie Nicci,' Sage pipes up after a pause.

'Sh.' I think that's Mum, or Cheska. 'She can't see you. Gabriel, don't you dare say a word.'

Matt removes the blindfold and stands to one side of me, holding my shoulders as if he's worried he's going to have to catch me.

'Happy Christmas, Nicci.'

The light is dazzling at first, but I soon work out that I'm outside Dark Star's old stable and Delphi is holding onto him. He's wearing a red rug trimmed with white faux fur and matching bandages, a new leather head-collar with brass buckles and tinsel plaited through his mane and tail.

Sage can't contain herself any longer. She's tugging at my coat.

'Auntie Nicci, isn't he the best Christmas present you've ever had?'

I turn to Matt. 'Dark Star? But he's been sold.'

'Yes, to me and I'm giving him to you,' he explains patiently. 'Maybe it's against my better judgement . . .'

'Oh, Matt, I thought I might never see him again. I can't believe it.'

'Well, you'd better because you're riding him from now on. I expect to see you both at Badminton in the near future.'

'Thank you.' I can hardly speak. Hot tears are running down my cold face at the thought of what Matt has done for me, because I know how much it's taken for him to do this. There's so much I want to say, but Mum wants a photo of me with Dark Star and Delphi wants to drink a toast while everyone is together.

She hands me Dark Star's lead-rope.

'I hope you'll be very happy with him,' she says. 'I'm glad he's staying on the yard – and that I don't have to risk my neck on him any more.'

I stroke his shining chest. He's been bathed and clipped out. He lowers his head and rests it on my arm as Mum takes pictures with her phone, gushing on about how this is the most romantic gesture she's ever seen.

Cheska is more sceptical – the horse-lover's gene has definitely passed her by. 'You have everything a woman needs,' she says, 'your dream horse and a mug to pay for it.'

'Matt's no mug,' I say, amused, 'and I'll be paying for my horses. Give me some credit.'

'Can I have a ride on him soon?' says Sage.

'One day. I've got to get used to him first.' With a touch of guilt, I look towards Willow's stable, where she's looking over the door and dropping strands of hay onto the newly swept yard. 'Why don't you give Willow a couple of mints?'

I keep half an eye on Sage while she's with Willow, but Willow is as gentle as ever. I wouldn't trust my new boy in quite the same way, but we'll get there.

Two of the grooms turn up with trays of mulled wine and orange juice. Gabriel tries to grab a mug of wine, but Sage stops him and swaps it for the non-alcoholic option.

'You're too young,' she says.

'Mummy says I can have some.'

'I said you can have a sip of mine,' Cheska says. 'Here.'

I watch Gabriel's face as he takes a big gulp of warm spicy wine and lets it wash around his mouth. Without flinching, he swallows it back and asks for more.

'I don't think that had the desired effect,' I observe.

'It was worth a try.' Cheska yawns. 'You were lucky

you stayed at Matt's last night. Guess what time the kids had me up?'

'I dread to think.'

'Two in the morning. Gabriel cried because he thought there was a strange man – i.e. Father Christmas – in his bedroom. I tried to persuade them to go back to sleep, but in the end I gave in.'

'We used to be like that. I'm not surprised they're excited, especially with Alan coming down. He is still going to Mum's for lunch?'

'He's texted me to let me know he's on his way.'

'Cheska, you're blushing.'

'I'm not.'

'Yes, you are. Are you two . . .'

She lowers her voice. 'I don't want to raise the children's expectations, but we *are* talking, and I'm hoping Alan finds that he rather likes it around here. He could set up a good little business – everyone can use a plumber now and again.' She pauses. 'Don't worry, Nicci. I'm making the most of the support and seeing the therapist Dr Mackie found for me. I'm not on some manic flight of fancy that Alan and I are going to live happily ever after. I'm crossing my fingers and everything else that today's visit could be the beginning, a fresh start.'

'What happened? What made him change his mind?'

'He missed us. Okay, at first he said he missed us like a hole in the head, but then he said the nicest thing . . .' Cheska's voice trails off. She touches the corner of her mouth and continues, 'He said he that he felt like he had a hole in his heart because we weren't there.'

400

I wish her all the best, not only for her happiness, but for Sage and Gabriel's too.

'Here's Shane,' calls Sage.

'Auntie Nicci's other boyfriend,' calls Gabriel.

'He isn't,' Sage says, scolding him. 'Matt only says that as a joke because Nicci spends all her time with him.'

'Very funny,' I say as Shane parks his four-by-four in the yard and jumps out. For once, he isn't wearing breeches. He's dressed in a sweater with a snowflake motif, dark trousers and black shoes.

'I'm not stopping,' he says. 'Michaela's not happy that I've left her looking after the turkey, but I couldn't miss this and I wanted to say Happy Christmas to everyone.' He walks over to me and Dark Star. 'Congratulations on your lovely new horse.'

'Were you in on this?' I ask him, my face aching from smiling.

'What do you think? I wasn't going to let this one get away. You're made for each other.' He kisses my cheek. 'I wanted to tell you – now you know Dark Star is yours – I've set up a meeting in the New Year with Topline, the local feed company who are really keen to sponsor a local rider, i.e. you, VB.'

'Me? Really?'

Shane nods. 'It'll take some of the pressure off you, financially, at least.'

'Shane, you are amazing.' I can't explain how I feel. I'm thrilled. 'How can I ever thank you?'

'It works both ways,' he says. 'I need the work. You're a good client.'

'You did get my present?'

'Yes, thanks. We're drinking it later. You know I can't wait to see you back in the saddle.'

Holding onto the end of the lead-rope, I give Shane a hug. Dark Star takes the opportunity to make a beeline for a tray of mince pies left on the trunk outside Willow's stable, but the Bobster gets there first and runs off with one.

Sage snatches the rest of them to safety, while I give Dark Star a tug on the rope, bringing him back to me. 'Good boy.'

'I must go,' Shane says.

'So must I,' says Mum. 'I don't expect Robert's remembered to put the potatoes in. Mind you, wild horses couldn't have dragged me away from this.'

Everyone moves on, including the grooms who are sent to make the horses' 'Christmas cake' for their evening feeds, a mixture of molasses, carrots, chaff and mix, topped with linseed jelly. Matt and I are left with Dark Star. I lead him back into the stable and take off his head-collar, at which he paws at his bed, sinks down and rolls on both sides until he gets up again, covered in shavings.

I close the door and watch him, laughing as he shakes himself, sending the shavings everywhere.

'He knows how to enjoy himself,' Matt comments, moving beside me and sliding his arm around my waist.

'I don't think you'll ever realise how much this means to me, Matt. I thought I might never see Dark Star again.'

'I know.'

'I can't believe you've done this for me.' It can't have been easy. Every time I compete, he's going to have to live with his fear that I might fall and not come back. 'How will you cope when I go out eventing next season? I really can't bear to put you through—'

'Sh,' he says. 'You said I was being furtive recently. Well, apart from negotiating with Delphi over the horse – she drives a hard bargain, by the way – I've had a couple of sessions of hypnotherapy to help me deal with my fear. I'm not sure I'll ever be cured as such, but I reckon it's worth a try.'

'You're doing that for me? Oh, Matt . . .'

'You showed me that you were willing to give up your dreams for me,' he goes on quietly. 'I can see how much the horses mean to you. I can't stand in your way, Nicci. And I really don't think I can live without you. So there you go. I'll take the chance and pray that you'll be lucky and always come home in one piece.'

My chest tight with emotion, I turn and throw my arms around him.

'I love you,' I whisper in his ear.

'Love you too,' he smiles.

'My present to you seems a bit small now.'

'I don't care,' he says. 'I am a very lucky man. I don't need anything else, darling.' He kisses me on the lips. 'All I want for Christmas is you. . .'

Trust Me I'm a Vet

Cathy Woodman

City vet Maz Harwood has learned the hard way that love and work don't mix. So when an old friend asks her to look after her Devonshire practice for six months, Maz decides running away from London is her only option.

But country life is trickier than she feared. It's bad enough she has to deal with comatose hamsters, bowel-troubled dogs and precious prize-winning cats, without having to contend with the disgruntled competition and a stubborn neighbour who's threatening to sue over an overzealous fur cut!

Worse still, she discovers Otter House Veterinary Clinic needs mending as much as her broken heart. Thank goodness there's an unsuitable distraction, even if he is the competition's deliciously dashing son . . .

Praise for Cathy Woodman's previous novels:

'Funny, truthful and original . . . I loved this book'
Jill Mansell

'Her style has a lightness of touch that can bring a smile, but also poignant moments that can bring a tear to the eyes'
Writing Magazine

arrow books

Must Be Love

Cathy Woodman

It must be love. What other reason could there be for city vet Maz's contentment with her new country life? The vet's practice where she's a partner with her best friend Emma is thriving, and so is her relationship with the gorgeous Alex Fox-Gifford.

But then circumstances force Emma to take a break from the practice, and Maz's life spirals out of control. What with working all hours trying to keep things going, fending off insults from Alex's parents, keeping one eye on the lusty locum – who's causing havoc amongst the village girls – and dealing with Emma's precarious mental state, it won't take much to upset the apple cart. So when she gets some unwelcome news, only time will tell whether Maz and Alex's love can withstand the fallout.

Praise for Cathy Woodman:

'Funny, truthful and original . . . I loved this book' Jill Mansell

'Woodman's warmth and wit are set to make her the next big thing in rural romance.' *Daily Record*

arrow books

The Sweetest Thing

Cathy Woodman

If only everything was as simple as baking a cake . . .

Jennie Copeland thought she knew the recipe for a happy life: marriage to her university sweetheart, a nice house in the suburbs and three beautiful children. But when her husband leaves her, she is forced to find a different recipe. And she thinks she's found just what she needs: a ramshackle house on the outskirts of Talyton St George, a new cake-baking business, a dog, a horse, chickens . . .

But life in the country is not quite as idyllic as she'd hoped, and Jennie can't help wondering whether neighbouring farmer Guy Barnes was right when he told her she wouldn't last the year.

Or perhaps the problem is that she's missing one vital ingredient to make her new life a success. Could Guy be the person to provide it?

Praise for Cathy Woodman:

'Funny, truthful and original . . . I loved this book' Jill Mansell

'Woodman's warmth and wit are set to make her the next big thing in rural romance.' *Daily Record*

arrow books

It's a Vet's Life

Cathy Woodman

Christmas is coming, and life is busy for vet Maz Harwood.

She has a beautiful baby boy, George, and she will soon be marrying fellow vet Alex Fox-Gifford. Frankly, though, life is not as rosy as it looks. Because between arranging the wedding, performing life-saving animal surgery, and taking care of George, Maz doesn't have much time left for Alex, and even if she did, he's working even harder than her so she rarely sees him. And as Alex won't do anything to make life easaier, Maz has decided to take matters into her own hands.

But Maz's solution has truly terrible consequences for them all, and as the wedding approaches, Maz realises that it will take a Christmas miracle to get her and Alex to the altar.

Praise for Cathy Woodman:

'I absolutely love Cathy's books. They are a treat to read.'
Katie Fforde

arrow books

ALSO AVAILABLE IN ARROW

The Village Vet

Cathy Woodman

**In Talyton St George, vet nurse Tessa Wilde
is on the way to her wedding . . .**

It should be the happiest day of her life. But then her car hits a
dog, and though the dog is saved thanks to the Otter House vets,
her wedding is not.

Animal welfare officer and part-time fire-fighter Jack Miller spends
his life saving animals and people. As one of Tessa's oldest
friends, he feels he has the right to interrupt her wedding and
rescue her from a marriage that can only end in tears.

But does he? Tessa is sure she doesn't need rescuing, least of
all by Jack.

When they begin to work together at the Animal Rescue centre,
however, Tessa begins to wonder whether being rescued by Jack
might not be such a bad thing after all.

Praise for *The Village Vet*

'A wonderful story about rescued animals and romance.
I loved it.' Katie Fforde

arrow books